Nyifie Brothers Publishing

FANGS AND FAME

THE VAMPIRE MAURICE (A FAT VAMPIRE SIDE SERIES) - BOOK 4

JOHNNY B. TRUANT

ONE

PROJECTION

The vampire hadn't spoken for a long time.

They hadn't even said hello. He'd simply arrived at Annabel's office just after sunset, nodded, then taken his usual chair opposite hers. He'd looked left for a few moments as if lost in thought (left was the direction of the window, with its stunning view of the parking lot), then twiddled fingers while looking down at his sneakers. Watching, Annabel couldn't believe she'd ever thought of Maurice Toussant as a teenager. He had the body of one, yes. The face of one, yes. But his manner was so somber. So serious. So unforgiving in all the ways that mattered.

"Uncle," she said.

Maurice looked up. He'd moved into a posture the world had mostly forgotten: feet planted, forearms on knees with hands interlaced, eyes toward the floor. It was what "waiting" had looked like before the advent of smartphones.

"'Uncle' meaning 'I give up,'" Annabel explained. "Meaning 'You win.'"

"Win what?"

"This staring contest we're having."

"I'm not staring," he said.

But he knew what she meant. Maurice was careful not to stare into her eyes unless he had to. He'd only done that a few times, and each had been a violation. Glamour was like an X-ray, leaving nowhere to hide.

"Do you know how Sigmund Freud worked with his patients?" Annabel asked.

"No."

"He didn't direct them. He waited for them to speak. Then he kept nudging them to *keep* speaking, adding nothing to the conversation. The patients did all the talking. They directed themselves."

"I can do that without you," Maurice said.

"So sometimes I make a game of it," she said as if he hadn't spoken. "I see how long it takes for my patients to talk first."

"Really?" This was news to Maurice. Probably because it was untrue and they both knew it. They'd never done that before.

"Because the thing is," she went on, "eventually everyone says *something* — even if it's just 'Are we going to say anything?' Silence is too weird."

But it was as if Maurice didn't understand. He looked like he'd bitten into something sour — or maybe like he was talking to a drunk. "I didn't even know we were playing. How long were you going to wait?" he asked. And now he *was* staring. Not glamour-staring. Wary-staring.

Something snapped as Annabel felt a change inside. She turned to the clock and was shocked to see that fifteen minutes had passed. She charged by the hour. She'd just wasted a quarter of one — and a lot of Maurice's money — for no reason at all. It wasn't victory, or even a vindication of Sigmund Freud. In truth it was little more than embarrassing ... and confusing as hell. What had she been thinking?

Yeth — what were *you thinking?* asked a lisping voice inside her head. *What hathe gone wrong in that big, juicy brain of yours, Dr. Rithe?*

Why was she playing stubborn, now for the first time? It was like she wanted to defeat Maurice instead of working with him. To bend him to her will: her own form of glamour.

"I'm sorry," Annabel said, all-of-a-sudden meaning it. "I ... I guess I lost track of time. To tell the truth, I haven't ..." She hesitated, then said it anyway: "I haven't felt like myself lately."

"What do you mean?" Maurice asked, now leaning forward. His eyes had grown intense, as if the comment wasn't as idle as Annabel meant it to be.

Under his gaze, she giggled again. Like a schoolgirl. And Annabel wasn't a giggler.

"I won't charge you for the time," she said, composing herself. "I guess I spaced out when you came in."

"Have you spaced out before?"

"It's been a long day."

"But ... Have you spaced out before?"

She deflected. "Let's talk about you. What were *you* thinking about, sitting there unspeaking for a quarter hour?"

But her inner Freud had turned against her. It said: *You're projecting because what just happened has you scared. Maurice is silent by nature. All that dead air is on* you, *Miss Annabel.*

Maurice hadn't looked away. She wished he'd go back to examining his laces.

"Have you ever lost time, Dr. Rice?" he asked.

"Everyone loses track of time now and then."

"That's not what I meant. Have you ever blacked out?"

"Only when drinking." And there was that giggle again. She barely drank.

He kept staring.

"I'm sorry, Maurice," she said. "I was distracted, was all. Let's not make this whole session about me. We're here for you. So let's begin by talking about why—"

He cut her off. "How did you find me?"

"I didn't. You came in and sat down."

He shook his head. "I didn't mean today. I meant before our first session. I never asked. I want to know how you found me in the first place ... as a patient."

"That was weeks ago. Why are you asking now?"

"Answer the question," he said.

There was menace in his voice — menace that surprised her. Annabel shifted in her chair.

"Maurice. I *didn't* find you. *You* found *me*. Doctors don't seek out their patients."

But his gaze didn't falter. There was an almost-imperceptible shake of his head. "I only called after I found your business card in my mailbox. You'd written on the back that you specialize in patients who don't think they can be helped. Patients who are ... *special*."

"I'm sorry, but you're mistaken. I didn't put a card in your mailbox. Until you filled our your paperwork, I didn't even know where you lived."

"I still have the card. I could show you."

Even though Annabel was sure of what she was saying (she really *hadn't* given him a card; what was she, a door-to-door shrink?) she still felt flustered. It wasn't a new feeling. The vampire had been flustering her more and more lately: when he'd asked if she knew her birth parents and why she was so preoccupied with aspects of him that had nothing to do with psychology. Most of all he'd flustered her the day he'd casually asked if he could sample her blood.

But she wasn't just *flustered*, was she? There was reality to this. Annabel *had* lost time. She *had* blacked out. More and more, she hated being at home for reasons she couldn't explain or understand. That phantom sense of not-well was why she spent so much time at the office, if only to avoid her husband. She came in early unless he stopped her. She stayed late. Sometimes she even slept on the office floor. It struck her as instinctual. It was compulsion: panic without a cause.

"I did some promotions in the past," she said, lying and defensive. "Half-price sessions. Things like that."

"And you advertised them by walking around handing out business cards?"

"I've handed out business cards!"

Yes. You have. Five years ago, at a convention. Or maybe not even then.

"The card I got didn't say 'half-price,'" Maurice told her.

"Well, then, you should have asked, shouldn't you?" She made as if to move toward her desk. "If you want it refunded, I'm happy to do it. *You* were the one who asked for an after-dark appointment, offering to pay whatever I wanted if I was willing to—!"

"*Sit,*" he said.

It wasn't quite a command. Not quite glamour. But it was stronger than a suggestion. She sat.

"Do you like treating me, Dr. Rice?"

"It's not a matter of 'like.' It's my job." *Too cold.* So she said, "It's my calling. To help people."

"Do you think I'm making progress?"

"You seem to be."

"In what way?"

"Well, do you still think of yourself as a monster?"

"They've made 'monster movies' about creatures like me," Maurice said. "I've killed people. I drink blood. I only come out at night."

"*Bad* people, though. The ones you've killed."

"Are you asking *me* if *I* think I'm a monster," Maurice asked, "or was the question for yourself?"

His question felt aggressive. She parried. "The fact that you're analyzing it at all feels like progress to me. There's more than 'death' to the definition of 'monster.' Do you agree?"

He looked hard at her. He said, "Oh yes." Then he finally looked away.

A beat of quiet passed between them.

"So, if we're ready to—" Annabel began.

"I killed Holmes," he blurted.

"*What?*"

"H. H. Holmes — the serial killer from the World's Fair," he explained. "He wasn't just a man. That was the missing piece: He was supernatural after all. So after our last session, I dug him up and killed the demon inside him."

"But ... How ...?" She could only sputter. According to the history books, the Chicago World's Fair serial killer had been dead for more than a century. Maurice had said so himself. Yet he was dead earnest right now. He'd learned something after they parted, it seemed. There were a million questions to follow his out-of-the-blue proclamation, and most were prerequisites of each other. She felt blindsided by what he was saying — and certain somehow that *blindsiding her*, exactly, had been Maurice's intention.

"Something has awoken," he told her. "Something troubling."

"What's awoken?"

"Something in me. Something I feel in you. Or around you. Or *behind* you. Something I've ignored because you've helped me. Because you're a friend. Something I've turned a blind eye to for much longer than my blood wants to allow."

He stopped, thought, and resumed.

"I won't force it out of you. I owe you that much. But Holmes was the final straw. Seeing what was inside him answered questions I've had for a hundred years, but seeing what was *behind* him changed everything. I see pieces of a puzzle coming together now every time I sleep."

"What exactly are you—?"

"I thought that coming here, for our sessions, was changing things for the better," Maurice pressed. "You asked why I didn't talk for fifteen minutes? It's because I was thinking. Because I've had a bad feeling for a while that I can't ignore any longer: *Things haven't changed for the better.* No. What we've unearthed in these sessions ... it's changed things for the *worse.*"

Annabel wasn't blinking. She said, "Wait. What was 'behind Holmes'?"

"Ophelia," he answered.

"You think *Ophelia* was behind Holmes?"

"I know it. I can feel it."

"The vampire who nearly killed your wife before you came along to turn and save her? 'Ophelia,' who traumatized Celeste so completely that she's hidden whatever happened that day inside a mental box?"

Maurice nodded, but it was a knowing nod — a kind of knowing that Annabel didn't understand. "Celeste's mind buried what Ophelia did to her. Locked the box and threw away the key. These days she sees the pain, but not what's causing it. It's the kind of pain that changes a person — that leaves a scar that will never heal. And *yes*. Ophelia is behind it. Behind Holmes. Behind … *everything.*"

In the pause, Annabel thought Maurice might say something else. He'd talked about their sessions, then about Ophelia as causing his ills … so had he almost said *behind YOU* before changing his mind to say *behind everything* instead? Certainly not. Ophelia was just a concept here … and clearly nothing was "behind" Annabel.

She said, "You told me about Ophelia last session, but I don't see what she could possibly have to do with what we're talking about now."

"Who's in your bloodline, Annabel Rice?" he asked.

Annabel hadn't seen that coming. She stumbled, then rallied. "In *my* bloodline? Ordinary people. Dentists. Bankers. My grandmother managed an H&M when she was a kid."

"H&M wasn't around when your grandmother was a kid."

"I'm sorry. I mean my sister."

"You haven't mentioned a sister."

"What's this about?" Annabel asked, careful to keep her tone curious rather than defensive. "Maybe we've gone too deep too quickly with you. For most patients it takes *years* to get to the root of things, and in those cases we're talking about a lifetime of forty, fifty, sixty years. But with you, we've gone to the roots every single time and you're two millennia old. I'm starting to think your 'blood memory' might be hurting this process more than it's helping. I should have thought of that before now. Maybe you remember *too well*. You remember photographically. Forgetting is a blessing sometimes, but because of your nature, it's not like you can just—"

Maurice stood.

"What ... What are you doing?"

"Do you still have my Black AmEx on file?"

"Of course."

"Charge me ten times the usual fee for this session."

After he went silent, still standing, Annabel understood. She almost leapt from her chair to join him.

"Wait. You're *leaving*? But we haven't even started!" She felt the concern in her voice, realizing oddly that the idea of Maurice quitting was more bothersome *for her* than it was for Maurice. She wanted very badly to know more about him, and if he quit therapy, that wouldn't happen. She needed to hear more stories — to delve deeper instead of shallower, no matter what she'd just told him. The farthest back he'd gone was the 1890s. She wanted to know what he'd done in medieval France. She wanted to know where he'd been during the crusades — and if he'd known Vlad the Impaler, rumored to be the legendary Count Dracula.

Worse, Annabel's need to know about Maurice wasn't just curiosity. It also felt — now that she thought about it — like a lifeline. If she couldn't keep plunging Maurice's mind, she might suffocate. But why would she feel that way? Why would she need (not *want*; *need*) to hear his stories? Was Maurice's history somehow protecting her? Would it be dangerous for her to stop learning all about him ... somehow, some way?

Absurd.

And yet the feeling within her, whenever she thought about him leaving, was easy to name. *It was panic.*

Maurice moved toward the door at a human's pace. He wasn't even going to give her the pleasure of one last vampiric act: flashing to the door faster than her eye could see as he'd done the first time they met, or perhaps turning into a bat — or mist — and flying away.

"I ... I *have to know*," she told him. It sounded like begging.

"I know you do," he said. Then he nodded. "Goodbye, Doctor Rice. You did your best. Thank you for trying, but you won't see me again."

He left the door open when he disappeared. Annabel's mouth hung agape, wondering what had just happened.

You know exactly what happened, said a voice inside her.

But it wasn't the voice of her terrible husband this time — the voice that usually controlled her.

This was a different voice.

A woman's.

TWO
SHADOW

Maurice returned to his mansion, attempting to not drag the darkness with him.

He walked home from the psychiatrist's office at human speeds, taking long breaths of cool air in an attempt to improve his mood. It didn't work; he still sensed a boogeyman in the shadows.

The ill feeling had been with him since he'd killed the demon Holmes last week. Only: *No, no;* it started before Holmes. The first time he'd felt it was after his first chat with Annabel. Which was strange. She really *had* helped him. After their sessions, he *did* feel better. It wasn't until daytime, as he slept, that the fears and worries came. But from where? Maurice could almost grasp the sources of his ill-ease, but not quite. His fears were shadows. They were specters that stood at the edge of his vision, retreating if he looked right at them.

Celeste was waiting for him in the hallway.

"You're early," she said. "I was watching reruns of *The Jersey Shore.* I wanted to watch them in peace, while you were gone."

"You're kidding."

"Of course I'm not kidding. I'm a vampire. I'm into pain."

He couldn't tell if she was kidding.

"It was a short session," he explained.

"How short?"

"So short, it's done forever."

She made a sympathetic face.

"Stop it," he said.

"I thought she was helping you."

"No offense, Celeste, but it's possible our kind is beyond help."

"You don't believe that."

He sort of believed it. Or at least, half of him believed it. He was a man divided these days, sure on one hand that life was getting brighter and sure on the other hand that it was falling apart. Reginald wasn't helping. Maurice had told his progeny to lay low so he wouldn't anger Logan and the Vampire Council any more than he (and Maurice, of course) already had, and for the most part Reginald was doing as he'd been told. But a problem remained: Reginald stood out just by *existing*.

Reginald thought he'd dodged suspicion by transferring to the night shift, but that just proved how naive he was. Treadmill companies didn't *have* night shifts. Maurice's glamour had created one, and Maurice's influence (not really glamour this time) had put Nikki on the night shift too, to keep Reginald company. That was good, because Maurice was poor company these days. He spent half his time astonished by Reginald's vampire-enhanced mind and the other half waiting for the other shoe to drop on the issue of his continued living. "A good mind" wasn't as important to vampires as it was to look the part. Smarts wouldn't save him forever.

Reginald didn't look or act like most vampires. Not at all.

And that meant Logan *would* eventually kill him. It was almost a certainty. Maurice had already delayed and delayed Reginald's trial, but soon he wouldn't be able to delay anymore. Once Logan got his hands on Reginald, they'd hold that trial, and it would be rigged — not that Reginald needed a disadvantage to fail. Logan had always had a strange way of bending the rules in his favor. He seemed to wield power beyond the usual power of Deacon. Some ace that asshole always had up his sleeve. It meant Logan would win. It was just a matter of how long Reginald had left to live ... not *whether* he'd live.

"I guess I don't believe it," Maurice said. "I'm just in a bad mood."

"Would you like me to beat the shit out of you?"

"No thanks."

"I meant sexually."

"Of course you meant sexually. I appreciate it, but I'm not in the mood."

She looked concerned now. Who didn't want sex bruising?

"Are you okay?" she asked.

No, Maurice thought, looking into her eyes. *I'm not okay. My progeny is about to be murdered, and when that happens it'll feel to my blood as if I've been murdered, too. I felt it with Daisy. The pain never goes away. And it will hurt you, too, Celeste, because our blood is entangled. I feel like there's a shadow behind all of us, and I can't quite find it. I feel that shadow most around Annabel: some great beast moving unseen.*

I feel like my presence is making it stronger. I'd swear staying with Annabel puts us all in danger ... but by leaving Annabel, I may have put her in danger too deep to remedy. It's all falling to pieces, Celeste. I thought I could control things around my imperfect vampire, but I was wrong. Trying to hide him is like trying to smother a brushfire with a handkerchief. Todd at work has seen too much. I think he's talking, and he's just one of many. We're trying to plug a leaky dike with not enough fingers. I fear our secret is out. Maybe everyone's secrets.

Even in his own mind, Maurice didn't want to think the rest of it. The thought came anyway.

Maybe this is the beginning of the end, Celeste, and maybe I can't bear the weight of it. The weight of waiting. Maybe Holmes's box should have stayed closed. I went to therapy to purge my demons, but now I fear that by looking deep inside myself, something from the deep looked right back at me. Now it sees us. Now it's chasing us. Now it KNOWS.

"I'm fine," he lied.

"Have you eaten?"

He nodded. "Some goth kids offered themselves to me under the Lane Street bridge."

"They knew what you were?"

"When they came at me, I hissed. My teeth were down because ... Well, it's been a hard day. But it's okay. They were DTF."

"DTF?"

"'Down to Feed.'"

That happened more and more recently. Humans had been enamored by vampires for a long time, but usually their adoration came at arm's length. In recent weeks, however, that love was practically in the open. Maurice hardly needed stealth to feed these days. New victims came to him of their own accord.

"I just want to be home for a while," he told Celeste. "I want to rest and not think about anything."

Celeste nodded. But there was something in her eyes — something dark and deep that, like Maurice's odd mood, had only grown in the past few days. She was usually so cheery. Usually the kind to bake cookies full of plasma and stuffed with scabs. She could make a man not vomit when eating human food; that's how good her cooking was, and how infectious her happiness. But recently that had changed.

"Don't," Celeste said, watching Maurice as he watched her.

Maurice pretended he didn't know what she was talking about, but he was fooling nobody. He was prying. Prying into her blood using his mind. It was like reading her diary, and she didn't like it one bit.

"I'm sorry," he said. "You've seemed down. I don't like that we're both like this. The air around here is ... *intense.*"

"My business is my business," she snapped, "just like your business is your business."

"But ..."

"I can tell you're hiding something, Maurice, so don't give me shit for doing the same. I feel your fear. It's like you're trying to protect me by keeping me in the dark. Like you think telling me what's worrying you will worry me, too. I don't like it any more than you do. But unless you're prepared to tell *me* everything, I'm not prepared to tell *you* everything, either."

"I've *told* you everything," he said.

"Then tell me why you stopped working with Dr. Rice.

Who you said was helping you. Tell me why you quit in the middle of a session without any warning at all."

He half stuttered. Then he said, "My issue is complicated."

"Then so is mine."

"It's Ophelia, isn't it?"

Her eyes widened, then contracted again. "I told you not to pry," she said, turning away.

"I didn't. I know because she's been on my mind, too."

Celeste turned back to him, not quite as angry. Maurice felt safe to continue.

"I think when I killed the demon in Holmes, something back-traced to her," he said. "Ophelia used black magic to defeat the necromancer. That's magic I don't understand. So what if when Holmes died, Ophelia felt it in her blood? What if my killing him reawakened some old connection, like activating a sleeper agent? Something of her is in you — an echo of the blood Macht slipped you that evening. And if it's in *your* blood, it's in mine. That's how I know I'm not just paranoid. None of this is coming to me from the outside. It's coming from the *in*side. Through you."

"So it's true," Celeste said. "Ophelia is still alive."

Maurice didn't answer right away. There was murder in his wife's eyes. It was clear she'd done more than *think* about Ophelia; Maurice saw that much just by watching her face. It'd been a week since he'd killed H.H. Holmes for good — a week since Maurice first began to feel the cloud above them thicken. He believed what he'd said: Destroying Holmes had set deadly clockwork in motion. A week was a long time for Celeste to feel it happening. To dwell on her traumatic, locked-down past. To obsess. To plan, in some way, to seek revenge on Ophelia or die trying.

Maurice wouldn't insult her by lying. "Yes. I think she's

alive. And if I had to guess, she knows we're here, undoing what she's done."

Celeste didn't reply. She'd already known. Already spent innumerable hours knowing.

"Please tell me we don't have to watch *The Jersey Shore*," Maurice said, attempting a smile that felt far too small.

"Maybe I feel like punishing myself," Celeste replied. "Maybe I don't feel like feeling good right now."

He laughed.

But she wasn't joking.

THREE

ONLINE

A gigantic tower of meat stood outside Maurice's door.

"I'm just getting ready for bed," Maurice told it.

The enormous man — Brian — seemed to be wearing his Council robe under a trenchcoat large enough to cover a blimp. Brian was the approved definition of "large" in the Council's eyes: broad shoulders and a huge, muscle-decked chest able to bench press buildings. Reginald's weight sat lower, making him round instead of Brian's breed of top-heavy. Strange that they probably weighed about the same.

Brian looked at his watch. It was analog but made to look like a sundial. Some sort of vampiric irony, Maurice assumed.

"It's only 3am," Brian said.

"I've had a rough night."

"Are you trying to avoid Celeste?"

"Celeste's had a rough night, too."

"Are you depressed? You can tell me if you're depressed, Maurice."

"Good to know. What's up, Brian?"

But he wasn't letting it go. "Because, you know, I hear

you're seeing a shrink." He lowered his voice. "A *human* shrink?"

Maurice looked both ways outside, then grabbed Brian's tree-trunk arm and pulled him inside the house.

"Who told you that?"

"Not Logan. Don't worry."

Brian's words had the opposite effect than intended. He wouldn't have led with "not Logan" unless there was a threat that Logan would find out soon. *Not Logan*. But to that, Maurice heard a silent appendix: "... *yet*."

"Who, then?"

Maurice waited. Was it *Charles* who knew his secret? Please don't let it be Charles.

"Paulina."

Maurice exhaled. Paulina was okay. She wasn't on the Council, which was good because Brian was the only pro-Maurice member of the Council right now ... and even then Brian only got away with it because he was too massive to piss off. Paulina was more like Council-adjacent: the advisor of someone's secretary's wife or something. Paulina liked Maurice and Maurice liked her — a rarity in vampire politics. Of all the vampires Maurice knew, Paulina was most likely to suggest that psychologically disturbed vampires (meaning most vampires) should seek professional help. No one else would be as understanding. Any other vampire would think Maurice was weak for seeing a thera-pist (let alone a *human* therapist) .... *and* a risk to the secrecy of the vampire world. His seeing Annabel would be more than a black mark if others found out. It'd be a target.

"How did she know? And why the hell did she tell you?" Maurice asked.

"So it's true?"

"It *was* true. It's over now."

"Really? Why?"

Maurice made a face. He wasn't sure how to answer that, coming from Brian.

So Brian said, "Because, you know, I was thinking about it for myself."

"You're kidding."

"I get nightmares. Do you think seeing your guy helped?"

"Girl."

"Do you think your girl helped?"

Maurice took a beat to answer, despite the earnesty in Brian's gaze. The sessions *had* been helping, yes. But there was more to it than simple the issue of helping or not — always more to the story with this paranoid and plotting community.

"It's complicated," he said. "Why are you here?"

"Aren't you glad to see me?"

"You're a giddy handful of excitement, Brian. I love having you around. If I'd known you were coming, I'd've—"

"It's your fat vampire," Brian interrupted.

Maurice stopped with his mouth open. He closed it slowly and said, "Reginald?"

"Yeah. Sorry. I don't mean to use the F word. I used to be F as a motherfucker when I was a kid."

"I'm not sure you know what 'the F word' means."

"It's just that it's all Logan calls him. 'That fat vampire.' I don't think he knows his name."

Maurice really had been getting ready for bed, but Brian's words woke him right back up. It wasn't Logan's reference to Reginald that bothered him. It was the fact that Logan apparently spent enough time talking about Reginald to the rest of the Council that 'what Logan usually calls Reginald' had meaning.

"See, the other day, at Council, someone—"

Now it was Maurice who interrupted. "Do you want to come in?"

"I'm already in."

"I mean, do you have anywhere you need to be?"

"I had to be *here*, Maurice," Brian said. Then: "You need to pay more attention."

Maurice invited Brian into the parlor, which Celeste had decked out in gold leaf and gold everything else just because the look was so hideous and gaudy. The room was grand and made mostly of marble, hung with tapestries and floored with a thick white rug to absorb echoes. The combined effect was terrible, as if pimps had been allowed to decorate Versailles. It was a crime of interior decoration and Maurice's favorite room in the house.

Maurice sat in a chair made to look like a bear risen on its haunches. The only chair large enough for Brian was a throne-type thing that was usually ornamental, topped with skulls of what looked like rappers with elaborate, bejeweled grills across their teeth.

They were just getting settled — and Maurice about to ask what Reginald-centric event had sent Brian his way — when Celeste entered the room wearing a gold and black-velvet robe that matched the decor. She was carrying a decanter full of brandy.

"Oh," Maurice said, moving a table upon which she could set it. "Thank you."

Celeste looked at Brian with surprise. "This is for me. Hello, Brian. What a pleasant surprise."

But Maurice could read his wife through her blood even if he hadn't already read emotion on her face. She was as alarmed to see Brian as Maurice was. Brian was friendly to the Toussants, but they'd never had him over and he hadn't had them over, either. Theirs wasn't that kind of relationship. Whenever the Council had voted against Maurice in the past, Brian was the only consistent vote in their favor. Their bond was practical, not recreational. So if he'd seen fit to visit unannounced, that told Celeste two things. The first was that Brian was here off-the-record, planning to come and go without anyone else knowing. The second was that it couldn't be anything good. Good news was delivered by phone, or through an amusing Hallmark card.

"Hello, Celeste."

She pulled up a chair without being invited. If this hard news concerned Maurice, then it concerned her, too. She centered the small table Maurice had grabbed in the center of the three of them, then set the decanter on it. She moved to grab glasses from the bar, listening as Brian began speaking.

"There's been a development with ... with your man. 'Reginald,' right?"

Maurice nodded.

"He's been seen."

"Where?" Maurice asked.

"Everywhere. Logan's people with the Columbus Police say there were reports of some creeper chasing joggers down on the jog trail. Some people are saying he was offering them money for blood when he couldn't catch anyone."

Maurice put his face in his hands. He'd heard the gist of this, but not the humiliating detail.

"During the day, no less," Brian went on. "One of the people reporting said he screamed at one point, then ran to sit below a tree. They said he burned when the sun hit him. That he smelled like ham."

Maurice nodded, embarrassed. "He told me about that.

It was when he still had some human blood. He didn't listen too well when I told him he needed to avoid sunlight."

"He was seen chasing joggers at night, too. They just sped up and got away from him."

Maurice looked at the rug. He'd known that, too. A natural hunter, Reginald wasn't.

"So the cops thought maybe he was some homeless guy living under the bridge. They went to check it out and found that some of the *actual* homeless people under there had seen him, too, but just the one night."

"Yeah."

"So you knew?" Brian asked.

Celeste set glasses on the table, then poured three two-finger glasses of amber liquid. She handed two to the men and sipped her own. "We both knew," she said.

"Look ... Maurice ... Celeste ..."

"He has other abilities," Maurice said. "His mind—"

"The Council doesn't see hearts and minds and intentions," Brian said. "Beauty is skin-deep and that's a good thing to them. Reginald presents pretty badly, you guys. He's not strong. Not fast. Not charming at all as far as I can tell. I've been trying to give you and him the benefit of the doubt, but ..." He trailed off.

"Come on, Brian," Celeste said. "You know better than to judge a book by its cover."

"I know. But I'm also a realist. I'm tolerated on the Council. *Tolerated.* They know my views, but I look the way they want vampires to look, and having a radical on the Council makes it seem like it might be balanced instead of rigged. I'm good for the rest of them as long as I don't make too big of waves." He sipped. "You know they'll take him to trial."

"They've already summoned us," said Maurice. "I've been filibustering for weeks."

"You know you can't delay forever. When it finally happens, you know they'll convict him. And sentence him. You know the rules of this world, Maurice."

Maurice did, but he'd hated it forever. Or, more accurately, he'd hated it since Logan took over and the whole world changed.

"It's not supposed to be this way. In the old world, we weren't elitists. We were creatures and we came in all shapes, sizes, colors, and forms. Now look at us. Now all vampires are vapid red-carpet Met Gala douchebags."

"You can thank *Interview with the Vampire* for that. You can thank *Twilight*," Brian said. "Now instead of being afraid to look at us, humans want to *be* us. You've seen the kids out there. It's not Year Zero anymore, Maurice. You're the oldest of the Old Guard, but you aren't and never were *American* Old Guard. You don't make the rules, no matter how '*it used to be.*'"

"What's really going on here, Brian?" Celeste asked, curt and all business. "None of this is new. Maurice and I talked all day after he sired Reginald. He knew the risks then and he knows the risks now. Reginald was always going to be an outsider because he doesn't look like a Hollywood leading man, and now, yeah, he's an outsider. They'll try him. He'll lose. It's a problem we haven't solved yet, but it's not a new one. You wouldn't have come here if something else hadn't happened."

Brian took a long breath before speaking. He frowned with resignation and his head bobbed: a look that told Celeste, *Of course you saw right through me.*

"You're right. There's a new twist on your 'old problem.'"

"What twist?" Maurice asked.

"Two twists, actually. Two new ways your man is twisting Logan's titty. One is that he's drawing attention from the human population, like I said. He's no good at hiding, and he doesn't seem to understand that he should. He had no advance training, like all the other new ones have."

"Come on, Brian. It used to take every new vampire time to find their feet."

"*Used* to," Brian said, giving Maurice a look that said, *I understand where you're coming from, and maybe I even agree with you ... but you're still wrong and it's time you face facts.* "But this is 2013. The Age of the Internet. The Age of Cell Phones. I'm not saying people have seen him running through the shadows like a creeper in some feudal village. I'm saying people have *caught him on video.* He's on *YouTube,* for Christ's sake."

"What's 'YouTube'?"

Brian — turned in the last century and a bit more friendly with technology, took a cellular phone from his pocket. He typed something into it, then handed it to Maurice. A video was paused on its screen. Maurice pressed Play and watched what unfolded: Reginald walking down a city sidewalk in the pitch of night, stumbling and falling every few steps.

"That video is called 'Fat Vampire can't get enough hamburger,'" Brian explained as Maurice, alarmed, handed the phone back. "He falls on his face over and over, clearly starved to death, all the way down the block. If you watch to the end, he stops at a house and some girl gives him one of those grocery store packages of raw ground beef through the window. He licks the cellophane."

Maurice said nothing, trying to act surprised. He could

feel Celeste's blood inside him, kicking his own blood knowingly below the table. Reginald may have gotten lucky. The way Brian was talking, it seemed the video of Reginald being handed rations by the girl who'd taken pity on him was the only one out there. Maurice, for one, wasn't about to admit to Brian what Reginald had already admitted to Maurice: that the girl's pity had turned into an odd sort of big-brotherly friendship, and that Claire was someone he visited regularly. Maurice had even met her. Smart girl. Absent, vacant-eyed mother. Might be the victim of an incubus. He tried not to think about it.

"There are other videos, too," Brian went on. "'Fat Vampire sucks on rats. Fat Vampire singed by watch reflection. Fat Vampire says, 'Joe Biden.'"

"Who's Joe Biden?" Celeste asked.

"The point is, he's been seen. But that's not even the worst part. Would you like to guess the worst part?"

"Not even a little," said Maurice, rubbing his scalp.

"The worst part is, *he's got fans*. At first it wasn't that big of a deal. Someone would catch him on video doing something funny and post it on YouTube, and people would laugh and share it. Then I guess the videos were shared enough that people started realizing some of them were of the same guy. There's blood-drinking in a few of them, so they started calling him a vampire. Then he became 'Fat Vampire.' Capital F capital V, like it was his name. So of course word made its way to the Council. Logan's furious. He already knew what you'd done, in turning him, from Charles. He already hated the idea of you not *just* committing wanton creation, but committing it to make someone so completely opposite of what vampires are 'supposed to be like.' He already hated you for Reginald, Maurice. But this?" Brian held up the phone, full of damning videos. "This pushed him over the edge."

"But you said Reginald has fans," Celeste said. "Not 'a following.' *'Fans.'* Doesn't that mean people like him?"

"*People,* yes. As in *humans.* But you both know the Council's opinion of humans. To Logan and the others, this isn't fame. It's infamy. It's making vampires a laughing stock."

"Oh, come on, Brian," Celeste scoffed. "Nobody actually *believes* he's a vampire."

"It doesn't matter. *This—*" Again he indicated the phone. "—is now part of our image. And a growing one. One the humans really seem to get a kick out of. I've seen entire write-ups on the Internet about what it would be like to be a fat vampire, based on Reginald's videos. Podcast episodes. One podcast in particular, called *Better Off—*"

"I get it," Maurice said, waving his hands for Brian to stop.

And he did, really. Before now, Reginald had been the American vampires' dirty little secret. He was like a pregnant teenager in the 1950s, sent off to live in another town. He was a mentally ill relative, hidden from sight in the 70s. The world was supposed to be better than that now, but it wasn't. Even in 2013, keeping Maurice's mistake carefully hidden mattered more to the Vampire Council than the fact that Reginald existed in the first place. Now, the fact that any humans at all were considering vampirekind's biggest misfit as representative of their race — even if only to laugh at him — twisted the knife in Logan's pride. Logan wanted vampires to rule over humans, or at least to be feared. Reginald's apparent popularity ran counter to both of those things.

This was very bad news for Reginald. There was now

no chance he'd be allowed to keep living. They'd have no choice but to grind him out like a spent cigarette.

"Why haven't I heard about any of this before now?" Maurice asked Brian.

"Because you're a philistine and don't use computers. Reginald's 'fans' are mostly misfits and nerds: fringe types without much of a voice who've found each other online. The vampires who know are keeping their mouths shut because they're as embarrassed by your guy as Logan is. For now, you still have to know where to look if you want to find 'Fat Vampire.' But mark my word, his popularity will only grow ... and then you *won't* need to know where to look. The videos and articles will end up in front of your face. You understand what I'm saying, don't you?"

Maurice did. And he could tell with a glance at Celeste that Celeste did, too. It didn't matter that humans didn't believe in vampires. The videos would still change how humans thought about them, imagining them now in shapes they'd never before considered. Soon vampires, too, would begin to imagine the same things ... and when *that* happened, the unravelling of Logan's perfect vampire society wouldn't be far behind.

A line from an '80s movie came to Maurice, summing things up perfectly: *We have news for the beautiful people: There's a lot more of us than there are of you.* There was no greater horror for Logan's kind than to realize they were outnumbered. No greater threat to the status quo ... and the power that came with it.

"Tell me you're on this, Maurice," Brian said. "Tell me you'll do whatever it takes to get Reginald in line and out of sight. Somehow. Some way. Not just for his own protection, but for your own. Logan already hates you, and he sees this as a huge black eye. It's not something he'll allow. If this goes on any longer, he'll have no choice but to skin you alive."

Maurice told Brian he'd do what he could. He'd solve this, no matter what it took.

But the truth was, the bad-news ship had sailed long ago. Maurice had kept all vampire news from Reginald, but it was clear there would be no protecting him now — no way to put the lid back on Pandora's Box once the Internet opened it. Reginald would be erased without ceremony, and chances were decent the Council would be angry enough to kill Maurice along with him. Logan would enact some of the weird power he had to affect the world after that, and would take the secret of the videos to his grave. Everything would simply *end*. Nobody but a clutch of online geeks would even know that "Fat Vampire" ever existed.

Reginald was digging his own grave and he had no idea. He'd die without knowing the depth of the crime of pride he'd accidentally committed.

FOUR
THAFE

Annabel had never noticed before how small her husband was. How unattractive. How repellant, both inside and out.

She'd known she hated him, of course. Thoughts of her husband's terribleness plagued her on a daily basis. She spent so much time at the office because she'd learned to hate spending time at home when he was home, and he was home constantly. He was home all day every day. He never *ever* left — at least not when the sun was shining. And it's not like he worked from home. Not like he had hobbies, not like he kept busy. He didn't even sit around playing video games like a cliche layabout. No. Instead, he slept. *All the time*. She couldn't think of a single daytime moment he'd been awake and around. He never mowed the lawn. Never ran errands.

In fact, now that she was thinking about it, she almost never saw her terrible husband because he was only awake at night. Why hadn't she realized that before? Why hadn't she connected those particular dots?

Truth was (and she was just now realizing *this*, too), her husband was *very* active at night. He left the house at the oddest hours. He rattled around and made noise, uncaring that she was trying to sleep. It used to bother her, but then they had a talk and she more or less stopped noticing. Just like she'd never noticed before now that her bed was a twin mattress. That was a little strange. She had money, so why did she sleep on a twin? Why did she sleep in the basement instead of the bedroom? And why did he, too, sleep in the basement — but under the bed rather than on top of it?

She hadn't thought about those things for some reason. Just like she'd never realized how ugly her man was, nor how detestable his personality. She thought back to the day they'd met, searching for an explanation as to why she'd gotten together with this horrible man in the first place. He must have been nice at some point. Or handsome. Or funny. Or charming.

Right?

But it turned out Annabel couldn't remember the day they'd met. Or their courtship. Or *anything* more than a week or two ago, really.

She went into the living room, to the mantle where she kept her framed photos. She looked through every one of them, knowing from the start that there were no photos of her and her husband on their wedding day — none of them together at all. Even stranger, she *knew* there were no photos despite *knowing* there must be photos. She believed both things equally and completely, even though they were contradictory.

Weird. She hadn't noticed how full of holes her assumptions were before now. She'd just never thought to consider it.

Keep looking. Keep picking the scab until something bleeds. It was the same woman's voice she'd heard in her head after Maurice left her office.

She searched the house, plagued by more contradictory beliefs:

There must be pictures of us somewhere. *In albums. Online.* And at the same time: *There are no pictures of us anywhere. Why would there be?* The pair of knowings were equally plain to Annabel. She'd never seen before how incompatible they were.

Odd.

It was as if she'd been living inside a dream. In dreams, a person doesn't think much of being inside and outside at the same time. She doesn't think it's strange that her desk is actually an elephant. In dreams, it makes perfect sense to (for instance) be married to someone she couldn't remember meeting and didn't like (and had never liked) at all.

The feeling now was like becoming lucid. Once you see what cannot possibly be, you start to awaken. You start to see the dream as a dream.

Talk to him, said the woman's voice. Not her own voice. It was a voice she'd been hearing for weeks. Maybe for years. *Go talk to your husband ... and when you do, touch his skin.*

The thought was repellant. She didn't want to touch him. She was pretty sure she'd *never* touched him. She hadn't touched him in ... How long had it been?

The woman's voice laughed inside her, as if this was all one big joke at Annabel's expense.

She returned to the basement.

She stopped with one hand on the naked 4x4 to which the bottom of the basement railing was affixed. The basement was unfinished and cold as balls, making it even stranger that she slept down here. Had she *always* slept down here? She wondered this as she looked at the man on the floor under her bed, visible beneath the bedskirt. It was easy because there *was* no skirt. No sheets, either. Her bed was an uncovered mattress that she was pretty sure had been down here when she'd moved in, set atop an old frame that was half rust. A ratty old blanket was all that kept her from freezing.

Even in shadowy silhouette, her terrible husband was small and grotesque. No wonder everyone back then used to make fun of him. Although, she couldn't remember when "back then" referred to.

She was still trying to figure out how long it'd been since she'd touched her husband, knowing it to be never. That's why this was an experiment worth doing: The voice inside seemed to know that when she finally *did* touch him, she'd notice something she'd never noticed before.

In the same way she'd never noticed that she slept in the basement.

And that her husband slept on the floor beneath her.

And that she only knew his name because she'd read it on an old ID in his wallet one night, sought because it'd dawned on her that she didn't know what to call him. His name turned out to be Victor. His ID had expired a while ago. In 1941, to be precise.

And lastly, she hadn't realized that she *did* now remember sleeping upstairs. It felt like a long time ago. The memory of it came back to her like a dream forgotten upon waking.

Confused, Annabel sat on the basement steps and closed her eyes. Then, ever so carefully, she pulled at the threads of her knowingness. Old thoughts returned to her slowly: memories she'd forgotten she had.

The first was that vague memory of sleeping on a king bed upstairs, alone and able to hog the entire thing. With it came recollection of an alarm clock. Of breakfasts. She remembered sitting in a room with a nook, reading.

She never read anymore. She'd forgotten reading was a thing. How long ago were those memories? Her mind showed her a holiday. Her mind showed her a friend

(*alicia*)

coming to her on that holiday, then coming back the next day. The second day, her friend had been bothered by something Annabel had said or done. Something out of character for Annabel. And when Annabel didn't answer her phone because of whatever else had changed her character that day, the friend

(*alicia*)

had visited the house. Annabel hadn't answered the door; some compulsion made her ignore it. So the friend had come back later. And again later. Eventually one of her returns had come after sunset, and that time Annabel *had* answered the door with her husband beside her. The friend had been surprised and asked for an introduction. Then after talking with Victor, her friend had lost all interest in ever speaking to Annabel again. They'd both forgotten about each other, apparently, forever.

Annabel squinted, trying to focus. Was there more? She seemed to remember something else about that friend. Had she heard something about her later? Annabel came up with nothing. She recalled only a mood, and the mood felt like doom.

What was the holiday she seemed to remember?

The Fourth of July, said the woman inside her. Not Annabel and not the friend. She didn't wonder whose voice it was.

Yes. Yes, it was the Fourth of July.

Annabel had forgotten all about the Fourth of July. Not

just what she'd done, but the fact that the holiday existed. It was a loud holiday. Loud, particularly, in this neighborhood. She usually hated all the noise, which was why her friend (What was her name? Annabel didn't know why she couldn't recall) had taken her away that night. They'd gone where there were no fireworks. The evening they'd had together was downright peaceful.

There was no way she'd missed a Fourth. They were too noisy to miss, and by now Annabel was thinking hard. That meant the Fourth of July she was half-remembering now was the *most recent* Fourth.

She pulled her phone from her pocket and looked at the lock screen. Today was August 2nd.

Annabel closed her eyes again. Focused again. And then it came to her.

Alicia. Her friend's name was Alicia.

But not just any friend.

Her *best* friend.

More came in a torrent. She'd known Alicia since high school. Unlike with her husband, Annabel remembered exactly how she'd met Alicia. Alicia had been moping down the B-Wing hall and accidentally collided with Annabel, who also hadn't been looking. After books fell from both of their hands, it turned out they were both carrying copies of *Catch-22*. It hadn't been assigned in Lit class. The book was simply Annabel's favorite at the time ... and Alicia's too.

They'd hung out at Starbucks the next day, making fast friends. Halfway through Alicia had gotten a call from her mother, who was drunk and off with a man that Alicia said was bad news. She explained that her mother needed AA but refused to go. So Annabel said, *We're AA. Alicia and Annabel. She's got AA because she's got us.*

Of course that meant nothing; Annabel's instinct to

help people (the same instinct that led her to becoming a therapist, in fact) was just pie in the sky and Alicia's mother hadn't wanted one iota of two teenagers' help. She eventually had a bad end, dead in a fall down the stairs. But the fact that Annabel wanted to try to help when nobody else cared meant everything to Alicia. They'd been peas in a pod ever since.

Jesus. How the hell had she forgotten Alicia? How the hell had Alicia forgotten *her?*

The oversight felt more than absent-minded. It felt more than *disturbing*, in a neurological sense. It felt, in fact, downright profane. You don't forget a bond like that, and yet for the last month Annabel had done just that. Before July 4th, her memories were crisp and clear — not that she could reach them all, but she could at least sense their light. After the Fourth, everything was foggy.

Had Alicia really asked for an introduction to Victor only a month ago? How was *that* possible? Annabel had married a guy — been with him for years — and yet her best friend hadn't even met him?

Although ... *had* she been with him for years?

Come on, girl, said the voice inside. *Put it together.*

Her eyes came open. She blinked. And she thought: *I* haven't *been with him for years.*

I've never *been with him.*

Then: *He's not my husband.*

The dream collapsed — not entirely, but at least halfway. In that moment, Annabel felt cold, and it had nothing to do with the temperature of the basement. She had the near-miss feeling of realizing something incredibly obvious and incredibly important ... but only at the very last second. It was the feeling of stepping off train tracks — purely by coincidence — right before a train screams by. It was the feeling of almost leaving a baby in a hot car, then realizing just before beginning an hour-long meeting.

Oh. Oh my God.

Annabel saw it now. She'd been living in a fugue. Going to work in a fugue. The man under the bed was her jailer, not her lover. Somehow she'd been duped into believing in a life that wasn't true: that they were married and had been for years, that all she did was work and sleep and that was perfectly normal, that she'd been operated like a puppet and, until seconds ago, had had no idea about any of it. She'd been made to forget everything. She'd kept her family from wondering thanks to believable phone calls in which she lied about things even her fugue-self hadn't done. She'd kept Alicia from wondering because Alicia came to the door when the ... the *thing* under the bed had been standing right beside her. He'd done something to her, hadn't he? He'd made Alicia forget just as Annabel had forgotten.

Annabel even remembered what Victor said after the door was closed and Alicia was gone:

Glamour is easy if you understand that everyone chooses the world they live in. We all decide what we wish to believe, even if it's not a conscious decision. I did nothing for your friend other than open a door. I showed her a way to 'know' a different set of lies. Nothing is objectively true, Annabel, and you're a fool if you believe it is. What I gave Alicia is no more powerful than the propaganda of everyday life. No more influential than the brainwashing of the ordinary world.

But wasn't there more to it? Wouldn't there *have* to be? Victor's instructions to Alicia were simple and dismissive. He'd told her to go home and sit in a chair, then never leave it. That was all. How long would she sit there? Was she allowed to go to the bathroom? Was she allowed to read?

Annabel stood from the basement steps, suddenly filled

with urgency. Suddenly terrified. She had to get out of here. How had she spent a full month this way? The near-miss of it was bone-chilling. If you can't even trust your own mind, what *can* you trust? She was lucky she'd realized the truth just in time.

But ... it wasn't luck, was it? There'd been that voice inside her. That woman's voice, always nudging her toward clarity. She'd disobeyed Victor before because of that voice — only for a while, and never reliably. She'd wondered about things she shouldn't wonder because that voice had spoken to her. But whose voice was it? It wasn't hers. It wasn't Alicia's. It was a voice that had its own mind. *Almost* had its own mind. Because although Annabel hadn't remembered why yet, she was quite sure the owner of that voice couldn't *literally* have her own mind because ... because ...

Because I'm dead, silly.

"Annabel."

The voice from behind made her jump. She spun. If she'd been holding a weapon, she'd have attacked with it.

"Victor!" She blurted. "I ... I didn't hear you. You ..."

He moved too fast for you to see, the dead woman finished. *Remind you of anyone you know?*

"What are you doing down here?" he asked. "You should be at work."

But he didn't say *should*. He said *thould* — the same word with a lisp. It'd always annoyed her.

So stop hearing the lisp, said the dead woman inside. *It's your mind. It's your choice, how you see this man. You have the power, Annabel. Victor said it himself: What you believe is your decision.*

But thinking wasn't a choice, was it? He'd somehow controlled her thoughts for weeks now.

Yes, said the woman, *and together, we resisted. It might not come easily ... but keep your focus, and it will come.*

Try, she told herself. *I can at least try.* This wasn't about her hatred of his lisp. It somehow felt much more important than that: vital that she take the reins of her reality, and choose one that suited her better than the one he'd given her.

Thould, she repeated inside.

In her mind's echo, the word became *should.*

"My client cancelled," she told Victor.

He was immediately alarmed. "Maurithe—

(*maurice*)

—canthelled?"

(*cancelled*)

"What did you say?" Annabel asked.

"I said, '*Maurice cancelled*'?"

The words arrived in her ears totally normal. The voice inside smiled. *Atta girl.*

"He showed up. But then he left."

"He *left?* Why the hell did he *leave?*" Victor

(PUFFED WHEAT *in the twenties they called him* PUFFED WHEAT)

demanded, shaking her hard by the shoulders. He was shorter than she was; the fury in him struck her as almost comical. "Why the hell did you let him leave? He *can't* leave! We need him!"

She slapped a hand over his, angry for the first time in what felt like forever, and almost recoiled the second their skin made contact. She understood now why she'd never touched him before. He was stone cold, his skin so pale it was almost grey. His touch was a block of ice.

She looked him in the eye, gritted her teeth, and said, "Fuck *WE.* You mean *you* need him."

He started back for a long moment, seeing the change in her. Seeing this new resistance. This new attitude. This new sense of infuriating independence. She wanted to spit in his face, but lost her resolve when his mouth opened and a pair of razor-sharp canines descended.

"You'll forget I said this," he cooed, "but when this is over, I'm going to cut you up into little pieces."

She struggled, but his grip was like iron. He was looking into her soul. She closed her eyes and held them shut like a stubborn child refusing to acknowledge the boogeyman. But then he began to whisper, and soon enough her eyes slid open. Then it was all soft tones. Quiet suggestions. And soon after Annabel felt much better, her troubles forgotten.

Everything was okay. She was in the arms of her loving husband, after all.

"Nothing to worry about, Annabel," he told her with a sly — and perhaps knowing — smile. "You're safe."

Safe.

Not *thafe.*

Didn't Victor used to have a lisp? She didn't recall ever hearing a proper S from him before.

A woman's voice — one Annabel didn't remember hearing before but that also felt extremely familiar — spoke up inside her.

You're hearing him how you choose to hear him, the voice said, sounding pleased. *He's in your world now, Annabel ... and breaking free will be easier next time.*

FIVE

THE BOND

Maurice felt the point of a stake press into his back. Someone hissed, *"Hands up, bloodsucker!"*

He spun on his heel, hands hooked into claws as he faced the vampire hunter who'd sneaked up behind him while he was staring at the house ahead, completely distracted. But it was only Celeste, wearing black slacks and a black turtleneck too small for her curves. *His* turtleneck, probably. She'd also donned a black beret he didn't remember owning. The get-up made her look like a beatnick. *Dig it, baby — like coolsville.*

He lowered his hands. A squirrel jumped from one tree to another across a gap of branches, unnerving him further. The relaxing errand wasn't working. He'd been more on-edge during this "walk to clear his head" than he'd been inside, pacing the mansion's long halls and going stir-crazy.

"I could have killed you," he said.

"You left your sword at home," she replied.

"Then I could have maimed you."

She shrugged. If he maimed her, she'd heal. There'd be

a bleat of pain and one ruined turtleneck that was, honestly, too stretched out already. Worse things had happened.

He looked down. What he'd taken for a stake in his back was actually the corner of her wallet.

"Going shopping?" he asked. Then someone passed on the sidewalk, and he waved her down behind the hedgerow.

"Stalking one troubled husband," she said just above a whisper.

"If you're just following me, why do you have your wallet?"

She made a *pssht* noise. "It's just common sense to be prepared.." She slipped the wallet back into her purse, which she was also wearing. It was burgundy. Close enough, in these nighttime shadows, to pass for matching black.

"This doesn't look like walking," Celeste observed, glancing around. She was playing along, but the way Maurice had ducked a moment ago wasn't going to pass for casual. She looked toward the house he'd been surveilling. "Are you planning to rob those people?"

"It's nothing."

Celeste's head cocked. Maurice knew he'd screwed up. Stay married to someone for a millennium and they learn to read you like a book.

"You know when 'it's nothing' is believable? When someone says it in response to a question that didn't imply it might be 'something' in the first place."

"I just meant I'm not casing the house."

"You know when it's believable that a person isn't casing a house? When they volunteer the word 'casing' in response to a joke."

"I get it."

"Clearly you don't." She peered through the hedge —

easy, because it wasn't tightly grown. "I could be suspicious. In fact, I just might be."

Maurice peered, too. Someone was in the big picture window of the house across the street now: staying up late, for a human.

"See? It's just some woman over there," Maurice said. "Nothing to be suspicious about."

"Then maybe I'm jealous."

Maurice considered her, then both of them looked through the hedge again.

"Who is she, Maurice?"

"Nobody." But that answer went nowhere. "Okay. Fine." A heavy sigh. "She's ... That's Dr. Rice."

The answer genuinely startled Celeste. The look of surprise on her face was substantially better than the morose look of doom she'd worn after Brian left — the look they'd probably *both* worn, if Maurice had thought to look in a mirror. It seemed for milliseconds like Maurice had given her a present. The kind of present a cat gives its owner when it delivers mouse organs to the door.

"*Your* Dr. Rice?"

His shrug said the answer was yes, but also no big deal.

Celeste wasn't having it. "Are you seriously going to make me ask why you said you were going for a walk ... then went to your therapist's house to spy on her from the bushes?"

"This is a hedge," Maurice answered.

Now it was Celeste who said nothing.

"I didn't lie," he said. "I did *walk* here."

"On purpose?"

No. He *hadn't* walked here on purpose. That was the really strange part. He'd walked, but it was a vampiric walk: faster and with a lot more range than a human one.

Annabel's house was around fifteen miles from Maurice's, if he had to guess. He hadn't known where she lived. He'd just come to this neighborhood at what felt like random, then just as randomly had ... *seen her*. Her blinds had been wide open, and for the past fifteen minutes she'd done little more than sit in the exposed room's middle, facing forward at the dining room table, writing something down on a piece of paper. It was like she was a window display. Like she *wanted* to be seen.

At 4:22am.

Fully dressed, not in her bedroom, not ready for bed, with every light on in the house.

Maurice shook his head, but his eyes were looking into the distance. It felt like he was answering a question nobody'd asked instead of the one Celeste just had.

"I don't know what brought me here," he said. He was just now accepting that, and he didn't like it one bit.

"Is that the truth?"

"Well," he said a trifle defensively, "what brought *you* here?"

"Your blood."

"But I didn't call you," he said.

They looked at each other, no longer accusatory or defensive. The same wariness that Maurice felt seemed to be dawning on Celeste. There was too much coincidence here if both of them were telling the truth, which Maurice was and he guessed Celeste was, too. It wasn't a good sign, and it came at the end of a night filled with bad omens.

They kept staring at each other in puzzlement. It was true; Maurice hadn't called to Celeste through his blood, and calling-to was usually required to draw one vampire, through blood ties, to another. The only other reason a vampire's sire bond might call out from maker to progeny would be if one or the other was in danger: In dangerous situations, the call happened automatically. But Maurice wasn't in danger, and yet Celeste had still felt the call. She probably hadn't realized until now. She'd simply obeyed the bond as anyone would, and come where blood beseeched her. So what did it mean? Was it possible that Maurice *was* in danger and didn't even know it?

"I don't like this," Celeste said.

"I don't like it either," Maurice replied. He didn't like that he'd come to Annabel's house without meaning to and without looking for it. He didn't like that on arrival, he'd found Annabel acting strangely, practically waiting for him. He *really* didn't like that Celeste had come to him through a channel that should only open in times of peril. The uncertainty of it set his senses twitching.

"Who is she?" Annabel asked, looking again through the hedge.

"I told you who she is."

"I mean, Who *is* she? She's not just your doctor, is she?"

"As far as I know, she's just my doctor. I don't understand why I came here — or you followed me — any more than you do."

She seemed frustrated. Maurice was all action, often dismissing thought entirely.

"Think, Maurice. Look inside. *Something* told you to come here. What did it feel like?"

As he thought, Maurice realized he already knew the answer. He just didn't like it. They'd even discussed this already, more or less — but relating to Celeste following Maurice, not Maurice following Annabel. The only real problem was that the answer to "What made you to come here?" was ...

Well, it was unthinkable.

"It felt ..." Maurice inhaled, then exhaled. He was going to have trouble saying this. It felt absurd on his lips, like saying *Aliens did it*. "It felt like her blood called to me. As if *she* was in danger, and I came because of it."

Celeste seemed to try very hard not to dismiss his answer right away — or, if they'd been under less frightening skies, to laugh in his face. Then she said, "In movies, I always hate it when people say 'That's impossible.'"

"I know."

"But ... that's impossible."

Together they looked at the woman sitting at the dining room table, now staring straight out with nothing to do. She couldn't see them with her lights on and darkness outside, but Maurice would still swear she saw him plain as midnight.

"She's a vampire?" Celeste asked.

"No. She's human."

"You're sure?"

"One hundred percent. I saw her just a few hours ago. If she's vampire, she's freshly turned. And I do mean *freshly*. She's still full of human blood. The smell of it was all over her."

He was still looking at Annabel when Celeste took his head in her hands and turned it to face her. "Maurice. Listen to me. Her blood *can't* have called out to you. Not on purpose and not by accident. Not if she's human."

"Supposedly blood ties can pass through humans."

"Only in theory. Even then, you'd have to share a tie. A *vampire* tie. A close one. Who's close to you, Maurice? Me. Reginald. Your brother. None of us even know this woman. You don't exactly cast a wide net."

"Maybe I came out looking for Reginald without meaning to," Maurice said. "Maybe *that's* what did it —

maybe he's the 'close blood tie' I'm feeling. It kind of makes sense. When I left the house, I couldn't get my mind off of Brian's story. I was worried before, when I thought Logan just found Reginald 'unacceptable,' but this video thing makes it a thousand times worse. Logan will burn the world before he lets word about Reginald catch on in the human population. If Reginald is starting to get popular on YouTube without even trying …"

Celeste's head was already shaking, already dismissing the answer. And with good reason. Even as he said the words, Maurice knew them to be bullshit.

"Why would thinking about *Reginald* bring you to your therapist's house?"

"Maybe they know each other," he said, digging deeper into bullshit as if willing it to be true. "I had this idea that maybe I could catch him out walking around. Drag him back home before someone else took a video, then give him a lecture. I've told him a hundred times: *You only go out to feed until I say you're ready to do more.* Instead, he keeps going to that girl. Claire. He's intuitive as hell, Celeste. It scares me a little. He'll be good at blood ties, mark my word. Maybe great. And glamouring; he'll be great at that, too. It all makes me think that *he* thinks the girl is in danger. I think he feels, somewhere deep down, that it's his job to protect her."

"No," Celeste told him.

"*'No'*?"

"You might have left the house with Reginald on your mind, but instead blood called you here — and we both know damn well it wasn't Reginald's blood." She turned again toward Annabel. "It was the blood of someone in that house."

Maurice, if he was being honest with himself, would

have gone further than that. It wasn't just "the blood of someone in that house" that'd compelled him to come. It was *Annabel's* blood. He was sure of it, even though it was impossible. He knew because of another thing that was equally impossible until he'd experienced it himself: He could *smell* the blood that'd called him: a psychic scent he'd never noticed before. The smell was human — no doubt about it.

"I believe that all things happen for a reason," Celeste went on, "but a random tie between Reginald and Dr. Rice? A tie that called you out tonight of all nights — *here*, to this place? To find *this* waiting for you?" She'd gestured toward the house, and now made an exasperated face. "Honey, that's too coincidental even for me."

Maurice said nothing. A very fragile sensation had begun coming to him over the past handful of seconds, and he didn't want to risk disrupting it by speaking. It felt like he was balancing something very tall and precarious on the tip of his finger. If he so much as breathed wrong, the whole works would fall.

"I don't like it," Celeste continued. "We need to go. We need to leave and never come back."

"No," Maurice told her. "That's not it."

"*What's* not it?"

When he didn't answer — still balancing the now-massive fragile thing inside him, more afraid than ever that he'd drop it — Celeste repeated herself. Then she repeated herself again, using different words: increasingly urgent, increasingly scared words. Dread had its hooks in her, same as dread had so recently had its hooks in Maurice. But he was above that now. Farther away. He felt distant: floating in a place where although he could see his wife panicking, he couldn't hear or feel her at all.

Instead, he felt hunger.

Insanely strong hunger — strong enough to eclipse everything else. *Unnatural* hunger. It was an intense, undeniable force of need that dragged him like an electromagnet drags iron. The sheer *want* of it filled Maurice's every sense, intense enough to block out the world itself. He'd kill whoever he had to, to satisfy the desire.

But then a new thing interposed itself between Maurice and the feeling. When it happened, his distance from it grew and he was able to see the sensation for what it was instead of being consumed by it. And in that seeing he realized it wasn't truly *hunger* that'd almost taken him away. It was *addiction*.

But not his own addiction. This was an addiction that belonged to someone else. Someone in his bloodline.

What's more, none of it was just *coming* to him. The calling-out, the blood tie, the hunger, the addiction itself ... these were things Maurice was being *shown*.

His fugue dissolved bit by bit. When he was himself again, he woke to find Celeste shaking him like a man in a trance — which, he supposed, he'd just been. He blinked. She stopped shaking, waiting for him to respond.

"*Maurice?*"

"There *is* a tie between us," he droned.

"Of course there's a tie between ..." She stopped. "You mean between you and *her?* A blood tie between you and Dr. Rice?"

He nodded, but more to himself than to Celeste. His certainty was growing the longer he sat with the fugue's memory. He thought he'd understood what was going on a moment ago, but now he was absolutely sure of it. It didn't matter that humans didn't typically express blood ties; what mattered was that it was *possible* if the human was exceptional — which Annabel was ... somehow, in some way. And it didn't matter that as a human, Annabel would have no logical way to call out to Maurice for help; what mattered was that there *were* ways even if they were illogical. But most of all none of that mattered because it wasn't really *Annabel herself* who'd called out. The real person who'd called to Maurice lived deep inside Annabel: an ancestor they shared.

Strange as it seemed, the blood memory of one of Maurice's ancestors ran within Annabel's veins. That ancestor's memory had hijacked her subconscious mind, speaking to Maurice through blood.

It was possible because although Annabel was human, the person her blood remembered had been vampire.

It was a relative as close to Maurice as Celeste and Reginald.

A vampire who'd been deeply addicted to the only thing vampires had *ever* been addicted to in the history of their kind: *Thrilloglobin*, the synthetic blood manufactured in 1929 by the Chicago Vampire Mafia. *Thrill*: the scourge that Maurice's killing spree had erased from existence.

"Not a tie between me and Annabel," Maurice explained, "but between me and the vampire in her bloodline."

Celeste waited, watching him. As impossible as it all seemed and felt and was, Celeste was already beginning to believe it too ... though Maurice.

"It can't be," she said.

But Maurice only nodded. "It's Daisy," he told her.

SIX

WHAT HAPPENS NOW?

Daisy.

She was Maurice's second progeny, made between Celeste and Reginald. The only other being he'd saved by cursing with eternal life — this one used, tormented, and eventually murdered during their time under Prohibition. Daisy was the reason Maurice had gone to Annabel in the first place: to purge himself of guilt over her death. They'd already spoken of coincidence. Was it coincidence, now, that Maurice had thrice spoken all night to a relative he hadn't even known Daisy had?

Not on his life.

Not considering the way Annabel's business card had been slipped to him despite Annabel claiming not to have done it: probably the only therapist willing to see patients in the middle of the night. It was like Maurice had told Annabel mere hours ago: *He* hadn't found *her*. It was she who'd found him.

"I don't understand," Celeste said.

She was sitting in her favorite chair in the living room: a subconscious attempt to find comfort amidst all this frightening uncertainty. After the two of them accepted the impossible fact of Annabel's lineage, the notion of staying anywhere near her had become far too worrying. So they'd run home, and while they ran, Maurice glanced constantly backward. He was sure they were being chased. Annabel's human blood had managed to call out through a connection she likely didn't even realize she had, and to Maurice that promised very bad tidings. Someone or something had planned this. It was now a race against time: a need to solve the puzzle before whatever-it-was sprung whatever trap it had in mind. Maurice had no plans to sit at ground zero and wait for it to happen.

Who hated Maurice Toussant? Who had reason to entrap and probably kill him? Maurice's life had made more waves than an ocean. The answers to those questions numbered in the thousands.

"Daisy had a child when she was very young," Maurice explained. "She told me she gave it up for adoption. The baby must have been Annabel's grandmother or something. Or great-grandmother; who knows. That's the only thing that makes sense. It can't be vampire kin. All of the vampires Daisy made died in '29. Even if she made one that survived, that wouldn't really work with Annabel. Annabel is human."

"But Maurice ... Daisy wasn't even a vampire for very long. How long was it? Weeks? Maybe a month before she died? She gave the baby up before she even met you. Even with back-tracing, to survive two or three or four purely-human generations ..."

"Time doesn't matter to blood," Maurice said. "It doesn't matter if she had the baby before she was a vampire; the blood still knows. I'd heard about this sort of thing before, but Reginald makes it crystal clear. He doesn't really understand blood ties yet, but I can see the ability inside him through my own senses. The things his mind can do … it's like everything he lacks physically was just shunted into enhanced mental abilities."

"Is that possible?"

Maurice shrugged. "Maybe everyone gets the same amount of the Dark Gift, and he got it all on the inside. I just know his bloodwalking ability far outstrips my own. When I look inside him, I see foggy outlines of everyone in his tree — human, vampire, past, possible futures … I can't get at them, but I know they're there. And the girl? Claire? I want to dismiss her as just some plaything he's got, but there's something in Claire, too. Something powerful. I can't tell what it is, and I don't think Reginald knows that he could probably figure it out, if he knew how to look. All of this is subconscious with him. I think he found Claire *because* of what a deep-down part of himself believes."

"What's this got to do with Daisy?" Celeste asked.

"If you look into me, I think you'll see the same sort of thing is going on with Daisy. Maybe our bond won't let you see what I saw outside Annabel's house, but I think you'll get the truth of it. *This is Daisy.* It doesn't matter if we understand how it happened — how her great-great grand-daughter came to be my therapist. The fact is, *it did happen.* I know it like I know my name. I went to her house tonight because the blood memory of Daisy called out to me … and the only way it could have done so is because Annabel is in trouble."

"But if it's really Daisy, why wouldn't she have spoken to you before now?"

Maurice made himself patient. Celeste was excellent at many things, but an in-depth knowledge of vampire lore wasn't one of them. Most humans didn't know *how* their own brains and bodies worked — just *that* they worked. It was the same with most vampires.

"It's not *actually* Daisy," Maurice explained. "Daisy is dead. There's no little *mind-of-Daisy* inside Annabel with a personality and soul of its own. This is an *impression* of Daisy, held within Annabel's blood, that her mind somehow recognizes."

"But if Annabel is human ..."

Maurice waved the question away. "We don't have to understand it. Humans can't usually read blood, but humans can't usually stay conscious while they're sleeping either, and Tibetan Yogis do it all the time. Either Annabel is unusual, Daisy was unusual, or both. All that matters right now is that it's true. And we know it's true."

Maurice was pacing, trying to work this out.

"Maybe it's like those stories of humans performing great feats of strength when shit gets real. Small women lifting cars because their kid is pinned under them, stuff like that. Maybe some small amount of vampiric power is always inside Annabel thanks to Daisy, but maybe it's usually too quiet to hear. But tonight isn't 'ordinary circumstances.' What if she really *is* in danger, and what if that danger is the only reason Daisy was able to rise up inside Annabel's mind and do anything? What if the fact that Annabel is in danger is the only reason she *could* call out to me?"

"But if she needs help, why aren't we helping?"

"Because you came to me," Maurice answered. "I didn't call you, and you came anyway."

"Which means that *you* were in danger, even if you didn't realize it," Celeste said, understanding.

Maurice nodded. "You felt the need to get the hell out of there even before I did. You wouldn't have come if the threat was only to Annabel. I would have, but you wouldn't.

No. This is a threat to me, not just her. That's why we need to figure this out before we do something stupid."

"Are you saying you think it's a trap?"

"I think it'd be a pretty big coincidence if Annabel and I were both in danger in the exact same place at the exact same time for separate reasons," Maurice answered. "If I had to guess, she's in trouble *because* of me. Someone sent me to her before our first session. I made my first appointment because someone slipped me her business card, and I don't think it was her who did it. That tells me someone is using Annabel to get to me. If there's danger, it's probably second-hand. I'm the real target. She's just caught in the middle."

"If that's true," Celeste said, "that 'someone' could have used *anyone* to get to you. It didn't need to be a therapist."

Maurice had been thinking on that one for a while. He kept recalling an obscure practice that psychopathic vampires sometimes used: a practice akin to mind rape. He'd even told Annabel about it. If you knew enough about a vampire, you could crash through the doors of their mind without needing blood ties — or permission — to do it.

If this really was a trap, his therapy must be part of it. Otherwise, whoever set this up wouldn't have bothered hooking him up with Annabel. Her vacant-eyed stare tonight meant she'd been glamoured, and the only reason to glamour her and send her to speak repeatedly with Maurice was to gather enough of his innermost thoughts to build a cypher: a way to break into his mind and, once there, to browse his brain like a library.

If that was true, Maurice wasn't even the real target. *His mind* was the real target. There must be something inside his head that someone wanted badly enough to jump through a lot of complicated hoops to retrieve. Unfortunately, Maurice had spent over twenty hours spilling his guts to Annabel. That might be enough. Whoever was behind this — if he had Annabel under glamour — might already have his key.

Maurice told Celeste his theory. Her hand went to her mouth, seeing the puzzle come together.

"Then why use someone with a connection to Daisy? They needed a therapist so they could learn all about you, but why bother finding Daisy's relative? Why *Annabel*, instead of some other therapist?"

"I don't know. Maybe Daisy's blood is part of this, too. I wouldn't even know where to start making guesses without an idea of what they're after."

"Well ..." Celeste tapped her chin. "What secrets do you know that a vampire psychopath might want?"

Maurice threw up his hands. "Who knows? I'm two thousand years old! It could be a treasure hunter looking for something I saw in some catacomb somewhere in the five hundreds. It could be someone who just wants my ATM PIN number."

He was half joking, but it was possible. A person doesn't live for two millennia without accumulating a lot of compound interest. Maurice's wealth — thanks to the passage of time — could buy countries.

"We have to help her," Maurice told Celeste. "But we have to figure out what's happening before we do. We can't just barge in without knowing what's going on. Chances are, whoever's got her glamoured is living with her. They'd want to keep her close because they've had her under glamour for weeks. But if we go in and confront them, that plays our hand. Right now we've got an advantage. It was Daisy who called out, so at least part of Annabel is resisting the glamour. That's good for us. If she's resisting and sending messages, her captor probably doesn't know about it. If he did, he'd find a way to stop it. Right now we know he's there but he doesn't know it. If we confront him, our advantage disappears."

"If we confront him, he dies," Celeste corrected.

"Yeah. But this is a lot of trouble for someone to go to in order to hack my brain. I don't think he wants my PIN number. It has to be something *really* important. What if it turns out to be bigger than we think? What if it's a group instead of just one person? We might storm in and kill one guy only to find out there's a hundred more, or there are things already set in motion that we can't stop because we have no idea what they are. It's too risky. We need to learn more. We *will* help her. Of course we'll help her, because somehow I'm the one who put her in danger. But we have to do it intelligently."

Celeste sat back, breathing slowly to calm herself. She seemed to be thinking.

"There's one thing that bugs me," she finally said.

Maurice stopped pacing and looked over. Celeste's voice was calm, but he'd just felt a jolt of alarm in her blood.

"You think someone was using Dr. Rice to build themselves a key to your mind."

He nodded.

"And she could help him do that because she's a psychiatrist. Because every week, you went in there and talked and talked and talked. You told her about us in Chicago during Prohibition. You told her about the time you spent at the World Fair, around Holmes."

"I told her about Michaud, too," Maurice said. "Michaud and the punks in Austin in the '80s. When you and I were taking our break."

"Lots of information. Lots of personal details he could

use to decode your defenses, if he knew how and was demented enough to do it. Week by week, thanks to your sessions with the doctor, he built himself a better and better decoder ring."

Maurice waited. He thought he knew where this might be going.

"So what I'm wondering," Celeste said, "is what he'll do now that you're no longer going to therapy? What happens to Annabel, now that you've quit?"

A hammer fell in Maurice's heart. *Why did I go to Annabel's house? Because Daisy called me. Why did Daisy call me? Because Annabel was in danger.*

But to that, now he could add:

Why would she be in danger tonight, but not before?

There'd *been* no blood-cry from Daisy before Maurice broke things off with his therapist. Why? Because as long as therapy continued, that decoder ring kept getting better and better. But maybe ... just maybe ... it was good enough to work already, and his fired therapist had just become dead weight.

Maurice's dead heart quickened its beat. He saw the truth behind Celeste's question.

What happens to Annabel, now that you've quit?

The memory of Daisy, at least, wasn't optimistic about the answer.

SEVEN

WARNING

Good God. I can warn her.

Maurice realized it so suddenly, he bolted upright. Celeste was beside him, still sleeping.

"Celeste!"

"Mmm."

"Celeste, wake up!"

"Mmm!" she said. It was the same non-word as before, but the first was confused and this one was annoyed. It was a versatile thing to say.

He shook her. The idea that'd woken him felt right, but Maurice didn't trust himself to judge anything with a lot of moving pieces. For that, he needed Celeste. She was details; he was blunt force. If she didn't assess his plans in advance, she usually ended up assessing the damage he'd caused.

"I have an idea!"

She removed her sleep mask, which was pink and frilly. Her hair was a bird's nest. One of her eyes must have been sleepier than the other because only one wanted to open. She seemed to be squinting, like a pirate.

"What time is it?"

He looked at the bedside clock. "One fifteen."

"PM?"

"Of course PM."

She groaned. "Your idea can't wait 'til sunset?"

"It's about Annabel," he said.

It'd been a long bedtime, but Celeste had slept deep once she finally slept. This woke her in an instant. She sat upright, face troubled as the night's worries returned to her.

"Tell me it's a *good* idea."

He nodded. "It's simple: We warn her."

"'We *warn her*,'" Celeste repeated. He couldn't tell if she was impressed by the idea's profundity or underwhelmed by how obvious it was. "Simple" was an understatement. *Warning her* was troubleshooting an appliance by asking if it's plugged in. It wasn't exactly Einstein.

"We make a phone call," he continued. "We keep our distance. Don't make contact. I'll just pick up the phone and tell her what we know. As long as she's the one that answers the phone, whoever's holding her won't find out."

"And if someone else answers?"

"I'll just hang up. There's a way to hide your number so nobody knows who called, right?"

Celeste was already letting herself fall back asleep, unimpressed. "I considered that already. Even if she picks up, she won't understand anything you say. She's glamoured."

"*Mostly* glamoured," Maurice corrected. "Not all the way. Whoever did this must be good at glamouring or I'd've seen holes in her story. I'd've sensed it if the glamour was less than complete."

"Right. So let me sleep."

He poked her until she opened her eyes again. He hadn't told her the wrinkle that'd woken him. Yes, Annabel was glamoured, and glamoured well. But that wasn't the whole story.

"No. Listen. No matter how good a job her captor did, the glamour *isn't* bulletproof."

"You just said—"

"I know. But think about it. If she was *completely and totally under his control,* we wouldn't know anything was wrong. We only know because Daisy called out to me, and that could only happen if she was free to act. So, you're right: *Annabel* is fully glamoured. But I don't think Daisy is."

"Is that possible?"

"Normally I'd say no, but here we are." There was precedent for impossibility, too. Blood ties didn't usually cross through humans, and yet they had. Somehow Annabel or Daisy or both were exceptions to the rule.

After a beat of thoughtful quiet, something else occurred to Maurice. Something that gave him hope.

"Actually, now that I think about it, even Annabel's glamour isn't perfect. It's good, but not perfect." He rearranged himself on the bed. "You asked why I left my session last night. It's because something's bothered me about her for a while. Something I couldn't quite explain. It felt like ... like she was hiding something. Looking back, I guess I can see she was glamoured. She hid her lineage from me. She wouldn't let me sample her blood, to check her bloodline."

"And that surprises you?" Celeste's face soured. "I don't like you sucking on other women, Maurice."

"I wouldn't have sucked on her."

"Sure sounds to me like you wanted to suck on her."

"Are we really going to have this argument now?"

"Hey. Your husband tells you he wants to drink another

woman's blood, a few alarms go off. I'm sure you'd be respectful. You'd probably use a sterile lancet on her finger and not get a raging boner at all."

"I had a hunch."

"Was it a hunch about her long, white neck?"

"You know what? Go back to sleep," he said.

She rolled her eyes and flapped her hands, not really waving away jealousy but putting on a show of it. "No, no. It's fine. Tell me your brilliant hunch."

Maurice waited to make sure she meant it, then explained. "The more I think about it, the more I'm sure I saw cracks in her glamour: ways that 'Daisy' was resisting, keeping Annabel from going all the way under. I think it happened because Annabel's a psychiatrist. She's on decent terms with her subconscious mind. I doubt she knew Daisy was inside her — or even that she had a vampire in the family — but Daisy *is* Annabel, right? That's the way it works. The real Daisy is gone. What we're calling 'Daisy' is really just a deep-down part of Annabel. Saying *'Annabel's asleep and Daisy's awake'* is splitting hairs. 'Daisy's resisting' really means *Annabel's* resisting. Somewhere deep down, Annabel understands everything. So maybe if we call, a part of her will hear us." He shrugged. "It's at least worth a shot, right?"

Celeste thought. Maurice could almost see her weighing the variables he hadn't considered.

"Okay," she said.

"'Okay'?"

"It might not work, but I can't see how it'd hurt."

"So we call first thing tonight."

Celeste shook her head. "Now. While any vampires in that house are sleeping. I noticed a landline phone just off her dining room. You can get the number from directory assistance."

"Annabel could be asleep, too."

Again she shook her head. "There's no way she's fully nocturnal. She might stay up late sometimes, but she's got clients to see. She has to keep up appearances. It's too suspicious if she just disappears."

"What if the vampire hears the phone ring?"

"When's the last time you've heard our phone ring during the day? I don't know any vampires who sleep that lightly."

So he got out of bed and together they padded to the kitchen. Maurice, who only owned a cell phone reluctantly, had a landline too.

He called 411, got the number of one Annabel Rice on Sherwood Street in Columbus, then dialed and let it ring. After twelve rings, he hung up and dialed again. He looked to Celeste, beside him.

"She's not answering."

"Keep trying. She was up all night staring into space. Maybe she's sleepy."

Maurice tried longer. He dialed and re-dialed.

"I don't like this," he said.

"We already covered that. This is an inherently unlikable situaiton."

"What if she's dead?"

"I don't meant to be blunt, Maurice, but if she's dead, she's dead. You calling won't change that."

His face made a scowl. "Then we have to do something. Something more direct."

She shook her head. "You were the one who said we *can't* do anything. Not until we understand what's going on. Besides, it's the middle of the afternoon. Unless you want a sunburn, we have to wait until nightfall anyway."

Maurice called once more. The phone rang twenty-two times before he finally hung up and sat on a kitchen chair.

Celeste sat beside him. She put a hand on his. "It was a good idea. Still is. If you want to stay up all day and keep trying until she answers, I'll stay up with you."

He deflected. Weakened by fatigue, he spilled what was truly bothering him. "I can't be responsible for another innocent life, Celeste. Not now."

"Why *now*? What makes *now* any different from yesterday?"

He laughed a little. "It's something Annabel and I were working on. Apparently I carry a lot of guilt over the deaths I've caused. I don't need to cause any more."

"You're an immortal. You've killed so many. It's a hazard of being what we are."

"Mostly I agree. Mostly, I've only killed assholes. Like Isaac."

Celeste's head bobbed. "Isaac *was* an asshole."

"But then I killed Daisy."

She squeezed the hand she'd been holding. "Honey. The Mafia killed Daisy."

"Because I put her in harm's way by turning her. I was just starting to get my head around it. The guilt. I half-wish I was still repressing."

"Listen to you," Celeste said with a little smile. "'Repressing.'"

"She has to live. She just *has* to."

Celeste took his other hand, now facing him fully. "We'll do our best to make sure she does. That's all we can do."

"If only she could talk to me. Tell me what happened so we don't have to waste time figuring it out."

"Annabel or Daisy?"

"Either. Both."

"Daisy's in *your* bloodline, too. *Can't* you talk to her?"

He smiled. Celeste wasn't good at this part. "That's a different Daisy. The 'Daisy' in Annabel is just Annabel's subconscious mind imitating the real Daisy. Talking to my Daisy would just be me talking to myself."

"Well, what did 'Annabel's Daisy' say to you before? When she put you in that trance outside the house?"

Maurice shrugged. "It wasn't really saying. It was feeling."

"Well, then, what did you *feel?*"

"I felt her addiction. That's how I knew it was Daisy. The real Daisy's Thrilloglobin addiction was ... it was like it became *my* addiction for a while." He shivered. "Jesus. Do you remember how bad it was? Thrill?"

Celeste nodded. They sat for a while. Maurice seemed to almost have a new idea — a new loose end to chase — but not quite. Whatever the thread of it was, he felt like he'd given it to himself when he'd spoken. But what kind of an idea could he possibly have prompted?

Addiction. How bad it was. No, he was just feeling guilty all over again.

Finally Celeste said, "I think we should try to go back to sleep. Tackle this with fresh minds after night falls. Sitting here and worrying about what can't be changed is a recipe for disaster."

Maurice frowned. There was that almost-idea again. He could nearly see it ... but not quite.

"What did you just say?" he asked.

"I said we should go back to sleep."

"No." Then he repeated the correct bit to himself: "'*Recipe for disaster.*'" As he said the words, a weak light lit, trying to brighten.

Celeste said something after that, but Maurice was too focused to hear her. He concentrated on what he'd just repeated. Feeling like a man rubbing a rabbit's foot for luck, he said the key word again: "*Recipe.*"

"What, is Reginald wearing off on you? It's like you want to bake cookies."

The corner of something emerged. Maurice sprang toward it with every bit of mind he had, grabbing and pulling. He repeated the word like a mantra as he did, trying to imbue it with power that words don't normally have.

Recipe. Recipe.

Then: *!!RECIPE!!*

"Oh my God," he said.

Celeste stopped patting his hands and faced him.

"Oh my God, Celeste. That's it. It has to be! There's nothing else important enough that Daisy and I have in common. That day. With Malone. The day we went went into my first distillery. There were three chemists. Just three!"

He'd stood. Celeste looked up and said, "What are you talking about?"

Maurice pulled her to standing, both of his hands holding hers. He'd been tired, but as the idea formed he grew wide awake. He was sure he was right. Daisy hadn't been trying to identify herself when she'd shown him addiction behind that hedge. *She'd been giving him a clue.*

"Thrilloglobin's recipe was a secret," Maurice explained. "They had three chemists who knew how it was made, but all three ended up dead. We burned the distilleries. Destroyed the entire Vampire Mafia. It was 1929, so it's not like there were computers. No Dropbox. No Internet. The Mob kept their records on paper and in the minds of the chemists because those were the only places you *could* store information. When those things were gone, the recipe was gone. In the twenties, something like a recipe could still be erased forever."

Celeste was waiting for the punchline.

"But someone must have survived; don't you see? I *didn't* kill every member of the Vampire Mafia. One of them must have lived ... and he's in Annabel's house right now!"

"And he's got the recipe for Thrill?"

"No!" Maurice almost wanted to laugh; the epiphany was that delicious. "If he had the recipe, none of this would be necessary! If he knew how to make Thrill, he'd be out there finding partners. They'd be making it already!"

"But because he *doesn't* have it ... that's why this *is* necessary!"

"Yes! Because the recipe was destroyed! Because anyone who could maybe have re-created it are dead! Because everyone in Santori's organization and all our Untouchables — anyone who might *possibly* have seen that recipe lying around somewhere on a desk or a chair in an office or one of their distilleries — is dead. Everyone, that is ... *except for me."*

Celeste's whole face changed. She understood.

"You saw it, didn't you? *You saw the recipe for Thrill."*

Maurice nodded. "When I went to the distillery with Malone. It was just a glance, but every vampire memory is photographic if you know how to get at it. Hell, Reginald can do it. You should have seen how well he did when I tested his speed-read of *The Shining.* He could have read every word of it back to me from memory, if I wanted him to. I don't think *I* could pull up that recipe; I'm just not talented enough. But if this Mafia survivor built himself a blood key with what Annabel got out of me?" He took Celeste by both shoulders. "Celeste. What if the blood key lets someone who *is* talented enough to get inside my head and take a good, hard look around?"

Celeste grew paler than usual. "You think this is about Thrill, don't you? You think whoever's got Annabel wants to restart the Thrill trade."

Maurice was nodding. "He needs the recipe to do it, and I have the only copy." He tapped his temple. "But he needs something else, too. He also needs a visceral experience he can compare his product to. How else will he know if he's got it right? He can't get an experience of Thrill from me. I never tried it. Neither did Santori's people. They knew how deadly it was. But we both know someone who *did* take it. Someone whose blood memories of Thrilloglobin were strong."

"Daisy," Celeste said.

"Daisy," Maurice repeated.

It all fit. *This* was why someone was using Annabel to hack into Maurice's mind. If he succeeded, he'd have all he needed to bring Thrilloglobin back to life. God help vampires — and the humans who got in their way — if that happened.

"What do we do?" Celeste asked.

"We had to warn Annabel before. Now we *really* have to warn her. But it's more than warning. We need her help, too. Maybe there's just one leftover gangster behind this, but maybe not. There are still things to figure out before we do anything, but at least now we know what's at stake. We still have our advantage. Whoever's doing this, he doesn't know that we know."

"I think there are some archives I can dig up that will help us," Celeste said, nodding along. "We—"

The doorbell rang. They went instantly silent, and stayed that way for long seconds.

"Expecting a delivery?" Maurice asked.

"Maybe it's a door-to-door salesman."

"We have a gated yard. That wasn't the gate buzzer. It was the front door."

"Then I guess it's not a delivery, either," Celeste said.

They waited, as if the world wouldn't see them if they were perfectly still. But then the bell rang again.

"Ignore it," Celeste said.

But then a man outside began shouting: *"Maurice? Maurice Toussant?"*

"Still ignore it."

Maurice moved toward the door. Celeste grabbed his arm.

"It's daylight," he said. "Whoever's out there is human. It'll be fine."

"You'll burn if you open the door."

"The stoop is shaded this time of day. If I don't stand there with the door open for a half hour, I'll be okay."

"I don't like it, Maurice. It's too weird. And that's saying something, because holy shit have we seen a lot of 'weird' lately."

Maurice gently separated her hand from his arm. "Keep trying to call Annabel and stay out of sight," he told her. "The guy out there came onto our property without us letting him in. I don't think the best choice is to go back to bed and hope he goes away."

"Be careful," she said.

EIGHT

IRONIC

The man on Maurice's stoop was human. And the exact opposite of threatening.

"Oh, hi!" he said, smiling as if Maurice was expecting him for a long-overdue reunion. He was moderate height and probably in his sixties. Maurice had lost the trick of judging human age. "I'm Harrison Cardiff. Is your dad around?"

"How are you here?" Maurice asked.

"Took a plane. Bumpy ride. You have a lot of clouds in Ohio!"

"No ..." Maurice was having trouble recalibrating after his doublet of worry and revelation. Whatever emotion he was supposed to feel now was a third thing unlike either of the others. "I mean, how are you inside my fence?"

The man swished his hand like waving away an insect. "Oh, I *jumped* that," he said. "Is your father home?"

"I'm sorry," Maurice said. He ducked further into the shadows, already sweating. Day like today, even the reflected UV was murder. "*Who* are you?"

"Harrison." He extended his hand. Unsure what else to do, Maurice shook it.

"And you are?"

"Maurice."

Harrison made a show of flapping his hands, demonstrating his mirth. *"You're* Maurice! I expected someone a lot older. They talk like you're a hundred years if you're a day."

"At least," Maurice said. "Who's 'they'?"

"Your bosses. At the staircase company."

"Treadmills. We sell treadmills."

"Same thing. Hey. You got a minute?"

"Um ..."

Harrison started rummaging inside a halfheartedly packed satchel. Detritus dropped to the stoop at his feet, totally ignored.

"I've got something you'll want to look at. We need a table. Say. Do you think I could trouble you for some water? Climbing that fence took more out of me than I realized." He gave a laugh that was nothing but innocent and genuine, if eccentric. "I'm sorry to just show up like this, but you never answer your phone."

"You could have left a message."

Harrison laughed again. "Oh, this isn't anything I want committed to a recording. You'll see. And ..." He trailed off as his eyes picked out something behind Maurice — something to which he yelled an over-the-top *HEEEEY!"*

Maurice turned. Celeste, apparently convinced by overhearing this bizarre conversation that her worries were overblown, had come up behind him. She was staying back, well away from bounced sunshine.

Harrison came right at her with his hand extended again, not waiting for an invitation to enter the foyer.

Celeste was baffled into shaking the hand, though she didn't seem happy about it.

"Harrison Cardiff. Hey. Are you Maurice's mother? Because I've gotta tell you, *your son here—*" He was wagging his finger at Maurice, apparently intending to conclude this sentence with something flatteringly affectionate.

But Celeste, who tended to be short with people who complicated her life, cut him off: *"Who* the hell are you? And *why* are you here, inside our fence, in the middle of the day?"

Maurice decided the threat of death by sunlight was worse than committing this cheery home invader to the inside of his home, so he stepped past Harrison and closed the door. The room instantly felt ten thousand degrees cooler.

If Harrison found anything strange in Celeste's implication that "the middle of the day" was noteworthy, he didn't show it. He was that unique kind of oblivious that was, when you got past frustration and irritation, was actually kind of adorable. He was also wearing a fanny pack.

"Harrison Cardiff. I sent you letters?"

That was no good. Maurice had lived in this house for hundreds of years if he included its time in France, and yet he had no idea where the mailbox was. Vampires didn't get much mail.

When Harrison saw the noncomprehension on their faces, he waved the issue of letters away. "Anyway. Who cares. I've been trying to get in touch about your friend the fat vampire."

A klaxon went off inside Maurice's brain. Celeste looked over in alarm. Harrison seemed oblivious to their shock.

"I don't know any fat vampires," Maurice said.

Celeste elbowed him. He really should be denying the existence of vampires first, then denying that he knew any of them second.

Harrison flapped that same hand again, this time as if to say, *Oh, you kidder*.

"Come on. This is just *us* talking. My tech guys can pull metadata from anything. They *tell* you YouTube strips it all out, but that's not what my people found. The videos of the guy I'm talking about are geotagged in a rough circle around your staircase company and all of them were recorded an hour or two before dawn. So our research people called every company with a night shift inside that circle asking if they had a guy about five-ten three-fifty with brown hair working for them. I had a theory those videos were recorded on his way home from work because he looks dressed for work. Not dressed well, by the way." Again he laughed. "Oh. Say — why does a staircase company have a night shift, anyway?"

"Treadmill company," Maurice corrected.

Harrison seemed to have an attention deficit. He didn't pause after his question, apparently uninterested in the glamouring work Maurice had done to keep himself and Reginald (and Nikki, and regrettably now Todd Walker as well) working without the ravages of the sun.

"In two of the videos, Fat Vampire's wearing unusual shoes," Harrison said.

"Wh ... *What?*"

"They look like Corthay Oxfords — Vendomes in creme brule color, if I'm not mistaken. For a big man, he sure has little feet."

Harrison paused to look down at Maurice's feet, which happened to be wearing their usual around-the-house

Corthay Pilat slip-ons in the exact same size. Damn his taste for fine footwear.

"Near as I can figure, your company pays ... what? Fifty, sixty thousand dollars a year?" Harrison said. "I mean, this isn't California. It's Ohio. So what's an average working Joe doing wearing a two thousand dollar pair of French shoes? That's when our guys started looking for a wealthy French benefactor in the same circle. What are you guys — partners?"

The truth was far less glamourous. Reginald had started experiencing existential fear when he realized he was going to live forever (joke was on him about that one, ha-ha) and for a while he'd been prone to crying jags in the breakroom. After he soaked his sneakers with blood tears one night (and after discovering they wore the same size somehow), Maurice had sprinted home to grab an extra pair of his own shoes. He told Reginald he could keep them; he'd had them forever and they were worthless. They basically were anyway. Vendomes were on their way out. Any decent Parisian fashion aficionado could tell you that.

"Are you a cop or something?" Maurice asked.

Harrison smiled. Even though this casual butting in to everyone's business made a pretty airtight case, he acted like it was just everyday curiosity. "No. I'm just a man serious about his next project."

"What next project?"

"Oh!" Harrison's hand shot into his pocket with the urgency of having forgotten something. He came out with a small ivory card. On its front was HARRISON CARDIFF. Below that: IRONIC PRODUCTIONS.

"'Productions'?" Celeste read over Maurice's shoulders.

"Yeah. Do you know *'Fuck Your Mother'*?"

"*Excuse* me?" Celeste said, but when she raised her arm

as if to come at him, Maurice pushed it back down. He didn't watch much television, but there was a lot of water cooler talk between shifts and a lot of his co-workers were talking recently about that exact Netflix show. It was supposedly like if a 70s sitcom had a baby with an off-color murder mystery. It didn't sound like a combination that should work, but apparently it did.

"I've heard of it," Maurice said.

"That's one of ours. What about *Superman is Gay?*"

"That one, I don't know," Maurice said.

"Oh, you should check it out," Harrison said. "Imagine *Sex and the City* with superheroes and light S&M."

When Celeste nodded as if she might be interested in such a TV show, Maurice found himself resetting. Harrison's style of interaction had somehow put them all on rails, guiding them effortlessly toward some inevitable destination. Because of it, the conversation had stopped being one Maurice wondered *why* they were having and instead become one he kept trying to understand. In a normal world, that wasn't the right reaction. This man had parked outside, jumped their gate, then barged in and announced the many ways he'd violated their privacy. Maurice should be angry, not interested.

"Look," he said. "I don't know what this is about or why you trespassed your way onto our property to tell us about it, but—"

Harrison didn't seem bothered by Maurice's accusation. He seemed more bothered that Maurice and Celeste didn't understand his purpose. He butted in.

"I'm sorry. I didn't say the most important thing. My partner and I want to make a TV show about your friend."

Maurice looked at Celeste. Celeste looked at Maurice.

Those words had meaning, but still Maurice couldn't make sense of them.

"What?"

"Your friend," Harrison repeated, as if that was the problematic part. "We got the idea for *Superman* by watching a queer chat group a lot of our writers are part of. Optioned a forum post. Can you believe that?"

It wasn't that Maurice couldn't believe it. It was more that he didn't know what it meant.

"*Fuck Your Mother* came out of a true crime story in a small town in Idaho. National news never really grabbed onto it, but a friend of mine grew up near where it happened. That's how we find our best stuff. We look for interesting stories that a small group of people are fascinated by but that nobody else has found yet. Then we fictionalize them: Write a story that fits into what actually happened. I like to think of myself as a 'cool detector.' I'm pretty good at knowing what a lot of people *would* like ... if they knew it existed."

"You want to make a fictional TV show ... *about Reginald?*"

Harrison stabbed a joyous finger at Maurice. "Ah! So you *do* know him!" He tried out the name. "'*Reginald.*' Yes, 'Reginald' is the *perfect* name for a fat vampire!"

Quite spontaneously, Maurice said, "Get out of my house."

Celeste grabbed his arm, then pulled him back with a warning eye so she could step front and center. It was clear she hadn't liked that last thing any more than he had, but as was usually the case, she was thinking of details and consequences while Maurice was busy reacting from the gut. He saw reason as she took control of the conversation: *When a man this persistent wants to publicize the thing you want publicized least in the world, it's not a good idea to just throw him out.* Like it or not, Harrison Cardiff had become a factor over the last fifteen minutes. They could deal with that factor and the damage it threatened to cause in a controlled way ... or they could dismiss it out of hand, and risk setting off a bomb.

"Harrison," she said.

"Yes."

"Maybe you can explain something to me."

"Shoot."

"I don't understand why you came here. If you wanted to track down this ... this *YouTube character* ... why did you come to us?"

"Because you weren't answering the phone." He looked around as if there might be other dullards nearby who'd missed that part of the conversation. "You have to act fast in this business. What if the SyFy Network or someone got to you first?"

"No. I mean: Why *us?* Why didn't you go to ..." *Sigh.* His identity was out of the bag anyway. "... to Reginald directly?"

"Oh! *That.* Yeah. I tried. Would you believe it — nobody at your company would tell me his name!"

Actually, Maurice believed it on a few different levels. For one, giving out employee names to random inquirers was a pretty egregious privacy violation ... although the company's HR department was a war crime and had clearly given out *Maurice's* name. The bigger reason was probably due to glamour. It wasn't that the humans who knew Reginald from work *wouldn't* give out his name so much as they *couldn't.* Everyone at the company knew his name, but Maurice had given all of them a very specific breed of aphasia to prevent them from saying it aloud to anyone outside the office. It was similar to what the Holmes spell had done to Maurice, wherein he was literally unable to talk to the police about the serial killer. And so, when asked for Reginald's name, the execs had probably only been able to moan at Harrison in reply. He probably thought they all had brain damage. It was just one of many ways Maurice had built isolation around Reginald for his own protection.

"Okay," Celeste said in a precisely measured tone, thinking this out on the fly. "Well ... now that you *do* know it, will you go to him directly?"

"Not if he forgets all about it," Maurice said.

Celese turned to him, then whispered low and fast. *"He's got a partner and a company. Unless you want to go find everyone who's heard this idea without missing even* one *of them, trying to glamour this away is just swatting flies. Now* SHUSH!"

Maurice shut his mouth.

"You were saying," Celeste told Harrison, though he hadn't said anything yet.

"Actually," Harrison said. "It's the weirdest thing. I couldn't read a lot of what I found, but it looks to me like you're this guy's legal guardian."

Now Celeste *really* rounded on Maurice. She stared into his eyes as if to say *You're in trouble, mister,* but what was Maurice supposed to do? Reginald was a risk to himself and others simply by existing, and he'd proven pretty obviously that he was unable to lay low and not attract attention — Harrison's presence in their foyer being the biggest proof of that.

And so, without Reginald knowing about it, Maurice had made Reginald a protected ward of the Toussant estate. Humans around him were glamoured in ways that would keep dangerous knowledge within a defined circle, while legal sleight-of-hand kept snoopers at bay. Although Maurice didn't like Harrison in his house any more than Celeste did, it did prove Maurice's precautions were working. If anyone broke through and tried to come at Reginald, they'd be deflected to Maurice. It was better than all of the alternatives, and vampire lawyers had been plenty shifty enough to make it happen.

Celeste inhaled, exhaled, and nodded to herself before speaking. The set of mannerisms was her way of resetting — of saying, *Well, where we are is a whole lot of bullshit ... but if bullshit is where we have to be, I'd better stop operating from sanity.*

"Thank you for bringing us this opportunity," she told Harrison. "We're flattered that you're interested enough to have gone to such lengths to give it to us."

Maurice shifted at that, but Celeste elbowed him in the ribs.

"We need a little bit of time. To ... talk to lawyers. And our advisors." Yes, that seemed right. As rich as time had made them, they must look to Harrison like the kind of people who had advisors.

"Oh. Of course."

"We'll get back to you."

"So we can tell you to f—" Maurice started to say, but again Celeste jabbed him and glared. She was steering this ship now that he'd run it aground, and that meant his role was to shut his mouth. Still, he thought he knew what she was doing. Her words would buy them time, nothing more and nothing less. They'd end up facing the same dilemma, but at least they'd've had time to think. Saying "we'll get back to you" would pause Harrison. He wouldn't keep investigating. He'd be quiet and wait for word.

"Okay," Harrison said. He sounded a little disappointed

to not be leaving with a golden ticket, but seemed to understand that'd been pie-in-the-sky anyway. He was a businessman, after all. "How long do you need?"

"Two weeks?"

"Oh, I don't know ..." he said. He seemed to be thinking about how far the Toussants might be able to shop their new options in that amount of time. "That's pretty long a time. I had this idea about Comic Con. Do you know Comic Con? It's sort of an anniversary for me, and it's coming up in just two months. I was sort of hoping to—"

"*It's not too long,*" Celeste purred, now staring into Harrison's eyes. "*You think two weeks is fair.*"

"Actually, I guess it's not too long," he repeated. "I think two weeks is fair."

"And when you talk to your business associates, if *they* think it's too long, you'll tell them that you want to give us all the time we need."

"If anyone back in LA thinks two weeks is too long to let you think on it," Harrison said, "I'll tell them I want to give you all the time you need."

"And if they press, you'll tell them we signed a letter granting you a month of exclusivity."

Harrison nodded as if deciding this was a good outcome after all, even though there'd been no letter. "And hey, if they won't let it go, I can remind them that we've got your signature on an exclusivity contract."

"Thank you, Harrison," Celeste said, opening the door while Maurice backed into the shadows. "It's been nice meeting you."

"Yeah," he said. "Thanks, Harrison. It's been nice meeting you."

When the foyer was silent and the TV producer who

wanted to expose their biggest secret was gone, Celeste looked at Maurice for a long time.

"At least he didn't go right to Reginald," Maurice said in a small voice with a small smile. "If Reginald found out he could be famous, who knows what he'd do?"

"I'm going to bed," Celeste replied.

Maurice followed. She turned and stopped him.

"You're going to the couch," she added.

NINE
AWAKENING

The phone had stopped ringing a while ago. Annabel was sitting by it anyway.

While it'd been ringing (and it rang quite a lot), she'd found herself uninterested in answering it for reasons she couldn't explain. She'd been curious who was calling, but unmoved to act and find out. Now, though, she was much more proactive. When it rang again, she'd decided to answer it. She was pretty sure how phones worked, but still just a little afraid of them. She didn't know why that was — something her husband once said to her, she thought.

She stared at the thing. It was almost four o'clock. The phone had been silent for a long time, but she couldn't shake a feeling that answering it when it eventually rang again was extremely important. She had a hunch about it. An internal voice kept telling her that answering was vital because of who was calling ...

... and ... ?

And the rest was vague. Like a dream just forgotten.

He's not going to call again, said that same voice. A

female voice. Annabel almost knew it like an old friend —
almost, but not quite. *You're going to have to go to Plan B.*

That sounded okay to Annabel, even though she wasn't
sure what Plan A had been. Did it have something to do
with the phone? She was sitting by the phone. She felt like
maybe she'd sat here a while, and that she had opinions
about the phone. Why would she have opinions about a
phone? Had it rung? She had no idea. She couldn't
remember the phone *ever* ringing, actually. She looked at it
now. Did she know how the phone worked? It was for
making food, right?

*Plan B is to walk out the door. You can do it, Annabel
Girl.*

Well, clearly *that* wasn't right. Annabel had gone on
some crazy adventures in the past, but walking out the door
was too crazy even for her. If she went outside, where would
she go? Did you need special equipment to go out there, like
a rope or a harness? There was a car in the driveway, and
she'd seen the keys, but she was pretty sure she'd never used
them. You'd have to go outside to drive a car. She didn't
want to do that — to walk to the car. She'd *never* do
anything like that. Not even to go to work. She'd gone to
work yesterday. In the car. She was very tired right now, as
if she'd been awake all night.

Fight him. You have to fight him.

Fight *who*, though? Annabel thought the voice's suggestion was probably a good one (she didn't know when she'd
tangoed with that voice before, but she had positive feelings
about it), but even if she wanted to fight, she didn't have an
opponent. The only other person around was her husband,
but he was sleeping like any other sensible person would be.
He'd be asleep for several more hours. Usually she'd go to

work at that point. On some days. She'd drive the car there. And once there, she often talked to a patient who …

That's it, said the voice, encouraging her.

But what was it about her patient that had almost felt familiar for a moment? She thought maybe they'd spent hours together, but those hours were hidden from her. They were inside some sort of a mental capsule.

Being at the office, talking to the patient in question … *that* struck Annabel as an interesting experience. She wasn't tongue-tied at work. She always felt a breed of openness and everyday ritual at work that struck her, here and now, as agoraphobic. It was hard to believe she left the house just to talk to someone. To anyone. Or that she'd ever drive the car. Or that she'd sit in a chair other than her usual chairs. She didn't really talk much otherwise. Her husband wasn't much of a conversationalist. He slept all day, then sometimes drank her blood. It was pretty much your typical marriage.

Maurice, said the voice. *Your patient's name is Maurice. Do you remember Maurice?*

No, she didn't. But then yes, she did. The memory had been hidden behind a partition, invisible. Now that she'd spotted it, she remembered Maurice indeed. Maurice might be her best friend right now. How could she have forgotten him? But he'd broken her heart. He'd … *quit?*

Only because he was worried for you. Worried by you. The unknown of you frightened him.

But the voice couldn't know that. The voice was probably wrong.

I'm not wrong. Think, Annabel. Fight!

Why would Maurice be afraid of her? Why would he be afraid *for* her? She was fine. All was well. She was a threat to nobody. She had an ordinary life. She—

A flash entered her mind: *a monster in the basement, grabbing her by the arms. A monster with sharp canine teeth. Teeth like fangs.* And atop the fear was worry. She was — or had once been — terrified for a friend of hers. But did Annabel even have friends?

Yes. Alicia. Alicia is your friend.

What was an Alicia? Was it like a phone? It was probably fine. It'd just been told to go home, whatever it was. To go home and sit in a chair.

But the monster. The monster in the basement ...

Then the flash of lucidity was gone. The startle remained. Her heart had quickened and not yet settled. Quite the contrary, in fact. Instead of slowing, that heart beat harder.

She focused. Tried to see the flash again. It was like gripping at gossamer. Like recalling a dream.

He came up behind you, said the voice. *Just as you were about to run away.*

She could see bits of it now. The monster looked like Victor. It'd come up behind her, just as she'd been planning to mount the stairs.

Her heart beat even faster. Why had she wanted to run away?

"What are you doing in here?" said a voice in the real world.

Annabel spun. The feeling gave her deja vu, because it seemed again that Victor had come up behind her ... and according to her heart, she'd maybe been just about to run.

"I can hear you in my head," Victor said. "You must know that."

"What?"

"Your emotions. They're so *loud.*"

"They're just emotions. And they're mine, not yours."

He squinted, considering her. She knew why: She didn't talk much at home, and now she was talking. The air around her seemed to be clearing. She didn't remember much in the moment, but something strange did come: *a memory of a remembering.* She had the sense that she'd just remembered something, but couldn't say what. It felt like the recent past. Like: maybe just earlier today, down in the basement. What had she remembered then that she hadn't yet re-remembered now?

(*Alicia.*)

Who was Alicia? She thought maybe she'd known an Alicia once.

"What's going on with you?" Victor said.

She was about to answer that when it dawned on her that the correct response (the one that was normal around here, the one Victor expected) was not to answer at all.

Just play dumb. Put a vacant look on your face. Smile at him vaguely.

She tried, but her heart knew better. It was still racing. Throbbing through her. Maybe even visible in the arteries in her neck, which she felt quite sure Victor paid attention to.

"I told you to sleep," he said.

She decided to try a gamble: "I was afraid."

"Afraid of what?"

"Afraid for you." She was careful to emphasize *FOR*, not *OF*. Even though right now, there was plenty of *OF* as well. Then she added another gamble: "... because of Maurice."

Victor considered her carefully, but Annabel's awareness was growing. She knew this was okay: to talk, if the things she said were about Maurice. Victor was *extremely* interested in Maurice. He wanted to know everything

Maurice told her after their sessions were over. He told her to omit no details, no matter how small they might be. *You never know when the smallest thing might make the key,* he sometimes said. She didn't know what that meant, but she'd been foggier then. Back then, she'd done everything she asked. Told him everything about Maurice, so he could build his "key."

Words of Maurice would be welcome, from her to him, whenever they came. She knew that now, so she dove in.

"That's why I'm up," she told him. "I was worried that Maurice is …"

Careful. Officially, you're just informing his hobby.

"… mad at me," she finished.

"Because he cancelled his appointment?"

Oh. Yes. Interesting. She'd forgotten about that. Now that clarity was returning to Annabel, she remembered some of the past windows in which she'd seen clearly. One time she'd managed to call Victor a nickname, provided by Maurice, that Victor hated. Other times, she'd defied him in small ways. She'd seen through her usual haze to see truth on occasion, though the haze always returned.

And just last night, Annabel had managed to tell him a lie. That same voice inside her right now had given her the strength to do it. The voice felt that telling Victor about how Maurice seemed suspicious (which he definitely had been) was a bad idea. The voice, actually, had felt threatened by the idea of telling Victor any of it. So it had given Annabel the strength to lie — to tell Victor that instead of becoming suspicious and storming out, Maurice had simply needed to cancel. For personal reasons.

"Maybe it's silly," Annabel said, aware enough now to play along.

"Is there any *other* reason he might be mad at you?"

She found herself able to improvise a new set of lies —
this time without the voice's help.

"No." She wanted to giggle idiotically to ram home the
idea of silliness, but her usual self didn't giggle. She made
her face a bit more dazed instead and said, "He rescheduled
the appointment. He said he had a really interesting story to
tell."

Rather than accepting this, Victor made a thinking face.
She wondered if she'd let slip that Maurice seemed suspicious some other time in the past. There was no way to
know here and now, because the fog so often ruled.

"It doesn't matter one way or the other," he said. "I
think I already have enough."

She couldn't ask what he had enough *for* because it
would prove she was less foggy than she should be. It was
important to keep playing dumb. She remembered events in
the basement more clearly now, including who *Alicia* was.
A lot of the same wheels were turning again.

She pushed it down. She had to keep herself from
looking too closely at those memories. If she remembered
while Victor was close, he'd see them, too. And he'd see how
much fear she'd recently grown deep down inside. Fear
of him.

*He came at me with his fangs down, ready to rip out my
throat.*

This time it was Annabel's own voice, not the other.

She repressed a shudder. For a horrible blink, she saw
Victor as a creature rather than a man. Because he *wasn't* a
man. Because he *was* a creature. The realization made her
want to run, but instinct kept her rooted. She suspected
Victor was extremely fast. He'd catch her long before she
reached the door.

"I have one last task for you," he said.

Last. Her fear boiled. Somehow she understood what "last" meant. Maurice was gone. Maybe Victor knew he wasn't coming back, and that was a problem. But what was she supposed to do, if her days had just become numbered? Victor was right in front of her, and the door was twenty feet away.

"Stand by my chair," he said.

Annabel did as he instructed. He sat in the chair.

"Give me your hand."

She did. She knew he was going to bite into her index finger before he did it, but she was playing dumb for now; there was nothing she could do to stop it unless she wanted to blow any remaining chance she had.

Her *last* chance.

He pierced her with one fang, not too deep. Then he shifted her finger so his fangs were no longer in the way and sucked on her bleeding digit like some weird fetish.

"Now keep your mind quiet," he told her. "I need to synthesize."

Annabel wasn't sure what that meant, but the voice inside was realizing something. The realization probably came from bits of a puzzle Annabel had observed ... but not yet put together.

There's something inside you that Victor has to meld with his "key," the voice explained. *Now, you* can't *run. Whatever he's going to do with Maurice, he needs your blood in his mouth if it's going to work.*

She was tethered to him. Literally *tethered*: her bleeding finger in his mouth.

Her awareness was almost complete now — almost entirely out from under his spell.

She was aware enough to know exactly how scared she should be.

TEN
DREAMS

It wasn't fair.

Maurice hadn't kept things from Celeste because he thought she'd disapprove. He'd kept them from her because things happened quickly and there wasn't always time for a consult. He took most things to her, didn't he? Just not this. Not this mess with Reginald.

Maybe he'd made snap decisions. Maybe he'd treated Reginald like a child who couldn't think for himself. But was that so wrong? Reginald *was* a child as far as vampire life was concerned — and when allowed to think for himself, Reginald thought poorly. His YouTube fame (strong enough now to attract Hollywood, apparently) was proof of that. The solution, for Maurice, had been to put Reginald inside an isolation bubble until the Council did whatever the hell it planned to do — and to not tell Reginald anything about it lest he screw it up. If he somehow survived his trial, Maurice would drop the legal guardianship and the many powers of attorney. He'd give Reginald back to Reginald, removing all the protections and glamour he'd put in place.

But now was not the time.

Until everything settled, Reginald needed a limited radius in which to do damage. Until that time came, Maurice would keep being deceptive and cagey. He'd kept Reginald almost entirely in the dark about the Council and all that'd been happening in Mauriceland outside of what related directly to Reginald — enough that Reginald probably thought his maker was halfway abandoning him.

Even now, Maurice stood by those decisions. Though maybe he should loop Celeste in from here on out.

He drifted off to sleep on the couch, hoping she'd forgive him when they woke at nightfall.

His dreams were unusual, full of blood ties instead of fancy. He dreamed of Daisy, but the dreams were more like real connections than memory. He dreamed of Annabel and Daisy together: his mind exploring their newly discovered confabulation, probably. He dreamed of the twenties in Chicago, his blood reaching out and wondering: *Who did I miss? Which one of Santori's gang survived, to chase Thrill today?*

He could think of nobody he'd missed.

His mind kept wandering. It crawled up and down the threads of his vampire family web. It lingered on Celeste for obvious reasons. She'd known Amadeus Macht's blood without knowing she'd consumed it, and Maurice had drank the blood of Macht's second progeny — the vampire absurdly calling himself "Dracula" in the late 1800s. Both of the weak, almost-dissolved blood memories (Dracula's directly, and Macht's through his tie to Celeste) sent Maurice's mind crawling toward Ophelia. Ophelia had killed Macht, her own maker, with the help of a necromancer. Somehow she'd killed the necromancer, too. She who'd planted thorns in Celeste's psyche, plaguing her forever.

How was Ophelia involved in this? Where *was* Ophelia? Had the vampire holding Annabel contacted her? Or was this sense of Ophelia's shadow coming from something else?

Then a new dream came. Only, this one didn't feel like a dream.

The new vision eclipsed everything else, forceful like a bludgeon. It took over his mind. Soon he found himself in a lucid nightmare, symbolically bound and unable to move. A new man stood before him, as clear as if this were real life. Maurice knew him instantly. In Chicago, the other gangsters had called him "Puffed Wheat."

With that, the penny dropped:

This isn't a dream. I'm being blood-invaded.

It was Puffed Wheat who was behind everything, he saw now: the lackey on Santori's crew, the punching bag for all the stronger gangsters. Had Maurice killed Puffed Wheat when he'd killed the rest of Santori's men? He had no idea; the kid was that forgettable. But obviously the answer was no. Because here he was now, shoving a fist into Maurice's mind.

The experience was so much worse than he'd imagined. It was psychically painful. It was *psychically and emotionally* painful. The man was deep inside him: hidden spaces meant to be private. These were places even Celeste didn't touch. To have the filthy, groping hands of Puffed Wheat in those spots? It was almost too much to bear.

He couldn't speak to the invader. The invader couldn't, or wouldn't, speak to him. Maurice could only be still. There was no chance of forcing the other man out. The attack was below the belt, no way at all to fight back. He could only lay there, motionless, and *take it*.

The scene, as it progressed, was vivid. Maurice could see everything that happened, and as such he saw all the places Puffed Wheat was looking and what he was looking for.

The invader found the memory easily.

A perfect re-creation of Maurice's visit to the Thrill distillery materialized around him. He could see the books on the foreman's desk, where the secret lay. They were in the thick of it now, minutes or seconds from the point of no return. Once the other vampire opened those books, he'd find the Thrill recipe. And once he saw the recipe, he'd have it forever. There'd be no turning back.

Resist, Maurice thought, turning his attention from his own discomfort to the bigger purpose. *You have to keep him from seeing the books or it's all over!*

But there was no resistance to be had. These were mental muscles that nobody used, or knew existed. Maurice had told Annabel so many personal details that the invader — adept or well-studied at such things, it seemed — had been able to form a perfect cypher to break into Maurice's mind. He seemed to be using Maurice's blood tie to Daisy as a conduit — probably through Annabel's tie to Daisy on the other end. Accessing Daisy through Annabel would have already given him Thrill's blood memory. All he needed now was one quick glance at the recipe.

At the recipe that was only inches away, as his psychic hands reached for Maurice's memory of the ledgers.

Resist. RESIST!

No way to resist. No way to move.

Celeste, he thought. If Celeste was here, she might be able to help.

But he was alone. Alone physically, alone inside his mind. There was no way to win.

It was too late.

Maurice had seen the face of his enemy, but it was too late to stop him.

Annabel could feel it happening; that was the strangest thing. She'd never believed in psychics or ESP. If she hadn't met one (okay, two) vampires, she wouldn't believe in them, either. And yet she was forced to believe in this.

Her mind was almost her own again, clear and unencumbered. That wasn't necessarily a good thing, because although she now understood the situation she was in, she couldn't leave it. She remembered all that Maurice had told her. Between that and what the voice inside her knew, she had a good idea what was going on. And it wasn't remotely cool.

This was mind-invasion: one vampire forcing himself into another's blood memory without consent.

Her own view of it was vivid and repellant. She could almost *see* Maurice on the other end of this, squirming in discomfort and pain. She could sympathize. For now, it was Maurice who was suffering. But when it was over, at least he'd be free. *Annabel*, though? After Victor had what he needed from Maurice, she'd be dead skin. The second it ended, he'd shed her.

So run, she told herself.

But the other voice inside her felt otherwise: *No. Don't run. He's a vampire. You can't outrun him no matter how fast you go.*

I have to do something. If I can't save myself, at least I have to try and stop this.

You can't. You don't have his mind. You don't have his abilities. Right now, he has you and Maurice in a snare.

Was it possible she could slip her finger from his mouth without him noticing? She doubted it; she got the very clear impression that whatever he was doing depended on that finger being there. If she pulled it away — even if his lips didn't feel it — it seemed likely that its absence would break the connection. And while that was what she wanted ("to try and stop this"), simply pulling out wasn't the way to do it. He'd round on her. He'd re-glamour her, just as Maurice had described vampires doing their glamour ... which, Annabel supposed, had been her own condition for months now. She was clear-headed for the moment and Victor didn't know it, but as soon as he *did* know it, he'd make sure she stopped being clear-headed. It was an impossible jam. What good was an advantage if she couldn't use it?

She tried not to watch as Maurice writhed in pain. Instead she saw symbolic representations of the effort at hand: her own mind stylizing the parts of the vision she couldn't see. She knew only that Victor was close to getting what she wanted. She knew Maurice was trying to resist, but *couldn't* resist. It wouldn't be long now. Soon Victor would be this situation's literal victor ... and although she didn't know which prize he sought, she did know bad things would happen once he got it.

Do something! Do anything!

Maddeningly, she had no options.

She couldn't run. She couldn't even step far enough from him to remove her finger from his mouth.

She couldn't fight him. She was human and he was vampire. He'd end her in seconds.

She couldn't help Maurice. She couldn't even imagine ways to do that.

She couldn't say anything sufficient to distract him: using guile instead of force. If she tried any persuasive words at all, he'd know her mind was free again. If that happened, he'd glamour her dumb, finish with Maurice anyway, and then probably kill her to stop her independence for good.

She had to do *something*. But what?

Her eyes spied an award she'd been given by the Columbus chapter of the APA, granted for exceptional patient care. It was a softball-sized marble ball engraved with her name and practice and the year of her prize. It sat atop an ashtray-shaped stand.

The shelf it sat on was maybe six feet behind her: too far to reach.

So she stepped back, careful not to jostle the finger between Victor's lips. As she did so, she leaned forward. She counterbalanced by extending her opposite leg behind her: the posture of a golfer reaching down to pick up a ball.

Further back.

Leaning forward.

Soon she looked like a yoga pose: upright on her right leg with her right arm forward, its finger in Victor's mouth. Her left leg was long behind her, her whole body in the shape of a T.

This will make noise, said the other woman's voice. *He's in a trance, but he still might hear it.*

Oh well, Annabel replied. *I'm dead already.*

As delicately but precisely as she could, Annabel jabbed the APA award with her toe. It wobbled but didn't move, and she almost lost her balance: something that *would* definitely draw Victor's attention.

Do better. Do it right next time or not at all.

She jabbed the thing again, but this time she hit it just hard enough, right in the center. The sphere left its base, struck the wall behind the shelves, then rolled forward again until it fell and thumped to the ground.

She had to lower her leg quickly, with extreme dexterity, to step on the ball and stop it from rolling away. With some work — and still without pulling her finger from Victor's mouth — she managed to trap it at the base of the chair.

Now's the easy part, she thought.

Yeah, said the other. *EASY.*

She reached down and took the heavy marble ball in her free hand. Then she straightened, raising it over her head.

Do it. Very very fast, and very very hard.

Just as her internal sight showed Victor reaching for his prize inside Maurice, Annabel slammed the marble ball as hard as she possibly could into the side of Victor's skull. There was a satisfying crack as he collapsed sideways, her finger out and the connection broken.

She couldn't help but stare. She'd never seen a fracture so bad. She'd never directly seen a person's brains before.

Go. NOW!

Her fascination broke as bone pivoted outward, already starting to heal. A second later his head was turning toward her, his eye so bloodshot it'd turned red.

Annabel ran as hard as she could. She could hear Victor

shambling to rise behind her ... but seconds before he reached her she was out on her front lawn, bathed in sun.

Victor's shape came near the window, parting the blinds just enough to wince at the ultraviolet. But it was enough. It was enough for her to see him — and for him to see her: in the middle of a wide-open yard, not a cloud in the sky.

He seemed to snarl.

Sure she shouldn't dally — not knowing every power vampires had — Annabel knew she should start running from this place as fast and far as she could. There'd been no time inside to grab the car keys, so she had only her feet beneath her.

But still she took the time to stop and face him.

Then very slowly and very deliberately, she raised her middle finger.

This was the worst.

After the human he'd been using ran out the front door, Victor was left in an intolerable situation. He was trapped in every way a vampire could be trapped.

He couldn't chase Annabel Rice, obviously, because she'd run into the sun. That made him trapped physically. He could try and find her after sundown, but by then it would be stupid to. Her glamour had broken (no idea how *that* happened) and that meant she probably knew everything. She'd already called him "Puffed Wheat," so clearly she'd ID'd him from Maurice Toussant's tales of Prohibition. And when a frightened human who already knows a "nice" vampire discovers she's in danger from a "bad" vampire from the Vampire Mafia, what does she do? She runs to the nice one for protection, of course.

Victor wouldn't kid himself by trying to believe otherwise: She'd go to Maurice now, no question about it. Victor had no desire to tangle with Maurice on even footing. Maurice was two thousand years old and Victor wasn't even two hundred. Even Maurice's wife was seven or eight times his age. If Victor went a-knocking at the Toussant home a few hours after Annabel told them everything they didn't already know, he'd end up a pile of ash. And besides, why bother? Rice was useless to him now. It's not like Maurice would return to her for therapy at this point.

But Victor was also trapped strategically, because Annabel's sucker-punch (or sucker-skull-cave-in) had broken his connection to Maurice, freeing Maurice from his bindings. Victor had had *one* chance to overpower Maurice, and it'd been with a sneak attack. A vampire knew when someone was trying to hack into his mind through blood; Victor had succeeded only because Maurice hadn't seen it coming and hadn't known what invasion would be like when it came — and therefore, had no clue how to defend against it. Now, however, Maurice *did* know it was coming. He *did* know what to expect. From here on out, he'd have his substantial defenses ready. Victor would never get into his blood now, even if he found a chance to try again.

So what was he supposed to do? He'd gambled and lost. He'd kicked a hornet's nest, and the chief hornet had seen him do it. What's more, Victor had been inside the distillery memory and leafing through books when Annabel hit him, so Maurice — who'd lived the memory along with Victor — surely knew exactly what Victor was after. Forget chasing Annabel at sundown. At sundown, it was Victor who'd need to be running for his life.

That left Plan N. "N" for "Nuclear Option." Which, to be honest, sort of trapped him socially.

Victor hadn't wanted to use Plan N. He'd wanted to get into and out of Maurice with the recipe for Thrilloglobin on his own, then dispose of Rice. He already had Thrill's blood memory from Rice's ancestor, and he'd planned to top-off on it before killing the good doctor. Maurice would still be after him in that scenario, of course. He'd've seen Victor just like he'd seen Victor today; the only difference was that he'd've seen him flee with the formula instead of seeing him flee empty-handed. If things had worked, Victor would have painted the same target on his back as was on it right now, but the difference would be that he'd have his prize. Instead, right now, Victor had nothing.

Well, not *nothing*.

He had knowledge. Nobody other than Victor knew Daisy's bloodline had endured and nobody else had tracked down her only remaining descendent. Nobody knew that Maurice had seen the Thrill recipe, and nobody else would have figured out such a clever way to get it. So Victor still had something to bargain with ... and that was good, because without some backup — and soon — his days were very much numbered.

Which was why Plan N was necessary.

He had to get to Logan. He had to cash in his chips before they lost all value ... and he had to do it before sunset, because at sunset Maurice (duly briefed by Annabel) would know right where to find him.

He peeked through the drapes and it was like looking at the sun. He lost vision in his right eye as reflected sunlight focused on his retina and burned a hole through it. He winced back, then tried again after stacking four pairs of Annabel's sunglasses from around the house atop one another. Seeing through them was like seeing through welding glass.

It was the brightest day he could imagine. Terrible luck. Ohio was usually so overcast.

He scoped the yard and the driveway, then decided he

might as well get about the unpleasant business ahead of him because he had no other choice.

He raided Annabel's closet and draped himself with enough garments that it felt like he was wearing a camping backpack. The garments included six long sundresses because Victor couldn't fit into her slacks, complemented with leggings underneath and two pairs of socks. He was able to squeeze his feet into a pair of oversized snow boots from the mud room. Over the sundresses he wore two winter coats, both with hoods. A cache of ski gear provided a neck gaiter and a hat that, when arranged just so and wrapped with a scarf, completely concealed everything but the skin around his eyes. He wore ski goggles over the bit that remained, their insides stuffed with paper towels. He tried to put Annabel's many sunglasses over the goggles so he'd be able to leave his eyes uncovered and hence be able to see, but there was no way to make it work. So instead, Victor studied his job very carefully. He might have to do this blind.

Wrapped like the Invisible Man, Victor opened the side door of the house and immediately felt like he'd walked into an oven. The warm day was doing some of it and his abundance of clothing was doing some of it, but the solar radiation not blocked by line-of-sight was doing the rest, baking him from the inside out like a microwave. He'd have to move quickly.

Working by feel, Victor was able to drag the comforters he'd taken from Annabel's bed over to her car and cover its top half completely. Fumbling in gloves, he then managed to secure the comforter to the car's panels with duct tape. This done, he climbed inside and pulled the last bit of comforter tight, slamming it in the car door to hold it.

Carefully, Victor removed his goggles. He did not

instantly burn to death. That was a good start. He opened the bag he'd brought with him and removed the keys, then started the engine to blast the air conditioning. The second item in the bag was his smartphone, which he now used to monitor the GoPro he'd taped to the car's hood before entering. He'd gotten lucky; the camera was straight and steady despite the fact that he'd mounted it blind.

He put his foot on the brake and shifted the car into reverse. Then he stopped.

Was he really going to do this? He hadn't given himself a back-up camera. He was going to have a pretty hard time looking both ways before crossing intersections, though the GoPro did blessedly have a wide-angle lens. And if anyone saw this blanket-covered car weaving down the street and called the police, he'd be in for more than a ticket.

Fuck it.

He backed up, tried to guess the distance of the street. He failed spectacularly and ran over Annabel's mailbox. Then he shifted into Drive ... and began making his way carefully across town.

He'd wanted to go to Logan and the Council with Thrill's recipe in-hand: coming to the powers-that-be already holding all the power. But this way of proceeding would be almost as good, wouldn't it? He didn't have the recipe just yet ... but he knew right where it was, and he knew how enough force could still be used to get it out of Maurice. That was information nobody else had. It meant he could still be a hero. He still could be strong. Still be wealthy. Still hold all the power ... still pull all the strings Santori had pulled back in the day.

If Victor couldn't have it all by himself, this was the next best thing.

Logan's muscle and influence could help Victor finish with Maurice now that the Nuclear Option had been engaged … and Logan would be so happy (*so, so* happy) to know Thrilloglobin was back in town.

Logan slept in a double-wide coffin that was barely a coffin. It was four feet deep and he entered it through a door on the side, not the top. Its footprint was the size of a king bed and the sides were padded. On its bottom was a mattress. He slept under covers. Those around him, Logan knew, privately thought he should make up his mind: Did he sleep in a coffin like their ancestors or in a bed like modern cousins? Logan pretended he didn't know the question existed and wouldn't have answered it if anyone dared to ask. Truth was, he slept in both. Like most things Logan did, the decision to sleep in a bed/coffin was political. The old ones liked him for using a coffin because it said he respected the past. The young ones liked him for using a bed because it said he wasn't stuck in the past and instead embraced the future. It was good, as a politician, to make stands only when they truly mattered. In all other things, it was best to pretend to be what everyone, everywhere, preferred him to be.

He was startled from sleep when one of the new aides pried the top off his bed/coffin with a squeaking of nails and snapping of wood. Asshole didn't know how the door worked. Asshole might not live to see tomorrow.

"Mr. Logan, sir!"

Asshole also might also not know if "Logan" was his first name or last. Yes, this guy was soon to be murdered.

Logan was on his back and looking up at the aide right now, hands crossed on his chest like the dead thing he was supposed to be. He hadn't moved other than to open his eyes. The lackey was gawking down at him like it was his first day on the job. He didn't smell human, so he must not be one of the daytime guards. Did that mean it was nightfall, and the vampires were stirring? No, Logan's internal clock said otherwise. He hated being woken when the sun was shining.

"Mr. Logan?"

"I'm waiting for you to say what the fuck you have to say," Logan told him. "Obviously you have my attention. And my curiosity as to why you're ruining my possessions." He looked to the vampire's hand. It still gripped the splintered coffin-top.

"An intruder breached the gate, sir," the vampire said. "He's—"

Shouting and arguing came from the hallway. The bedroom door had been left open.

"Anyway, sir," said the aide, "it's someone who insists he absolutely must see you right away."

"See me or kill me?"

"He says you know him. Or you knew his boss?"

"*Do* I know him? Or his boss? How dare you interrupt my sleep with more questions than answers!"

"Sir?"

There was much hissing and furor in the hallway, then hissing and furor closer to the door. Logan sat up, then stood to find a small, wiry-looking vampire trying to fend off two Eclipse guards still in their blackout helmets. The newcomer was wearing what appeared to be dresses and winter garments wrapped layer on layer like a cocoon. His scarf had been partially ripped off. Beneath, his face was blistered and blackened, trying to heal. Had this fool actually been out in the sun? Breaching his gate in broad daylight? The helmeted guards implied yes. They didn't lower their helmet shields unless to enter the sun.

The guards advanced on the blistered man, but a look from Logan backed them off. The new vampire turned to see him, then started blubbering like Logan's biggest fan. Logan ignored him until he was finished embarrassing himself. Only after he'd run out of words did Logan speak.

"Who the hell are you?" he asked.

"Oh. I'm sorry. My name is Victor Fratelli. I—"

"You," Logan said as if to complete the sentence for him, "are in my house."

"Oh." He didn't know what to do with this statement of the obvious. "Yes. Yes, I am."

"How did you know where it was?"

Victor blinked.

Logan explained, angry now. "The Council's location moves. *My home's* location moves. The process for learning where either one is at any given time is private and controlled by—"

"I worked for Santori," the vampire — Victor — blurted.

"What did you say?" Logan asked.

"I worked for Santori," he repeated. "You use the Santori system, don't you?"

Now *that* was interesting. Logan had been ready to behead the intruder, but the fact that he'd found the current location of Logan's home pretty much proved that what he said was true. Santori's position at the top of the Vampire Mafia had always made him paranoid, so to confuse his enemies he'd created an elaborate system: his homebase moved constantly, so his enemies couldn't track him down. Unfortunately he'd never been able to use it: Maurice had killed the whole Mafia before Santori's people implemented it. Logan's team later found the system in the rubble and repurposed it to keep Logan safe instead. Santori's system wasn't a tenth as complex and indecipherable as the algorithm that kept the Council hidden, but it would still be hard to hack unless you'd seen the system firsthand. The fact that "Victor" was here at all implied he really had worked for Santori. But how? The Vampire Mafia was supposed to be extinct.

Logan looked at the guards and the idiot who'd broken open his casket. "Leave us," he said.

"But sir," said the idiot. "He drove a blacked-out car through the gate. It's half in the fountain. He almost killed three—"

"I said *leave us*."

More slowly than Logan would have liked, they did. The door closed, and then Logan and Victor were alone.

"You worked for Santori."

"Yes."

"I don't remember you," Logan told him. "I knew Santori's entire crew."

"Some of us were only used in the special trade at the time," Victor said. "When you and Mr. Santori were partners. When the two of you were making Thrilloglobin."

That was a dangerous thing for Victor to say. Officially, Logan and the Council had had nothing to do with Thrill. It was illegal and a potential public relations nightmare, should word get out about the government's involvement.

But Victor saying it now was bold as well as dangerous, and maybe Logan even admired him for telling the truth. Now they could look each other in the eye. Now, each knew where the other stood: namely, on the corrupt and backhanded side of the line.

"Maybe I do know you," he said. An isolated group had handled Thrill distribution. Logan had just let its faces slip his mind, because Thrill was in the past. All of it was in the past. "They called you ..."

"... 'Victor,'" Victor finished.

"... 'Puffed Wheat.'"

Victor sighed. He'd been holding his shoulders high with importance, but now it sagged like a beaten dog's.

Logan looked him up and down. Talk about strange attire.

"I had to go out in the sun," Victor explained. "I'm sorry to have come uninvited. To have disturbed you. I wouldn't have if my matter wasn't urgent. It couldn't wait until nightfall."

Logan waited.

"May I speak plainly?" Victor asked.

Logan, curious, briefly dipped his chin.

"Sir. I know that the Vampire Council gave money, assistance, and protection to the Thrilloglobin trade in Chicago. Your cause was noble. Humans have been evolving and we have not. They cover the globe and our population is still small. I always agreed with you. With Don Santori. If we wanted to meet the humans on their own terms, it would take passion and a willingness to fight that modern vampires lack. Thrill was the only way to create soldiers. To force our aggression forward enough that the humans might start fearing us again."

Logan nodded. These were the right things to say. "I always thought of it as making monsters."

"Yes! And for a while, it was working. Thrill's addicts were disruptive. Change was on the way. The chemists' work had even succeeded in increasing their turning drive. For a few months there were more new vampires in Chicago than there ever had been, but they were addicts, so they burnt themselves out. Built-in expiration dates, so they couldn't get out of hand. I was never inner-circle enough to know for sure what you planned for Phase 2, Logan sir, but I have a guess. If I'm right, it's too noble a cause to abandon forever."

Logan's eyes narrowed. This vampire played a dangerous game. "What's your guess for Phase 2?"

"If it were my plan," Victor said, "I would be working with the Annihilist Faction. I would have encouraged the spread of Thrill frenzy until the humans finally accepted what they were facing and started hiding. Then I'd have Annihilist soldiers ready to perform sweeps. The addicts become the frontline soldiers because they're never afraid. Because you'd promise them a fix of Thrill when their job is done. But most of all, sir?"

Logan waited.

"Most of all, it was to restore our dignity."

"'Dignity'?" Logan said.

"Yes, sir. Vampires have become a joke. With the help of Thrill, we wouldn't be a joke ever again."

Logan moved to a chair and sat. With apparent permission, Victor did the same.

"You break into my home and interrupt my sleep talking about dreams that died long ago, telling me you have concerns too urgent to wait until morning," Logan said. "So what is it, *Mr. Wheat?* You've got my attention. I pray, for your sake, that you won't squander it."

Victor swallowed, then began telling Logan a story. It was a beautiful story about a lost vampire dream that maybe wasn't lost after all, that troublemaker Maurice Toussant, and a way that Logan and Victor might be able to do undo so much of the damage the modern age had done.

"I should kill you for keeping this from me for so long," he said, "but I'm choosing to see this glass as half full instead."

"I know where it is inside Maurice," Victor told him, "but now he knows I know. He'll lock down. I can't get to him on my own anymore, sir. He'll come for me. I came to you because *maybe*, just *maybe* ..."

Logan leaned forward to clap Victor on the arm.

"You were right to come here, my friend," he said. "Maurice's defenses are formidable, yes. But if leadership has taught me anything, it's that applying enough force will solve just about any problem."

"So that's it?" Annabel said. "Victor's not at my house anymore? He's just ... *gone?*"

The big vampire, Brian, nodded. Last month she hadn't known vampires existed. Now she seemed to be friends with three of them and on the run from at least one more. From what Maurice told her, there were vampires all over the city and country — all over the globe, in fact. He'd dropped the glamour he'd put on her during their sessions, and that meant that technically speaking, she could go out and tell the world. She wouldn't, though. This wasn't like in the movies.

"You can't go home yet," Maurice told her. "Especially not now."

"I'm not going anywhere," she said.

Especially not now referred to the news Brian had brought them. If Annabel understood the dynamics at play, Brian was acting as a double agent. He'd come with today's news for Maurice at great personal risk. The "Vampire Council" Maurice had told her about was on the other side of this fight, and Brian (who was on that Council) was on

Maurice's side. But Brian seemed the moral sort, willing to risk himself in the name of a greater good.

Annabel had been inside Maurice's mansion for two full days and nights now. The day she arrived, it was like they'd been waiting for her — which they very well might have been. Maurice already knew the story by the time she arrived at the front door. It proved that what she'd believed was correct: Victor really *was* invading Maurice's mind, and Maurice had known. Now Maurice was holding his mind shut, but that wouldn't mean much until someone tried again to invade him. Victor seemed to be marshaling his forces at the moment. It might take a while before another attempt was made, but Maurice was uncomfortable relaxing his guard even for a moment.

"Nothing's been disturbed," Brian said. "I don't think he's been back to your place. In my mind, that just confirms it."

Maurice nodded grimly. "It" didn't really need confirming. Maurice had gone to Annabel's house the first night, not at all surprised that the vampire she called Victor wasn't around. He'd known Maurice would come for him and he'd known that when it happened, Maurice would tear him to pieces. Annabel, because she'd freed herself of glamour before leaving the house, had been able to give Maurice some insights. She said that Victor struck her as a loner. And a coward. He was the kind of guy who'd egg on others to fight for him, then jeer from a safe distance. She wasn't surprised he hadn't stuck around to fight ... and, if Brian was correct, that he'd gone to hide behind a bigger bully.

Meaning Logan.

For his part, Maurice guessed right away that Victor would go to Logan. Logan had been a secret partner in the Thrill game back in the 1920s and was, therefore, Victor's most logical partner now. Maybe Victor had been working alone when he'd talked his way into Annabel's home and put her to use, but today he wasn't alone at all. Brian said that rumor claimed Logan had a secret visitor and a secret plan. Clearly the visitor was Victor. And clearly the plan was next-step to Victor's first plan: to bring Thrill back to life.

"So Victor is with your Council," Annabel said.

"I'd bet on it," Brian replied. "Logan's working on something and he's clearly getting information from a new source. The new source has to be Victor. Logan's pulled a few people aside for private consults. He's requested early mobilization of Council Guard to guard ... *something*. Or *someone*. He even relocated Council ahead of schedule. He hasn't told any of the rest of us yet where it was moved to, probably because he's got your guy there with a heap of Mentalists, all of them preparing to get what they want from Maurice."

"'Mentalists'?" Annabel repeated.

"Most people just call them 'Mental,' because that's what they are. They're *totally* mental. Nominally interrogators, but really torturers. It's not something I know much about. Supposedly Mentalists can get anyone to talk. You can't refuse to tell them anything because they use your own blood against you. You can't lie because at least one of them is always trained in Truthsense."

"So they could get it out of you," Annabel said, speaking to Maurice. "The Thrill formula, I mean."

"If they have Victor's blood key, yes," Brian answered before Maurice could. "Maurice can block out *Victor* for now, but not those psychopaths."

"Well, then ..." She felt like she was missing something. "If Victor's with those nut jobs, and if they all want what

Maurice has ... *If* they have all that, why haven't they done it yet? It's been two days. Why haven't they invaded Maurice's brain or whatever?"

"Because they'd need to abduct him to do it," Brian said. "They have to hook him up to special equipment. It can't be done at a distance."

"And ... What? Maurice is too strong to be abducted?"

Maurice laughed. "I'm strong, but they have guns that shoot silver and wooden bullets. If they want me, rest assured they'll get me if they can find me."

Still Annabel thought she was missing something. There was no question of *finding*. Maurice's home didn't change locations like Logan's or the Council meeting place. Everyone already knew where Maurice was.

Brian saw her look of confusion and answered.

"Thrilloglobin was illegal. Logan supported it behind the scenes, not out in the open. Synthetic blood isn't allowed, see. Everyone knows how dangerous it is. The Vampire Nation would turn on Logan if they knew what he was up to. So, yeah — eventually Logan's people will come for Maurice ... but *only if they're sure they can do it quietly.* They need to wait until they're sure nobody's paying attention to this house. Which won't be hard because Maurice is so antisocial." Now he looked to Maurice. "If you were better liked, hiding in plain sight would be easier. As it is, nobody cares about you, Maurice. You're *already* invisible. *Already* nobody's looking. Logan's just taking a few days to be sure. Mark my word, we don't have much longer before they break down your door. Like ninjas, of course."

"That's ridiculous," Annabel said.

"That's *politics,*" Brian answered. "Logan needs to be liked or others will start trying to convince rivals to topple him. He lives in constant paranoia. We can turn that paranoia against him by using public opinion as a shield. Problem is, public opinion doesn't like Maurice very much. If he were popular and a lot of people were interested in what he was doing, it'd be one hell of a lot easier to stay safe. A lot harder for anyone to mess with him."

"Whereas now?" Annabel asked.

"Whereas now Logan just needs to avoid a spectacle. Once they've got him, it'll be smooth sailing. Take him away, let the Mentalists have him ... they'll break right in and get the memory they need. Nobody cares enough about Maurice Toussant to notice when he goes missing."

"We'll just have to find a way to keep them from getting him," Celeste said. "That's the only way."

"An *impossible* way," said Brian. "Come on, Celeste. You know these people. If he runs, they'll find him. If he stays, they'll take him."

Into the silence that followed, Maurice said, "There's another option."

He stood up. Celeste must have had an idea what he was about to say, because she stood up beside him. As if she wanted to keep him from speaking.

"There's *one* copy of the Thrill formula," Maurice said. He tapped his head. "It doesn't exist anywhere else. If they get what's in my brain, it's over; they'll have it forever. If they don't, they'll *never* have it. They'd have to start over, and from what I understand, Thrill was almost impossible to formulate the first time around."

"That's why we're trying to figure out the best way to protect you," Brian said. "To keep them from getting the last copy."

Maurice was shaking his head. "How long are we going to do that? *Forever?* As long as Logan's in charge, he'll never stop trying to get it from me."

"Then we'll take the fight to Logan," Celeste said. "We kill the bastard, if that's what it takes!"

But Maurice had already explained how impossible it would be to get at Logan. Daisy's blood had had an idea at first about how to find him (the method Logan used to keep moving his home was apparently based on something Santori used to do), but Brian already confirmed that a security breach had caused Logan to change his method. As of this morning, Logan's house relocated using the unbreakable algorithm that kept the Council moving. There was no way to decrypt that algorithm and find him. No way at all.

"As long as Logan lives and I live," Maurice said, "this problem continues to exist."

"Maurice," said Celeste, but Maurice stopped her.

"As long as *this* copy of the recipe exists—" Again he tapped his head. "—everyone in this room is in danger." He looked toward the front door. "I ... I think the only choice might be for me to erase the last copy."

"Erase it how?" Annabel asked. "Have someone glamour you into forgetting?"

"Vampires can't be glamoured," Brian said. "It's been claimed, but never proven. Old wives tales or the claims of charlatans. Nothing more."

As Brian spoke, his eyes went to the door, where Maurice had looked. Annabel looked now too, and something clicked. It was daytime out there.

"How would you erase what's in your head, Maurice?" Annabel asked, afraid she knew the answer.

He took a breath. "I'd walk into the sun."

Celeste was immediately in front of him, barring his way. *"I said no!"*

"Then what are we supposed to do, huh?" Maurice spat back. "Before, it was just Victor, but now Victor's got Logan.

Brian says he's already putting resources into this. You know what a cold son of a bitch Logan is. He's not above using torture; he'll *absolutely* get it out of me if he gets hold of me. We can't have much time left. It's act now or let them act for us. And *win*. You *know* what a Thrill epidemic would do to the world, Celeste. You more than anyone."

Maurice looked at the clock. It was after six. They only had a few hours until dark, when wolves might come.

"Logan has the Council Guard. He's got the means to sway public opinion against me: make *me* look like the traitor for spilling my guts to a human psychiatrist. He's got the Mentalists. If we stay here and try to fight them when they come, chances are one or more of you — probably *all* of you — will be killed trying to save me. Who wins then? *Me?*" He shook his head. "No. It's too big a risk. I'm not willing to take the chance. There's only one way to be absolutely sure they never get their hands on it."

"You don't have to die!"

"We've already wasted two days!" Maurice said. His tone was an exasperated breed of noble that seemed to say, *Don't make this harder than it already is.* "Logan's not going to wait forever. The second he thinks he can rush in, he's going to. If we can't win that fight, which we can't without losses, our options are to get rid of Logan — which we can't even *begin* to know how to do — or get rid of me. If I run and you stay with me, you'll be in danger for the rest of your lives ... and *then* if they find you, they'll kill you out of hand. If I leave alone and you stay, you'll *still* be in danger because he'll grab you instead: use you to get to me. Our best-case scenario involves at least the three of us (Brian, you might be okay if they don't know you helped us) staying in hiding forever. *Forever!* We're immortal, Celeste. Forever is forever. I can't do that to you. To any of you. *I won't!*"

Brian put a hand on Maurice's shoulder. It almost looked companionable, but then he used the plate-sized hand to push Maurice down to sitting.

"Real talk, Maurice," Brian said. "Your speech makes sense, and it's noble of you, but I think we all know we're not going to let you kill yourself. We're not robots without emotions. We're decent vampires, and you know goddamn well that asking us to okay your plan is actually *more* cruel than just letting us choose for ourselves whether we want to fight and die. But atop that, Celeste would walk into the sun behind you if you did that. You know she would. She's much stronger than me. I couldn't stop her if I tried. And certainly not forever."

Husband and wife stared at each other like a grudge match, but Maurice broke first. Annabel had seen them together and believed what Brian said. Maurice's death sentence would be Celeste's, too. You couldn't live with someone for a millennium, then endure after they're gone.

Nobody said a thing. The room felt deadly, draped with a pall.

So that was it, then. They were at an impasse. There was no way out, no way to win, and no way to dodge. There was no good here; their choices were between different shades of bad. They could pin their hopes on one of the impossibilities if they wanted — try to believe it might work. But weren't they all adults here, rather than children who believed in fairy tales?

"Then there's nothing to do but wait," Maurice said. "We can't go after them and we can't stay. As soon as Logan's confident nobody's looking, they'll rush in and kill us all."

Celeste's head picked up.

"What is it?" Brian asked, seeing something on her face.

"Say it again," she told him. *"Why* hasn't Logan come for Maurice already?"

"Because if anyone sees the Council involved in a forcible abduction, vampires will ask questions. It'll shine a spotlight on Logan that he doesn't want right now," Brian said. "He's waiting for a quiet night when he can feel sure nobody's looking."

"A spotlight on Logan," Celeste said, turning the words over. "And Logan doesn't want the spotlight ..."

"What are you thinking?" Brian asked.

"Nobody really knows how Logan's held his power, do they? People talk like he's got a secret weapon. He seized power without effort and has always held it without effort. It's like he's got a sixth sense. Eyes everywhere, like having leagues of spies. You know the things people say about him. Logan likes to pull strings from the background, not hog the stage. He's not charismatic. He doesn't like attention. He's a manipulator. A manipulator who needs people looking the other way when he does his best tricks."

"Rumors," Maurice said. "He doesn't have any 'secret weapon.'"

"Rumors or not, Logan always operates in secrecy," Celeste went on, thinking this out. "He works in the dark. The Council didn't constantly relocate before Logan became Deacon. Logan started that because he's paranoid. There was never this much secrecy in the past. Logan's like a magician; he can't let the audience look too closely at what he's doing. His need to avoid attention and scrutiny," she said, "is his Achilles' Heel."

"Okay ..." said Brian.

"You said that if Maurice was better-liked, people would notice if he was abducted. If others were interested in him and curious what he was up to, Logan couldn't abduct him without stepping into the spotlight, right? There'd be no way to sneak in and grab him *without* attracting attention and scrutiny, if he wasn't so antisocial. Isn't that exactly what you said?"

"Well ... yes, but ..."

Celeste stopped him with a held-out hand. Then she spoke to Brian, to Annabel.

"What if Maurice *wasn't* in the shadows anymore? What if more people knew who he was, and maybe even liked him? What if the world was fascinated by Maurice? *What if there was a way they'd* never *really leave him alone* — a way for Maurice to become someone who'd done things people care about — a person whose abduction would be noticed, whose absence would be missed?"

The questions were rhetorical. Everyone was quiet while Celeste thought.

Then she walked out of the room.

"Wait," said Brian. "Where's she going? *Where are you going, Celeste?*"

She turned around long enough to say, "To make my husband famous."

FIFTEEN

COUNTER-MOVE

"Um, Logan?" said Bella, Logan's daytime familiar.

Logan was extremely busy. He'd been about to make a call to one of the dungeon cells when Bella interrupted him, and he couldn't make that call with anyone else around. He needed someone extremely persuasive for tonight's errand — a kind of manipulative savant — and although he couldn't admit it, Logan just happened to know one such person. That person's work explained why three different assassination attempts on Logan had failed in the past ten years, why he'd been able to subdue an anti-Council group in Detroit he'd nearly learned about too late, and why journalists kept deciding not to use videos they had of vampires acting like vampires. The things his acquaintance could do were more than glamour. Calling was like hiring a supernatural marketing firm to improve your brand … through any means necessary.

"Later," Logan told Bella.

"I really, *really* think you'll want to come now."

Logan huffed with annoyance, but there was little point

in brushing Bella aside. She was right too often. Odds were excellent he'd regret it later if he ignored her now.

So Logan followed. Bella led him into the smaller living room, which they found stuffed with the home's guards, cooks, and maids. It looked like the whole staff was inside, meaning nobody was on duty. They were all watching the room's TV. Logan's irritation doubled.

"What the hell's going on here?" he demanded.

Unbelievably, someone shushed him. The television was blocked. He couldn't see what had them so captivated, and nobody was making way.

He glared at Bella. He didn't have time for this. His sole focus today was closing the box on Maurice Toussant, and he couldn't afford distractions. He planned to send Guards to Maurice's mansion tonight, and there were a thousand loose ends to be handled before that happened. He'd run Victor's story by the Mentalists (careful not to reveal the stakes of what was in Maurice's head, of course), and they'd given him nothing but thumbs-ups. The real problem to solve was Maurice himself — and probably Celeste, who was twenty times older than the oldest member of the Council Guard. To solve those problems, Logan had spent two days hashing things out with Victor. Most of that time had been spent fantasizing about how rich he'd be once Thrill began to flow again, and how much his stranglehold on the vampire world would tighten.

Bella pushed through the crowd to reach the TV, then gestured toward it.

"Look."

Logan looked. Immediately he wanted to smash the screen.

The TV showed the eleven o'clock news, where reporters were covering a hastily-convened press conference. Logan knew it was hastily convened because the lectern was a pair of orange crates. A bouquet of microphones had been laid atop the crates instead of resting in holders. Maurice was behind the crates, and at his side was a man Logan had never seen before.

"So when will we get to meet the star?" one of the reporters called out.

"Well, um ... he's very private," Maurice said. A lower-third graphic on the screen's bottom read *MAURICE TOUSSANT — TALENT AGENT.* "You might *never* meet him."

The second man good-naturedly nudged Maurice aside, taking prime position. The lower-third changed to *HARRISON CARDIFF — PRODUCER.*

"What the fuck is this?" Logan asked.

Nobody answered. Onscreen, the man identified as Harrison Cardiff started speaking.

"Maurice here is the guardian of the man the world knows as 'Fat Vampire,' but the 'vampire' himself is a very private person. You asked about the 'star'? The *star* will be someone we cast, not the YouTube phenom himself. He's only agreed to let us create this story based on his online reputation on the strict condition that he remain anonymous. That's how he wants it, so I hope you'll all respect his wishes and keep your attention off of him and on our forthcoming show, where it belongs."

Fat Vampire. Logan felt cold.

"I asked what this is," Logan said again.

"Someone's shooting a TV show in Columbus," one of the guards answered without looking back. "About vampires."

"They're not shooting it *in Columbus,* idiot," said someone else. "That guy just lives here."

"*'That guy,'*" Logan intoned, meaning Maurice. "You don't know who '*that guy*' is?"

"Some kid?" a girl near the front answered. Then she turned to her neighbor — the sweeper of Logan's shoe closet — and said, "How d'ya think a kid gets to be the guardian of an adult?"

"Maybe he just looks young," said Logan's shoe-closet-sweeper.

Numb now, Logan felt a hand encircle his arm. It was Bella, who pulled him away so they could speak privately.

"They don't know," she said when they were effectively alone. "I got a tip and I turned it on. Staff started coming in when they heard the word 'vampire.' Most here are too junior to know Maurice. They know all about YouTube's 'Fat Vampire,' though."

"*They know about Reginald?*" Logan couldn't believe it. He'd done his best to keep Reginald under wraps for reasons of dignity, and thought he'd succeed as far as average citizens were concerned.

Bella shook her head. "They know about *Fat Vampire*," she repeated. "You have a young staff, and right now he's a meme. It's not a crisis. *Yet*. For now, as far as they're concerned, 'Fat Vampire' is human. He could be anyone."

Yes. But with this attention now on Reginald and Maurice, that could change. *Easily*. The thought of wide-spread exposure gave Logan hives.

"Why aren't these people at their posts?" Logan wanted to know.

"Things have been a little crazy since your friend came to stay," Bella said. "If you'd just tell me why he's here, I could coordinate the staff to better suit—"

"Never mind," said Logan. Bella's main job was House Manager, but she spent most of her time guessing at her duties because Logan's dealings were too secret to disclose. The arrival and tenancy of Victor was no exception.

He glanced past her shoulder and into the crowded living room. Maurice was onscreen again. The lower-third now read MAURICE TOUSSANT — DISCOVERED LOCAL INTERNET CELEBRITY.

"You didn't tell them Maurice is a vampire?"

"I didn't know if you'd want me to. Should I?"

Logan watched the group. They were laughing at the screen, discussing something he'd missed that had just happened. Whatever was going on with Maurice's announcement, everyone found it hilarious.

"No," he told Bella. "We're not supposed to attract attention. A vampire putting himself on the news sets a terrible precedent."

His mind wouldn't settle. Maurice was an antisocial recluse, so why *was* he on the news? And why so haphazardly, all of a sudden? The press conference looked more like a garage sale than anything professional, held on the front steps of Maurices's house with equipment visible in every shot.

Bella was watching Logan patiently, waiting out this daze he'd fallen into. Eventually she said, "Logan? You understand what's happening, right? Tell me you see how bad this is."

But Logan didn't answer. He was watching a new scroll creeping across the screen. It said, IRONIC PRODUCTIONS TO MAKE "FAT VAMPIRE" TV SHOW BASED ON COLUMBUS-LOCAL INTERNET PHENOMENON.

Logan's jaw dropped. There was no pretending this was innocent now.

"No," he said.

"'No' as in you *don't* see how bad it is, or—?"

"*NO!*" Logan said, pushing past her to advance on the TV again. He grabbed the screen by both sides and shook it. "*No no no no no NO NO NO!*"

"Hey," someone said. "Down in front!"

With a furious shout, Logan ripped the TV from the wall. He swung it around the room in a tantrum, slamming it into everything. Books rained from ruined shelves. Light fixtures exploded. The audience disbanded in a cartoon puff: vampires instantly, human familiars at a sprint. A huge spark from where Logan had ripped the cord in half caught the wallpaper on fire. Without comment, Bella walked over and extinguished the flame by swatting it with a pillow.

"You're upset," she said. They were alone now.

"How the fuck could he do this?"

"I asked around. It's too big a glamour for a contract thing, so my guess is this Harrison guy was already interested somehow. They probably got the news to come on zero notice using glamour, though. Maybe just the first few reporters, and then the rest came when they saw what the competition was up to. Nothing attracts a crowd like a crowd."

"I didn't ask *how* he did it! I asked how he *could* do it!"

"Oh," Bella said. She shrugged, not caught off guard so much as temporarily on the wrong well-researched page. "Well, I think that's straightforward enough. You threatened his progeny. You threatened Reginald Baskin."

"And his response was to ... *announce a TV show?*"

"Maybe he's going for a more body-positive spin on vampires. Body-positivity is a big thing right now, Logan. I was listening for a while before I called you in, and they're not playing the 'fat' in 'Fat Vampire' like a joke. That Cardiff guy says it's about time for vampires to break the 'slim and pretty' mold. He said it's time the world finally had a 'relatable bloodsucker.'"

Logan stalked out of the room, needing fresh air. The living room smelled like ozone and smoke. Someone had destroyed a television in there. Bella followed him with her usual tablet cradled in her arms like a press secretary.

Logan didn't buy Bella's theory. Maurice was even more of a vampire classicist than Logan: He wanted *less* exposure of their world, not more. Maurice didn't want to make a spectacle of hilarious overweight vampires. In truth, he didn't want a spectacle at all. That had to mean the spectacle now was incidental. Maurice's *real* goal was to undo the 'vampire beautification' that Logan's regime stood for. Nosferatu was, like, Maurice's hero or something. Maurice said vampires all used to be like that bald, ugly motherfucker and maybe that's how things should have stayed.

He was an underground crusader. A social curmudgeon who no worthwhile vampire liked. So what'd taken normal, furious, anciently moral and murderous Maurice Toussant and made him into a media patsy? What had possessed him to make "the Reginald problem" a thousand times worse by dragging Reginald further into the spotlight instead of trying to undo his YouTube presence instead?

Logan said this to Bella. Of course Bella had already thought it out. The girl didn't miss a beat.

"He's not really dragging *Reginald* into the spotlight, though, is he?" she said. "You heard that thing about how he was Reginald's legal guardian, and how Reginald had to stay anonymous. If he was just trying to piss you off, getting on TV with Reginald in *any* way would have done it. Or getting on Facebook. Or, hell, YouTube. The 'Fat Vampire' videos are already hot and he probably knows you know about them, so he could just post a new one. The way he's taking pains to *hide* Reginald from the press, though ..."

She made a face. Then she shook her head.

"It doesn't fit. What Maurice is doing really only draws attention to *himself*, not Reginald."

"Have him brought in," Logan said. "In silver chains."

"Not dead?"

"No. Alive."

"You're sure? Maurice will stop embarrassing you more if he's *dead*, Logan."

"I want him alive. I have to ..."

... to torture the Thrilloglobin recipe out of him. To embark on my illegal, keep-it-under-wraps, I'll-be-murdered-if-anyone-finds-out Thrilloglobin plan.

All of a sudden, Logan understood. He understood why Maurice would want the spotlight on himself at this particular moment in time ... not that he could tell Bella.

"Well, all right," Bella said. Then she hit on the exact thing Logan had just figured out. "But going for him now will attract a lot of attention given the press that's around. Unless you want to risk even more exposure, maybe it's smarter to give it a few days. Everyone's looking at Maurice right now. So maybe we hang back, unless we want them looking at us, too."

Everyone's looking at Maurice right now.

"What if the attention lasts longer than a few days?" Logan asked, already feeling cold. If he was right about why Maurice had done this, there'd be plans to *ramp up* attention in the wake of this announcement, not let it diminish.

"Then I guess we risk it," Bella said. "Go for him anyway."

Alarm bells rang in Logan's head.

"*No!*" he said too quickly.

Bella looked surprised. After a beat, she said, "'*No*'?"

"We need to wait until the attention is off of him. *Entirely* off of him."

"But that could take months." She assumed her take-command voice. "Logan, the Nation will understand. We can't have vampires exposing vampires. It's a capital crime. Nobody will question you if you arrest him after this."

True. But they *would* question Logan after Maurice, arrested in public by the large squad of Guards a sensational arrest would require, started talking about Thrilloglobin while they dragged him in.

Goddammit. That was it. That was the reason.

Maurice knew Victor had gone to Logan, and he knew Logan would come after the Thrill recipe with all fangs blazing. But he *also* knew that Logan had to work in secrecy. *Nobody* could find out about Thrill ... not Bella, and certainly not anyone looking in Maurice's direction because they'd seen him on the news.

For now, Maurice was untouchable. It was the perfect counter-move.

Logan would have admired it, if he didn't want to kill him so badly.

SIXTEEN

ISOLATION PROTOCOL

Celeste put her hand on the front door when Maurice touched the knob.

"No," she said.

"*No?*"

"We just broke a millenniums-long vow of secrecy in order to keep you safe. Any vampire who sees the news and knows *you're* a real vampire thinks we're blood traitors now. This might backfire on Reginald. Might backfire *for* Reginald if he finds out about it, and it's ridiculous if you think you can keep it from him forever. The same attention we hope keeps Logan off your back will make it hard for us to feed. Hard for you to visit Reginald without the press following you, because they're *dying* to know who the real YouTube 'Fat Vampire' is after the coy little show you put on, refusing to divulge his identity. The influential people you ran out and glamoured tonight might be doing their best to turn this little nothing of an announcement into some sort of 'story of the year' thing. Honestly, they're doing pretty well at it so far ... but the side effect is that we now have fans. *Look*, Maurice. Just *look* at the crazies out there."

She used two fingers to push back a section of curtain. Maurice could see spark lights beyond the fence where a group of people were shining around with their phone flashlights. Maurice's vampire eyes had examined them in detail earlier. They were a group of maybe a dozen, some men but mostly women, all wearing dime store fangs with dime store blood running down their chins. From his perch atop the roof, he'd heard their chatter enough to know the name the group gave itself: *The Chubby Chasers*. "Chubby" in a positive sense, by the way. Most were a little rotund themselves and proud of it, extremely excited that this unknown vampire represented a new Rubenesque hero in town.

"I don't suppose you glamoured any of them," Celeste asked, meaning the people beyond the fence.

He shook his head. He hadn't needed to. Maurice didn't think he'd ever hit a target so perfectly in his entire life. The goal, between the time Celeste called Harrison to say Yes and the time Harrison arrived, had been for Maurice to streak out into the night and glamour a few key people into being very excited about a random television deal announcement. His hope was that those people would talk publicly about the so-called "Fat Vampire," and that the people *those* folks talked to would blab on to others. He hadn't counted on what felt like mediocre news being so grandly received, and he definitely hadn't counted on it happening so quickly. Their little dog-and-pony show had ended up hosting three news vans, half a dozen print reporters with nothing better to do at night, and a fair-sized crowd of citizens. All that attention immediately, on signing day. Most shows didn't get this kind of attention after months of careful advertising. Apparently, the idea of a non-cover-model vampire had struck a nerve.

"I'm glad it's working," Celeste said. "Even with some

glamour, I was pretty far from sure. Harrison tells me it's really unusual for anyone but Hollywood insiders to care *at all* about a deal when it's new, let alone for an out-of-the-blue announcement to draw a crowd. Isn't that right, Harrison?"

Maurice had forgotten the producer was in the room with them. Celeste had glamoured him into believing he was a coat rack, and of course coat racks didn't believe in real vampires so he'd thought nothing of their conversation so far. Only now did he perk up, and become a human again.

"It's really unusual for anyone but Hollywood insiders to care at all about a deal when it's new," he recited, "let alone for an out-of-the-blue announcement to draw a crowd."

"Maybe it's catching on so quickly because everyone's tired of a small, pretty group acting like they're the majority," Maurice supposed. "A latent dork rebellion, just waiting for us to ignite it. You know, in *Revenge of the Nerds,* they said—"

"Yes, yes," Celeste said. "Again with *Revenge of the Nerds.* Let me guess. 'We have news for the beautiful people: There's a lot more of us than there are of you.'"

"I've never quoted that to you before."

"Oh, honey. You quote it at least once a week."

"Well, maybe people are finally realizing it's true!" Maurice heard himself becoming defensive. He did quote *Revenge of the Nerds* a lot. Sometimes he wished he'd quote something fancier like Emerson or *Citizen Kane,* but that's not who Maurice Toussant was. He'd been born this way: an '80s man from the time of Jesus. There'd been very few panty raids during the reign of Caesar.

"I'm glad it's working," Celeste said again. "I'm glad

we've at least bought some time. It's a huge risk, but maybe since nobody knows the show's about a *real* vampire, it'll be contained. People will focus on you for a while. Keep Logan from moving against you for fear of people looking his way, then seeing what he's up to with Thrill. If this goes well and moves fast, which Harrison and the executives and lawyers and bookkeepers we'll glamour are going to make sure it will, then okay. Problem temporarily solved. With luck we'll have a year or more to find another way to deal with the situation. But my point is—"

"Logan might find another way to deal with it, too," Maurice pointed out.

"My point," Celeste continued, eyeing the door to the outside that'd started this conversation, "is that *the last thing in the world* I'm going to let you do after all this craziness and risk and traitoring is to run off and find Reginald."

"I'm not going out to find Reginald," Maurice said, trying to step past her.

Celeste moved to block. "Doesn't matter. For now, leaving the house means leaving the spotlight."

"It is *Reginald-adjacent*, though."

Celeste gave an exasperated sigh.

"Well, what do you want me to do? Just *hope* he doesn't find out about this? I took time off this week, but Reginald didn't. He's probably at work right now. I made sure work's a black hole, but once he goes home, do you really think he won't see this on the news? They're showing clips, you know. He's going to catch one of them on his way across the living room and about crap his pants. He's not *trying* to be a YouTube sensation. Not *trying* to get nosy assholes recording him while he embarrasses himself. Finding out that's exactly what's been happening will embarrass the hell out of him. *At least,* Celeste."

She exhaled hard, considering. Embarrassment could be dealt with. The real concern was that Reginald's attempts to fix things — once he learned the truths Maurice had been keeping from him — would make things worse. He was a sweet guy, but a total loose cannon. If Reginald survived his Council trial, maybe Maurice could drop the isolation bubble and let Reginald interact with the wider world again. Dropping it now — or allowing it to drop out of neglect — would undo all they'd done tonight.

"I glamoured the bosses so Reginald could work when nobody else was around," Maurice told Celeste. "I got the night shift down to a skeleton crew so it'd be manageable. I conditioned the people he calls most on the phone to not think twice about the strange things he started doing, like calling at night because he sleeps all day. The people at the supermarket don't wonder why he buys so much meat, thanks to me. I'm the reason his calls and text messages are redirected. And yes, I'm the reason Harrison found *me* when he went looking for Reginald, and the reason I was able to make this deal on Reginald's behalf."

Maurice cleared his throat.

"But you get that we can't do this halfway, right? *Reginald can't know.* The people around him *can't know* — or if they find out, they can't be allowed to tell him. If Reginald knows, he'll try to bargain. He'll try to slim down so he won't 'embarrass the Vampire Nation,' which even he knows he can't do. He'll try to feed on humans even though it grosses him out, and that'll just make more YouTube videos if for no other reason than because local people will be looking for him more than ever — especially at night, since he's a 'vampire.'" He settled, moving closer to Celeste. "You're right. I *am* shocked by how well and how quickly it's catching on.

But that's why I *have* to go out and tie things up with Reginald; don't you see? As time goes on, it'll be harder for me to get out unseen, not easier. The more time I let pass without handling Reginald's loose ends, the more we risk catastrophic failure when he does the wrong thing while someone's watching. What if they find out *he really is a vampire?* What then?"

That made Celeste blink. Apparently she hadn't thought of it. But what Maurice described was a real threat; Reginald could easily expose the existence of vampires while someone had a camera pointed at him if steps weren't taken to prevent it. In fact, it was just dumb luck that it hadn't happened already. What if Reginald had caught one of his intended victims instead of hilariously failing, on-camera, to do so? What if one of the videos had caught him feeding? They'd be facing a very different situation today if that had happened.

"Fine," Celeste said. "Go for him. But I'm going with you."

Maurice shook his head. "You're the second-oldest vampire I know in America. The second-strongest. It's not out of the question that Guard still might come here tonight. Someone has to be here in case they do."

He was thinking of Annabel. She'd watched the press conference, then gone to sleep in one of Maurice and Celeste's many bedrooms. It'd been a hard day for her, but it'd get a lot harder if Victor or someone else came calling and nobody was around to stop them.

"Okay," Celeste said after another moment of thought. "I'll stay." She didn't look like she liked the idea, but her logical brain was making clear that there were no options. "At least keep yourself in plain sight until you get to wherever you're going. Lose anyone following you only if you absolutely have to. You earned yourself a spotlight tonight. Might as well use it."

Maurice didn't like the idea, but maybe it was smart. He'd be faster, stealthier, and more agile alone, but he'd also be a lot more vulnerable to the exact things they'd done all of this to avoid.

"I'll go by car, then," Maurice said, hating the idea.

"And take Harrison with you."

"Harrison will go with you," Harrison echoed, deadpan.

Maurice nodded, knowing this was as much permission as he was going to get. He said to Celeste, "Guard the house. Guard Annabel. Keep her safe."

"I'll just sit right here," Celeste said, indicating the parlor table, "doing my homework."

Maurice's stomach dropped. He'd felt okay about everything until right now. "Homework," before Harrison showed up and Victor entered their lives, had been Celeste-code for her quest to find Ophelia. Ophelia had been a peacefully-sleeping dog in Celeste's heart for a hundred years, but Maurice's re-engagement with Holmes (even to kill him) had woken it up with a vengeance. She'd become obsessed. Sometimes he feared she'd never give up. Not even if it killed her.

Worse, his blood told Maurice that Ophelia had started thinking about Celeste, too.

"Be safe," Celeste said, not seeing his worry.

Meaning Ophelia instead of Annabel, Maurice replied: "You, too."

SEVENTEEN

WORTH THE RISK

Maurice looked sideways at Harrison, assessing him as they stopped at a traffic light. Celeste had released his glamour before they left, but Maurice had decided Harrison always acted a little bit glamoured anyway. He was sharp in show business, but smiled too much for what Maurice thought show business was. Wasn't Los Angeles a city of jackals? Didn't they eat each other's children just to get ahead? The fact that the only LA emissary they'd met was so friendly and pleasant threw off Maurice's compass. He was surprised to find how much he liked the man.

"Harrison."

Harrison turned his head. "Mmm?"

"I'm curious about something."

"What?"

"Don't you think any of this is strange?"

It was a risky line of questioning, but he supposed if Harrison realized strange things now that Maurice was asking, he could always re-glamour him.

"*What's* strange?"

"We called a press conference with two hours' notice. A

successful one, complete with fans cheering outside the fences. Now we're going out in the middle of the night to meet some people, and I haven't told you who they are or why. You just made a deal with me — a guy who looks eighteen or so — for the life rights of a man twice my age who I won't identify or let you meet. None of that's weird to you?"

Harrison laughed. "Oh. It's *all* weird to me."

Maurice waited. He prompted on with, "... and?"

"I live in LA. People walk cats on leashes there."

"Oh."

"And it wasn't life rights that you gave me. You'd have to identify him for us to need his *life rights*. We're not actually doing a story about your guy. We're doing a story based around a quirky character we saw online ... more *inspired* by your guy than *about* him. We'll film all new scripted stuff, not use the real videos. My partner and I already made little deals with the people who took the videos of him, but that wasn't hard because legally they're not supposed to profit off of a video of someone they don't know and didn't have permission to record. Technically speaking, I didn't have to come to *you* at all, Maurice. I could have just 'made a story about a fat vampire.'"

"Then why *did* you come to me?"

"It seemed like the right thing to do. And besides, getting publicity is hard without a hook. Linking the real show to the already-popular clips online makes for a good hook. When you said you'd help us promote it — sort of be a public face, you know; add a backstory to whatever we make up, since you know the original guy — that made this trip worth it to me. Makes it more than worth the expense."

Maurice considered what Harrison had said. It made sense. It was, he thought, one of the more rational things he'd heard recently.

The traffic light turned green. Maurice drove on. Then he said, "One more thing."

"Shoot."

"I told you I'd help with publicity, but only when it's dark out."

Maurice waited then, knowing he was courting a confession. But he had to know. Harrison had accepted that condition without glamour, without a blink.

"I just assumed you're a vampire, too," Harrison said.

Another stop light. Maurice looked over with his dead heart pounding.

"*What?*"

"You know. One of those kids who go around in black all the time. Hang out in cemeteries. Drink red wine like it's blood. Hey. I don't judge. In my day we were wearing bell bottoms and having key parties."

Maurice relaxed. Harrison didn't mean "vampire" literally. But his answer told Maurice that he was — and this was a bonus — extremely open-minded. And that was convenient, because he'd been wondering for a while how he'd get rid of Harrison in order to meet with the people he'd come to meet.

He had a hunch, too. For once, it was a positive hunch rather than his usual foreshadows of doom. Something deep down told Maurice that Harrison would be a friend to him one day — that if Maurice took a small leap of faith now, they'd build a partnership strong enough to help everyone later. And hey. It'd make for a better TV show, too.

"Would you like to meet my familiars," Maurice asked, "now that you've met a vampire?"

EIGHTEEN
YES

Maurice's usual way of losing pursuers was to run really fast, but with Harrison present he had to rely on movie cliches to shake any tails they'd picked up while driving. He made a lot of turns, went into and out of parking garages, then went through a late-night Taco Bell drive-thru because Harrison was hungry and had pointed out that Maurice's erratic driving was apt to attract more attention rather than less. The pursuers they were trying to lose would be human anyway, not vampire — if there even *was* any pursuit, which they both doubted. Humans just weren't that clever most of the time.

"Don't let the fans outside your gate give you a big head," Harrison said. "You're not even an executive producer."

After Taco Bell, they drove to Maurice's place of business, which was also Reginald's place of business. Reginald's nemesis Todd was on vacation for the week at some gross-sounding swinger's resort, leaving Reginald and his girlfriend and co-worker Nikki alone in the office. At some point, at Maurice's request, Nikki had run out to get ten-year-old Claire, whose mother was at her own night-shift job.

Nikki was in the break room and Claire was playing with the Xerox machine when Maurice and Harrison arrived.

Maurice looked around. He whispered to Nikki, "So where is he?"

"Asleep in the supply room."

"You got Reginald to take a nap?" Maurice had asked her to get Reginald out of the way so they could speak plainly, but he'd assumed she'd just convince him to stay home.

"It's a food-and-sex coma," Nikki explained. "Trust me, he won't wake up."

Maurice's eyes ticked toward the hallway that led to the supply room.

"You don't want details," she added.

So they called Claire back, ready to get down to business. But first, there came the question of glamour.

"Harrison," Maurice said, drawing Harrison's eyes. "You're going to listen to everything I say."

"I'm going to listen to everything you say."

He dug deep, trying to remember how he'd first glamoured Annabel. He wanted this to be like that.

"You're going to be your usual self. Nothing about your personality will change. Nothing about your business will change. Nothing about the deal we signed tonight will change, and your attitudes and prejudices and lacks thereof will remain the same. "

"What are you—?" Nikki started to say, but Maurice held a palm toward her.

"The things you hear here, although you will find them hard to believe, will strike you as true. They will not alarm you. You will believe in vampires on my word alone. You will not need me to demonstrate and convince you. But you will not be any more afraid of us than you would of anyone else. You will not discuss anything you hear in this room with anyone outside this room, except for my wife Celeste. You will not tell your partner or anyone you work with. It will not be hard for you to keep our secrets, and to know they are secrets. You will learn my friend's name but will have no desire, ever, to share it or to let anyone else know you know it. You will pretend as if none of what's about to happen ever happened, but you will remember it just the same. You are free to make your own judgements and have your own reactions, in the exact same way you would judge and react if I wasn't talking this way to you right now. If any of those natural reactions bother you — if you are afraid or anxious or anything other than accepting — you will speak to me about it so that I can make those feelings go away."

Maurice then eyed Nikki. He said, "Think that's good?"

"Why are you asking me?"

"Because you think like a lawyer. I want him to be himself in every way, but not freak out and not tell anyone about anything we're about to discuss."

She thought for a moment. Then she bobbed her head and said, "I guess it sounds good, but isn't that a pretty precise set of instructions coming from an admittedly bad glamourer?"

Maurice looked inside himself. He thought of Annabel, and the complex glamour that she'd embodied perfectly.

"I think we're going to need him," Maurice answered. "And if my gut's worth anything, I think the glamour will be just fine."

He looked back to Harrison. "Do you understand?"

"Perfectly," he said.

AFTER THAT, it was introductions around. Nikki had seen the news and knew who Harrison was, and she'd told Claire all about it on the drive over. If Maurice hadn't called her, she'd've called Maurice. Sending Reginald's story to TV had seemed as reckless to her at first as it had to Celeste. The difference was that Maurice and Nikki had only known each other for a few months, whereas Celeste had known him for a thousand years. It was easier to convince Nikki that things would be fine because she hadn't lived through ten centuries of well-intentioned promises that seldom worked out.

Whether it was due to failures or successes in Maurice's glamour felt up for grabs, but Harrison was absolutely fascinated by the things he heard within the first sixty seconds. Maurice prefaced Nikki's intro by saying flat-out that YouTube's "Fat Vampire" was named Reginald, and that Reginald was *actually* a vampire — and that Maurice, of course, was too. This gave Nikki's introduction some delightful context. Harrison wasn't just meeting a pretty woman who worked the night shift at a company that didn't need a night shift; she was a bona-fide vampire's girlfriend.

"And this is Claire," Maurice said, introducing the girl.

Harrison sat on a chair across from Claire after shaking her hand, which Maurice took to be a deft move of courtesy. Standing above her would be unintentionally intimidating, but squatting before her (and this was particularly true of Claire among all children) would have seemed condescending. Sitting was a nice compromise.

"So you're the one who feeds him," Harrison said.

"I just gave him some meat we had in the fridge. Mostly we just hang out. It's not creepy."

Harrison seemed amused and impressed at the same time. Claire was nothing if not precocious. "Why would it be creepy?"

"People in the YouTube comments seem to think it's creepy. It's not. My mom works at night and Reginald needed a friend."

"I'll bet people say he should have a friend his own age."

"Yeah. But if you ever meet him, you'll understand. He's not slow or anything. He just ... has nobody." Then she looked up at Nikki and Maurice, who Reginald also had. Harrison looked to Maurice then, and they shared a thought. Maurice didn't need to be psychic to read the understanding on Harrison's face: *You don't just look like a family. You really ARE a family, aren't you?*

Maurice couldn't help a smile. Yes, letting Harrison in on this was the right choice.

"Tell you what," Harrison said. "You know I'm making a TV show based on your friend. On Reginald."

"Yeah ..."

"What do you think about us adding a 'Claire' character? So we see his other side. So he's not just some big fat joke."

Claire smiled. "I'd like that."

"And maybe instead of him coming over to your house in the middle of the night to watch cartoons—"

"*Columbo*," Claire corrected. "We watch reruns of *Columbo*."

Now Harrison gave Maurice and Nikki both a look that said, *Okay. I get it. I'll stop treating her like a little kid now.*

"Maybe instead of that, we'll have you work together."

"You want your 'Claire' selling treadmills?"

"Maybe somewhere younger. Somewhere more mini-mum-wage. Do you like ice cream?"

"I like Slushies."

"So maybe some sort of Slushy Shack."

Claire liked that, too. The other three sat around the break room table, the four of them now in a rough circle.

In the beat of silence that followed, Maurice decided the best start, in the limited time they had before Reginald woke up, would be to get everyone up to speed. So he told Nikki and Claire (without censoring himself for Harrison's presence or Claire's age) that Logan was gunning for him and that agreeing to the TV show was Celeste's way of creating camouflage — of putting a spotlight on Maurice and Reginald so Logan couldn't attack them without drawing attention to himself. He didn't tell them about Annabel, Victor, Daisy, or especially Thrill; that part had to remain a secret for everyone's protection. Instead, he left it at "threat from Logan," wondering only after he said it if he should have admitted his reasons for signing in front of Harrison. But it was no problem; the glamour on Harrison had woven perfectly into his demeanor — more like an atti-tude adjustment than something he'd been commanded to do. Harrison nodded along, satisfied after hearing about this "Logan" fellow that signing a TV show was a sensible way to escape him.

Then he told Harrison the things that Nikki and Claire already knew: that Reginald's inputs and outputs were being filtered by the three of them without Reginald's knowledge. It sounded bad at first, but the nodding of ladies' heads seemed to justify it. By the time the trio was finished explaining Reginald's delicate position within the vampire world and the ways their filtering was meant to protect him, the whole thing didn't sound quite so insulting. If Reginald spoke too much with his human friends and relatives in an unchecked way, he'd slip up and make his situation a whole lot worse. In the same way, Reginald had mostly been sheltered from vampires. His world was little more than work and home, wake and sleep: Maurice, Nikki, Claire, repeat.

Harrison hadn't understood the most difficult part until now. When it dawned on him, he looked confused and doubtful.

"Wait. You're not just saying that you don't want me to meet Reginald. You actually think you can *keep all of this from him?* Your plan is to black him out *totally*, and just hope he never hears from *someone, somewhere*, that a TV studio is making a show about an overweight vampire?"

Maurice nodded.

"Well, how the hell is *that* going to work?"

Maurice sighed before speaking: his concession to the difficulty of it all. "We'll do our best. We don't really have a choice. I love Reginald, but he's no good at being a vampire. Not yet, anyway. If he hears, he'll be embarrassed. He'll try to 'be more like a proper vampire.' He might even try to argue his case with other vampires, and that'd be a problem because other vampires don't like him much right now. My guess is, there are a *lot* of TV shows out there being made that I've never heard of. Until a show gets a lot of PR or goes on the air, how excited does the public actually get?"

Harrison's head was shaking slowly — not denying this so much as trying to wrap his head around it. He was glamoured perfectly. All of his wits were still intact.

"You're right that the average person doesn't know about most of what's in production until it airs. But you just said you're using this as a smokescreen. You *did it* to create a fuss. That's the *reason* you did it. You called a press conference to bring all the local media to your doorstep. How's that supposed to jibe with the goal of keeping quiet?"

"We just have to keep it quiet from Reginald," said Nikki.

"Yes, but it'll still be out there!" Harrison argued. "Other vampires already know about this 'unfit vampire' you made, right? They were already mad at you about it before I showed up. Even if humans just think you're some random guy, at least a few vampires will know who you are, and which 'fat vampire' the TV show is about, right? People who haven't seen the YouTube videos before will find them now. *Someone's* eventually going to tell Reginald, and that's assuming he doesn't just get a bunch of emails from people who know who he is and connect the dots."

"Email isn't a problem," Claire said. "Just like Facebook's not a problem and text messages aren't a problem."

Harrison looked over.

"I'm pretty good with technology," Claire explained.

"You did something to his phone?" Harrison's head whipped between the three of them. "Well, what about his TV? What about his home computer? What about his *work* computer? He might use any machine here!"

"I'm *very* good with technology," she said.

"Look, Maurice," Harrison said, looking over. "No offense to you, Claire, but if the stakes are as high as you say, then trusting a ten-year-old hacker to—"

"It's not hacking," Claire said. "This is ... something else."

Harrison seemed far from convinced, but when nobody spoke and instead just looked at him, he let it go.

"Okay," he said. "If you're vampires, then far be it from me to think I know better."

Maurice didn't bother to correct him. Claire wanted to be a vampire but they'd never turn her. She still had a mother, absentee though she was. And Nikki ... well, her ascendency was yet to be determined.

"We're here to make sure we're all on the same page," Maurice told them. "Until Reginald's trial is over, he needs to be protected from himself. If the show takes off, we can bring him in later, but for now this is how it's going to happen. So I need to know that you can add 'TV show' to your list of keep-aways, ladies."

"No problem," said Claire. "Filtering is filtering."

Maurice wasn't sure what that meant, but Claire's scary ability with all things electronic was a mystery for another day.

"I've got him in as much of a cocoon as possible already," Nikki said. "I'm with Claire. Blocking is blocking."

"You understand that there's a chance someone will recognize him out on the street. And if he realizes ..."

"I'm pretty good at keeping his attention, Maurice." Nikki said it as if he'd insulted her. It was true, though. Reginald kept telling Maurice that Nikki was out of his league. All she had to do was exist and he'd look at nothing else.

"Harrison?" Maurice asked.

He half shrugged, half put up his hands. The gesture said, *I'm not convinced, but what the hell.* "Well, yeah, okay, but I don't see why you brought *me* into this discussion."

"I guess I should ask how you feel about all of this."

"In what way?"

"You thought you were making a funny show about some guy who comes off like an atypical vampire. Now you know he's real — a *real* vampire, not a delusional human. And *we're* real. And the people who want to erase him and kill me? Also real. I could probably force you to make the show no matter how you feel, but I don't have a great track record at that and I don't want to anyway. You seem like an interesting guy, Harrison. If you still want to do this knowing full well what it really is, I feel good about it. I believe in magic. I trust my gut, and my gut tells me I should trust you."

Now Harrison laughed. "Are you kidding? Knowing all of this makes the show a hundred times better. I get that I still need to pretend that Reginald is fake. And that I don't know his name is Reginald. I understand everything I can't do. But *I'll* still know what all of it is actually based on, and any good creator will tell you that the parts of the story that never leave your head are just as important as the parts you put on the page or screen. *I* know I'm making a story about a real vampire misfit. It's not just a comedy, is it?" He thought, then answered his own question. "It's actually a *dramedy*. It's ... *it's an underdog story!*"

Maurice smiled at that, for the first time in what felt like ages. Yes, Harrison understood perfectly.

"So you're in," Maurice said.

"In like Flynn. I have some ideas how to keep it low key. You understand I have to circulate it in my circles. That's how we make our money. *Hollywood Reporter*. *Variety*. Probably *Bloody Disgusting*."

"Of course."

"And eventually, you know we'll want to widen that circle. This is a for-profit thing. The financiers won't want us playing small on purpose."

Maurice was trying to find a way around that — but yes, he understood.

"We have time to figure it out," Harrison said, reading Maurice's face. "The non-Hollywood networks won't care yet anyway, so we just won't reach out to them yet. No more local media. You'll just rile people up if you do that. I think the best way to serve both masters — keeping the media footprint small so the risk of Reginald (or anyone who knows Reginald) finding it stays small, while also giving you protection from this Logan guy — isn't to make the spotlight bigger. It's to move you closer to it."

Nikki's face changed. "Are you saying you don't have to make a big splash and create a ton of publicity to do what Maurice needs?"

Harrison shook his head. He seemed positively invigorated by the challenge of his career's first supernatural job. "Not yet. Not if he's willing to come with us."

"'Come with you'?" Claire repeated.

"Yes," Harrison told her, giving her his full attention. "That's better anyway because it keeps the rest of you safe. Unless you think Logan will try something while Maurice is away?"

Maurice had been thinking that at first, but now he dismissed it. "He won't as long as he can't get at *me*. He knows that if I hear about him doing something back home, I'll make a big stink about it. Going after someone I love will make me spill his secrets *more* than going after me."

"So you'll come back with me," Harrison said, nodding as if it was a done deal. "Back to LA. Stay with us while the production gears up."

"How long will that take?" Maurice asked.

"You want it drawn out, right? So attention's on you for as long as possible?"

"Actually, faster is better," Maurice said. "I can't postpone the trial forever. One way or another, it'll happen within a few weeks. Maybe a month. *Maybe* two, but definitely no more. If there's a way to get as much momentum as possible as fast as possible, that'd be ideal. But I know everyone says things move slow in Hollywood, so maybe that's not—"

Harrison waved it away. "Money solves everything. You were saying earlier how much money you have and how you can't find things to do with it."

"When did I say that?" Maurice asked. It was true. But he hadn't said it to Harrison.

"When I was a coat rack."

"Oh."

"I'll just say it. Can you pay for this?"

"So I can bribe people to move faster?"

Harrison shook his head like he was impatient. "So you can fund the whole thing. Financiers and lawyers are what slow projects down. I figure your glamouring trick can help with the lawyers. We can keep things boilerplate."

"If I fund it, can we skip the lawyers? I'm guessing the contracts are mostly for insurance, legal troubles, stuff like that?"

"Exactly. But we can't skip it. We *need* insurance, Maurice. The unions require it."

"Then I'll fund the insurance. I'll be the insurer."

"You have money for *that?*"

Maurice took a second to enjoy Harrison's reaction. The simple answer was yes. He'd accrued for two millennia and, outside of the home he'd bought almost literally forever ago, he had simple tastes. He'd need a calculator just to figure out how many worldwide accounts he had, let alone how much was in them.

"I'm not nineteen, Harrison. I'm a vampire. I've been

around for a long time. How much money are we talking about?"

"I'll have to get back to you on the cost of insurance. But we'd need a few million dollars an episode for the show itself. Ten hour-long episodes for the first season."

"And that gets it moving how fast?"

"Let's say forty million budget for the season. That might get us up and moving in a month. *Might*."

"We can't go faster than that?" Maurice asked.

"A month is *stupid* fast by Hollywood terms. You should be laughing at me for even saying it. In this business, people work a year out or more. The geek sector is kind of a mess right now as everyone starts planning for Comic Con. I wish I could get *that* for us, Maurice, but unless you can do magic ..."

"What slows it all down? Why's it take so long? Red tape? Will more money solve it? Because I can pay more."

Harrison shook his head. "Writing scripts takes time. You understand we have to *have a story* before we can shoot one?"

Maurice exhaled. "Okay. Fine. I'll drag my feet. What else?"

"Deal-making. We need partners."

"Why?"

"Well, who the hell is going to buy the show and air it?"

"Does it matter, if I'm footing the bill?" Maurice asked. "Film it all, *then* sell it. Or *don't* sell it; who cares? We just need activity. Something we can show the world."

Harrison tapped his chin. "There's also scheduling. The people we'll want to hire are probably in the middle of other jobs, so we'll have to wait for them to finish. Although a crew I've worked with before in Victoria, actually ..." His voice faded as he seemed to be remembering what might be a fortuitous gap in schedules. "There may be a way. But *cast*, Maurice. Cast really matters, and even neglecting the time it takes to find them, they're busy people."

"*Someone* must be between movies. *Someone* who'd be perfect for the role. Tell me you haven't already been casting Reginald in your head, at least."

Harrison smiled a little. "There's someone I'd love to get. But he's not available for several months."

"Why? Is he shooting a movie?"

"About to."

"Then we do better. Make our deal more attractive so we get to go first."

Now Harrison's smile said Maurice was naive. "Maurice. It's a *superhero movie*."

"What are they paying him?"

"He's third on the call sheet. Trades say somewhere around $1.5 million."

"So we offer him three."

"It's not just about the pay," Harrison said. "There's a whole lot of cachet that comes with being in a superhero movie right now, and—"

"Then offer him ten."

There was silence. Nikki and Claire were just watching, entranced by this high-stakes dealing.

Then Maurice said, "I'll give you one hundred million total budget for the season. Spend what it takes to get it done and to get it done well, so people love it, and love us, and most of all love and are sympathetic toward Reginald." That was starting to feel like an almost primary reason to do this show now that it was on the table: not just to keep the Thrill recipe out of Logan's hands, but as a way to humanize Reginald in advance of his trial. "You can keep the rest of the money. So. Tell me. This guy you have in mind. The superhero guy. Is he awesome?"

"He's the best."

"It doesn't have to finish faster than it can finish," Maurice said. "I just need it to start ASAP. To get underway. To generate some good vibes — enough that if the worst happens with Reginald's trial, we can release some footage and show off those vibes. That's why it doesn't just need to happen, but to happen *well*. And be wonderful. I'm starting to see: This is going to come down to a fight for hearts and minds."

Harrison seemed to be thinking about it.

"One hundred million dollars to find a way to start shooting this thing within a month," Maurice said. "I can have the money wired the second you need it."

Finally Harrison said, "Okay. I'll start getting it together immediately," he said. "No promises, but I'll see who I can get on board. No glamour for the crew and cast, though, Maurice. I have to insist on that. This needs to be legit. I don't want anyone involved who doesn't want to be there."

Maurice didn't understand, but didn't ask. Harrison's rule sounded like an integrity thing. Maybe Maurice had spent a bit too much time forcing people to do things his way. If Harrison thought he could get people involved in the project without glamour, maybe that was best. Give the world a chance to support him for a change, instead of twisting their arms. Who knew? Maybe humanity — and even vampirekind — would surprise him. Maybe not everyone had to be coerced into doing good.

Harrison was still thinking. He said, "I think we'll shoot in Canada, far from prying eyes."

Maurice couldn't believe what he was hearing, though he'd been digging hard for it. Yesterday he'd been laying low, and a few months from now he'd have a TV show underway.

A grin crawled across his features. He looked at Harrison, who'd make it happen, and Nikki and Claire, who'd play defense on the home front.

They were really going to do this.

"Is that a yes?" Maurice asked.

Harrison shook his hand. "It's a yes."

NINETEEN
PROBABLY

Annabel was making her bed. Bed-making had always struck her as beyond unnecessary (it was *her* bed, not anyone else's, and she was just going to sleep in it again 16 hours later), but as a stranger in a strange house she couldn't help but feel she should make an effort. For one, it felt discourteous not to — maybe because it implied she took her stay here for granted instead of respecting it; she really wasn't sure. But for another, Maurice and Celeste had the opposite schedule as Annabel. When she woke in the morning, they'd already gone to sleep. There were just a few hours in the evening after the vampires woke and before Annabel went to sleep, and in those hours she didn't like the idea of them passing her room and seeing housekeeping undone.

The whole thing was probably Annabel's imagination. They'd told her to make herself at home and not to fuss over anything. It was strange, to think of vampires as welcoming and courteous, but either way she wanted to make herself worthy of it. She tried to express how thankful she was that they'd taken her in. To Maurice, who Annabel knew well, the imposition seemed no problem. But to Celeste? Although Celeste had been perfectly kind, Annabel couldn't shake a feeling that she didn't want her here.

There'd been tension between Maurice and Celeste, and the first day she'd been angry with him because he'd kept something from her — something involving Reginald, it seemed. Did that mean that Annabel, too, could be a source of conflict? Surely Maurice hadn't told Celeste *everything* about his therapy, seeing as discretion was part and parcel with therapy. You didn't blab about your innermost baggage. To anyone.

To solve the maybe-not-a-problem, Annabel had done her best to stay out of Celeste's way. They smiled and said hello, but always in passing. When Annabel entered rooms, it seemed to Annabel that it wasn't long before Celeste left those rooms. And yet more than once Annabel had expressed her desire to leave — to get out of Celeste's hair. Celeste always poo-pooed the idea, saying Annabel was their guest; she should stay as long as she liked.

But now Maurice reported that he'd be moving to Los Angeles to perpetrate his TV show smokescreen. He'd run back to Ohio at least once a day so Reginald wouldn't be suspicious of his absence (literally *run*; he could make the trip from Columbus to LA in just over 20 minutes, which Annabel calculated to make him faster than the fastest jet in existence), but most of the time he'd be on the other side of the country. Most of the time he *was* in Columbus, he'd be at work at the treadmill company: a ritual of ordinariness Annabel found baffling at a time like this. He'd almost never be at the house. The mansion would therefore be Annabel and Celeste only: two roommates just distant enough to make things uncomfortable.

"Oh, I'm sorry," Celeste said, poking her head into the reading room. "I didn't know you were in here."

She had a book in her hand. It seemed she'd planned to read by the fire, same as Annabel had.

Annabel hadn't yet sat. She'd been perusing their volumes. The books on the shelves seemed impossibly old and valuable — and there were a *lot* of them, filling shelves that ran on four large walls from floor to ceiling. The room she was standing in might, by itself, be worth $100 million. Enough to fund a priority-schedule TV show.

"I was actually going to go read somewhere else," Annabel said. "Please." She gestured at the best chair — the one she'd been planning to use when she'd thought she was alone.

"Don't be ridiculous. Have a seat."

"I honestly didn't plan to read here. It's fine."

"But you have a book," said Celeste.

"It's your book. I borrowed it from the shelves on my way back to my room."

Celeste approached. She looked at the book Annabel was holding. "So from our shelves of pre-French-Revolution hand-bound volumes, you chose ... *Twilight.*"

"Maybe it's Maurice's," Annabel said lamely.

"Annabel?" Celeste said.

"Yes?"

"That's *your* book. You came in here to read it."

"No."

Celeste took the volume, then set it on the end table between the big, high-backed chair and its almost-as-plush neighbor. Then she said, "Sit."

Celeste sat, but she took the lesser of the chairs as if leaving the first for Annabel, maybe because she was here first.

"I see what's going on here," she said. "You're uncomfortable."

"No," Annabel lied.

"I'm sorry."

"Because I'm reading *Twilight?*"

"That too. But mostly that you're uncomfortable. It's my fault."

Annabel laughed. "I'm not uncomfortable. And even if I was, it wouldn't be your fault. You've been nothing but wonderful."

Celeste put her book on the table beside Annabel's. She set her knees primly together with her legs to the right, then folded her hands on the outside of her thigh. She was wearing a knee-length skirt, and was one of the few people left in the world who wore pantyhose.

"It's because you remind me of her," Celeste said.

Annabel stood for a moment longer. Then she sat. "Daisy?" she asked.

Celeste nodded. Her eyes cast down, then back up.

"I can't have children," she said. "I'd have to *make* them. I'd have to take them from the life they knew and curse them with this thing of ours. It's terrible, to want a child as a vampire. If you make a child, she never grows up. Never grows old. If you keep her human, she grows old so fast that she dies without you. Neither option is any good. You can't know what it's like, to never see change in the mirror. It has a curious way of making days feel pointless. Even if you learn something, you look in the mirror tomorrow, and ten years later, and a hundred years later, and half the time your mind makes you forget what you learned because of the dissonance. *How can I have changed,* you start to think, *if I haven't changed at all?*"

Annabel said nothing at all.

"I never would have made Daisy. I have a hard enough time committing to a dog or a cat, which is why we haven't had one in forever." She looked over. "It's not that I don't like them. In fact, I'd argue it's because I like them too much. Bringing an animal into a home changes the dynamic. The whole family changes, whether you think it will or not. If it *doesn't* change, you're doing it wrong. Animals need love. They need attention. If you're going to get a pet and then just carry on exactly the same, it's not fair to the pet. Babies, I always thought, would be a thousand times that. Turning someone so you'll have a companion? That's an even bigger deal. Because they will live forever. Or are *supposed* to live forever. Because you've taken away their life and given them a different life, and that means you're responsible for them. Until the end of time, the good things that happen to them are partially your doing and the bad things that happen to them are partially or entirely your fault. So as much as I wanted a child sometimes, I don't think I'd have ever pulled the trigger as a human. And I certainly wouldn't have done it as a vampire."

Celeste looked at her hands. Annable saw that she was crying, and her tears were made of blood.

"But I loved Daisy just the same, Annabel. *Oh God,* how I loved her. I didn't think I would, but she became Maurice's daughter and that made her my daughter, too. Even when she was infuriating, I loved her. Even when she was in trouble — maybe *especially* when she was in trouble — I loved her. That's an impossible, desperately painful sort of love: a feeling like part of you is in peril and yet you can't pull it back to safety. She defied us. She was addicted. *Born* addicted. It wasn't her fault. She was only with us for a short while, and in a life as long as mine, that while went by in a blink. But I think about her all the time. I wake up forgetting she's gone. I'd do anything to have her back — anything. The fact that I know I can't is the worst, most cruel sort of torture. So mostly I just try to look the other direction. I try to forget."

She looked up, the sockets of her eyes streaked with gore, her fingertips red from wiping. She managed a small smile. "But over the past few days, I can't forget her. Because of you."

"I ... I don't know what to say."

"You don't have to say anything. I'm telling you so you understand, not so you can apologize. Do you have children?"

Annabel shook her head.

"Then I don't suppose you can understand how when it comes to them, even the pain is good. It hurts to remember her, but I wouldn't take that pain away. Seeing you is like seeing how she might have grown up, if vampires hadn't crossed her path. You look so much like her. Did Maurice tell you?"

"He said he had no idea we were related."

Celeste gave a dismissive laugh. "I guess he wouldn't. If he'd shown me your website, I'd've known right away. Saved us all this trouble." She laughed again. She was being hyperbolic for sure; if they were true ringers, her lineage wouldn't have been a mystery for so long. "I don't suppose he ever showed you a picture."

"Of *Daisy*?"

Celeste nodded. "We had one taken. Maurice might not remember. Or might not *let himself* remember." She reached for a small cigar-style box on one of the bookshelves, then opened it and begin sorting through old black and white pictures. "Back then you couldn't just point and click. People had to sit perfectly still, looking like someone had forced them to be there. Back then nobody really smiled in photos, but of course Daisy did."

She found the one she was looking for and handed it to Annabel, who took it carefully by the edges. It probably measured 5x7 and showed the little family together. Given their respective ages, they must have told the photographer the portrait was of a widow with her two children. As promised, Maurice and Celeste were stone-faced in their throwback finery. Between them was a smiling girl who looked to be in her early twenties, hair short in a flapper cut.

"Here's one of just her," Celeste said, handing over another photo. This one was smaller but showed Daisy from the shoulders up. She really did look like Annabel, but even more she looked like Annabel's mother. Mom had some photos from when she was in high school, and so much was the same: eyes, nose, the shape of her smile.

"She's beautiful," Annabel said.

"She was our Daisy. Our little flower, no matter how old she was and no matter what she got into."

Annabel tried to hand the photos back, but Celeste gave a wave. "Hang onto them for just a minute if you would." She laughed down at her blood-smeared hands. "Look at me. I'm a mess."

"I'm sorry," Annabel said.

"I told you. Don't be sorry. It's a blessing, having you here." She reached into a box on one of the tables and came out with a restaurant-style hand-wipe packet. She laughed as she tore it open, sniffing back tears. "Pro tip if you ever become a vampire. Don't carry a handkerchief for when you get emotional. Carry moist towelettes."

Now Annabel laughed. When Celeste was finished cleaning and drying, she tenderly took the photos and placed them in the box as if they might crumble. Even replacing the box on the shelf had the careful feel of a mother's nighttime tuck-in.

"I'm done," she said. "It's over. So let's stop being strangers, me and you. If it's not insulting, I'm going to pretend that your history is Daisy's history. Maybe she didn't get to grow up, but her genes did."

"That's not insulting at all," Annabel told her.

"Good. So. Ever been married?"

"What?"

"I'm a very old woman, Annabel. I'm old-fashioned in some ways. Is it uncouth for me to ask about marriage as my first question?"

"Only if you imply that I needed a husband to get by in life."

"Oh. No. Of course not. Daisy wouldn't think that way, either." Celeste patted the table. "Strictly a question of romantic butting-in."

Things felt easy now. Annabel already knew she liked Celeste ... just a few days delayed.

"I haven't, no. But it's strange."

"That you haven't been married?"

"That it feels like I have. I keep forgetting that I'm not. That thing you do. That 'glamour'? It's a real mind-job."

"It's not just that," Celeste said. "If the glamourer does it right, it causes your own mind to invent false memories to fill in the gaps."

"Yes! Like *Total Recall*. I feel like I've gone on the vacation, but my 'vacation memories' are just implants."

"I haven't seen *Total Recall*."

"You don't need to. Although Arnold Schwarzenegger does pull a thing the size of a golf ball out of one nostril. And there's this really ugly puppet. And a lady with three boobs."

"Maybe I *do* need to see it."

"But yeah. My head's full of false memories. I remember a time that Victor refused to wipe his feet outside our rental when we were in the Bahamas. He tracked mud all over, and I got really mad at him. But we never *went* to the Bahamas. Obviously. It's super sunny there. And as far as I can tell, he only got me about a month ago. We never even left my house together."

"I'm glad you got out of it."

"Yeah. About that," Annabel said. "How *did* I get out of it? When I told Maurice what I just told you, about the filled-in fake memories and whatever, he said Victor must be really good at glamour because he certainly couldn't do as good a job. But if the glamour was so good, how did it break?"

"Must not have been as good as it seemed."

Annabel shrugged. "I guess it's like you said. Our girl's got moxie."

"What girl?"

"Daisy."

Celeste blinked at her.

"*Daisy,*" Annabel repeated.

"I heard you. What *about* Daisy?"

"I thought ... Didn't I tell you both?" She wondered now if she had; things had happened so incredibly fast that first night.

"Tell us what?"

"Well ... I didn't break out of the glamour on my own. Daisy helped me. I mean, her 'blood memory' helped me, is how Maurice described it."

Celeste was still dumbstruck.

"The legacy of her blood that's in my blood," Annabel went on. "Maurice called it 'blood ties.' He said that sometimes you can see echoes of your relatives' lives from the past, and it's like they have their own voices inside you, and …"

She stopped on her own. She was suddenly sure she'd committed a huge *faux pas*.

Way to go, idiot, she told herself. *You finally clear the air with the host, then screw up and pee on her flag.*

Celeste didn't seem angry or offended, though. She just seemed not to understand.

"That's how it normally is with vampires," she said. "Something in you called to Maurice, telling him that you were in danger. That happened through Daisy's tie. And when he was waiting outside your house one night, wondering what to do, a feeling of Daisy came so strongly to him, it's like it took him over for a while. He said it was like she was speaking to him. Like she was trying to show him something. But that's for *vampires*, Annabel. You're human."

"Maurice said it could happen in humans."

"Sometimes. *Maybe*. And if so, just a little. It's pretty far from accepted wisdom. The way I understand it, it can pass *through* a human more than be felt *by* a human. So if you had a kid and that kid became a vampire, he might feel all of your ties through you even if you couldn't feel them yourself. But you're saying that Daisy was *loud enough inside you that you could hear her?*"

"Well, I know it's not *her*. I know it's just my subconscious mind putting together little bits of blood memory and—"

"And she was strong enough to help you break through an elite glamour?"

"She kept poking me until I noticed how much strangeness I was accepting as normal." But Celeste was still staring, so Annabel said, "Is it really that weird?"

"Did Victor know this? Not that you could break through, but that Daisy was *that* strong inside you?"

"I never heard her until after he did whatever. So no, I don't see how he could know."

"And you never told him."

"No. I didn't want him catching on."

"Even when you were glamoured, you didn't tell him."

"Yeah." Which was weird. Because she was quite sure she'd kept Daisy's phantom voice a secret despite having no way to keep secrets (or know that she *should* keep them) while glamoured. Looking back she remembered many times that "a voice inside" had pushed her to disobey Victor's word, starting with the first time Annabel had reminded him that his nickname used to be "Puffed Wheat." He'd commanded Annabel to stop speaking once he realized what was coming, but Daisy had poked her to say those loathed words to him anyway, just to piss him off.

"What?" Annabel asked. "Does it mean something? Is it bad?"

"It's just that ..." She seemed to be seeking a political way to say whatever she had in mind. "Well, Victor picked you instead of some other therapist because of your tie to Daisy, right?"

"Because Daisy has ties to Maurice," Annabel said, sure she was talking out her ass. "I *thought* that was why. Victor needed to go through Daisy to get to Maurice."

"He didn't, though," Celeste said. "Having a tie through Daisy would make it more convenient for him to reach out from a distance, but a blood key on its own would let him into Maurice's mind. He could have made that key through any means that told him enough about what made Maurice tick. He could make it by reading a detailed-enough diary, if Maurice kept one. I'd been assuming that Victor followed Daisy first, *then* Maurice, and *that's* why he started with you. Like he used Daisy's family line as a guide. But what you're saying now, about Daisy being this strong inside you … It makes me think there was more to it."

"Like what?

"Like maybe your connection to Daisy is more than ordinary blood," Celeste said. "Like maybe somehow Victor knew it, and hoped that connection would give him an advantage in making the key he needed to break into Maurice's mind."

Annabel didn't like the nerves this gave her, but she tried to talk it away.

"I guess it doesn't matter now, though, right? His key failed. I hit him over the head and broke it off, and now Maurice has his dukes up so he can't use it again."

Celeste pondered for a second, then nodded. "You're right. It's probably nothing." She smiled. "Forget I said anything."

Probably nothing.

Annabel didn't like that *probably*. Not one little bit.

TWENTY
CONTINGENCIES

Victor kept Plan B at the ready. Like those Boy Scouts he'd once eaten, he was always prepared.

Usually a person's Plan N — N for Nuclear — was their last resort. Once you went nuclear, you never went back; that's how the expression went. A typical amateur created one last-ditch exit in the event of emergency, understanding that using that exit meant giving up control to someone else. In Victor's case, seeking the Vampire Council's protection meant handing the Thrill ball to Logan and allowing him to carry it the rest of the way. It was a trade of control for security. He'd've been dead if he'd stayed on his own, so he'd opted for company. Plan N meant nuking his solo plans in the name of survival. He'd *wanted* to go it alone as far as Thrill was concerned (and become kingpin all by his lonesome), but after circumstances required bringing Logan in as a partner, Plan N accepted that Logan would hog all the glory.

That's how nuclear plans usually worked: You gave something up when you used them because otherwise you'd never see tomorrow.

Not for Victor, though.

The others used to make fun of him back in Chicago — always the shrimp, always the whipping boy for all the tough-guy gangsters — but now those tough guys were dead and Victor was still breathing. When Maurice came for them in 1929, the egomaniacs faced Maurice while Victor hid inside a cabinet. Maurice came, Maurice killed, Maurice left ... and then Victor crawled from the blood-soaked rubble and walked out of town. His self-respect did not demand revenge or satisfaction. It did quite the opposite. It wasn't true that Victor didn't have a backbone. In fact, he was the only one who *did* still have a backbone. All of the braver vampires' backbones had turned to ash more than 80 years ago.

Tigers got all the glory as undisputed kings of the jungle, but it was the smarter and sneakier animals (like the fox, or possibly the roach) that survived.

So Victor kept his private Plan B warm. He didn't yet know if he'd need it. So far Logan was playing mostly fair, treating Victor like the partner he'd asked to be. This way, if it held, was better than Victor's solo plan. Victor had few resources. After he'd gotten the recipe from Maurice, if his first plan had worked, he'd've faced the daunting task of finding vampire chemists willing and able to actually make Thrill. If Victor remembered right, it was more delicate than throwing ingredients in a vat. He'd've needed the vat, too, as well as at least a bathtub-gin-scale distillery with all the right equipment installed in all the right ways. Knowing how to make the stuff, per the recipe, was only half the battle. The rest came down to project management and leadership of what would become a large team of workers. Victor had known all of that was coming, but hadn't wanted to face it. Now, with Logan's help, he wouldn't have to.

And that, in theory, made this partnership worthwhile. Using Logan's power, resources, influence, and network, they'd definitely ship more than twice as much Thrill as Victor could ever have hoped to ship alone — and that assumed a short setup time, zero losses, and the vampire authorities being willing to look the other way. Split 50/50, Victor would end up richer and more powerful partnered with Logan than he ever could have been on his own. So in theory, all was well. As long as Logan kept his word, all would *stay* well.

The problem was that Victor had little faith that Logan would keep his word.

So far, Victor still had all the power. *He'd* made the blood key to Maurice's mind, and Logan couldn't make his own key without repeating Victor's work — on an aware and guarded Maurice this time, who by the way seemed to have inexplicably left town. That meant that until they got the recipe from Maurice by force, Victor would *keep* his power.

What bothered him was that the second Logan had Thrill's recipe in-hand, he'd almost surely cut Victor out of the mix.

Maybe cut him out of *life,* too — *probably* out of life, in fact, because Victor would be the only one able to reveal the extent of Logan's rulebreaking. Logan liked deniability. With Victor gone, Logan would be able to deny everything. He'd be able to pretend he had nothing to do with the addictive synthetic blood soon to be flooding the streets. He'd be able to pretend there was no connection between himself and Maurice. After the recipe was in-hand, Logan would probably stop seeing Victor as an asset and start seeing him as a liability.

The recipe was, after all, the only thing Victor had to offer. The rest of the work would be Logan's ... with Victor standing by doing nothing after that, collecting half the dough.

Logan could easily erase Victor's part in this. Evidence that he'd done worse was all over the house — all of it highly suggestive, none of it definitive enough to nail Logan on anything illegal. The man was slippery as hell. He wasn't just influential; this was more than that. His rise to power (and holding of that power) should have been impossible without widespread insider help.

When Logan overthrew the last Deacon, Council Guards had helped him. Those Guards died soon after.

When he'd made a trade deal with the Asian Vampire Nation, it'd been so unfavorable to Asia that none of the vampires abroad should ever have agreed to it. Yet somehow they had, and Logan's power had grown.

That sort of thing had happened again and again. Vampires here said that nobody defied Logan because Logan always — *always* — got what he wanted. If the Council threatened to overrule him on something he wanted badly enough, whispers said he'd deploy a secret weapon ... and the next day every Council vote would fall the way Logan wanted it to fall.

Logan had something up his sleeve. Victor just hadn't worked out yet what it was. Only a stupid man would trust him — especially on anything as high-stakes as the return of Thrill, especially when Logan had nothing to lose and everything to gain by slitting the throat of his partners once things were underway.

Hence Plan B.

Hence Annabel.

There was something about Annabel Rice. Victor had never quite put his finger on it. She hadn't laid down at his command like a good zombie, and she'd exercised more independence than he'd liked in her sessions with Maurice. The stories she told Victor after those sessions made it sound like she was actually curious about Maurice instead of just acting as Victor's spy. She was making her *own* decisions, asking her *own* questions. More than once, Annabel had even asked Victor those same questions. And of course, in the end she'd broken his hold on her like flimsy handcuffs.

But it wasn't all bad news. The more he thought about Plan B, the more Victor thought he could still use Annabel to his advantage. There was more than one way to skin a 2000-year-old vampire.

He hadn't thought much about it when he'd begun this venture — a quest that went back to the twenties in theory, but began in earnest twenty-some years ago when Annabel was in her teens. That's when he'd become interested in her as more than a way to keep tabs on Maurice Toussant and the priceless information Victor was sure had found its way into his head. He had no idea how he'd ever get that information back then (the "blood key" plan ended up requiring years and years and *years* of study), but he'd kept watch on Daisy's descendent nonetheless. Because Victor was thorough, and because he'd tracked down the adoption records for Daisy's baby while sloppy Maurice hadn't bothered, Victor had known exactly what he was looking at when he looked at young Miss Rice. And so he'd felt the blood tie reaching out from Annabel to Maurice (something he could sense but not decipher, like standing too near a magnetic field) despite the fact that she was human. He had a hunch that one day he could use that tie to get at Maurice, but the "how" of it only appeared the day Annabel enrolled in college with psychology as her major ... and then amplified when she entered medical school as a budding psychiatrist.

Not that Victor's influence had anything to do with that. He hadn't whispered in her ear at night. He'd never passed her in the hall, held her gaze for too long, and then suggested how much she wanted to be a therapist. Not at all.

He'd ended up with a tool he could use in two different ways. Her skills at psychiatry would get Maurice to spill his guts if both of them could be steered toward one another, but even if the blood key failed he'd still have that strange, shouldn't-be-possible connection between them. How could a human and vampire tie so tightly? Was it because of Daisy — because of something special within her? Victor didn't care. All that mattered that the tie existed. Worst-case scenario, it could be leveraged to make Maurice and his wife care nearly as much about Annabel as they'd cared about Daisy, so he could use her as a hostage. Worst-case scenario, his own skills at glamour and blood-tie manipulation might make the threat of Annabel's death feel like an echo of the heartbreak they'd had when losing Daisy.

He hadn't fleshed out his alternate plans yet, but it was nice to know he had options. Those options meant that just like Logan, Victor had a secret weapon. He'd told the Deacon all about Thrill and his quest for the recipe, but there'd been no need to tell Logan much about Annabel. As far as Logan was concerned, Annabel was just a random human Victor had chosen to use as his prybar on Maurice's thoughts. Logan didn't know what Victor knew about the ties that bound them like an unbreakable tether.

Plan B was just a concept for now. But give it time, and Victor would turn it into an ace up his sleeve.

Wandering Logan's mansion, he found himself strolling down the administrative corridor. The layout of the place was exactly the same every time it was moved to a new location. He'd watched the last move happen, thinking of the way roadies stripped down the enormous setups required for in-the-round arena concerts. Hundreds of roadies could disassemble monoliths in one city and rebuild them in a new city the next day. That's how Logan's relocations worked: *unbuild, move, then build again.* The only difference was that Logan's roadies had vampire strength and vampire speed. You'd swear from inside the house that it'd been where it was forever.

"Victor!" Logan said, spotting him and waving him into a room at the corridor's end.

Days ago when he'd waved for Victor, he'd done so with a huge fake smile, as if Victor was his best friend in the world. Now — after the announcement of Maurice's absurd television show and Maurice's subsequent leaving town — Logan called with more command than mirth. He still managed to make Victor feel important, as if Victor's arrival was about to save everything. That's how politicians worked: They made the people they used feel good about the using, then stripped them to the bone.

Victor entered. He was still thinking about Annabel. Everyone assumed she'd run away and hidden, but only Victor cared enough about her to have a theory as to where she was. She was still at Maurice's place, of course. She'd gone there after their little daytime incident and she hadn't gone back home — just like Victor had run to Logan, then never gone back. He could still reach her at the Toussant home if he wanted to. Maurice was gone. Annabel's only companion, in all probability, was Celeste.

"Come," Logan said, still waving. "Come meet Sergei. Our chemist."

Victor shook the cold hand of a vampire wearing a lab coat as Logan introduced him.

"I've told Sergei all I can remember about how our product is made, but I was never close to it," Logan said to Victor. "We hope you can fill in the gaps."

"You have formula?" Sergei asked.

Logan answered before Victor could, eyeing Victor to let him know he should follow his lead.

"Victor doesn't have a formula," he lied. "We're not even sure there *is* a formula. We have a lead, but that's all."

"Is a lot of work," said Sergei, "for not being certain you can make."

"I'm confident we'll get the recipe," Logan said. "We'll leave it at that."

He looked again in Victor's eyes, and his message was clear: *Nobody finds out what we have, you hear? Nobody even finds out if we have it. Nobody gets a clue about where we'll get it, or how. Everyone's on a need-to-know basis, and unless the Earth burns, nobody but me and you need to know.*

So Victor began speaking, watching Logan for signs that he might be saying too much. He kept his report observational and avoided all mention of formulas, seeing formulas, or even being sure formulas existed.

"So we will need bleed chambers," Sergei concluded when Victor was finished. "How many Santori use in Chicago?"

"Forty? Fifty? That's for one facility," Victor said. "I don't think it matters exactly how many humans are being bled, though. If you get more blood, you can scale faster."

"Plan for an even hundred," Logan told the chemist.

"That is many humans and is not as easy to take them as in American Prohibition. You have plans to get?"

"Just worry about the equipment," Logan told him.

Sergei unrolled large sheets of paper that turned out to

be black and white photographs of a Thrill distillery busted up by vampire do-gooders back in the day. He started pointing at tanks, lines, and other machines.

"In concept looks simple," he said. "Lines in from bleed chambers." He traced the lines with a callused finger. "Was direct but today we will filter. Human pathogens will not hurt your customers but may be irritants and better experience is better for repeat business, yes? So centrifuge, separate, wash, recombine." He'd listed equipment not in the photos, so they must be in his mind. "But I think this is just fancy way to take blood from here and put it here." He tapped a large mixing vat. Then he tapped something else. "This, I do not know. But line going in tells me it is another ingredient. Lines out are here, which go to—" He shuffled to another photo. "—here. You can see this is only dispenser. If you ask me it is simple. Not like baking cake. More like making cocktail. Pour in, mix, pour into glass. I see no heating, no cooling, No equipment for incubation, fermenting, or distilling. You call this place distillery?"

Victor nodded. "Yeah. But that doesn't mean they actually distilled. I think it was just a word. Compared us to the other bootleggers at the time, who did distill their spirits."

"Makes sense," said Sergei, nodding. "I wonder how anyone distill blood. You boil her, she clots. Take out platelets and boil, water comes out and left behind is sludge, but is also what makes blood *blood*." He slapped the photos, then looked at Logan. "You ask me, making is easy. Next step is formula. Formula will show amounts and ingredients and what is not easy. You will want testing. I can learn how to test and what to test when I know all ingredients. You will want gas chromatograph. You have access to gas chromatograph?"

"Anything you need."

"Vampires I know who use this and still alive say it felt like drugs that cannot be gotten in much supply. Government watches supply. If this is true, will not be easy to get and hold supply."

"Bribes solve things like that," Logan told him.

"Is not just matter of bribe. You know? Is complex. Controlled by underground and government the same."

"I said, *I'll get you anything you need.*"

Now Logan sounded annoyed, because Sergei had been told once and hadn't gotten the picture. Victor could understand Sergei's disbelief, though. Logan was giving him a pat answer: *I can get anything from anywhere.* That might turn out to be a pointless promise; for all Victor knew, the other ingredients might turn out to be water and over-the-counter children's cough syrup. What piqued Victor's attention, though, was the surety Logan seemed to have that even if one of the ingredients was all the world's purified Uranium, he'd be able to get it in unlimited supply by morning.

Sergei leaned back on a high stool, crossed his arms across his chest, and then gave a little shrug.

"So. Is it, then. From what I see, Thrilloglobin could be mixed in a bucket. Need only to know what is in it."

"I'll get your recipe," Logan said.

Sergei clapped his hands. "Good. Then I will build you more than a bucket. My organization has contractors able to operate under cover of human institutions. They will pull permits as if making restaurant that never opens. As part of deal, will also glamour building inspectors and health inspector and others as needed."

"How long until the first distillery is ready?"

Sergei frowned. "Month? Two? But this does assume no supplies are, how you say, bottlenecked. I understand you will glamour humans and use network, but is possible they will encounter vampire institutions that cannot be glamoured and cannot be bought."

Logan looked even more annoyed. "You worry about building as fast as you can," he said. "Let me worry about the rest."

Which was to say, *I'm not worried about anything. Anywhere. Ever.*

Again Victor wondered: What was behind that certainty? Nobody should be as confident as Logan. It made Victor nervous ... and that much happier that he at least had a chance, if Logan betrayed him, of doing an end-run around him using Plan B.

You have to get Annabel back somehow, Victor told himself. *Her blood — her tie to Daisy and then to Maurice — is the only advantage you might end up having when Logan finally stabs you in the back.*

TWENTY-ONE
BALLS

The next weeks passed in a blur for everyone.

For Maurice, the surprisingly intense demands of being a Hollywood financier warred with his need to be at home with Reginald. It wasn't that Reginald needed him; it was more that Reginald needed not to notice that Maurice was missing. Claire and Nikki were doing their best to isolate Reginald and keep everything from him (it wasn't difficult so far; with PR on hold, only people "in the biz" had any idea the show was happening), but if Maurice disappeared, Reginald would start to ask questions. So between night-time meetings in Los Angeles, Maurice buzzed back and forth to Columbus on foot for the most anticlimactic use of a rush-back-home ever. All he did at the office was to exist, pretending to do work that'd been glamoured out of the bosses' heads. Meanwhile he prepared Reginald for trial as best he could, acting as the mentor he was supposed to be. Still, he couldn't help being aloof. Being home was distracting at a time he couldn't afford distractions. He always felt the clock ticking back in Los Angeles, always needing his attention.

To make things happen quickly, Harrison went into a mode he called "guerilla on-spec": *on-spec* because they'd be shooting for no buyer in particular, *guerilla* because the speed of things had him cobbling a rag-tag group that probably wouldn't end up working by the book. Entire legal departments usually worked around the clock on leases and location permits, but that way of doing things could be slow. Harrison was prepared to dodge the letter of the law whenever he had to.

To move things along, Harrison reached out to networks he'd worked with before. Maurice thought involving new parties would slow things down, but Harrison argued that unless they got more hands in the mix, they'd never get it all done. Soon one of the three-letter networks (Maurice didn't know which and didn't care) apparently found the story interesting enough to take a meeting, but they wouldn't involve their people — and, more importantly, start swinging their network weight around — without a signature guaranteeing them a piece of the action should they later decide they wanted one. It was an easy yes, and helped tremendously. Apparently networks were able to do things faster when someone else (Maurice, in this case) was footing the bill, and hence didn't have any financial risk themselves. The three-letter network ended up going all-in effort-wise in exchange for a simple contract granting them first right of refusal on the finished project.

The network's primary liaison was a man named Jerome Waika, who Maurice hated immediately. He was a cliche cut from the show-biz-exec coloring book. He told Maurice he looked fabulous just for something to say. He laughed too hard at comments that weren't funny. He tried to make boneheaded criticism look like an effort to help the poor dumb people who didn't know how to make good TV, even though Harrison and his partner Ella very much did.

Jerome was especially full of thoughts about a TV show that dared to call itself *Fat Vampire*, which was what Harrison liked best as a working title because it was so attention-grabbing.

"We've seen all kinds of vampires before now," Jerome said at an overpriced lunch, a white napkin tucked into his collar over his tie. "Tall ones, short ones, white ones, black ones, hetero ones, gay ones, of course lots of lesbians and bisexual vampires, non-binary vampires, old vampires, young vampires, vampires who turn into bats, vampires who sparkle in the sun, and George Hamilton."

"What?" Maurice said. He hadn't been listening. In a half-drunken reverie full of why-the-fuck-not a few days prior, he'd dropped Harrison's glamour and let him see the truth without it. Turned out Harrison didn't care one bit that Maurice drank blood and burned in the sun, and that Reginald did, too. He swore he'd never tell — not about vampires, not about Reginald. Nobody else knew — certainly not Jerome. Jerome, in fact, didn't seem *able* to know more than what didn't track well with key demographics and if cameras were shooting him from his good side. So all throughout lunch, Maurice had been drinking wine and ignoring the entree Jerome had ordered for him without being asked. He hadn't fed for real, so the wine was accumulating quickly enough to make him drunk.

"But you know what vampires have never been?" Jerome went on. "They've never been fat."

This went on for a while. Jerome seemed torn between twin ideals: a need to capitalize on the lack of corpulence in the vampire community and the fact that using the word "fat" might make him look like a bigot. It was extremely unwise to be a bigot in television circles these days. Bigots had to hide their bigotry or risk losing corner offices to more woke candidates. Jerome was on the fence about just how bigoted the world knew he was.

"I'm down with it," Jerome said. "With people being fat, I mean. A lot of people are fat these days. So I say, 'bring on the fat'! The fatter the better. *Slather* on the fat. Maybe our whole crew should be fat. Is there a fat-advocacy organization we can call, to make the fat people think we accept them?"

Maurice leaned toward Harrison and said, "Maybe we shouldn't call this thing *'Fat Vampire'* after all."

"It's meant to be ironic," Harrison countered. "The title is what *the world* thinks, not what *we* think as creators."

"Fat fat fat," Jerome said. "I just wanna put my face between some big, fat titties!"

"Maybe we don't call it that anyway," Maurice said to Harrison, eyeing Jerome, "just in case of douchebags."

WHILE JEROME WAS DOUCHEBAGGING the wrong way down the body-positivity highway, Logan was enjoying the less commercially relevant aspects of Maurice's work — the aspects that didn't get more eyes on a future TV show but did get more eyes on all things vampires.

And by "enjoying it," that meant "hating the living fuck out of it."

Work on the first Thrilloglobin distillery was already underway. Sergei's people were in the process of purchasing a warehouse in the ever-popular heroin district and had only needed to kill one stubborn zoning inspector to do it.

The deal was a quit-claim tied into a more traditional purchase. This was necessary to begin construction, because as long as the building was officially owned by humans, vampires couldn't get inside to begin construction unless those humans invited them in. The owners were hidden by three layers of corporations. It was easier to convince their representative to quit-claim the place now and pay for it later. That rep was resistant at first, but came around when his first testicle was painfully removed.

It happened faster than anyone expected. On the same day that Maurice was signing his first contracts, delivery trucks were arriving at the would-be distillery with steel mixing tanks and sheets of drywall. They'd even put a sign up out front, announcing it to be the future home of the Kluski Factory restaurant. Victor had seen the place and the part of town they'd put it in. He wasn't sure why they bothered pretending it was an eatery. Clearly it wouldn't fool anyone.

By the end of the second week, with drywall already finished and more tanks and tubes arriving, Logan cornered Victor and said, "Enough fucking around. We have to get that goddamned recipe."

"For Thrill?"

"Of course for Thrill. Sergei wants to try some small test batches. He doesn't want all those blood lines installed without having some idea if some lines need to be made of non-reactive metals or plastic. He says this is like working in the dark."

"They *are* working in the dark. They're vampires," Victor said.

"Is that a joke? Because I don't see you spending any money. I don't see you laying out bribes to keep people looking the other way."

Yes. People really *were* looking the other way, weren't they? Victor had been watching *that*, too, while he tried to work out a way he could abduct Annabel without being murdered. The part of town in which the Thrillery was being built (a combination of *Thrill* and *distillery*, though Victor thought it sounded like a family fun center) was thick with vampires. Homelessness was big there, and that meant it was easy to feed without attracting attention. Yet no vampires visited the construction site and none raised questions through official Council channels once construction began. Why?

"Okay, then," Victor said, standing from the chair he'd been sitting in. "Let's go. Now, Maurice is two thousand years old, so I'll need at least five Council Guard to go with me. If you want him alive, I suggest silver harpoon guns. With trailing filaments. Diamond ones. And chains. A lot of silver chains. Now, if you want to go with us, that's great, or I can just—"

Logan was aghast. "You can't go after him *in force!*"

"I thought you wanted the recipe?"

"Not in an open abduction! Find another way!"

But there was no other option, and Logan damn well knew it. Both of them did. There was exactly one way to extract the memory from Maurice's head, and it required bringing Maurice in for torture. Bringing him in, of course, wasn't something that could be done unseen now that Maurice was in the public eye all the time, so they were at an impasse. Logan knew his protests — his tendency to yell at Victor about this exact same thing every few hours — were pointless. It was just venting steam. Truth was there was no way to grab Maurice without vampire eyes seeing it happen. If they saw, they'd ask questions. Maurice might open his mouth about Thrill. Officially, Logan was supposed to follow the law — and in no uncertain terms, experimentation in augmented blood had been banned, such experimentation punishable by imprisonment and execution. After Santori and Capone and the ravages of the first Thrill epidemic, the vampire world refused to take chances. Logan would be finished. Done. Fodder for an empty ashtray.

"I've been considering the possibility of grabbing him while he's at work," Victor said. "He comes back most nights to work his usual job. I don't know why he's doing that, but he is."

"Probably wants to keep an eye on that protege of his," Logan said.

"But every time I think we might be able to do it, I remember the Chubby Chasers."

"The anti-Reginald group?"

"They're actually pro-Reginald. Apparently they're determined to 'take back "chubby."'"

"They want to cut off penises?"

"Not that kind of *chubby*. It means they're changing the meaning of the word."

"What's the new meaning of 'chubby'?"

"Same thing," said Victor, "only now it's affectionate. One of their chants says, *'We're here! We're chubby!Get used to it!'*"

"I don't get it."

"It doesn't rhyme either. They should say 'hubby' instead of 'here.' But I guess some of them might not be husbands, so 'here' is safer, if nowhere near as much of an earworm."

Logan didn't seem interested in the chant's rhyme scheme. He was more interested in why the group's existence was keeping Victor from trying to grab Maurice at work.

"Are you saying those people are watching Maurice when he's in Ohio?"

"Constantly. Maurice is a hero for the rotund on both sides of the Mississippi. They love him to death. They just stand outside Maurice's office and chant all night."

"Glamour them, then," said Logan. "Glamour them and make them go away so we can do what needs doing."

"Can't."

"Why?"

"Because they're vampires."

Logan's jaw fell. He looked like one of those carnival games where you squirt water into a plastic clown's mouth to inflate a balloon.

"What."

"I said they're—"

"I fucking heard you," Logan told him. "I fucking heard every fucking word you just said. Even the ones that fucking said even *our own species* wants a fucking fat misfit representing us."

"That's actually all the words," Victor said. "The words I told you don't say anything else."

"Unbelievable."

Victor said, coyly: "Can't you just ... *you know* ... to get rid of them?"

"Can't I just *what?*" Logan asked.

"Use your *whatever* to get them to leave. Get them to go somewhere else."

"What the hell is a 'whatever'?" Logan demanded.

"You know. Whatever's keeping vampires from being interested down at the Thrillery?"

Then Victor waited for an answer. Officially, Logan

wasn't doing *anything* to keep prying eyes away from the warehouse, so this was one of those wink-wink games where nobody actually says what they're after. Victor for one couldn't figure out how it was being done at all. Yet the rumor that Logan held some secret power was legend. Everyone believed Logan had at least one huge dirty trick up his sleeve, and had had it from the beginning of his Deaconship.

"*You know,*" Victor said again.

Logan shook his head and walked away. As he went, Victor thought he heard him say something that didn't make sense. Something about how the bubble couldn't be in two places at once.

Two fucking places at fucking once, to be precise.

AND MEANWHILE CELESTE and Annabel stayed inside the Toussant mansion, doing their best to kill time. There was very little else to do. Annabel didn't feel safe leaving during the nighttime hours for fear of vampires, and just to play it safe she'd stayed put during daytime hours, too. So, locked in, the two of them read, and they watched TV and movies, and Celeste taught Annabel how to play a game so old, Annabel had literally never heard of it before. It was played with sticks and pine sap. If you rolled the right combinations, you earned the right to take some of your opponent's sticks. Or you could put them on the rack.

"Now it's just taking the sticks," Celeste said. "Not many people have racks and iron maidens anymore. It's a very old game."

Personally, Annabel thought maybe Celeste was making the game up. Celeste had a weird sense of humor in part because she usually seemed the type of person who had no sense of humor at all. Annabel took the whole thing as flattery. It was better than when Celeste acted cold around her. Now, without meaning to, she often acted like her mother.

When reading got old and TV got old, Annabel tried her hand at Sudoku. At these times Celeste disappeared behind a stack of books so must-covered, they smelled like time itself. The books were in the front room where Annabel did her Sudoku, not hidden away in one of the home's many studies or libraries. Annabel suspected it was because Celeste didn't want to let Annabel out of her sight for safety reasons.

Celeste had a rather annoying habit that cropped up whenever she did ... *whatever* it was she was doing behind the musty old books. She reacted to what she found in an audible way that Annabel, nearby, had to hear over and over again without context.

So after two days of intermittent gasping-in-shock and *a-ha*'ing-with-realization, Annabel finally walked over to Celeste's book fort and said, "What the *hell* are you doing over here?"

Celeste was surprised when Annabel approached — not because she had anything to hide, but because although Annabel hadn't been able to see it before, Celeste turned out to spend a good amount of her time behind the books in a semi-catatonic state. Her eyes rolled up, appearing veiny and almost grey. Her eyelids stayed open, but fluttered. Her mouth hung open. *That's* why she didn't know how loud she was being. It looked like maybe she had no idea about anything when she was in her trances.

"I'm sorry," she'd said that first time, coming back to reality. "I was bloodwalking. It's a way of using your mind to walk up and down your family tree."

"Why don't you call it 'treewalking,' then?"

"I don't know. That's just what we call it."

"You guys have a whole lot of compound words with 'blood' in them," Annabel said. "No wonder society doesn't accept you. Let's compare how often I say 'blood' to how often you say it as a percentage of total words. I think like ten percent of the words you say have 'blood' in them. And it's even more for British vampires."

"What?"

"Because they're *bloody good* at being vampires."

No reaction.

"'*Bloody good*,'" she said again.

"I heard you. It's just terrible. You tell terrible jokes."

"*So*," Annabel said, trying to pretend the joke didn't exist. "'Treewalking.' Am I intruding? I thought you were just being weird over here. If it's like meditating, I can leave you to it."

Celeste laughed. Then she told Annabel a story.

It began long ago in a European village, when a young human named Celeste de Beaumarché was walking home from an errand and was attacked by a then-unknown vampire she now knew to be named Ophelia. The story somehow took a turn a handful of weeks ago when Maurice forcibly exorcised a demon living inside the long-dead body of serial killer H. H. Holmes.

The story turned on that day. It definitely hadn't ended. Not for Celeste.

"I know this story," Annabel said. "Maurice told it to me. I know about Ophelia. I know she's the reason you almost died and the reason Maurice had to turn you to save you. I know you've blocked it all out, so that even you can't see what happened. I know Maurice now thinks Ophelia was somehow behind Holmes — not just back then, but now, too — but he was suspicious of me that night and wouldn't say why or what he meant. I *didn't* know that Maurice drove into the country after our last full session and dug Holmes back up. That one's news to me."

"That's what he did," Celeste said, "and it woke something somewhere in the bloodline. Ophelia's not my maker, but I think that when she nearly killed me, I might have fought back. I think our blood touched, if only for a little while. Maybe it made a connection." She indicated the books. "That's why I've been trying to find her in history, matching what I think I know to what someone wrote down. That's why I'm ... *treewalking*. I've repressed what my deeper mind knows of her, but now I think I'm ready to see. She's in here somewhere." Celeste tapped her own head. "But she hides."

Celeste and Annabel had talked about Celeste's quest ever since. Vampire matters were supposed to be vampire matters and human matters were supposed to be human matters, but the two women were alone together so all that division went out the boarded-up windows. It was just the girls these days. Maurice hardly had time to visit the house what with all his attention-seeking and dealmaking and Reginald-lying-to — resentment about which Celeste didn't try hard to conceal. She'd had plenty of downs to go with her marriage's ups, and right now it felt like she was trending down. Maurice was doing what he had to do to protect them all: That was the fairest way to see it. But in Celeste's opinion, he didn't need to enjoy it so much. He didn't need to "talk in LA-speak" so much. And he didn't need to dismiss his wife as extraneous while he was saving the world from Thrill. He *could*, if he wanted, come and visit them more. He could come and stay, if he wanted, for a while.

By the time Victor was making plans to visit Annabel (and Maurice was just making plans), Celeste knew all about the Sudoku game that Annabel played and Annabel knew all about Celeste's maybe-obsessive search for the vampire who'd so traumatized her — who'd broken her at a formative time, then left her to die alone.

"I know it's ridiculous," Celeste said. "It was a very long time ago. I know I should just give it up."

But Annabel didn't find it ridiculous at all. Celeste had described Ophelia's actions as "traumatic," but as a psychiatrist with good instincts, Annabel suspected "trauma" was an understatement. The event seemed to carry the emotional baggage of a violent rape by someone who should have taken care of her. Someone she should have been able to trust.

The other reason Annabel didn't find the quest for Ophelia ridiculous was because Ophelia sounded like extremely bad news, even now. According to Maurice, she'd once partnered with a necromancer in order to kill her own maker, Amadeus Macht. Then somehow she'd killed the necromancer. Along the way she'd left bodies and minds, like Celeste's, in ruin. If Maurice thought Ophelia was again relevant at the same time Celeste realized on her own that Ophelia was again relevant, that wasn't just coincidence.

Annabel knew it because through Daisy's blood — through a tie stronger than it had any right to be — *she* could feel that Ophelia was relevant again, too.

They searched book after book. Bloodline after bloodline. Celeste narrated as she navigated her family tree with her eyes closed, knowing that for those who could walk blood very well, all vampires were ultimately connected. But the books gave no sign. And the blood gave no sign.

And even after the two women compared all they knew of Holmes and Macht and the joke called Dracula and everything Maurice had said about any of it, no clues presented themselves.

"It's possible I'm missing something," Annabel said, half-apologizing for what was surely no reason. "I haven't shaken off all of what Victor did to my memory, I don't think. Usually it feels like I remember everything, but then I'll be surprised by something I've forgotten. Usually it's an inconsequential thing like the combination to my luggage, but once it was my dad's name. I had to look through his company director. *My own father,* and I had to look him up."

But there was more: Friends she suspected were now just black holes inside her, never to be recovered unless she met them again. Childhood experiences that were simply missing. And worse: tiny, dark knowings she found impossible to put a finger on — dark tidings hiding like minuscule bombs inside her mind. Sometimes Annabel felt a sense of terrible loss, but couldn't figure out what she'd lost. Even recollections of Alicia came and went. Why hadn't she contacted Alicia, post-glamour? Was Alicia even *now*, or was she someone from the past? Just thinking of her best friend sometimes made Annabel desperately sad, and she couldn't even say why. No wonder she couldn't remember the few things she'd learned about Celeste's tormentor.

It put them both on edge, not knowing where to look for Ophelia. Only two things were surely true: Ophelia was alive, and Ophelia could be hiding anywhere. She was a threat today in a way she'd never been before — maybe because of Holmes, maybe because Maurice had finally dispatched the demon she'd helped summon. And both knew she'd made herself invisible: protected by something or someone, unable to be seen as she made her deadly approach. And that was another thing both seemed to agree on: Ophelia was not laying low anymore. She was definitely *approaching*.

Annabel wished she hadn't asked about any of it. She could have let Celeste keep right on gasping annoyingly. Instead she'd wanted to know everything, and of course she'd learned too much.

But.

Perhaps it was fortunate that Annabel had ended up here, now, while Celeste was troubled. Annabel was used to the depths of the mind. And Annabel — perhaps alone amongst human psychiatrists — had experience plunging deep into the psyche of the vampire.

"Sometimes the answers aren't out here in the world, even in books," she told Celeste when frustration (and a *will-this-ever-end* feeling of desperation) settled upon them particularly thickly. "I keep thinking there's only one place left that we haven't looked. One place left that we know for a fact we can find her."

Celeste sat up. She'd been in slumber-party-cookie-over-dose posture, her body tossed across messy cushions and her hair a mess behind her, one arm slung over her eyes.

"Where?"

"Exactly where you want least of all to look," Annabel answered. "Inside the memory you've repressed."

WHILE CELESTE and Annabel prepared to go deep, Maurice's company kept him shallow.

"Look, M," said Jerome, who'd become Maurice's most common companion and had begun calling him "M" inexplicably and without permission. "You're not considering the big picture. I get that you want to be cool to the people who got you this far—"

"*I* got me this far," Maurice said. They were in a restaurant that served little more than water in highball glasses garnished with sprigs of herbs. They cost seventeen dollars.

"Exactly. It was you. Not them. You."

"There's actually no 'them,' either," Maurice pointed out.

"But you can't let Midwest sensibilities hold you back. You *invented fat vampires, man!* Nobody else *invented fat vampires.*"

Maurice was getting tired of hearing it. He'd never thought much of the word "fat" until after he'd heard Jerome revel in it approximately five hundred thousand times.

"That's not entirely true," Maurice told him.

"So it's like I said. I dig that you're loyal. It's the best thing around, loyalty. And not just best — *good.* But you don't know everything. You can't. How old are you, again?"

"Two thousand."

Jerome went on as if he hadn't heard, because he never really did. "Eighteen? Nineteen? You're fresh out of high school. You've got mad talent, kid. *Mad* talent. Together with Cardiff, you've got *mad mad* talent. But, and don't take this the wrong way, I like Harrison."

"Why would I take that the wrong way?"

"But he's old. Out of touch. What you've got here with this fatass vampire, this big fat guy, it's cutting edge. Now think on this: Right now, you and me are on a first-look deal. First right of refusal. I know you want total control of the creative process—"

"I actually don't."

"—and I know Harrison feels like the best partner for you and your fat friend."

"You know, maybe we should just come up with a name for him. Like 'Marty.' We could call it *Marty the Vampire. Fat Vampire* worked in 2012, but that was a different time. Hearing you say it in 2013 is changing my mind."

"Yeah, man. It's the same with everyone. Everything changes with new mouths, new ears."

"No, it's really just you. Really I only hear 'Fat Vampire' in new ways when *you* say it," Maurice explained.

Jerome continued. "So anyway, you and Fat Marty think Harrison can do it all because he was the first one to come up to your door in *Ohio.*" Jerome said "Ohio" the way most people would say "anal fungus." "But this is LA. It's a whole big world out here. So. Listen. This is just you and me talking. I could probably swing my dick and *get some shit done already* whether Harrison likes it or not — in your best interest, of course, whether you *know* it or not — and just one little signature will let me EP this thing. Not even solo. If you want Cardiff to stay on as an EP too, cool. But I can make you a *star*, M."

That much was tempting. Maurice did like the star life, now that he'd spent a while living it. He liked it, in fact, a lot better than he'd thought he would. LA moved quickly and partied on throughout the night, whereas Ohio rolled up the sidewalks at 8pm. In Ohio he'd always hidden himself away because he was an outsider even among his kind, but on the West Coast everyone was already half-vampire and Maurice fit right in. They'd managed to nail down location and crew and cast using his huge pile of money (and a tiny bit of glamouring, but that was only for people who didn't matter, like lawyers), and were scheduled to start shooting two Mondays from now. The enormity of the project and its timeframe was finally starting to hit Maurice, after about a thousand contracts signed and initialed. Jerome was an idiot, but he did seem to know what he was doing. Maybe it was wrong to dismiss his business sense out of hand.

"Listen," Jerome went on. "You don't want to be in bed with the same dude forever. Rubbing the same dude's sweaty, smelly balls against your face forever."

"Ugh," said Maurice.

"You won't be sorry you gave my balls a chance." Then he extended a hand. "Come on, M. Reach out and grab my balls. Giving me a bigger role in this production won't change a thing. It's *adding* my balls to your ball party, not removing or switching anyone else's balls around. Do you really want all of your balls in one basket? Of course not. You need to be sure the person who's got your rights is the right person for the job. You need someone with network connections. That's me. Not Cardiff, not Ella, and not some woman in Ireland."

"Who's talking about some woman in Ireland?"

"Exactly," said Jerome.

Then they said nothing.

"Tell you what, man," Jerome said after a pause. He stood and put on his sunglasses even though they were inside. "I need to go. I'm training a new mascot."

"What?"

"So all I want is your hand."

"But that would leave me with one!"

"Shake, and I know that a good, loyal guy like you won't change your mind without a damn good reason. We don't need paper, do we? Just tell me you want what's best for your project and I'll make sure it happens."

Maurice hesitated, then gave Jerome's hand a shake. It wasn't pen on paper. Officially speaking, he'd committed to nothing. He should at least explore his options. He should at least consider that maybe he didn't know it all, and that maybe adding a seasoned network mind — even a dumb one — might give this wobbly behemoth Maurice had launched with barely a thought a whole lot more stability. Was he really willing to bet a hundred million dollars — and his life, and Reginald's life, and maybe Celeste and Annabel's lives, too, not to mention the future of the vampire and human worlds — on the one and only producer he'd ever met? Harrison was great, yes ... but he was only one man, and he didn't have a media empire behind him.

"We'll talk about it," Maurice said. "There's just one thing."

"What?"

"Stop calling him fat."

AS MAURICE MADE HIS DEAL, and as the last of the big tanks moved into the Thrillery with plans for electrical and plumbing and painting and the rest scheduled for the next two weeks, Logan paced and thought about something Victor had said.

Can't you just ... you know ... to get rid of them?

Meaning turning vampire heads. Meaning imposing undue influence. Logan wielded a lot of power in a lot of quarters of the vampire world in an official way, but he wielded additional power in a way that wasn't strictly kosher. It was true, what people said about him: He really *did* have a secret weapon. He really *did* have a way of changing minds *en masse* — but that came through an asset he'd gained control of, not from himself. It's how he'd tipped the balance in his favor several times in the past and how, if he wanted, he could tip it again.

He'd never really thought about that secret weapon before, regarding the Reginald situation. Reginald's was such an absurd and embarrassing state of affairs that the whole thing should have self-evidently self-destructed. Logan shouldn't need force, or persuasion, or violence, or *any* extra use of resources to deal with Maurice and Reginald. All it should have taken, for Reginald to go away, was for Reginald to exist in the first place. Logan shouldn't have had to point out the fact that Reginald needed to be destroyed. Every vampire alive *should* have seen it as plain as the fangs in their mouths.

But was that what had happened? Nope. Instead, Maurice had stumbled along with his misfit progeny, and the vampires who heard about it had shrugged as if to say, *What're ya gonna do?* But that wasn't the right reaction. What're ya *gonna do?* You're *gonna* put a stake through his heart! You're *gonna* erase the skidmark Reginald had left on the image of what was once a proud and fearsome race!

Vampires had gotten soft; that's the way Logan saw it. That's why stamping Reginald out was so important: to minimize instead of maximizing their softness. That's also why returning Thrill to the world was so important: Nothing would scare humans into line quite like an outbreak of psychotic vampires. Nothing would restore vampire pride as quickly, if messily. Logan could contain the spread of Thrill. He'd done it back in Chicago. The trick was to keep it in the undesirable neighborhoods. The trick was to let *them* get addicted to it, while more respectable vampires stood up and decried the drug, pretending to stamp it out.

But things had spun out of control. What should have been simple had grown complex. Now every idiotic problem overflowed into every other idiotic problem.

Things had been an embarrassment ever since Baskin was created.

And *now?* Now there was this fucking TV show. The buzz remained low-key in the wider world, but it was big among vampires. The vampire community in America was comparatively small, so once a few of them had gotten a whiff of Maurice's original publicity stunt, they'd spread the word. Now everyone had Google search alerts set. Now everyone knew about this vampire show, based on Reginald, that only Hollywood insiders were supposed to know.

Worse, the idea of the show was already gaining popularity. Almost nobody seemed to be aghast that this ... this *Reginald* ... was how their species was being presented to the humans. It was worse than an embarrassment. It was collusion, was what it was.

Logan had to do something to stop the show from being made, and definitely keep it from airing. Stopping the show would kill so many birds with one stone. It'd kill the spotlight currently on Maurice, enabling Council Guards to abduct and torture him without being noticed. It'd kill the spreading disease that was this fat vampire's popularity. Lastly, it'd allow the not-entirely-fair trial that Maurice kept postponing to kill Reginald himself. Without the TV show to create support for Reginald, he'd be a goner.

So yes. He had to stop it. He might even know how.

He just had to move the focus of his secret weapon. That weapon could cast a weak spell over a large and populated area as it was doing right now for the Thrillery, or it could focus on just *one* mind and turn it completely. The Thrillery didn't need hiding anymore, did it? Logan could send Council Guards, not in uniform, to defend it now that the walls were up and the most sensitive equipment had been delivered.

So he made a phone call.

He told the person who answered, "Your talents are needed elsewhere."

Gave an order. Logan was in control; he made the choices for both of them.

Hung up.

And felt a whole lot better.

Annabel thought she was following her gut. Turned out she was following her blood.

Blood memory is like a trance. Use more than your words, Annabel.

It was Daisy, still awake and aware within her.

Annabel's plan was to crack Celeste's repressed memory of Ophelia. As a practical doctor, she assumed she'd do it with talk therapy, same as she'd done with Maurice. Even repression cracks, given enough time … and recently it'd seemed they had all the time in the world.

But that wasn't true. In truth, time was short. Maurice's updates suggested the TV show would be underway in no time, soon to be shining spotlights of all sizes. It sounded to Annabel like Maurice had managed to make it happen against all odds, self-funding in excess and unfreezing squeaky wheels. Even passion for the project had begun to bloom. According to Maurice, the actor who'd been offered the superhero movie actually preferred what'd been ludicrously named *Marty the Vampire* to taking the superhero gig. "I'll do that next," he'd supposedly said. "This feels more important."

Important how? Annabel had asked him.

The answer was both fortuitous and interesting. *Marty the Vampire* "flipped the usual type of vampire story on its head," Maurice said, and had somehow managed to do it with perfect timing. The industry had, in recent years, grown tired of the all-pretty, all-white, all-mainstream image usually portrayed in vampire lore. Tom Cruise didn't need to be Hollywood's only poster boy. Nowadays, audiences were hungry for characters who looked more like themselves. Not every actor needed to look like they were fresh from the gym, fresh from the hair stylist, fresh from the tanning salon. Heroes could be a little overweight and still be heroes. They could be Filipino, which Reginald's actor was. They could look more like average Joes than the stereotypical leading man, or woman.

The TV show had begun because Maurice needed a smokescreen: a way to keep himself relevant so Logan couldn't snatch him without being seen. It'd begun to threaten Logan's secrecy and ruin his "proud vampire image" — all in the name of keeping Thrilloglobin off the streets. But already it'd become more than a smokescreen. The TV industry, at least, seemed to be embracing *Marty* as a milestone of much-needed evolution.

"Change was overdue," Maurice told them one dark night while wearing sunglasses indoors. "Not long ago, I'd've cast myself as a late-90s Joseph Gordon Levitt. But that's not what happened."

He said it with pride, but seeing as Maurice didn't finish the story, Annabel had no idea what he was proud of or who *had* been cast. She just nodded along. Celeste, rubbed raw by what struck her as posturing by her full-of-himself husband, left the room without comment.

Atop the show's breakneck pace, Annabel (probably through Daisy-mediated, quasi-vampire intuition) couldn't shake a feeling that bad tidings were ramping up at Camp Logan as well. As far as she knew, Victor was still with him. Victor certainly wasn't at her house, where a friend of Brian's now lived 24/7 as a precaution. If Victor had gone to such great lengths to steal the recipe for Blood Crack (as she thought of Thrill), she doubted he'd give up after his first attempt failed. Logan was protecting him; she was sure of it. And if Celeste's characterization of Logan was accurate at all, Logan wouldn't protect him without expecting something in return. The Deacon knew about Thrill by now, of course — and would eventually come at Maurice with all guns blazing.

Logan frustrated? Victor furious? Both of them wanting Thrill more than anything? It felt like extremely bad news to Annabel. It was only a matter of time before one or both of them launched some sort of sneak attack. Would it come at Annabel, hoping to still use her somehow? Would it come at Celeste, hoping to use her as a hostage? Maurice's (really Reginald's) new fans still hung out at the home and reporters still poked around from time to time, so an outright seize would be difficult if Logan wanted to lay low. But they'd do *something* in time, Annabel felt sure … and they'd do it soon.

So no, she and Celeste *didn't* have all the time in the world to find Ophelia — a task that also felt urgent, if what Maurice said in his last therapy session was to be trusted. That's why Daisy was speaking up: They couldn't afford the time that talk therapy would take. They needed a faster way to break the lockdown in Celeste's brain ... and that's where blood came in.

Blood memory is like a trance. That was what Daisy kept reminding her. But Celeste was skeptical as they settled in.

"Hypnosis?" she asked. It was what "trance" conjured most for Annabel.

"I know. But it's legit, with the right set of expectations. Hypnosis can't program you to kill the queen unless you're already planning to do so—"

"I'm far too busy right now," Celeste joked.

"—but it's great at making your mind receptive. It's not something I'll do *to* you; it's something we'll do together, with you as the subject and me as your guide. And Celeste? Keep in mind that hypnosis is something you do to yourself already."

"I do?"

"All of you do it, I think. Blood ties, blood memory ... You said that when you and Maurice were outside my house, Daisy talked to Maurice so intensely that his mind went bye-bye for a while. And when I came around your mountain of books and saw you 'bloodwalking' ..."

Semi-convinced, Celeste laid down and they began. Instead of swinging a watch, Annabel asked her patient to focus on the ticking of a metronome app on her phone. She told her to relax every muscle one by one. To breathe slowly, and picture the journey of her breath. Beneath her eyelids, Celeste would de-focus her gaze. She'd watch for smears of color. For flashes of dull light.

And ...

.   .   .

AND THEN CELESTE WAS UNDER. She found herself in an all-black room, her body visible to her internal eyes despite the fact that whatever was lighting it spilled no light elsewhere. There were no echoes. Maybe no sound at all.

She knew this place, though. Maurice was mediocre at bloodwalking and Celeste was downright bad at it, but in her few successes she'd come to a foggy version of this place. It'd never been this crisp before. Never this clear. She knew she was nowhere real (whenever her focus slipped, she felt the weight of her hands on her belly in the actual world), but if she let herself *be* here, she remained here. Annabel's voice was present and absent at the same time. Celeste somehow knew what Annabel was saying without consciously hearing the words.

You're back in time. Back to the last day you were human.

The world around Celeste changed. She found herself wearing sandals, standing on a bare-dirt road. The sun was just above the horizon, low but still risen. She was not burning. Her hypnotic human skin felt warm and pleasant, the light around her in reds and oranges. This was sunset. Her very last sunset.

But she wasn't alone. There were two other women with her, younger than Celeste looked today in the mirror. She had no idea who either of them were. Small, primitive huts formed a village ahead — a horizon Celeste guessed was maybe two miles distant.

"Almost home," said the woman on the right. She was compact and just a little bit round, like Celeste. She spoke ancient French — but for Celeste, more used to English now, the words translated themselves before she truly heard them.

Distant clouds were slowly eclipsing the sun. The burning red ball was so low now, its bottom seemed to have been sheered by the hills. It took little to halve its rays, and soon what remained of the light became the color of Caucasian skin shown through with a flashlight.

The girl on Celeste's other side took her hand. She looked to be in her twenties, practically still a girl.

"I do not like it," she said.

"What is it you do not like?" Celeste asked, though she knew.

"The world is like blood. We must hurry. It is the hour of the wolf."

"I will protect you, Anna," Celeste said with a smile. But she knew with some of her mind that Anna's fears were justified, that her own humanity was about to end.

They're your sisters, aren't they?

Annabel's voice came from somewhere else. From far away, in some future time, when Celeste was immortal.

But yes, it was true. They were sisters: the oldest, Celeste, in the middle; the youngest, Anna, to the left; and Nell, between them in age, to the right. They'd gone to the next village to trade. They were not supposed to walk alone, but Celeste had done so many times before. The area was safe, though it sometimes felt otherwise when night fell. The children in both villages feared the night. They'd heard things in it. Seen things in it. And there were rumors from afar, of people who'd strayed too far and gone missing.

They hadn't meant to travel so near to nightfall.

The clouds moved on. The wan sun returned. It was a half-circle now, its fattest portion sliding below the surface.

They quickened their pace. Anna wanted to run, but their burden was not light. Celeste urged calm. Shadows were merely the absence of light — nothing, in themselves, to fear.

Soon enough, the sun became a fraction of itself. At its very last gasp, some trick of the atmosphere rounded the remainder's edges, creating a dull red lozenge. Then it was gone and the distant hills glowed red, illuminated now only from beyond the land's edge.

The memory suddenly stuttered. The world blinked away, and then there was nothing. Celeste found herself no longer on the village road. She was blackness again, same as she'd been when she'd first gone under.

She lifted her hands in front of her face, discovering that she could see at least that much of herself. She rubbed her eyes to fix them. Her fingertips came away red. Tears.

Let it come, Celeste, said the voice of her hypnotist. *Let yourself see this.*

The dark road returned. She was again walking with her sisters — two sisters that, until this vision, she hadn't remembered she'd had. Her dream hand went to her dream belly without volition. That was another thing she'd forgotten: the new pregnancy she'd been carrying.

They walked on. Then, suddenly, they were surrounded by racing shadows that moved too fast for the eye to see.

Anna clung to Celeste. Nell did as well. It felt unfair. Celeste was the rock here? No. Celeste was just as terrified.

The dark forms circling them stopped. Four people appeared in a diamond shape around them: One woman at the front, dark and beautiful. Three handsome men in black cloaks to the sides and rear.

"H-hello," said Celeste.

The woman did not speak. The men eyed the travellers, smiling to one another.

"A-are you from the monastery?" The answer was obviously no; women were not allowed at the monastery. But the men were in cloaks, and she had to say something.

Still the newcomers did not answer.

"Apologies for my impoliteness," Celeste said, taking a step, "but it grows dark, and we dare not tarry."

The woman let her halve the distance between them before she said, "Why dare you not tarry?"

"We are expected," Celeste said. Then, because the mood here was foul, she added, "The swordsmen who protect our village might be unduly alarmed if we do not arrive at the expected time, which is already overdue."

"*Swordsmen,*" said one of the men.

The woman turned to Celeste. "I understand your predicament. But surely you would not deny three travelers in need of food?"

"Apologies, Miss. We carry candles and spice. We do not carry food. But if you care to inquire with our governor at—"

The woman stopped her. "It is not that you *carry* food."

Now the men were very close. Touching close. Celeste had not seen them move. The tallest of them picked up a clutch of Anna's long blonde hair and put it to his nose. He inhaled, sighed with delight, and said, "*Oh,* how they smell."

"It's that you *are* food," the woman finished.

Celeste turned toward her eldest sister as if demure — as if to whisper for her not to be afraid. But then she lunged toward the man closest to her because men had an easy weakness. She drove her foot hard between his legs. He was unable to dodge in time, even for what he turned out to be.

The man fell. Celeste dropped her bags, grabbed her sisters by their wrists, and dragged as fast as she could. Nell and Anna's legs quickly got the message, and they managed to shamble and sprint a few large steps before the woman and remaining men surrounded them again in less than a blink, scowling this time.

"Naughty naughty," said the woman. "Unkind of you, to take Rafi in his babymakers."

Celeste clawed at the woman, but she dodged as if she'd never been there in the first place. A moment later she was behind Celeste, pulling her hair and tilting her head toward the night sky.

"Do not fight," she said. "Fighting will only make them more excited. It will linger. You will—"

Celeste turned sideways and spat in the woman's face.

"So you would choose punishment," she said, handing Celeste off to one of the men and pulling a cloth from her bodice to wipe her face. "So you would prefer this is made the most of?"

"Kill me if you'll kill me," said Celeste. "But let my sisters go."

They all looked at Nell and Anna. They'd collapsed to the dirt, sobbing in each other's arms.

"There is," said the woman, furious-faced and glancing at all three men now, "something I'd prefer we do instead."

CELESTE WATCHED it all happen again.

She remembered each thing fractions of a second before it occurred again in front of her, but she was powerless to stop it. At some point she left her body, now an observer and unable to so much as throw kicks, unable to so much as squirm and fight. She became an interloper, watching with eyes held open.

They'd made her choose which of her sisters died first.

When she refused to make that choice, they chose for her: Penelope, but the men violated her first.

Then Anna, who bled slowly with pleading in her eyes, violated just the same.

Celeste, held back by whoever was not torturing her sisters at the time, struggled and fought, horrified at the way the creatures drank their blood. She could of course do nothing. And when both sisters were gone — pale and drained — the woman came to her and asked how she, herself, would like to die.

Quickly, Celeste had answered. *Please, I beg of you. End me quickly, and end this pain.*

She'd been in no physical pain at first — only an empty-chested feeling that left her soul screaming. Physical pain came next, though, and it took its time. The woman had not yet drunk blood, so she drank from Celeste all by herself. She licked her lips and pointed teeth as Celeste finally began to drift away.

Go now, the woman said, *while you stare at the dead Heaven that awaits you.*

BUT CELESTE HAD NOT GONE to Heaven. Nor to Hell.

In the real memory, after the vampires departed, she'd found herself still alive. She'd been in unfathomable pain, with just strength enough to drag herself on. She'd made it halfway to the village before collapsing for good — far enough that her sisters' bodies would no longer have been visible if there'd been light, far enough that Maurice hadn't seen them when he arrived to find her bleeding — and then instead of finishing her off, had stolen her away and saved her. Her baby — too young to survive on its own and unable, once it had vampire blood, to develop further — had not been as lucky. It'd been a girl. Celeste had no idea how she knew that, but she knew it now.

But this was not a real place anymore. Celeste was not scared anymore. Instead, she felt herself become the Reaper.

Her nightmare body, in this new and rewritten story, was not pained at all. Quite the contrary; it was strong enough to stand. The mental Celeste looked one last time at her sisters' mangled bodies, willing them to become whole again. They healed before her eyes, then smiled sweet smiles and evaporated like steam. The road disappeared. And then for the third time, Celeste entered in the pitch-black void, not standing still this time. Instead she was running without ever intending to run ... and the beautiful woman in black ran ahead of her.

It was no longer a memory. Now she was in the blood, and it was real, and the connection was happening now. The connection that had been hidden. The connection Celeste had been unable to find consciously, but her furious mind had found, just now, without effort.

It's the right branch of the tree. By God. It's her. It's really Ophelia, here and now.

Ophelia, still dressed by Celeste's mind in the garb she'd worn the day she'd done her murders, looked backward. She saw Celeste in pursuit, and her smug face lost its smugness.

She ran.

But Celeste ran harder.

THE BLACK VOID became an enormous tree with branches like avenues.

Celeste ran faster than the wind, faster than Ophelia

with the gap between them quickly closing. The memory had ended. This was *now*; this was reality. The tree whose branches she ran was *hers*. It was Celeste's tree of bloodlines, where she — and no one else — was in control.

And Ophelia, who Celeste had scratched during the attack and who'd bled into Celeste's wounds that night a thousand years ago, was an interloper here.

Celeste ran faster. *Faster.* She couldn't believe she'd ever been afraid. She was nothing now but furious. She wouldn't just *kill* Ophelia when she caught her. Instead, she'd sever her head mostly from her neck, then block the wound from healing by shoving a silver plate into the gap. She'd remove Ophelia's body's parts again and again and again. She'd pump liquid silver nitrate into her veins, tie her down and only halfway stake her. She'd leave Ophelia in shaded sun all day every day: not enough to kill her, but enough burning pain that she'd lose her terrible mind.

My sisters. My child. How had she forgotten?

Ophelia no longer looked confident and dangerous, as she had the night Celeste had met her. Instead she looked afraid. Afraid of Celeste, and the wrath in her eyes.

Celeste was almost on her when Ophelia leapt from the metaphorical tree, landing on lower branches. She descended quickly, limb to limb. Celeste followed. She didn't know what this was, this space she inhabited. It was *like* blood ties, but not. It was *like* memory, but not. What would happen if she jumped from the tree of her own blood? Was it only figurative? Or was it real?

She landed on hard black dirt. Ophelia's lead had dwindled to almost nothing, but now it seemed she was running toward a target. A pair of enormous gilded doors had materialized ahead. They were a metaphor for some *other* vampire's blood-bound protection, just across the in-between place where one family tree touched another. Ophelia leapt that gap, then was through the doors in a flash. Immediately the doors began closing.

NO!

They were shut by the time Celeste reached them, herself now the trespasser on another vampire's land.

She looked around. Whose lineage had she crossed into? She couldn't care less. She banged her fists raw against the gilded doors, but no avail. They were impermeable, the intruder kept outside where she belonged.

Celeste stopped, then looked up. She took in the impossible height of the strong, golden doors. She could feel the power behind them. She could feel the vast network of force behind the one who protected Ophelia. And that's when she understood whose blood they'd crossed into. That's when she understood whose blood gave Ophelia refuge — and perhaps had always given it.

Logan.

She was sure of it. It was *Logan* who protected her now. *Logan* who'd hidden her away all along. No wonder Celeste had never been able to find Ophelia: She'd never had enough strength of anger to draw her enemy from this fortress. Celeste's blood had been holding back her entire life, afraid to unleash the emotion required to bring Ophelia forth. It took pain to send echoes across blood, and for so long Celeste's pain had been locked deep inside, unable to emerge.

Unable to help Celeste find the one who'd ruined her. Unable to help even the score. Ophelia was older, but not by much. Celeste's anger was enough, now, to outmatch her on even ground.

So was this the answer she'd been seeking? If so, it was a sour one. If Logan was hiding Ophelia, there'd be no way to reach her unless she came out on her own. What's more, Celeste got the feeling Ophelia *couldn't* literally come out; this little dream of emergence was the closest she came. In the real world, Ophelia could stay inside Logan's fortress forever. She might not have a choice. After Ophelia killed Macht (and after she'd somehow, against all odds, found a way to also kill the necromancer who controlled them), she'd been wanted in a way few vampires had ever been wanted by the vampire authorities. It was beyond taboo to dabble in the black arts the way Ophelia had. She'd hired a magician to control a vampire she wished to kill. That alone was punishable by a thousand deaths.

But Logan had hidden her from the authorities. Why?

As Celeste stepped back from the golden doors inside her mind — doors that her hardest willpower would forever be unable to breach, now that Ophelia was aware of her rage — she thought she might know Logan's reason. People said that Logan had a secret weapon. He was persuasive in the extreme, able to convince any vampire to see things his way ... a bit *too* persuasive to be possible without a cheat.

Now Celeste knew the rumors were true: Logan *did* have a cheat. He had a secret weapon after all, and that weapon was Ophelia.

Had she learned a bit of the necromancer's vampire-controlling art, and learned how to use it for Logan's benefit? That fit what others had seen of Logan, and it explained how he could do what he'd been able to do. How he'd risen to power. How he'd held that power for so long. And besides, Ophelia must have *something* Logan wanted, if he'd chosen to protect such a wanted criminal ... same as Victor had something Logan wanted, in exchange for his protection.

But was it a *trade* they'd made? Were Ophelia and Logan *partners?*

No. Ophelia had run inside Logan's protection to save herself, but the fortress Celeste saw now was only symbolic, able to be breached here in the playground of mind. But that fortress stood for *real* walls, in the *real* world. Even in here, its walls were large. Solid. Impenetrable. So no, Celeste was willing to bet they weren't partners.

It seemed more likely that Ophelia was Logan's pet.

His prisoner.

Logan was a snake, slithering and weaving toward whatever got him what he wanted. If Ophelia was his prisoner now, surely she hadn't begun that way.

I will keep you hidden, Celeste could imagine Logan telling her when she first came to him seeking asylum. Logan hadn't always been Deacon but for most of his life he'd held some sort of power; even long ago he'd had asylum to give — if elicit, if in trade for a price. *In exchange, you'll use your ability to push obstacles from my way. You will stay in my shadow, enjoying my spoils. You'll help me become Deacon, and after it's done you will be the power behind the throne: the only way you can still* have *power in this world of ours. And you will have wealth ... all the wealth and power you'd ever want, through me, by proxy.*

But over the years, the bloom had faded. She'd done his work and her options had faded. How could she leave now? Logan couldn't allow it, seeing as he'd built his empire atop her shoulders.

So now Ophelia hid. Like a coward. And now she served him. Like a slave.

When Maurice killed Holmes, the necromancy tie between them must have broken. *That's* why Ophelia was back; she'd felt the tie break. *That's* why her head had turned toward Celeste's world all over again: the payoff of an old grudge, nothing more.

Oh, Maurice, Celeste thought. *The box you unwittingly opened.*

She must have been communicating all of this to the surface world where Annabel sat over her, because Annabel spoke next with full understanding:

What's Ophelia doing now? Can you see anything through the doors?

Celeste looked at the doors. They were solid as stones.

But ...

But this was still a mental place, and anger still had power.

So she turned her mind to her sisters, raped and dead on the ground. First came dispair. Then rage returned.

A gap opened — not between the doors, but in the world itself.

In the next blink Celeste found herself behind the eyes of someone new. She'd crossed blood, now a passenger in the mind of another. She was a spy. She was seeing through the senses of ...

... of *Ophelia.* She'd been weakened by surprise and fear; that's the only reason Celeste was able to enter her. It wouldn't last ... but for now she could see everything.

Something was happening. A memory of a memory. A memory of Ophelia's

Celeste's mind saw Ophelia: not now but very recently, shifting the power she had from one focus to another. Logan had commanded her to do it — to shift the laser beam of her necromancy to a brand new target. And he was angry. Logan was angry about ... *something.* And he felt that ... *something* ... was even more urgent now than it had ever been. He'd called her on the phone. Called *Ophelia* on the phone, down in the dungeon in which he kept her, bound and unable to flee. Celeste heard his command in the way Ophelia thought about it: Ophelia's self-talk, telling herself what to do:

Remove the bubble from the Thrillery. The Thrillery is protected enough now. Let the vampires nearby look at the Thrillery now, if they want to look. Instead, move the bubble to the show. Move it to the TV show, he says.

Celeste's internal ears — if that's what she was hearing with in here — perked up. *TV show?* Was Logan making a move on Maurice in the full light of publicity?

But no, Celeste's Ophelia-mind told her he wasn't. He didn't *need* to move against Maurice directly. Not if he had Ophelia, who could shift the attention of scads of vampires at once. So ... did "shifting the bubble to the TV show" mean Ophelia was commanding vampires in Los Angeles to attack the show somehow? Asking random vampires to abduct Maurice, so Logan didn't have to?

But Celeste, temporarily holding some of Ophelia's instinct, knew that wasn't right.

It was necromancy that Ophelia commanded, not a death ray. Black magic could work like either a laser or a diffuse spotlight: It could affect a lot of vampires a little bit, or it could affect one vampire a lot. That wasn't an Ophelia rule. It was just how necromancy worked.

Shift the bubble to the TV show. That's what he wants.

Dark eyes appeared in Celeste's mind-vision. They stared right at her, seeing through her. Celeste felt a whiff of fear coming from Ophelia's blood-mind, then confidence and anger. Ophelia was back in her own house now, not exposed in the open. Inside Logan's protection, she was not weak and fearful. Inside, she was strong.

There was no chance for resistance. With a mighty

shove, Celeste was forced out. Doors slammed. She awoke with a start, Annabel beside her.

"'Shift the bubble to the TV show,'" Celeste repeated, feeling her eyes widen with undirected panic. "That's what he wants!"

"What?" Annabel asked.

"He uses her like a weapon. Ophelia." But she was freaking out; she didn't need to tell Annabel this because she'd already said it in her sleep. "Logan wants Ophelia to focus her power on destroying Maurice's TV show!"

Annabel leaned in. Perhaps she hadn't heard *everything* from her fugue-state patient.

"He's threatened by the show," Celeste went on. "It's screwing up all his plans." She had to get these words out quickly; though she'd gotten no detail, she knew this was urgent; this was bad; this was already happening. "It's not just about getting Thrill out of Maurice anymore. Vampires *like* the idea of the show. They're embracing the idea of Marty, of Reginald, of whatever they think his name is. Logan's hold on the vampire population is based on us being an elite, Annabel! To Logan, what Maurice's show threatens to do is just like the French Revolution!"

Annabel understood right away, given that metaphor. "Proletariat takes down bourgeoise," she said. "He thinks heads will roll."

Marie Antionette. Let them eat cake. The queen's head in a basket as the people stormed the palace: crowd justice for being an elitist motherfucker.

"How's he going to do it?" Celeste demanded, as if Annabel would know. "How will Ophelia destroy the show for him? What could anyone possibly do at this point to stop it — throw Maurice back into obscurity so those butchers can grab him?"

"You said she's able to control vampires," Annabel said. "If she learned any necromancy, that's something she can do."

Celeste nodded. "Vampires and other supernatural creatures."

"Okay. But how exactly is even a 'supernatural creature' going to stop the freight train they have going in LA? Even killing someone won't stop it; you get that, right? Show business is a *business*. What could possibly undo 'the show must go on'?"

They stared at each other, both with no idea whatsoever. Celeste was sure of only one thing: Logan meant to undo the show and capture Maurice as it failed, using Ophelia's power to do the dirty work. The rest was anyone's guess.

Annabel's phone vibrated. She picked it up and looked at the screen.

"It's from Maurice," Annabel said. "He says he signed with a network, and decided to give this guy 'Jerome' broad, sweeping power so that the show can, and I quote, 'Finally stop screwing around out here and get some real work done.'"

When Annabel looked up, Celeste was staring at her wide-eyed.

"What?" Annabel asked her.

TWENTY-THREE
A MATTER OF TIME

Victor knew he could climb the fence without a problem. Maurice had added the thing to keep humans out rather than vampires, and even then it was flimsy protection — ornamental, really, and a deterrent only to those who cared about obeying rules.

Crossing the grounds would be easy too, because Maurice had no guards. No cameras either — maybe because without guards, cameras were useless. Maurice's mansion did have a rudimentary security system (*just motion sensors,* Logan had told him back when home-invading the place still felt possible) that would alert him if someone crossed the lawn, but given what Victor had heard about the producer-man walking right up and ringing Maurice's doorbell, those systems either weren't always on or didn't always work. There were deer in Ohio, and deer seemed to get past any barrier. They probably triggered the motion detectors constantly. Maurice may have disabled the sensors so he could get some sleep.

Victor kept thinking. Kept planning. If he was going to do this, he had to be thorough.

Victor wasn't the fastest or strongest or even the smartest vampire in the world, but he was definitely one of the most methodical. Apex predators were sloppy; they counted on raw force to get their jobs done. Scavengers, however, went extinct when they were sloppy. Victor (elite even among scavengers) wasn't *remotely* sloppy. He was precise and careful and double-checked every detail. That's how he'd survived in Chicago, while the rest of the Vampire Mafia died.

Maurice was sloppy, though. He hadn't even traced Daisy's lineage.

And *Logan* was sloppy. All it'd taken, for Victor to learn about the Deacon's secret weapon, was to eavesdrop on a single phone call.

Victor knew now that Logan had someone at his disposal who could do a bit of necromancy — someone he was using to nuke Maurice's TV show — and that their power could *influence* a lot of supernaturals or outright *control* one of them. And he knew that Maurice, who'd experienced necromancy before, would be immune to it.

Working so sloppily, did Logan really think he could cut Victor out of the Thrill deal? There wasn't a chance in the world.

Right now, Victor had all the power because he had the blood key. Logan might turn the necromancer on Victor and force him to hand that key over, but again ... Logan was sloppy. Victor's plan, therefore, was to outwit, outfox, outthink. Those were skills at which Victor excelled.

His plan was simple.

All he needed was to get ahold of Annabel. Annabel's blood tie to Daisy had called out to Maurice once before. Failing to anticipate it was the only sloppy move Victor had made — but because he was crafty, he could turn his mistake into an advantage.

All he had to do was put Annabel in danger. Once he did, Maurice would come running, leaving his spotlight to do it. With Annabel under the gun and Maurice afraid for her safety, Victor would hold all the aces. He wouldn't even need the key to get the recipe then — a good thing because he couldn't use it without Logan's Mentalists anyway. To save Annabel and the Daisy inside her, Victor figured Maurice would tell Victor anything he wanted to know.

Then it would be *Victor* who had the recipe. *Victor* who kept the power. *Victor* who'd then leak news of the necromancer, get Logan ousted, and replace him as Deacon.

The smart defeats the strong ... every single time.

He just had to figure out how to get to Annabel. It shouldn't be difficult. He could sneak out of Logan's place, then into Maurice's. If he was very careful and very quiet, he could make sure Celeste Toussant was occupied elsewhere in the house before making his move. If Annabel's blood cried out, it'd cry out to Maurice, not Celeste. And where *was* Maurice? Why, he was a continent away, making deals and unable to get home fast enough to stop anything.

Break in.

Grab her.

It was okay if other vampires saw him do it. That would be ideal, really. Logan couldn't smash and grab because he didn't want to be seen, but Victor could turn Logan's fear of exposure to his advantage. If Victor was seen, people would blame Logan, right?

His plan was almost complete.

It was only a matter of time.

Celeste decided to just get Maurice on the phone. It didn't feel particularly *vampire* to speak to her maker and husband of a thousand years using telephony instead of telepathy, but blood wasn't always precise. The way Maurice's head had been in two worlds recently, he might interpret her blood cry as a complaint that she'd burnt some cookies.

"You just ... You've seriously never used Facetime before?"

Annabel took her phone back from Celeste with thinly disguised frustration — an "oh, for fuck's sake, just give it here" sort of mannerism. Celeste had been using the phone backwards, pushing on the rear-facing cameras as if they were buttons.

"Vampires aren't good with technology," Celeste explained.

Annabel, who hadn't felt the urgency of hypnosis from the inside out, wasn't moving quickly enough for Celeste's tastes. Annabel seemed to think Maurice's text about this Jerome person meant nothing. *So he brought on a new producer. So what?* her expressions said.

It didn't bother Annabel that "Jerome" would be able to steer the show however he wanted. She was acting like Celeste was hysterical — like Celeste only assumed this new producer was bad news because the text arrived just as they were trying to work out Ophelia's scheme. Celeste, on the other hand, knew otherwise.

How could a necromancer destroy the TV show that was keeping them all alive?

Why, by turning someone close to the show into Ophelia's puppet and using them to torpedo it, of course.

"The twenty years these things have been around is like ten seconds to me, you know," Celeste snapped while Annabel connected the call with an irritated glance.

Annabel handed the phone back to Celeste. Maurice's face appeared onscreen. He was somewhere dark, filled with flashing lights. And it was loud.

"Celeste?" he said, clearly surprised. "Why are you using Annabel's phone?"

Dummy. Because Celeste didn't have one of her own. Because she wanted to look Maurice in the eye while she told him this instead of using the house phone to talk only to his ear.

"What's this about a new producer?" Celeste asked instead of answering.

Maurice laughed and threw his head back in a very un-Maurice way. Behind him, between strobing lights, Celeste could see people dancing. A bass thump confused his microphone, warbling the audio.

"It's great, right?" Maurice said, failing to sense Celeste's tone. "Tell you the truth, I don't like him much, but he's got a lot of experience. Even though Harrison's a good guy with a good plan, I sort of decided he wasn't mean enough by himself to crack the whip on this thing in the way it needs to be—"

"Logan has a necromancer," Celeste interrupted.

Maurice looked like he'd just been asked to perform complex math. "What?"

"He has a necromancer. It's Ophelia. I chased her down my blood tree."

"Ophelia's not in your bloodline."

"Annabel helped me find a repressed memory. The day I was turned, her blood … It doesn't matter!"

"What?"

"You don't believe me?"

"No," Maurice said, "I can't *hear* you." He was shout-talking, probably to compensate for the noise on his end. "This DJ is really fucking serious! You know?"

Why was he acting so weird? Maurice was dour, never into the club scene. Never one to talk about how serious DJs were.

"How the hell can you not *hear* me? You're a goddamned—"

"I'm also kind of drunk!"

"Drunk?"

"And maybe on a little molly."

"Who's Molly?"

"Ecstacy! It doesn't last long in my system. I've had to take hits every few minutes to keep the love going. Nobody here can believe it. They're calling me 'Mr. Molly'!" He laughed again.

"You're *high?"*

"Oh, it's *fine,"* Maurice said. "So Annabel showed you my text. Did it make sense? I'm kind of high. They call me—"

Celeste's fear, and urgency, and frustration, and leftover pain from her unearthed flashback focused into one huge ball of anger. She threw it at her husband. *"I know what they call you! Get to a fucking bathroom if you can't hear me!"*

"All *right*, all *riiight* ..."

Celeste fumed while Maurice made his way through the nightclub without hurry. Once inside a graffiti-covered restroom, things quieted down. Behind him, a man was at the sink snorting cocaine.

"Okay," he said. "Why so serious?"

"Don't interrupt. Just listen," Celeste told him.

Then she explained everything she'd seen under Annabel's hypnosis, all the way through to the end. To Maurice's otherwise-oblivious credit, he stopped looking like a party asshole and looked properly crushed when she told him the story — one he hadn't known because he'd found her a mile from where it happened. When she was finished, he waited for the punchline as if she hadn't already given it.

"Don't you see?" she said. "It's this Jerome guy. *He's* the way Ophelia's going to do it. The way Logan will pull the rug out from under you."

"The rug hasn't been pulled."

"Well, I assume he can't do it right away!"

"Celeste. Listen to me. You're—"

At this point the cocaine-snorter finished up, approached from behind, and photobombed their Facetime session with his tongue out. He yelled, *"ZERO POINT ZERO FUCK YEAH!"* Celeste had no idea what it meant, if anything.

"Get the hell out of here," Maurice said.

The party guy instantly became serious. "Hey, fuck you, Junior!"

So Maurice turned to face him. The camera slipped away, but she heard Maurice say to the guy in an even, glamour-heavy voice, "You're going to go back out into the club. You're going to find that guy in the green thong and get him to pee on you."

The view returned. Without explanation, Maurice continued where he'd been interrupted.

"You're not thinking straight," he said.

"I was hypnotized! I just re-lived the worst trauma of my life!"

With maddening patience, Maurice said it again: "Exactly. That's why you're not thinking straight. You're being hysterical."

"*Hysterical!*"

"You don't know how things work in this business. We've thrown a hundred million dollars into this IP. The ship is already sailing. It can't just be stopped just like that."

Celeste was pretty sure it could *definitely* be stopped. Projects everywhere were cancelled all the time.

"Jerome is keeping us on track," Maurice explained. "That's it."

"But you said he had 'broad, sweeping powers.'"

"I was being dramatic. I told you; I'm a little high right now. The guys who operate at this level, they don't just agree to the parts of contracts you want them to agree to. The kill clauses are there because lawyers need to know exactly what will happen in every conceivable circumstance. But the number of things that'd have to go wrong before anyone could do anything to screw this thing up are—"

"Did you hear me say I found Ophelia?"

"Of course. And I know how emotional you must be, after all the time you've spent searching."

"*I'm not emotional!*" Well, okay, she was. But that didn't invalidate anything.

"Celeste ..."

"And did you hear me say Ophelia is *working for Logan?* That he's been hiding her at least for as long as he's been in power?"

"You *think* she's working for him."

"I was inside his blood! Inside *her* mind!"

"You *think* you were inside her mind."

"Goddammit, Maurice; you're not—"

"Celeste, listen. I'm going to explain this situation."

"*What* the fuck did you just say to me?"

In the corner of Celeste's eye, Annabel flinched. Celeste almost never swore, and yet she'd done it a few times tonight. People said Celeste didn't seem the swearing type. She was more of an "Oh golly gosh" type.

"You just re-lived something terrible," Maurice said. "Then you saw something you can't *possibly* be sure of. If you think you saw Logan's blood fortifications, okay, fine. I'd believe he has them. But if Ophelia's been hiding behind him, why would she come out so you could see her in the first place?"

"I *dragged* her out! With my emotions!"

Maurice nodded condescendingly. She really shouldn't have said "emotions."

"Even if you *did* see Ophelia instead of some sort of manifested echo—"

"Which I did."

"—and even if she *did* sneak back in to Logan's protection—"

"Which she did."

"—and even if *somehow, some way, even though I've never heard of it before,* you actually managed to push your way into her *without blood ties* and then *saw her thoughts—*"

"Which I *did!*"

"—you can't possibly be sure you read them right! I mean ... a *necromancer?* Necromancers are human!"

"It's a *skill*, Maurice, not a trait," Celeste snapped. "You said yourself that you couldn't figure out how she got one over on the necromancer *she* used to kill Macht. What's to say she didn't pick up some of what he knew how to do? What's to say she didn't somehow convince him to *teach* her?"

"And even *then*," Maurice pushed on, "you think she's got her hand up *Jerome's* butt? You don't even know Jerome!"

"Did he not convince you to give him 'broad, sweeping power' over the same TV show Ophelia was ordered by Logan to destroy?"

"He didn't *convince* me to do anything. I—"

"Even though you didn't want this guy involved *at all* at first ... and now he can do whatever he wants?"

"I was *going* to do a neutered deal — just add him as another EP, with no power — but what's the point if he can't actually do anything? If he couldn't be of use?"

"He can cancel the damn show if he wants, Maurice!"

"A technicality! And not even an accurate one! He can make creative decisions. He can bargain for us. He can't *cancel* it. I'm the only one who can *cancel* it."

"Can he fire the crew?"

"Not really. Not without—"

"Can he screw up what's being told to the press, so everyone hates you?"

"I guess, but why would anyone—?"

"The contract you signed sounds *perfect* for a saboteur, Maurice."

His ecstasy must have worn off again, because now he looked angry. *"Jerome isn't a saboteur!* You aren't here to see how much he's helping already! You're leaping to conclusions, and you don't know half of what you think you know about what's going on out here, and honestly it's starting to piss me off!"

Celeste was out of words. She wanted to reach through the line and claw his face off.

"You didn't even hear Ophelia say his name," Maurice said, more evenly now. "You didn't even hear her talking to herself about one specific person. Even if *everything* you said to me is true — every *tiny little bit of it* — you have *zero* idea about *how* Ophelia's 'necromancy' would be used. Did you hear anything about a network executive being hired? *Did you,* Celeste?"

She kept her face hard. "No. But—"

"So you heard nothing about using her *scary powers* to control a guy who technically has all sorts of control, but in practical terms can't do more than annoy us with network notes?"

"You said 'broad and sweeping.'"

"Not in any way a judge would see things."

If Celeste wasn't using one hand to hold the phone, she'd've put both hands on her hips. "So that's it? That's all there is. You know everything because you're Mr. Hollywood, and we girls are just back here being 'hysterical.'"

"Don't turn it into that," he said. "It's petty."

"You're not even going to look into it. Not even going to question this Jerome guy."

"He's not a vampire, Celeste. His Instagram is full of pictures at the beach."

"Then he's glamoured."

"You're mixing your logic. If the danger is Ophelia, why would Logan use her to glamour a human? Anyone could do that. And besides, he's not glamoured."

"How do you know?"

"There's a way. I told Harrison about the thing with Logan and he actually brought glamouring up based on what I'd already told him about vampires, for story reasons. Everyone here is taking this seriously. It's not just entertainment to us; we know it's life and death. I've been testing every human involved. Not that you'd care, but figuring out if someone's glamoured is actually based on the test they used to detect Replicants in the movie *Blade Runner*. Only for real."

"You're saying you're sure. You're *positive* Jerome isn't glamoured."

"I'm positive."

"Then he's something else," Celeste said. "What walks in the sun?"

"Humans."

"Dammit, you know what I mean! There are all sorts of supernaturals that can—"

Movement behind Maurice. He turned his head and the camera slipped again as he spoke to someone who'd just entered the bathroom. Then his face returned and he spoke to her again.

"I've gotta go. Someone needs to talk to me. But I hear you, okay? I'm being careful. Jerome is fine. In fact, Jerome *loves* the show. One hundred percent in support of the show. If I'm wrong and you're right about him, why would he be so supportive? Wouldn't he need to be doing something to harm it for any of this to make sense?"

"Maybe Ophelia is just now getting to him. Just getting started."

"If that's the case, things will start to change. If he suddenly starts doing things to sabotage the show, I'll look into it more."

"You promise."

"I promise," he said. "Look. Everything here is fine. The show is fine. The show's *great*, actually. All engines firing. Full steam ahead. So. Celeste?"

"Mmm."

"Please don't worry. I love you."

"Mmm."

She killed the call and handed the phone back to Annabel.

"I guess we girls will just to have to handle this ourselves," she said.

The big day arrived. Mountains were moved.

Maurice hadn't dismissed Celeste's concerns. Not at all. In Maurice's mind, Celeste was this situation's canary in the coal mine: closer to the epicenter and hence more attuned to Logan's treachery than Maurice could possibly be. But the thing with canaries (the reason they made good sentinels in the first place) was that they were more sensitive than other animals. That made them *data*, not decisions in and of themselves. Threats that endangered canaries weren't necessarily threats that endangered human beings — or, more relevantly, vampires.

A canary's death told people to be careful, nothing more. And Maurice was already being careful. No problem there.

He had no doubt Celeste had been frightened by her vision. No doubt she had good *reason* to be frightened. But just because Ophelia was still out there in the world (Maurice already knew that) and just because Logan was plotting to get him (he knew *that* too; it was the reason they'd started the show in the first place), that was no reason to throw logic out the window. Maybe it was true that Ophelia was working for Logan. Maybe it was even true, somehow, that she'd learned necromancy and could influence supernatural minds. But the idea that Jerome was Ophelia's puppet? Maurice *worked* with Jerome. He'd seen Jerome do his job, and do it well despite being an ass. Caustic or not, Jerome was working *for* the show, not against it. Maurice saw that much every day.

Jerome wasn't supernatural. He wasn't glamoured. He just had an everyday personality that wasn't for all the Lord's children. Keeping her concerns in mind, Maurice told Celeste he'd keep an eye on Jerome — on everything, really. He told her there was no reason to worry. Maurice was on this. Maurice *had* this.

And so the show kept rolling.

Just a month from the plan's inception (maybe even in time to present at Comic Con if they were allowed to publicize, Harrison kept pointing out with irrational dismay), the hastily-thrown-together production office had already managed to coordinate several hundred crew members in the small city of Victoria, British Columbia. Most were locals, Harrison told Maurice. They were a crew he'd worked with before: eager, fun, hard-working, and most without the need to relocate for the job.

Teamsters took over a parking lot ten minutes from the main office and transformed it into what they called a "circus": dozens of truck trailers and equipment set to provide essential services: on-site offices, makeup, hair, and wardrobe trailers, first aid and general medical, administration, and more. The shooting itself had to get creative. The production design crew, unable to locate studio space in the not-usually-a-show-biz-town town, had rented an empty Home Depot and built sets inside it. There were three or four "locations" as well: real places around town at which scenes would be shot. All construction had been done on quadruple rush for roughly quadruple the budget. Looking over the numbers, Harrison joked that *Marty the Vampire* would end up being the most expensive moderate-budget show he'd ever seen. "Looks like fifteen million, costs a hundred million," he said. But Maurice hadn't been paying for spectacle so much as speed.

Shortly before shooting began, Harrison asked Maurice if he wanted to read any of the scripts.

"'Scripts'?"

Maurice said it like he didn't know what the word meant. Somehow, in all the hubbub of getting the show off the ground in what felt like a profane amount of time, he'd forgotten the show actually needed content. He'd earned himself enough attention to keep Logan from snatching him like a ninja in the night. He'd managed an impossible production, getting wrapped up in the impossibility of it along the way. He'd made new friends. Learned a new world with all-new jargon. Somewhere along the way, the effort itself had become the horse Maurice was riding. He'd lost track of the fact that the core of the show was a story — *Reginald's* story — and that of course there were scripts; of course there were writers.

Harrison put a stack of papers in his hands. Maurice had the distinct impression that the stack was something that would normally be sent digitally, and that he'd printed them out to impress Maurice with their sheer weight with this exact moment in mind.

"Ten episodes," he said, "each an hour long. Well, forty-four minutes. It's a broadcast hour. We need room for commercials."

"I thought it was a half hour," Maurice said.

"You paid for a summer blockbuster," Harrison told him. "The least we could do was give you a lot of content."

Maurice wasn't a writer, but still he was impressed with the amount of writing in his hands.

"They're good, too," Harrison continued. "Solid story. 'Marty' is an underdog with lots of heart and soul. He's not a doormat. He's just a guy who's yet to find his strength. It's funny, you know. I asked myself the other day what this show is really about, and I decided it's about Marty coming to understand life ... after he's technically dead."

Maurice flipped through the pages. Harrison knew Reginald's real name, of course, but to everyone else, Reginald would be Marty.

"I know I asked you to do this," Maurice said, "but that was before I knew how any of it worked. I can't believe you found a way to pull this off so quickly."

"We haven't pulled it off yet."

"Still."

Harrison shrugged. "Creativity can happen on a deadline, no matter what a lot of creatives say. One advantage of working fast is you don't have time to second-guess yourself. You don't have time to get in the way of your instincts."

Maurice wondered what happened if your instincts sucked. Harrison must have trusted something deep in the hearts of his team, to push them this fast and still be satisfied with the results.

"Only two of those are finals, by the way," he said, meaning the scripts. "Episodes three through ten are still in various stages of rough draft. I'll tweak them as we go, assuming your timeline hasn't changed."

It was actually Jerome's timeline at this point. Harrison and his partner Ella, who Maurice still hadn't met, would be splitting the job of showrunner, and that made them the creative heads of the project. Jerome, however, was in charge of cracking all the whips. He had spreadsheets for everything, from budget to schedule to plans for eventual marketing.

"There's no rush to finish shooting," Maurice told Harrison — something he felt confident saying because the biggest reason to move fast was money, and there was no lack of money here. "Once we start, the spotlight on me stops being an issue. We're making a show, sure. But keep in mind the reason we started this was to keep me in the spotlight for as long as possible."

"Yeah. Well, you definitely got your spotlight," Harrison said.

It was true. They were standing at a crossroads in the small Victoria suburb of Saanich after dark, and even so there were plenty of onlookers. Two weeks ago, the building behind them (the building at which the onlookers were looking) had been a derelict auto repair shop. The crew had transformed it into a bright yellow building that a new sign at the corner declared to be "The Slushy Shack." Locals kept stopping to ask when said Shack would open even though on the inside, the Shack remained little more than an unheated muffler shop. The interior set was six miles away, inside the Home Depot.

Tomorrow, the Slushy Shack would be surrounded by cameras and lights as filming began. The local news was so confused. Word was only now getting around that there was a new production in town.

"Those are yours to keep, if you want them," Harrison said, again nodding at the scripts. "We might have to ping-pong around instead of blocking the way I'd prefer because most of the episodes are still being finalized, but otherwise we've got the all-clear. It's less efficient to start tomorrow than if we wait until we can block better, but if you want to get started and still don't care about money ..."

"I don't care about money," Maurice said.

"Then it's no problem. Usually you want to spend all day at one location, but we can do mid-day moves if we have to. You lose a few hours every time you do that, but since you said you don't care about money ..."

"I seriously don't care about money, Harrison," Maurice repeated.

"Good. Good." Harrison nodded, forcing himself to accept what Maurice was saying. Maurice had spent enough time talking shop with him over the past weeks to know just how unusual this situation must be for him. Harrison was being told *just get it done and don't worry about wasting money*, whereas usually he was told not to waste money even if it meant not getting it done.

"If you read the scripts," Harrison said, "you'll see that we made a lot of changes to your story."

"It's not really my story," Maurice replied.

"Marty is younger than the real Reginald. And Nikki is now two different characters. We kind of split her down the middle."

"That's okay. It's not meant to be a documentary."

"When I adapt authors' work, a lot of times they're protective of the original story. They don't want anything changed. Their fans will contact them and say, 'I hope the TV show or movie doesn't change anything!' But the format's entirely different, book versus TV show."

"I'm not an author, Harrison. There isn't an original story."

"There's Reginald's real life."

"Yes. But I don't want Reginald to know the show

exists. The goal is to create noise around both of us *without* actually pointing at the truth."

"I'm just glad you're not precious about it."

"I'm not precious about it at all, Harrison. You're doing great."

"Oh. And ..." Harrison seemed to be caught on something, forcing himself to get it out. "... you're gay."

"I am?"

"The real story isn't very diverse, Maurice. Diversity matters. So you're gay now."

"Oh. Okay. Do I need a new bumper sticker?"

"I mean your *character* is gay."

"I figured that out."

"If anyone asks, thinking the *real* you is gay ..."

"I don't mind being gay," Maurice interrupted. "I'm down with being gay."

"You were also sired by a vampire named Angela."

"Oh. Okay." He didn't know any Angela.

"In the 1970s."

"Harrison ..." Maurice flipped through the scripts. "I'm *two thousand* years old."

Harrison was suddenly defensive. "I thought you weren't precious about the real story!"

"I'm not. I'm just wondering what I should say in interviews. I know almost nothing about New Wave music. I really only know Rick Astley. How am I going to pass for a child of the 80s?"

"I don't think I'd characterize Rick Astley as New Wave."

"Then I know *absolutely* nothing about New Wave music."

"Maurice," Harrison said, "you don't even look old enough to drink."

"So?"

"So you weren't going to be able to tell interviewers that you grew up in the 80s anyway. Or, for that matter, that you grew up during the Crusades. The fact that we changed your backstory doesn't matter because people won't assume the *real* Maurice is a vampire. Only the fictional Maurice. The real Maurice Toussant, as far as the world is concerned, was probably born in ... like ... 1994."

"Oh. Right." Maurice had forgotten that. Maybe he should have asked Harrison not to include a character-version of him in the TV show. Dealing with the shadow of a fictional doppelgänger was already confusing. Unfortunately, using much of the real-life circumstances about Reginald and his actual life was what had allowed Harrison and his writers to put the scripts together so quickly because they hadn't had to make most of it up. This, right here, was the downside.

Maurice told himself to relax. He could be a gay thirty-something. Celeste might even like that it broadened his horizons. Most vampires were omnisexual anyway. That was even more sexual than pan.

"So what do you think?" Harrison said, turning around so they could look at the Slushy Shack together. It looked entirely authentic and not newly constructed at all. Its quasi-stucco, yellow-painted exterior was stuck with large, circular, various-colored lenses that glowed from the rear, giving the building an eccentric look. The sign, like the building, glowed at night.

Maurice was nodding, surprised by how much the sight of the thing — the whole show, really — pleased him. The Shack really did look like the kind of place a younger version of Reginald (the actor was in his twenties) could easily work. It definitely looked like the kind of place Claire would frequent. He didn't know if Harrison had actually made her character an employee as he'd said he would, but even beyond that (even without reading the scripts), he liked what he'd heard of the plot so far. The YouTube videos that'd kick-started "Fat Vampire's" popularity were mocking: they made fun of Reginald. The show, however, had made him the hero. Some of the "underserved underdog stories are important" vibe that'd attracted the cast was now making its impression on Maurice.

This wasn't something Maurice should have been forced into, given the need for vampire secrecy ... but now that he had, he was glad for it.

"I think it's brilliant," he said.

TWENTY-SIX
STALKERS

Monday, ten-fifteen PM.

Victor watched from a distance. Maurice, of course, was just as sloppy now as he had been back in the day. He was as sloppy as Logan, who hadn't bothered to keep a guard on Victor because he never thought Victor would dare to leave the protection of the house — poor little defenseless Victor, who'd *never* dare move against Logan.

Well, he's *going to move against* me, Victor thought as he laid on a grassy knoll three hundred yards from Maurice's home, using vampire sight to look directly through the windows. *He's left me no choice.*

It wasn't a rationalization. It was one hundred percent true. Victor wanted nothing more than to do as Logan expected of him: to lie still like a dog, letting Logan handle all the doing. That's how things would be if Logan was less scheming or if Victor was dumber, but Logan schemed plenty and Victor was no idiot. If Victor lied like a dog today, he'd eat a stake tomorrow. With a necromancer at his disposal (a necromancer he'd carefully hidden from Victor, no less), Logan didn't really need Victor's permission for anything. A good necromancer could open Victor's mouth and get him to babble out the blood key. A good necromancer, if they got to Victor before Victor's mind could assimilate and adapt, could probably walk Victor onto a beach at noon.

After that there'd be no more problems for Logan. Nothing but glory for Logan, and Logan alone.

So, true, what Victor was up to right now was far from ideal. He *didn't* like being out of Logan's palace. He *didn't* like exposing himself to Maurice's almost-as-deadly wife. He also didn't like working alone when the odds were so low. But this was the only way to save his skin now: to not just survive recent changes, but also to thrive after they'd collapsed. Victor, for one, didn't care much about the fat vampire. So the public liked the idea of a bloodsucker who didn't look like an old-school leading man. So what? Victor could abide it. If things with Reginald distracted Logan and allowed Victor to do his work, that was even better. All Victor needed was to get his claws on one frail human psychiatrist. That made his job a thousand times easier than the job occupying Logan's time right now.

So Victor figured: *Let* Logan do his thing. *Let* Logan believe that he — and he alone — would control Thrill when its formula came to light. Logan had already finalized his first Thrill distillery, which Sergei said needed only the recipe to begin producing. Logan was also building distribution channels, and attracting parters, and paying bribes. Logan's necromancer had kept vampires away from the Thrillery during construction and could probably be turned to make other impossible tasks possible. Victor was more than happy to let Logan do all those things. That way Victor could step into Logan's position and use all of it to further *his* Thrill empire when this was over, beating Logan to the punch and getting Logan arrested by his own Guards in the process.

Victor lay on the knoll like a spy with binoculars, except he required no binoculars. He simply watched the wide-windowed rooms on the visible side of the house. And he wondered: *Where the hell did they go?*

As far as Victor could tell after three nights of observation, Maurice's wife Celeste and Annabel were the only people in the house. Maurice didn't even have a staff.

The last three nights, Victor had visited Maurice's mansion three separate times. In between, he ran back to Logan's place and made his presence known by walking past guards in the hallway and bugging Logan for things that didn't matter. When Logan tired of seeing him, Victor ran back here. With all his research, he'd gotten a good feel for the women's routine. They spent most of their nights in a book-lined study, Annabel finally having taken on the vampire's awake-at-night schedule. The pair struck Victor as people plotting something. They shuffled papers; they made notes; their lips moved in ways that looked like constructive debate rather than arguments or casual chat. But if that was true, *what* were they planning? Something futile, no doubt.

Today, their usual routine had broken. Annabel and Celeste were in the study for a while, but they didn't shuffle papers and they didn't debate. Instead they seemed to be gathering things together: organizing, maybe. After, they'd gone into the hallway. About a minute later he'd spotted them three rooms down, passing a window. Since that, there'd been nothing.

Victor's intention was to move on them tonight. Logan's plans seemed to be reaching a plateau, unable to move forward until Maurice was in-hand. Once no more planning was required on the Maurice front, Logan would likely turn his energy to another aspect of the plan. That meant one of two things: Either he'd work with his necromancer on whatever-was-happening to bring down *Marty the Vampire,* or he'd go ahead and cross "get the blood key from Victor" off his To-Do list. All of that meant Logan's backstabbing could happen any time ... and *that* meant Victor needed to shit or get off this particular pot.

The only way to prevent Logan's backstabbing was gain leverage on Maurice. He had to get ahold of Annabel, and he had to do it tonight.

He moved closer and watched from a new angle. The women reappeared, now four more rooms down.

He already knew they were alone.

He'd already done his planning.

He could do this.

So he moved in closer, and began to.

GO WITH HER.

Annabel stopped with her hand on the doorknob. Her other hand held what could only be described as a bandolier full of wooden stakes, which she'd been about to hand to Celeste. Celeste didn't look like the kind of person who'd wear a bandolier. Celeste, rather, looked like a person who should always be carrying cupcakes.

"What?" Celeste asked.

"It's nothing."

She handed Celeste the stakes. But she must have paused again, still listening to the air itself, because this time Celeste asked more pointedly. "*Annabel.* What is it?"

"It's—"

"Don't say it's nothing."

So Annabel just closed her mouth.

"You should actually answer the question, though."

Annabel took a moment. She'd gotten used to hearing a foreign voice inside her head during the time she'd spent under Victor's glamour, but that was different because during that time she hadn't been herself. She'd learned since to label her internal voice as "Daisy," but even then Celeste and Maurice had been careful to explain that it wasn't literally Daisy. Ever since she'd thought of the voice more like an internal monologue, like a song that wouldn't leave her head.

"I still hear Daisy sometimes," she said. She said it lamely, expecting Celeste to laugh. Annabel was human, after all. She was probably just absorbing vampire lifestyle, Celeste would assume: a deep part of her wishing she got psychic blasts like the vampires got.

But Celeste didn't even smile. She put the bandolier around herself, then perched on a stool in the mud room to consider Annabel carefully.

"You're hearing her now?"

"It's just a thought. One of those random thoughts that run through your head."

Instead of responding, Celeste reached out and put her hand over Annabel's. She was trying to feel Annabel's emotions and see some of her thoughts. She'd done it before over the time they'd spent together. Maurice and Annabel were both connected to Daisy, making them connected to each other. Celeste's first-degree connection to Maurice meant that Celeste, too, could sometimes feel all the way into Annabel if Annabel let her, and it was easier with physical contact.

"It's not 'just a thought,'" Celeste told her. "What did Daisy say to you?"

Annabel didn't want to believe any of this. She'd tried many times over the past month to disavow all of it. For a while she'd been fascinated by the vampires, but mostly that was therapy hangover: the old way she'd had of participating in vampire adventures, through Maurice's stories, while keeping her distance. Recently, though, the peril had become real. The supernature of it had grown too close for comfort.

"Seriously, it's nothing," Annabel repeated. She knew it *wasn't* nothing; the voice had spoken as directly as it ever had. "She's just 'me,' right? Because she's not alive anymore."

"You have a vampire in your family tree," Celeste said. "It's not like having a juggler in your family tree. Vampire blood is special. It carries gifts, no matter how distant. Most humans don't feel that connection at all, but you do. I don't think we should ignore her if she's talking. Because yes. She's *you*. But you are more than you think you are." Her eyes narrowed, as if her next question was taking a shot. "Tell me. Have you always had good instincts? Like ... *scary* good instincts about what was going on or what was about to happen?"

That was an uncomfortable question — uncomfortable because it was undeniably true. Annabel had once decided not to board a plane because of a bad feeling, and the plane had crashed. She'd changed her normal route to work on impulse, then learned later of hundreds dead on her usual route, trapped in their cars by a flash flood.

Annabel didn't need to answer. Her face must have done it for her.

"Mmm-hmm," said Celeste. "So. What did she say to you just now?"

"She said I should go with you."

Celeste looked almost confused. "That's ridiculous. You won't be any help against Ophelia, if I manage to track her down."

"Maybe I'm supposed to hypnotize you along the way," Annabel guessed. "She's back inside her fortress now, so maybe you need my help to draw her back out like we did the first time."

Celeste was shaking her head. "We already know she's trying to shut down the TV show. Going back into my memories is a totally different path. I'm going to LA. This is more like being a detective than some sort of blood explorer."

"I don't know. You asked what Daisy said to me. That's what she said. She said, 'Go with her.'"

"With me."

"There's nobody else around."

"You can't come to LA with me. Even if I carry you, it'll take forever if I have to slow down to a speed that won't liquify your skeleton."

"Hey. You asked."

Celeste was stumped. Thinking, her eyes ticked toward the ceiling.

"Maybe we're supposed to snoop Logan instead," Annabel said. *"Don't* go to LA. Stay here, and search Ophelia out at the source instead of going after that Jerome guy. Would she be close to Logan?"

Celeste shrugged. "Maybe? If I knew, I'd start there. But when I was inside her mind, I felt like Logan called me — *her* — on the phone. If that's true, she could be anywhere. Come to think of it, *Logan* could be anywhere. He's paranoid. His entire home is moved by vampire roadies every few days. Unless you're already inside his circle, nobody knows where it is."

"Is he in town, at least?"

"Maybe. But not for sure."

Now they *both* stopped to think.

"Maybe we should just ignore Daisy," Annabel said. "Maybe it's nothing."

Again, Celeste put her hand on Annabel's. She said, "You don't believe that."

Deep down, that was true. Deep down, she realized she was scared to death.

So it's for protection, then. I'm not supposed to go with her to help her, so much as I'm supposed to go so I'm not alone.

"Grab the crossbow out of the lodge room," said Celeste, pointing two doors down. "And let's not dawdle."

IT WAS EASY TO APPROACH. Easy to leap the fence. Easy to cross the grass. Sixty seconds after leaving the knoll, Victor was behind one of Maurice's rose bushes with his back to the east wing, but he was starting to wonder if there was any point to hiding. There seemed zero chance anyone would pay him any attention.

He'd reacquired Annabel and Celeste on his way toward the bush, spotting them in a shoe-and-coat filled room while they pulled on gear as if preparing for a mission. Annabel was holding a crossbow. Celeste wore a sword on her belt that he'd previously seen Maurice carry. Maurice didn't carry the sword these days. Apparently people with swords bothered Los Angeles, even though he'd gotten away with being a weirdo for so long in Ohio.

What are you up to, Annabel?

Victor moved a little, but he could only see them in glimpses and couldn't hear any of what they were saying. If he came too near the room, Celeste's superior sight and hearing would pick him out better than any security camera or motion detector could. He couldn't swing out onto the grounds to spy the window from afar for similar reasons. So mostly he hung back, being very still. Unfortunately the only way he could be sure Celeste wouldn't hear him was if he couldn't hear them, either.

He had no idea why they were gearing up. Why they'd put on boots and coats. What they possibly hoped to accomplish by sneaking out past the adoring fans who still hung around the grounds most days — the fans comprising the best anti-Logan protection they had.

But did it matter? If Annabel and Celeste left the house, it meant leaving anyone who might be watching them. So maybe this was good. Maybe it was better than the old plan. He wouldn't have to hide anymore. If he could just find a time when Annabel was away from Celeste — even for just a second — snatching her from the wild would be child's play.

He waited until he heard the back door open. It was a subtle sound, but easy for Victor to hear. He could tell by the slow swing of the hinge and the lightness of their footsteps that they were trying to be covert. But why?

Victor hardly cared. The women were together right now, but sooner or later they'd separate.

That's when Victor would make his move.

A BLOGGER NAMED Saul Boveneq happened to have his night vision scope trained on the rear gate when Celeste and Annabel approached it. He startled when he saw them, then elbowed his partner.

"Gabe."

Gabe was sleeping. The two of them had been on the world's dumbest stakeout for almost two weeks now, and the only way to keep Gabe coming back was to engage in a lot of role-play: they were spies in Cold War Russia, watching agents cross the tundra. There was much sex involved, always with one eye on the scope. Gabe slept when they were finished. It meant he slept a lot.

"Gabe!"

"Mmm."

"Celeste Toussant just went through the back gate."

"Lemme sleep."

Saul elbowed him harder. "God dammit, this is why we're here!"

"I thought we were here for Russian agents."

"Well, now we're Saul and Gabe again." But that wasn't right, was it? There were other alter-egos he could call on that would rile Gabe better. So he said, "Actually, we're *Svekla and Vlad.*"

Gabe sat up straight. When you played as many games and immersed in so many facets of geek culture as Saul, Gabe, and their friends did, sometimes identities got confused. They hadn't done any true live-action role play in a long time, and even then it was usually medieval LARP. Neither was a huge fan of medieval. The swords were either cardboard or flimsy aluminum, or they were real-seeming replicas that were way too heavy. Gabe's usual medieval character was an elf, but one who'd been stripped of immortality, magic, and everything else that made elves special in a rather embarrassing battle against the Sofia Guild. As a result, he was a liability, and as a further result he'd lost his taste for most kinds of LARP until a reset happened — and Saul, who couldn't leave Gabe behind, had lost it too.

That applied to *most* kinds of LARP. Most, but not all.

They were still both fiends (no pun intended) for *vampire* LARP. Which, Saul had hoped since this whole Fat Vampire phenomenon began, was secretly the reason they were here.

"Then tell me, Svekla," Gabe/Vlad said. "Where is the woman going?"

"*Women*," Saul corrected. "There's someone with her."

"A vampire?"

"Hard to tell. Both are moving like humans."

Which, of course, was obvious. Gabe was a real sucker for fantasy play (which is probably why it was such a huge part of their sex life), but secretly Saul had a hard time doing some of it with a straight face. They and the others had been pretending that the so-called "fat vampire" on YouTube was a real vampire because it was part of the fun, but once under life's microscope the whole thing honestly became a little silly. When you did medieval LARP, the swords and shields often looked real enough that they didn't need to suspend much disbelief. Celeste and Maurice Toussant, however, turned out to look like normal people just like the fat vampire (whoever he was) looked normal. The house was too far to see into (unless you had vampire vision, ha-ha) so they'd never seen more than vague shapes since this ridiculous stakeout began. Gabe pretended he saw vampire-type things (Celeste moving too quickly to be seen, for instance, though Saul suspected she was just moving out of sight), but mostly the whole endeavor had been a bust. If Maurice came and went, he did so using an invisible helicopter or another unseen mode of ingress. Celeste never came outside. It'd been nearly impossible for Saul to keep his game face on, to keep believing the fantasy. Their time outside the Toussant home so far wasn't like being vampires. It was like being stalkers.

"Should we follow them?" Gabe asked.

"I guess that's why we're here?" He wasn't sure. He'd gotten bored days ago.

"If we don't follow them," Gabe said, now using his serious voice, "Volika and Simone will find him first."

That changed Saul's mind. They weren't the only vampire aficionados whose lives had gained new meaning after they learned from Maurice's press conference that the fat vampire lived right here in town. It was very important to the many vampire clans in their on-again, off-again LARP that they find the fat vampire. Finding him would prove for once and for all that misfits like themselves could be special.

Before now, real vampires had felt like an unobtainable ideal. Saul and Gabe and Volika (Nellie) and Simone (Wendy) had always needed a lot of faith to LARP as vampires before the fat vampire became a thing. They'd had to avoid looking at their geek faces in the mirror and pretend they were classically beautiful (not to mention strong and tall with big, lean muscles) instead. Fat Vampire was the opposite of that. Pop culture had embraced him despite — and possibly because of — his total lack of remarkability. He wasn't handsome or fast or chiseled or strong. He couldn't even catch someone jogging or riding past him on a bike. It was the perfect vampire ideal for Saul and his friends to aspire to. That made finding him first the ultimate LARP goal ... and something worth picking up shop right now and moving for.

Saul's walkie-talkie crackled. They didn't like to use cell phones because vampires didn't use cell phones and all four of their LARP characters were vampires. Vampires didn't use walkie-talkies either, but walkies felt somehow more acceptable. The players pretended the walkies were a form of telepathy. Everyone knew vampires were telepathic.

"Vlad! Svekla!" came Nellie's voice. "This is Volika! Do you read me? Over."

"You don't need to say 'over,'" said Saul. "Over."

"But you just said 'over,' over."

"Well, don't say it anymore," Saul told her. "Vampires don't say 'over' when they're using real telepathy."

Nellie didn't answer.

"You there?"

"I'm sorry," Nellie said. "I didn't know if you were finished—"

"Yes. I w—"

"Over!"

Saul sighed. He tried to keep his head in the fantasies that Gabe took to so easily, but he'd been born too logical for that to happen. Saul was in the unenviable position of wanting very badly for life to be more fantastical (*Avatar, Harry Potter*) but knowing how unrealistic it was for those fantastical things to actually happen. It made him a curious breed of role-player: skeptical and optimistic at the same time. Gabe, by contrast, was able to make himself believe for long periods of time that they were real vampires in pursuit of real vampires: that he and Saul *actually* ran up walls and drank blood, and so did the big guy on YouTube. Saul did his best, but knew disappointingly deep down that every one of them was just a different breed of deluded human.

Gabe was practically jumping up and down. It was after dark on a Monday and both of them had early shifts at GameStop tomorrow. They were hiding in the bushes outside the home of a guy who'd sold a story to Hollywood, pretending the supernatural was real. Remembering this,

Saul had one of those moments, wondering what he was doing with his life. But then he caught sight of his partner's innocent enthusiasm, reminded himself that their LARP friends and his stupid little horror blog gave them more joy than everything else in life put together, and decided that as long as he was in someone's bushes this late for no good reason, he owed it to the universe to take the gam all the way.

Maybe this was the break they'd been looking for. Maybe Celeste was going to meet with the fat vampire, who Maurice claimed to know. Maybe, if Gabe and Saul followed her closely, she'd lead them to him. And *then* just think how happy his blog readers would be.

"Holy shit, Saul ... *Svekla*," said Gabe, putting his eye to the scope. "The lady with Celeste? Did you see what she's carrying?"

Saul shook his head.

"It's a crossbow. She's a *hunter!* Who carries a crossbow in boring old real life, man? I told you this might be real!"

Saul tried to be enthusiastic as he slung on his backpack full of play-vampire gear and prepared to follow.

He was not successful.

TWENTY-SEVEN
TEETH

Maurice had never had use for a smartphone before. When Harrison bought him his first so he'd be reachable, Maurice had rolled his eyes. But he'd quickly seen how easy the thing made it to connect with Nikki and Claire about All Things Reginald, then to turn around and send updates to Celeste without the trouble of a call or blood communication. He'd asked for Annabel's number with a sigh, then asked if she wouldn't mind letting Maurice track her phone with an even larger sigh. That was one Celeste had sighed at, too.

You're a vampire. You can track us with your mind.

Yes, he'd said. *But my mind's got a lot going on right now.*

She'd shaken her head and walked away. Annabel had hesitated at that point, reluctant to let Maurice track her after all when Celeste was clearly so against (or just annoyed by) it. He told her he just wanted a way to know they were safe. He couldn't look out for them from LA using his eyes, but he *could* with an iPhone. Oh, what great things the future had brought them.

Thank you, Maurice told Annabel when it was done. *Now I can keep watch. I'll know where you go if you get in trouble.*

And then Celeste had said, loudly and sarcastically, *My hero!* The voice she used was a lilting one, as if she were putting on the persona of a damsel in distress. If Maurice had stuck around, she'd've started crooning about what a big, strong man he was, and how small and frail she and Annabel were.

Maurice heard his phone ding now, then looked down to see a notification: *ANNABEL HAS LEFT HOME.*

Why would she be leaving? Was Celeste with her? Maurice didn't like it — not now, and especially not with Celeste still mad at him, which she clearly still was. He'd run home yesterday after skimming Harrison's scripts even though it wasn't a work day for Reginald and Nikki, making the trip specifically to make peace. He was not successful. Celeste had remained single-minded, asking him what he'd done about Jerome. Maurice answered that he'd done *cocktails* with Jerome while Jerome was making some very market-astute notes on the scripts: not messing the story up as Harrison seemed to feel, but instead making the story track better with key demographics and making the show more appealing to potential advertisers. Celeste hadn't thought that was funny, especially since they weren't supposed to advertise. Maurice reminded her that Jerome was on their side, not Ophelia's — and that assumed Ophelia even *had* a dog in this fight, about which Maurice was far from convinced. He wasn't even sure Ophelia had poked her head back up at all. For all they knew, their guts were wrong and Ophelia was dead.

Celeste told him to sleep on the couch. He ran back to his Mulholland flat instead.

And now Annabel was on the move, leaving the mansion. Why? What could possibly compel her to leave Celeste's protection? Unless Celeste was with her. But Celeste wouldn't leave the house now of all times ... *would she?*

He pulled up his contacts, finding Annabel. His thumb hovered above her number, preparing to call. But then someone said, "Maurice. You got a minute?"

It was Harrison.

"I just need to make a quick phone call."

"Sure," said Harrison. "No problem."

Maurice looked at the phone, then at Harrison. The man was just standing there like waiting in line.

"What's it about?" he asked.

"I'll wait."

"Is it about the show?"

"Turns out they don't have the right kind of vampire fangs in Canada," Harrison said. "I wanted to get your opinion on some options."

"Wait. What options?"

"Well, look," Harrison said. He'd printed sale listings for various prosthetic teeth, now handing them to Maurice. Maurice set his phone down and looked at the top page. "This is all they seem to have in terms of vampire teeth. See where they're pointy?"

The listing showed the teeth in someone's mouth. The mouth, with the teeth, looked like an aggressive rabbit rather than a vampire.

"Wrong sharp teeth, right? I don't even get it." Harrison sounded offended. "Those are lateral incisors. Are *your* fangs on your lateral incisors, or are they on the canines where they belong?"

"Canines. Obviously."

"Well, this must be how Canadian vampires work. Maybe it's a better arrangement for eating poutine."

"What's 'poutine'?"

"Nobody knows. But, look. Ella's up there and she says they're ready to roll at ..." Harrison looked at his watch. "Well. Shit. They *were* ready to crack the first slate at ten, but I guess that didn't happen. You know how this works. We get twelve hours of work. *Twelve.* I don't want to run over time on the very first day. We've got a 5pm call time tomorrow and people are going to need time to sleep. That means the clock's ticking. Jerome wants on-location Slushy Shack exteriors tonight because we've only got the spot for a few weeks before they need to tear it back down. Then sunrise shit with Marty's last morning, at magic hour. I hate to lose the day."

"I don't see the problem," Maurice said.

"Problem is the first scene requires fangs. Shouldn't have been a problem, except that we don't have the right kind of fangs. We just have these stupid-looking narrow fangs. Until they get the right kind of teeth — and they've already hunted around and found zilch — the whole day is dead in the water."

"Can't they just do a different shot? One that doesn't require fangs?"

"Sure. But the only other shit anyone's prepped for is going to require a complete re-set, moving dolly tracks and the crane arm, and apparently there's some issue with wardrobe that means they can't—"

"I get it," Maurice said. "I assume you have an idea? You're not just here to tell me."

"I want them rolling in a half hour," Harrison said. "I

don't like to make this kind of a first impression. First day sets the tone. Amado's really amped up. He's got everyone laughing already. Gonna make a great Reginald, you know. Or I guess a great 'Marty.' Anyway. I don't want to ruin the mood by telling them all to huddle up and sit still while they break everything down and set for something else. Right now there's momentum. Day One. I want to capture it."

"Okay."

"You could be there in ... what? Fifteen minutes?"

"You want me to run up to Canada?"

Clearly that was *exactly* what Harrison wanted. He'd already reached into his pocket and come out with a pair of prosthetic teeth — with the fangs in the right place this time.

"Yeah. I figure you run up there. Take a bunch of pairs of these teeth. I'll tell them you were already in Victoria scouting or something. Like, 'Oh, hey, no problem, man! Maurice is right down the road and he just so happens to have a bunch of the kind of teeth we want!' I haven't answered Sally yet. What do you think?"

"You think they'll believe that?" Maurice asked.

"What, you think they'll believe you're a vampire instead?"

"I'd have to leave right now."

"Okay. That expose you to Logan or anything, if you run up there alone?"

"Only the endpoints matter. It's busy here and it's busy there. Nobody can catch me when I'm actually in motion."

"So ... yes?"

Maurice's phone was on the table. He felt like he'd been meaning to do something with it, but he couldn't remember what. He put it back in his pocket, then took what turned out to be a whole backpack full of vampire teeth from Harrison.

"Sure," said Maurice, pulling it on. "Tell them I'll be there in twenty."

TWENTY-EIGHT
NERVE

Annabel felt like they were being watched. She had no evidence of it whatsoever, though. In fact, she had quite the contrary. The places they'd gone were wide open. Celeste had a hundred times her vision — as well as some sort of a vampire Spidey Sense — and hadn't mentioned a thing.

You're being stupid. You're jumping at shadows because you're out in the dark. But it was Annabel's own voice saying those things, not Daisy. Daisy, as far as Annabel could tell, was refusing to comment. Her opinion was inside, but it hadn't taken sides. The sensation that so bothered Annabel was a back-of-the-neck thing: instinct, not sense. Celeste had implied earlier that Daisy herself was a form of instinct, but this was deeper. No part of Annabel's sensible mind knew what to do with it.

Just be careful, Daisy seemed to say.

"You okay back there?" Celeste asked.

"Y-yeah."

But she'd hesitated. Celeste turned fully around to face her.

"Yeah?"

"Yeah," Annabel repeated.

"Because you don't sound okay."

"I'm just spooked." She was, too. She'd been afraid of the dark as a kid. Hadn't liked it when her bedroom closet was ajar, but hadn't liked it when it was closed, either. Closing the closet door didn't keep the monsters inside. It just prevented you from seeing them. There'd been many times, after her parents were asleep, that Young Annabel had flipped on the light and thrown the closet door wide and slept that way. Monsters didn't like light. It was the only way to defeat them. Everyone knew that.

"If Daisy's telling you anything ..."

Annabel shook her head. "It's nothing like that. I actually wish she *would* weigh in, but she hasn't. I think this is just vintage Annabel. Or vintage human." She laughed uncomfortably. "This is my first time outside in the dark since I learned the truth, you know."

"What truth?"

"That vampires exist. Until the night I came to you, I was under Victor's spell. This is the first time I've been clear-headed, knowing you're real, and out at night like this. I feel like a kid again."

"Not in a good way."

"Not in a good way," Annabel agreed. Then she waved it away. "It'll pass."

Something rustled. They both looked over, but it was only people. They were in a valley in the park. Some walkers were up above them, probably making out in the bushes.

They walked on. Celeste, who could see perfectly well in the dark, didn't want to use a flashlight. She hadn't really explained what she was up to, but Annabel got the feeling a flashlight would break her concentration. She knew that somehow, in some way, Celeste was on the trail of Ophelia. She had no idea how it worked at all, or even if it did.

"What are you doing, anyway?" Annabel asked. "I mean, I know you're looking for Ophelia, but how? You don't expect to just find her under a bench or something, do you?"

This seemed to shine a light, for Celeste, on her own actions. She suddenly seemed to see herself from Annabel's perspective ... and how ridiculous this looked.

She sat on a rock.

"It was just a question," Annabel said.

"A good one," said Celeste. "To answer your question, I was looking for signs of necromancy. The first plan was to go to Los Angeles and check out Jerome, but once you came with me ..."

"I'm sorry," said Annabel.

"Don't be. If he's really under Ophelia's control, confronting him would be just about the worst thing I could do, I guess. He'd be her puppet, nothing more. Even if he turned out to be what I'm pretty sure he is, and even if I made him *not* a problem anymore, Ophelia would still be out there. Except that she'd know for sure I'm after her. *Then* what do you think she'd do?"

The question seemed rhetorical. Ophelia was working from inside a blind, and Celeste had no idea where it was. Hard to defend against an attack when you have no idea from which direction it might be coming. Celeste was probably right: Going after Jerome probably *was* about the worst thing she could do. This was a weed that had to be killed root-first. Lop the head off and the weed just grows back stronger.

"I'm not taking your thoughts at face value," Celeste

told Annabel. "It's Daisy I think we need to listen to, not you. No offense."

"No problem." Annabel wouldn't listen to herself either.

"I have to know what I'm dealing with. I have to know if it's true that Logan's really protecting her, and I have to know where she is. I have to know what she *wants* — is it just shelter, or is it something else? I can't go into this with my eyes closed."

"Okay."

"But I'm not a detective. You want to know what I'm looking for? Well, so do I. I did a bunch of research on necromancy, hoping it'd give me some idea of what it looks and feels like and how a person can chase it, but all the information out there conflicts. As I'm sure you can imagine, it's not a topic about which vampires want information readily available. It's a huge taboo. Even *looking* for information on it is a red flag, so I've had to stick on learning whatever's in the books I already own. You'd have to be a scholar to know how it *really* works."

"Well, what *did* you find?"

"Just about the only thing everyone agrees is that 'controlling the dead' amounts to 'controlling death.' Necromancers are actually re-animators. So for instance, supposedly supernaturals that are being puppeted by a necromancer don't shed nearly as many dead skin cells as unaffected people do."

"Well, *that's* easy to measure," Annabel said. "All you need to do is go to LA and collect Jerome's skin on the sly. Or you can hold a microscope against his forehead."

"There's more — side effects that some people say necromancers leave in their wake whenever they pass by. Lines of ants that don't seem to be going anywhere. Spiders gathering in groups for no clear reason. You can supposedly watch roadkill that a necromancer's been close to *un-rot* if you look at it close enough, like watching time-lapse in reverse. Problem is, I don't know if any of those things are true, or if they're just old wives' tales. Every source book I've come across is full of *thees* and *thous* and religious rhetoric, or it's been censored. I just ..." She readjusted her bandolier of wooden stakes, which now struck Annabel as optimistically tragic. "I'm just *tired*. Who the hell knows anything about necromancy except the human necromancer Ophelia killed?"

"Macht does."

Celeste looked up at Annabel. She hadn't meant to speak. Hadn't even known she was speaking in the first place. The words just came out, as if spoken by Daisy.

"What?"

But now she saw it. Now Annabel understood what her own argument was supposed to be, even if she didn't entirely understand it.

"*Amadeus Macht.* Ophelia's maker."

"How do you know about that?"

"Maurice. Maurice told me the whole story."

"But why ...?"

"I'm just saying that Macht *would* know, wouldn't he? It's thanks to a necromancer that Ophelia was able to kill him."

Celeste shrugged. "I guess he would. But he's dead."

"Yeah," said Annabel, starting to understand more. "But *Daisy's* dead too ... and I'm pretty sure she's the one who's giving me this idea in the first place."

. . .

LOGAN PROWLED the halls of his home. He had a man missing.

"What do you mean he's gone? Where the hell would he be?"

The Guard either didn't understand or refused to. Sensing there was no correct answer to the question of "Where is Victor," he was opting to stonewall: shaking his head in small arcs in front of the raging Deacon, saying nothing at all.

"I asked you a question!"

"I ... I don't know, sir. I've been outside this door the whole time. I haven't left my post, just like you asked. As the Captain of the Council Guard ordered me, sir."

Logan wanted to rip the vampire's head off. He didn't, though, because the cleaning staff had retired for the evening and he didn't know where the vacuum cleaner was. Death made so much ash.

Instead, he called to the Captain — a vampire called Nightshade.

"I want him found," Logan barked. "Do you understand me?"

"*Yes sir!*" Nightshade replied. Then she ran off like her life depended on it, because it did.

Shitty-ass timing. Someone was playing games with him.

Maybe he was being paranoid (and he always was), but it struck Logan as a pretty big coincidence that Victor had disappeared right before Logan came to his room with a palm injector full of silver nitrate solution. He'd been planning to slap Victor on the shoulder in congratulations for a job well done (the Thrillery was finally one hundred percent finished; all they needed was an opening on Maurice), then drag his vomiting corpse to a chamber where

Ophelia could do her work in secret. After the blood key was out of Victor, Logan figured he'd just hit the him with more nitrate and be done with it. It'd be okay if he expired in the silos. There was already ash in there.

But fucking Victor must have figured it out. Or, more likely, someone had leaked. Nobody knew about Ophelia other than Logan, but half a dozen people knew Logan was planning to kill Victor the second he wasn't needed anymore. Betrayal was par for the course around here. It was just how business was done. So had someone said something? It was hard to believe Victor was smart enough to guess this twist on his own, seeing as he struck Logan as little more than a sniveling weasel. But who knew? Stranger things had happened.

Logan paced with his hands interlaced behind his back — the posture of a furious dictator — while his minions scrambled. It wasn't really possible for heads to roll around here (combustion, once the spine was severed, made that impossible), but still the expression was romantic enough to hold sway. The whole house was terrified now that the master was displeased. They'd return to him with good news soon enough, or there'd be Hell to pay.

Nightshade was back ten minutes later. She came in a blur rather than walking, as befitted the situtation's urgency.

"So? Did you find him?" Logan demanded.

"Partially," she said. "The cameras show a motion blur we've determined must be Victor leaving the grounds."

"That's not *finding,*" Logan said. His neck had tightened into knots. He was in a killing mood, and he still wore his palm injector.

"No, sir. But there's more."

"'More'?"

"The eye in the sky detected movement at Toussant's house not long after."

"What do you mean 'movement at Toussant's'? How the fuck's *that* relevant right now?"

"Well, sir," Nightshade stammered, "it looks like Maurice's wife has left the building."

"So what?"

"At a visible pace, sir. If she left at her normal speed, it's doubtful we'd've seen her."

Logan wished Nightshade would just spit it out. He already knew that cameras couldn't capture the Toussants; that's how Maurice was probably coming and going without being seen. Logan already knew Maurice was still showing up — on and off, and more "off" than "on" this week — at his job with Fat Man Reginald, that whole area smeared with far too much attention for Logan's people to take rogue action. Same went for the house, where humans and the occasional vampire traitor waited in fandom.

"So fucking what?" Logan asked.

"She left with Rice, sir."

"Really." He sneered. "*And* eggrolls?"

"Not the food, Deacon. The woman. Annabel Rice. Maurice Toussant's doctor?"

Nightshade was waiting patiently for Logan to connect the dots the Guard Corps had already connected. Anyone who worked closely with Logan knew how much he hated being handed an epiphany. He liked to believe all ideas were his ideas. All realizations came from Logan and nowhere else.

"That's where he is! That's what Victor's after! *He's chasing Dr. Rice!*"

"Oh my God," said Nightshade. Her tone of fake realization wasn't at all convincing. "You must be right. Brilliant deduction, sir!"

"Keep eyes on Rice," Logan said. "Same rules apply for her as for Maurice and Celeste. *Don't touch her*; you understand? I can't afford the way that would look if anyone saw it happen. Stay low and don't be spotted. It's *Victor* you're after; do you get me? *Victor!*"

Nightshade ran off. Logan continued stalking the halls, congratulating himself on his brilliant idea.

SAUL AND GABE — having donned black capes and false teeth to embody their LARP characters Svekla and Vlad — watched the women. They'd been following them for a while. So was someone else, though — maybe more than *one* someone. Saul had seen a man rushing through the bushes. And in fact he could see the man now: on his own, crouched low, watching the taller woman very closely. Not Celeste Toussant, but the one with the crossbow.

"*Gabe,*" Saul hissed in a near whisper. "Do you see that guy?"

"Who is Gabe?" Gabe asked.

"Okay. *Vlad.* Do you see that guy, Vlad?"

"Yes." Gabe put on his best Transylvanian accent. "He is a vampire."

"I think he's some sort of rapist."

"Who's he raping?"

"Nobody yet. But look at him. Tell me that dude's not rapey."

Gabe looked. It was hard to say. At least half of the world's straight men had that look to Gabe. He'd said it before.

"Maybe he wants to suck her blood," said Gabe.

"Maybe this is a time we don't do the vampire thing."

"What? Why?"

"Because look at him. Come on, Gabe."

Gabe looked, but seemed heartbroken. He knew this was serious; the creeper in the bushes had definitely been watching the tall woman in a way that might have included one hand down his pants. But at the same time, the guy *really did* look like a vampire. He was pale and dressed in black. Not terribly handsome or muscular, but Fat Vampire had proven that not all vampires were pretty. He'd moved a few times in vampiric ways: tricks of the light that Saul would swear caused him to blur from one place to another. Atop it all, the woman he was stalking held a crossbow. Who carried a crossbow, if they weren't hunting or chasing vampires? The situation in front of them was a vampire LARPer's dream, and yet Saul was asking Gabe to assess it like a boring old human.

Now they might have to save the day in a purely conventional way. Saul had pepper spray. Even if he chickened out and couldn't get too close to the guy, he was willing to bet that spraying it in the general area would have at least a deterrent effect.

What made it worse was that the women were clearly lovers. The pervert was watching it all, rubbing one out while he did so. Apparently Celeste was closeted and this was her lover. Although ... they'd both just been in a very private house together, so why had they come *here* for a rendezvous? Must be some adventure-seeking thing. That much, Saul could understand.

"Fine," Gabe said. "You wanna call out to them or something?" He looked sympathetic. "Look at them. It's gonna embarrass the shit out of them if they realize anyone's watching."

"Not yet," said Saul. "Let's check on the creeper. He's just one guy."

DESPITE BEING JUST ONE GUY, Victor had been pretty sure he could handle this situation until Celeste and Annabel started getting cozy. He wondered if he'd misread the situation. They'd left the house on a mission, then snooped around very carefully ... then had come to this dark section of park so that Celeste could sniff up and down Annabel's neck. He didn't like it. It was going to be much harder to grab Annabel if she started getting frisky with Celeste.

He moved carefully until he was one bush closer. Then another. He wondered if he could circle all the way around. If he found a strong enough piece of wood, he could ram it through Celeste's ribcage from the rear, maybe before she even knew it was coming. Probably, actually, if they were horny. Maybe this was a blessing in disguise: two ladies swinging in an unexpected direction while Victor, sly and clever as always, took the advantage.

He was wondering how he'd fashion himself a stake without making noise when he found one ready-made in the brush. A short branch had been sheared off, leaving a sharp point.

He moved forward another bush, now making his way to their side and eventually to the rear.

Not much farther now.

CELESTE'S FANGS WERE OUT. Annabel's skin, at the neck, was intoxicating. It was rare that humans offered themselves so willingly. Making this sexual would make it weird — *especially* since Annabel reminded her so much of Daisy — so she kept trying to do what human men did in movies to banish their erections. She thought about baseball. She had no idea how baseball was played, so at first the strategy was difficult. Then it got easier because she realized she'd seen the game played before. There were two teams on a rectangle. One threw the baseball down the field, dodged and weaved, then scored a touchdown before jumping up to slam the baseball through a circular thing.

That's when her eroticism finally departed. She was too confused to be aroused.

"Tell me it won't hurt," said Annabel.

"It won't hurt," Celeste repeated.

"Is that the truth? Tell me the truth."

"Do you want the truth, or do you want me to tell you it won't hurt?"

"I want you to tell me both."

"Okay," Celeste said. "Both." She wasn't at her cognitive best. She was still thinking about baseball and wondering when players were supposed to spike it.

"Celeste!"

Celeste pulled away.

"Can't you just bite my finger? Victor bit my finger."

"Victor needed a crutch. *I'm* trying to mingle a memory you aren't even sure you have with a memory I definitely don't. To do something like that, if it's even possible, I need arterial blood. That means your neck or the inside of your thigh. I figure this is less awkward, but if you want to take off your pants and—"

"No, no," Annabel said, blushing. "This is fine."

Celeste leaned in. Her bloodlust was building. Right now, it would take all her willpower not to rip out Annabel's carotid and dance in the gore. If Annabel didn't stop teasing, Celeste couldn't be held responsible for her actions.

Annabel pulled away again.

"Maybe I could numb the area with ice," she said. "Poke it with a sterile lancet."

"Try to do it without my clotting agent and you'll bleed to death," Celeste said. "Be a man."

"I'm not a man."

"It's an expression."

"Not a very enlightened one."

Celeste moved in, mouth opening. Then Annabel said, "Hang on."

"*What?*"

"Let's think about this. What do *I* know about vampires?"

"Jesus Christ, Annabel. Tell me if you've changed your mind. This was your idea. I don't mean to be gross, but if you aren't going to let me feed at this point, I'm going to need to run off and get off with a jogger or something."

They faced each other. The plan was simple, if a longshot. A very long time ago, Amadeus Macht had slipped a little bit of his own blood into Celeste's drink in order to show himself, vampirically, to Celeste. That blood was still in her because vampire blood never left, but any memories Macht once gave her had grown vanishingly weak by now. The voice of Daisy, however, seemed to think that imparting some of Daisy's Thrilloglobin frenzy — an addictive *need* so heavy, it'd driven Maurice into a trance outside Annabel's home that first night — would cause Macht's blood to wake up. Celeste was to be the crucible for combining those two things: Macht's old blood tie plus the memory of what it felt to be jacked up on Thrill. She'd seen what Thrill did to vampires who drank it. If Daisy's experience of it couldn't wake Macht's memories, nothing could.

Annabel nodded. Celeste leaned in again, brushed her fangs against Annabel's skin, then pulled away on her own this time.

"Oh my God, just do it already!"

Celeste was looking around the park. She said to Annabel, "The day Daisy called out to Maurice, when she invaded his mind, it messed him up a little. Basically incapacitated him. It made him sort of crazy, like he was an addict himself. So I was just thinking: It's possible that'll happen to me when I drink your blood if there's really Thrill memory in you. Thrill wakes the senses in a pretty extreme way. Chances are I'll zone out. That means you'll be more or less alone until it's over."

Annabel hadn't realized that. She tried to pretend she was okay with it, but she wasn't.

"I have my crossbow," she said.

"Maybe we should go back home. Where it's safe."

Annabel shook her head. "You said to obey my intuition. My intuition tells me there's not a lot of time. Something's happening with Maurice."

Celeste wanted to dismiss that idea, but obviously she'd had the same thought. She had a mainline bond to Maurice, and she too couldn't shake a feeling that this needed to begin soon so it could end soon. If their longshot worked, it might even lead her to Ophelia *tonight*. Whether Macht knew anything about necromancy or not was up for grabs, but he was one thing for sure: *He was Ophelia's maker*. Sire bonds were the strongest bonds vampires had — and based on what she'd seen Thrill's memory do to Maurice, Celeste was willing to bet that a dip of Daisy's addiction would light up the Macht-Ophelia bond like a blazing neon sign.

"*Maurice,*" said Celeste. She'd had an idea.

"What about him?"

"We should at least ask him. He's done this. He's felt Daisy's need for Thrill. He can help."

"Celeste ..." Annabel said. "He doesn't even *believe* you."

"He's my husband," was all Celeste would say.

Then she closed her eyes and breathed in, thinking of him. The trance came quickly. And why not? The sire bond burned brightest when one of the pair was in danger. It didn't matter what Maurice had said to her. It didn't matter how he'd acted. Celeste needed his guidance, and there was no time to waste. The falling of hourglass sands felt to Celeste like boulders.

Something was happening. And it was happening now.

Her blood sniffed toward Maurice, faithful as any telephone connection.

Maurice, she thought at him, through the bond. *I need you. I need your mind. Your progeny needs you. Your wife needs you. Show yourself to me in blood. Show me your face, and show it now.*

But again like a telephone connection, Maurice gave no answer.

This is vital. This is life and death. You have to tell me what I will see. Teach me how to gird myself. There's no time. I feel eyes over my shoulder. An enemy's breath on the back of my neck. You can give me that knowledge. See me, Maurice. See me as I need you.

But there was nothing. When Celeste returned to Annabel, her emotion was indescribable.

"Do it," Annabel said, seeing her. She'd turned her face, exposing her neck. "Do it now, before I lose my nerve!"

So Celeste did.

Maurice felt like he was forgetting something. But then again, he'd had so much on his mind recently.

These teeth, for instance.

The fact that the set didn't have the right teeth was, in truth, a tiny bit Maurice's fault — and not just because he was still running, still hadn't arrived. Harrison had asked him to look through a bunch of different prosthetic vampire teeth and narrow the field to those that looked most realistic when held up to Maurice's own teeth in the mirror. Problem was, Maurice didn't love his teeth. They struck him as small and crooked. His plan, therefore, was to take the teeth with him when he next went home and compare them to *Celeste's* teeth. Celeste had always had good teeth — even when she was human, even that long ago, even in France. Becoming a vampire had made them stellar. He'd even thought the idea of running her through all those fake teeth would be a good bonding experience at a time when they needed bonding most. But then Maurice had forgotten, so the production had guessed.

That was the first ball he'd dropped. Not that it was the only one.

Soon after, Maurice dropped another ball with the 1st Assistant Director. He was supposed to meet the man Jerome wanted for the job last Thursday, but of course Jerome didn't know Maurice was a real vampire and had only left schedule slots open during the day. Maurice meant to circle back to iron things out, but the task got lost in his head. He'd had a reason; he'd needed to run back to soothe Reginald's nerves after Nikki let him know that Reginald had grown restless, foolhardily considering running away from his Vampire Council problems. The AD issue ended up being solved without Maurice's help, but it'd meant a one-day delay. The production was still catching up from that delay, hobbled by its ultra-tight schedule.

And it wasn't only dropped balls that besieged him. Plenty of what'd occupied Maurice's head of late went well, if in a frenzy. There was script approval. There was an issue with the sound crew to be dealt with. The actor playing Maurice was the son of a great actor and had inherited his father's chops, according to the second-block director and (again) the 1st AD Maurice had failed to meet with. He'd do well just by existing, Harrison told Maurice, but he'd do even better if he could talk to Maurice about his character.

Apparently he had all sorts of questions in mind that were difficult for him to imagine but would be simple for Maurice to answer. Real stumpers like, "If you were a vampire, how do you think you'd get by being out only at night?" and "My character is old, but I'm not. Any idea how you'd act if you were a lot older than you looked?" There was also, "Do you think you could kill people and still be able to look at yourself in the mirror?" but Maurice figured defer to Annabel for the answer to that one.

Maurice had taken all those meetings and done all those tasks — but a lot of other chores, he'd missed. He decided he needed to prioritize. *Some* failures were going to happen regardless, so the least he could do was to make sure he failed at the correct things. He learned the 80/20 rule, reminding himself that a select twenty percent of the things he could do for the show would yield eighty percent of the results. The trick was to figure out which tasks were important and which could be dismissed. In the end, he had no idea. He ended up dismissing a lot of tasks with no clue whether they were the right ones.

And so, true to form, Maurice was absolutely certain he'd forgotten something as he crossed the US/Canadian border with a backpack full of false teeth. The only question was whether it was something that mattered.

It'd been a chaotic, tumultuous run. His mind was occupied the entire time, juggling schedules and checklists he hadn't thought to write down. Then, in the middle of all that tumult, halfway between LA and Victoria, he thought he'd felt Celeste calling him. He wasn't sure, though. He couldn't focus with all his exertion. There were too many inputs at once: too much mental noise lately to hear the mental signal.

He'd been passing Seattle at the time, dodging his way around a big evening festival. He stopped to listen for her once he was past, but by then Celeste was no longer calling ... if she'd been calling in the first place. He tried to call out from his end, but by then her mind was occupied somehow. What he got back was a sensation he'd never seen before: something like a busy signal. It had to mean Celeste was concentrating. Focusing intently on something and unwilling to be bothered. A big flashing sign saying, *Do Not Disturb*.

Not much he could do about it, in any case.

He told himself that if Celeste *had* called (and he was in no way sure she had, though he hadn't been thinking straight), it struck him as a low-grade thing: closer to "Ahem, do you have a minute?" then a red-hot "I NEED YOU." It was probably nothing. *Almost certainly* nothing. When Celeste wanted to reach him, she eschewed the trouble of blood and just used the phone. She only called out through blood for emergencies, and this definitely hadn't felt like an emergency.

Still vaguely troubled ten minutes later, Maurice stopped outside the production circus and tried to focus. He sat in the dirt with his delivery yet undelivered. Then he closed his eyes and whispered inside himself: *Celeste?*

He got the same weird busy signal. And then:

"M?"

He looked up to see Jerome standing over him.

"Why are you sitting in the dust, man? We have a chair with your name on it."

Even with Jerome above him, Maurice took one final moment to glance into his void of his blood. He was terrible at this. He'd never had any subtlety in his mental communication at all. He could yell at the top of his psychic lungs when a war cry was required, and he could hear related vampires' war cries from a whole world away. Anything less — anything on the order of an inquiry or a simple reach-out-and-touch — was doomed before it began. That's why these days, he carried a cell phone.

In the darkness of his mind, looking for Celeste and whatever she may have wanted of him, Maurice found nothing.

"You okay?" Jerome asked.

Maurice stood, brushing himself off. "I'm fine. I was just ..."

He wasn't sure how to finish that sentence. What would make sense in this situation to a slick-suit from LA?

"... meditating," he said.

"Oh, for sure," said Jerome, instantly nodding. "I meditate every day. I need it to organize my whole life. It's a great time to rehearse conversations for the day. Especially when you're about to fire someone."

"I don't think that's how meditation's supposed to work."

"Hey," Jerome said, putting an arm behind Maurice's back and ushering him toward the brightly lit tractor trailers. "I was thinking. We lost a lot of the magic when we stopped calling this thing 'Big Ass Vampire.'"

"I think it was originally '*Fat* Vampire.'"

"Whatever. Same thing. Anyway. Back in the day, it was much more about making fun of fat people."

"It really wasn't."

"I mean, the original guy, with the falling down and drinking supermarket ground beef blood, he was funny."

"He was."

"He was a guy we could all laugh at. And the story, at the start, made sense along those lines. Harrison invented that vampire chief. Lambert. And Lambert, he had the right idea. You take the fat guy, and you put him in a contest and then laugh yourself silly."

"That's ... not even close to correct," Maurice said.

"But now the story's all woke. It's Harrison's fault. He crowdsourced that shit. Asked too many opinions. Heard 'diversity' a few thousand times too many. Lambert became Angela. Now everyone's fat or gay or ugly."

"Are you really saying this to me right now?"

Jerome wrapped an arm around Maurice like a brother. "Here's my question for you, Maurice. Who's looking out for us? Who's looking out for straight white America?"

"Everyone? Everywhere? Since the dawn of time?"

"Exactly. We're lost in the shuffle. The message of this thing was supposed to be about optimizing. The story was originally a training montage. Like in the middle of *Rocky IV*." He said the letters rather than the number: *eye-vee*. "Remember in Rocky eye-vee, where Rocky's doing situps off a loft and throwing Russian grain around, and meanwhile Dolf Lundgren is killing that Black guy?"

"Are you talking about *Apollo Creed?*"

"Sorry. Spoiler. I guess that was after the training montage. He trains, *then* kills him. And they're making him punch this high-tech device that says how hard he punches. And he's using this chrome machine that goes like this." Jerome approximated whatever he was talking about. It consisted of keeping his lower half still and then whipping his upper half hard to one side while exhaling as if exercising. "And at the end they shoot him full of steroids. That was really the lesson of *Rocky Eye-Vee*: Don't throw grain. Use steroids. Like Rocky finally realized."

"I don't think Rocky used steroids," Maurice said.

"Please. You seen him recently? Tell me that guy's *not* on steroids."

"Do you ... Do you think Sylvester Stallone and Rocky are the same person? You know that's a character, right?"

"So anyway," Jerome went on, oblivious. "You get a movie like that, and it's about taking some little Italian guy and doing whatever it takes to turn him into Dolf Lundgren. That's the show we started out to make, here. That's the show we should *still* be making, Maurice."

"We ... What? No."

He slapped Maurice on the back. "No worries. I'll take care of the changes. I just needed your okay."

"Wait! You don't have it!"

Jerome nodded, pointing a finger at Maurice as if he'd scored a point. "Gotcha. That's smart. We'll leave the first episodes the same so they can stay on schedule. It'll be an arc. Tracks perfectly with our key demographic. Really, changes are only needed further in anyway."

"Jerome. Are you listening to me? Don't change *anything*."

Jerome was wearing a Chiclet smile exactly like Todd's back at the treadmill company. "Of course not." Then he winked. "You've told me. You're the good guy. I'm the bad guy. I never told you any of this."

"No. I'm *actually saying this to you* right now: *Don't change anything*."

"Oh, hey, and another thing," Jerome said. "We didn't have time for focus groups, but I did an informal one. The women are way too bitchy. Sarah has too many lines."

"She ... *What?*" He had to think who "Sarah" was, then remembered that in the TV show, Sarah was the girlfriend half of Nikki. Nikki's badass half had gone into another character. Named Nikki, he thought. "No, Jerome. She has exactly the number of lines she needs."

"Well, yeah. If you like her having an *opinion*."

Maurice wondered if he could kill Jerome without remorse. Probably. But then the production would have to slow down to bury him, and that would be inconvenient.

"Jerome," Maurice said.

"M," Jerome answered.

"I can fire you, right?"

"Not really." Then, seeming to think Maurice was

joking, he slapped him on the shoulder, gave that too-white smile again, and walked away.

"*Jerome!*" Maurice called. But Jerome was gone.

For some reason Celeste came to mind. Something she hadn't liked. Something she'd raised that'd felt like an absurd, too-far-from-things-to-know flag about, regarding Jerome.

What was it? He knew it wasn't small. How fucked *was* his head these days?

He pulled his phone from his pocket. There was something he'd forgotten about the phone, too. His list was too long these days. He couldn't keep track of everything. Or, really, anything.

The vibe of tonight was all wrong. Something in the air. Something in the way.

He decided to slash the Gordion knot and just call Annabel. He'd call her quickly, right now, and then at least he could relax. He didn't like this sensation of something gone missing, something overlooked. It had the feel of watching traffic approach from the front, not thinking to check the rearview while a semi barreled full speed toward him.

"*Maurice!* Is that you?"

A woman was coming toward him, crossing shadows between the trailers.

"Oh, thank goodness," she said, moving into the light. "I'm Ella, Harrison's partner. We haven't met." She smiled and they shook hands. "Harrison said you have our teeth? They're entirely blocked, rehearsed, and lit. Ready to shoot as soon as they get the teeth."

Maurice was in the process of taking off his backpack when Ella seemed to have an idea.

"I just realized. You haven't met the cast and crew, have you?"

Maurice shook his head. He was supposed to, but it was yet another ball he'd dropped.

Ella waved him toward a pool car, fishing keys from her pocket. "Come on," she said. "I'll drive you over."

THIRTY
AUTOGRAPHS FOR EVERYONE

"WHAT ... THE ... FUCK?"

Victor had the sharp branch aimed and ready when the cry came. He'd gotten himself nice and close to Annabel and Celeste unseen, raising his ad-hoc spear in preparation for the thrust. He'd have to leap to do it but that was okay; he had one knee bent, that foot pressing into a tree. As soon as Celeste bit Annabel (which was what now seemed to be happening, though Victor had no idea why), both women would be beyond distracted. Celeste would be buried in the ecstasy of feeding and Annabel would stop noticing the world for more obvious reasons. That was the moment in which Victor would push hard off the tree, flying through the space between himself and Celeste Toussant in a flash. All he needed was one little bite, and then Celeste would be gone ... and Annabel would be his again.

But that's not the way things happened.

At the last second, Annabel — who Victor had already heard worrying about the bite — flinched hard. Celeste's teeth were fully launched when she did so. As a result, the tips of Celeste's fangs must have just pierced Annabel's carotid artery as some pain-avoiding instinct wrenched her away. The effect of *jab-wince-jerk* was to tear incisions in Annabel's neck instead of piercing it.

Panic set in for Annabel, who threw her eyes wide instead of succumbing to the vampire sedative that would nudge her toward sleep. Blood gushed rather than confining itself to Celeste's mouth. It sprayed her lips, face, hair, and shirt. Enough must have made it down her throat, though, because as Victor paused his lunge, Celeste's eyes fluttered in rapture. Not all the way, though. She looked like a woman who'd taken two punches from a three-punch combination. She was swaying on her feet, neither peaceful nor agitated but instead both things at once.

Annabel, meanwhile, was fighting for her life. Whatever reason she'd had to invite Celeste to drink her blood, instinct had since revoked it. Over the next two seconds, she landed an elbow on Celeste's jaw and kicked her hard in the groin as if she had testicles.

Celeste went down. Vampires healed fast, but getting clocked still hurt.

That's when a previously-unseen third party started shrieking from slightly above Victor and to the left. There were two in that party, one more composed than the other, both watching the scene at the center of the park's open space. The smaller of the two had his hands on his face and was shrieking like a schoolgirl. The second seemed to be morbidly fascinated: a man watching an antelope dismembered by a cheetah but unwilling to turn away.

"WHAT. THE. *FUUUCK!?*" he repeated.

Victor retreated. He lowered his spear and removed his foot from the tree. He'd never land a good blow now, not with Celeste half-staggered, drunk and raising one hand to keep herself from taking another of Annabel's whirling fists in the eye. Annabel, meanwhile, had her non-swinging hand pressed hard against her neck wound. It was doing nothing to staunch the flow. She had a geyser under her fingers. She looked like the final scene of Stephen King's *Carrie*.

"Stop moving!" Celeste yelled at Annabel. "Sit the hell down or you're going to bleed to death!"

One of the nerdy kids watching the melee — the screecher, not the shouter — suddenly speared a finger at Victor.

"There he is! That's the masturbator!"

And Celeste yelled, *"ANNABEL! STOP RUNNING!"*

Annabel didn't hear her. She'd lost all sense. Instead of stopping, she sprinted directly away from Celeste and into a tree.

The smaller of the two shouting humans set his sights on Victor, then started running toward him like some sort of hero. He was brandishing what looked like a costume-store scepter, with a big fake blue jewel on top.

"Stop jerking it! *Get away from those women!*" he screamed.

Victor turned and bared his fangs. He made to leap after all, but this time at the kid who'd decided to be braver than he had any right to be.

"HEY!" yelled a new voice from the edge of the clearing. *"Hey, what's going on down there!"*

Victor's head whipped to see a new human walking by with a dog. Then the human then noticed Annabel painting the area red, crouched, and threw up.

Victor retracted his fangs. The kid renewed his charge with the scepter.

In the corner of Victor's eye, Celeste made her move on Annabel. She seemed not to have noticed anything else — not Victor, not any of the humans shouting. While Victor was standing down (best not to make any vampire move-ments if he couldn't kill all the onlookers), Celeste wasn't standing down at all. She sprinted like a vampire, then used her muscles like a vampire. She was atop Annabel in a second, pinning her hard and putting her mouth to the other woman's neck. It looked like assault, but it was prob-ably utility: If Annabel lost much more blood, the only way to save her would be to turn her. Celeste was probably biting her properly now, smearing vampire coagulent onto her wounds in the process.

The dog-walker was still vomiting.

The scepter-bearer reached Victor at a run, then seemed to have no idea what to do when Victor didn't even look at him.

Annabel finally went still. If Victor had to guess, half of it was due to the coagulent plus the sedative of a vampire's bite and half was due to something Celeste seemed to have whispered in her ear. This wasn't glamour. It didn't need to be. These two were in league, as unholy an alliance as Victor found it.

Everyone was looking at everyone. Mostly they were looking at the bloodbath in the center of the area, spotlit by a street lamp.

Annabel raised her head. Unconvincingly and inappro-priately, her make-it-all-right statement in this blood-drenched moment was an ill-advised *"I'm fine! It was just a misunderstanding!"*

Phones came out. Two of the humans began taking pictures and the third — the one closest to Victor — seemed about to make a call.

They'd have to clean this up. Victor couldn't be seen out-of-bounds and it'd do nobody good for a real vampire attack to make the internet. That meant grabbing all of them — all three humans. It then meant glamouring or killing them. But who would do it? The women saw Victor now. Annabel's eyes were like ice. If Celeste was ready to advance on anyone, it was Victor. Victor would never be able to outrun her. Never be able to out-fight her. Only the presence of humans was keeping him alive.

Then it got worse.

At the lip of the shallow depression in which the ladies had put on their bloody show, new dark figures arrived. They were in plainclothes, but the look of Council Guard was unmistakable. That was very bad. It meant that Logan knew Victor had left, and had sent these soldiers after him. It also meant that Victor was a man without a home. He was on his own again, no longer a guest of Logan's unless he wanted to die, and because of everything that'd just happened it would now be much harder to get his hands on Annabel. Logan would capture him now. He'd have the necromancer (or the Mentalists) suck the blood key from his mind and then kill him. Alternatively, Celeste — or Maurice, if he turned back up — would kill him. Even Annabel, in this moment, might kill him. She'd picked up her dropped crossbow. She'd been carrying it cocked and bolted, with only the safety's protection to keep the thing from firing.

Subtly, slowly, the bow raised until it neared Victor's chest, and clicked the safety off.

The only reason nobody moved was because there were too many parties in the mix: too many alliances, too many grudges, too many attacks held at bay with too many attacks waiting to happen. Omitting Annabel, there were only three humans here and a whole lot of vampires. Glamour would be easy. Killing would be easier, especially since the night was young and every vampire here was probably hungry. Beyond the humans, it didn't matter that none of the vampire groups were on the same side. Victor would be the next to fall. The only consolation was that they couldn't kill him just yet.

After that would come Annabel. With this many of Logan's people present, Celeste, too, would die for sure. There was only one way it could all end: with four human corpses and two piles of black ash.

The Guards seemed to be realizing the same thing, now baring teeth and hooking hands into claws.

"What's ..." said the larger of the human pair: the one who'd been shouting. "What's going on here?"

It was suddenly clear, to all three humans, that this would end badly.

Do something, Victor thought. *You can't escape. If you do nothing, you're lining yourself up for torture. Then death. You can't make it worse. Literally anything is better than this.*

Victor was clever. He prided himself on being clever — on outsmarting those who were older and faster and stronger than he was. The brain wasn't a muscle, but in times like this it was the only muscle that mattered. But what could he do? There was nobody he could attack to make this easier. No way to run without being stopped at the gate or followed. He couldn't take a hostage; the Guard in particular didn't care about hostages. He couldn't ally with Celeste because she wouldn't have him, and because even if she would, the basin was surrounded by two dozen soldiers.

Think.

He'd seen other humans coming in. They were far enough away to be missing this. Could he use them as fodder? As shields?

Yes. But not in the way he'd been thinking.

Stand up tall, Victor, he thought, deciding. *You're an actor now.*

With all parties motionless and the vampires ready to spring, Victor yelled, *"CUT!"* as loud as he could.

Vampire faces frowned. They looked to one another. Thank God Logan didn't seem to be here. He'd sent his militarized idiots but wasn't around to command them. And so the Guard did as they'd been told: With no new orders to obey, they followed their previous orders and erred on the side of caution. *Logan didn't want publicity.* Even the grunts knew that.

"THAT'S A WRAP ON LOGAN'S VAMPIRE ATTACK!" Victor shouted, not caring that the words he was saying didn't really make sense. What mattered was that the rest of the park's humans — those beyond the lip where he couldn't see — heard him. What mattered were the key words he'd said: *Logan* (because Logan wanted no spotlights) and *vampire* (because the humans had seen what they'd seen already, and there was no point in trying to deny it).

The Guard soldiers began openly talking to each other, confused about what to do next. The human nearest Victor was looking back at his buddy, their faces no longer angry or wrathful. Those two, at least, looked almost pleased.

Between and around the Council Guard, other humans began to arrive. Some had cell phones out, tiny flashlights illuminated on their fronts.

So Victor shouted more things, even more uncaring that they meant nothing.

"STRIKE THE SET! PRINT IT!" He was yelling to some unseen director that, as far as the humans were concerned, was hiding out-of-sight for reasons unknown.

"GET MAURICE DOWN HERE! MAURICE TOUS-SANT! FAT VAMPIRE YOUTUBE HERO SHOW OR WHATEVER, TAKE TEN!"

Now the murmurs were beginning in earnest among the humans. Victor had said magic words that, in their minds, explained everything:

It's not real! Look, the attacked woman isn't even hurt! It's just television. Someone is filming this, and the women at the center are actors. The blood's fake. Maybe we'll get to meet the stars. Appear in the background of a shot. Call Mom — we're gonna be famous!

It was just Maurice's famous little vampire drama, filming here in their very own town.

Forget the illogic of it. Forget that there were no visible cameras or directors. All that mattered was that the Guard had gone from a hive mind with a clear purpose to a bunch of confused individuals. All that mattered was that there were now too many humans around to kill or glamour ... and that simply by sticking around, the Guard was making it more likely that Logan's presence here would be noticed.

Logan's vampire attack. They'd all heard Victor yell those words. By sticking around, they would only make their Deacon's anger worse.

"Shit, I'm sorry, man," said the guy with the scepter. "We saw you back there and thought you were creeping on those lesbians. We didn't know this was part of the TV show!" His voice was absolutely delighted.

Victor looked at Celeste. Her eyes were onyx pearls. She seemed to see right through him — through his skin to his spine, which her hands had already tensed to snap. Then Victor looked at the Guards, who were already disbanding with eyes in Victor's direction: a promise to catch up with him later.

"No worries at all," Victor answered, returning his attention to the pair of men. He moved between them, then nudged toward the larger group of humans to secure his safety in numbers.

Then he turned, glanced toward Celeste, and smiled at his new fan club.

"Thanks for coming out," he said to them. "Anyone want an autograph?"

Ella handed the backpack full of teeth to a grip with instructions to pass them off to makeup. Then she snagged a man who turned out to be a producer and intro-bombed him and Maurice. His name was Kyle. He was a rotund man who, following pleasantries, grabbed his gut and told Maurice that he totally dug the show "for obvious reasons." He was a big guy, and it was about damn time the big guys of the world had a chance to be heroes.

It was nice to see, producer-wise, that Jerome was an anomaly. The way Kyle interpreted Reginald's ("Marty's") story was exactly the opposite of how Jerome saw it, and more or less the way Maurice would have written it had he been a writer. He'd skimmed Harrison's scripts; he knew the TV show had a victorious ending ... for this first season, at least. He wished he felt confident that the real story of the world's most underdog vampire would end the same.

Defeat the Deacon. Win the trial. Get the girl. Maybe, in time, find a way to save the world.

Considering the real oppression waiting for Reginald, such things were flights of fancy. But for now, Maurice finally had an excuse to forget life and think about fantasy instead. *More* than an excuse, really. Now that he was on-set, joining the fantasy was basically a mandate. He could (*should*) forget about Logan and the upcoming trial that Reginald would surely fail. He could (*must!*) forget Celeste's obsession with Ophelia, and his own suspicion that she was at least partly right, that Ophelia might still be a threat. And of course he really needed to (*and, for now, was required to*) forget that Logan and Victor had likely gathered everything they needed to make Thrilloglobin. All they still needed, to start production, were a few painful minutes of Maurice's time.

It was brass-balls cold in Canada, and today's "set" wasn't actually a set but instead the nighttime exterior work Harrison had mentioned at The Slushy Shack. Victoria's Pacific climate helped dull the chill a little, but all the humans were in coats and there were portable heaters everywhere. Black tents ringed the lot except at one side, where an upcoming scene required the girl playing Claire to ride down the street on a scooter. Apparently Claire rode a scooter in this version of reality.

Maurice didn't care about the cold. He felt cold much less than humans anyway, but the larger reason was because he was transfixed. Seeing his life become art erased all his problems.

He met the first-block director and both ADs. An associate producer named Cathy showed him around the scene: equipment up front, support in the rear. The gaffer had set the lighting crew up in one of the old auto shop's open garage bays around the corner of the Shack, out of sight. The sound crew was inside. Dolly tracks had been laid in front of one of the Shack's colorful sides, a camera dolly already on them. A crane held a second camera, and a third had been mounted atop a ladder. Cables ran from tent to tent. Cathy also showed him the rear, where there were more truck trailers and where a man named Ron ran a food stand the crew referred to as "Crafty." A large dining tent had been set up behind that for later.

"Harrison said they were ready to shoot," Maurice told Cathy, looking at the unmanned cameras.

"Makeup needs some time with the teeth," Cathy explained. "There's more to show you in the meantime, if you want."

Maurice *wanted* very much.

It was fascinating to think that one little "Yes" had done all of this. Another thing it'd done, Harrison had explained back in LA, was to turn Maurice into an author.

The YouTube videos didn't tell a story, so the production needed an explanation for how the story they were filming had come together so quickly. In truth Harrison had cribbed from real life, but obviously no one could know that Maurice was a vampire who'd lived a version of it. The simplest solution was to tell everyone that Maurice was a writer. Specifically, Maurice had written a book based on his friend from the videos. That nonexistent (and definitely not written-by-Maurice) "fat vampire book" was the story's source as far as the cast and crew were concerned.

And so Maurice was given a lanyard to hang around his neck, and on the bottom of the card hanging from it was written his official role with the production: *Author*.

Cathy handed Maurice off to a Teamster named Jack to continue his tour. Already Maurice was feeling like a VIP, now with his third escort of the evening and being given all-access.

"Show me everything," he told Jack.

So Jack showed him *everything*.

He learned from where the equipment drew power and what they did with the toilets when they filled. He learned what was on the lunch menu ("lunch" was served after six hours of work whether it came at noon, dinnertime, or four in the morning) and was introduced to too many techs and riggers to remember everyone's names. They were all friendly, all pleased to meet the show's "author."

After a while, Jack started forgetting to tell people who Maurice was and simply introduced him as "Maurice." Often the name alone was enough to raise eyebrows, drawing a connection to the fictional Maurice being played by one of the actors — but this was also Canada, and parts of Canada spoke French, and so it turned out he wasn't the only Maurice.

This caused confusion. At one point Jack poked his head into the makeup trailer where two of the actors were getting ready and asked "if it's okay for Maurice to come in and say hi." The actors agreed, but the woman in the first chair (Delilah, who played Sarah and *hated* Jerome) thought he was one of Jack's fellow Teamsters. When she realized her mistake, she leapt out of the chair, said "holy shit" a few times in a way that suggested it was her favorite expression, then hugged him. It was a much warmer welcome than he'd expected.

He learned to introduce himself properly after that.

Within fifteen minutes, it felt like Maurice knew everyone. The Trainee Assistant Director ("TAD," for those in the biz) showed him a small set built inside the Shack where later, "Maurice" would be burned in a coffin. Not fatally, of course. A sound tech gave him a wireless receiver and earbud that would allow him to listen in to official audio: production sound once they were rolling, but chatter that happened around any live microphone until then. He even met the other Maurice, which was surreal, and he met Claire, who had the same pluck and smile as the real Claire.

Then he met Amado: the actor playing Reginald ... or, in the language of the show, "Marty."

From Amado, he got another hug. He also got a reprimand because apparently Maurice should have let Amado know that he was coming to watch a day of filming so they could hang out together. They hung out on set instead. Then Alexander, who played Maurice, asked Maurice to run some lines with him. If he'd thought earlier that meeting an actor playing him was surreal, reading "Maurice's" lines was *doubly* surreal. They weren't exact words that Maurice had spoken, but they *were* Harrison's interpretations of conversations Maurice told Harrison he'd actually had. Rehearsing those lines was Uncanny Valley for Maurice: They weren't direct quotes, but they were close enough to be (and this was another in-the-biz term) *really fucking weird.*

His cell phone vibrated. It was Annabel. Maurice, with his sense already overloaded, didn't notice.

He decided to watch as much of the night's filming as he could, planning to leave with just enough time before sunrise to reach LA unburned. The schedule, once things began, was packed — something Amado said was a real change from the feature films he'd done before, where setups took longer and the number of scenes per day (they spoke in "pages" of script) were fewer.

Maurice watched Amado and Alexander re-create Reginald's making as cameras rolled. He watched Isaac die — something Maurice had done for real himself, using his wood-tipped sword. He watched Claire visit the Slushy Shack where Marty worked: a strange (but apparently less creepy) replacement for Reginald and Claire's real relationship.

Delilah pulled him aside at lunch.

"What's it like, seeing your book come to life?" she asked.

In truth it was closer to watching his *life* come to life, but obviously he couldn't tell her that. "Humbling," he answered.

"Well, we love it," Delilah said. "My agent brought this project to me when I was already sort of committed on something else. I'd just moved to LA and the thing I was going to do was basically within walking distance. I didn't want to move to Canada for two or three months. With, like, zero notice. I don't like the cold. And to be honest, the pay's not amazing."

"You're welcome," Maurice said.

"But the story spoke to me. I know that sounds like some sort of shitty cliche, but it's true. You and Harrison made characters that break a lot of barriers."

"Oh," Maurice said.

"So thank you."

"Sure," he said. It felt ridiculous to accept praise.

After lunch, Maurice watched Marty (he kept thinking of him as Reginald) contend with Todd pre-turning. Todd, like the rest of the cast except for Claire, was at least ten years younger than they were in life. TV-show Todd worked at the Slushy Shack with Marty. He was almost as big of an asshole in the show as he was in life.

Then came the introduction: Marty and Maurice meeting outside the Slushy Shack for the first time. Later, Maurice glamoured Marty to ask Sarah on a date. That hadn't happened with Nikki, but Maurice was getting used to the changes.

He visited Crafty. Met the digital imaging technician and script supervisor in the video village tent, with the camera monitors, where Maurice ended up spending most of his time during takes. He walked around. Drank coffee. Coffee wasn't really human food, just like wine wasn't really human food, and agitated his stomach only a little. Everyone else was drinking it. Drinking coffee with them made him feel like he belonged. He'd certainly been welcomed enough.

At 6am, it was time to go. The sun would be rising around seven. Maurice wanted to stay forever — and come back tomorrow — but real life awaited.

He stopped to say goodbye to Amado, who was dressed in his blue-and-yellow Slushy Shack uniform, before leaving.

"It's been a good first day, man," Amado said. "That's always a good sign."

Maurice shook his hand. Amado was wearing a hat and gloves, apparently not curious why Maurice hadn't donned so much as a coat all night long.

"You're a great Reginald," Maurice told him.

"Who?"

Shit. "I mean Marty," he corrected.

Amado smiled slyly. Then he said, "Mind if I ask you a question?"

"Um … sure."

"It's for my character. For … *Marty.*" Letting Maurice know he'd noticed the slip — that the real man's name was Reginald — but wasn't going to tell anyone. "Everyone knows that Marty's a misfit."

"Sure."

"And that he's an outsider."

"Yeah."

"And because of it, he gets bullied. By Todd. By everyone."

"Yeah?" Maurice wondered where this was going.

"But everyone knows the real Fat Vampire guy doesn't actually have to fear for his life. So I'm just wondering how I should play him. For maximum authenticity, you know?"

Amado was looking at Maurice funny. There was something going on here. More than he was saying.

"You're the actor," Maurice said. "I guess ... follow your heart?"

Maurice assumed that would close the issue, but it turned out Amado wasn't remotely finished. Instead, he seemed to be building to a punchline.

"I'd rather follow *his* heart," he said.

"Whose?"

"Reginald's." Amado paused and watched Maurice's eyes, letting him know he hadn't said that by mistake. Maurice was pretty sure he could read something else in Amado, too: It wasn't *Maurice* who'd let the name slip for the first time. Amado had already known Reginald's name.

"Harrison told you," Maurice said.

Amado nodded. "He told me other things, too. We go back a little, me and Harrison. He worked with my dad. I kind of grew up around him."

"I thought Alexander was the one with the actor father."

"He is. My dad's a DP. Director of photography."

Amado pulled a joint from his pocket and lit it, weed being legal here. He said, "Just a couple of misfits, aren't we? Me, an actor who's round and brown, suddenly starring in my own TV show. That's not supposed to happen, you know. 'Leading man' is a type. They usually look like Matt."

Matt was the actor who played Isaac until Isaac died. And Isaac was beautiful.

"I'm glad it worked out," Maurice said.

"And you."

"*Me?*"

"A vampire, with his own TV show."

Maurice was sure he'd heard that wrong. Or he'd heard a joke. And yet Amado didn't smile. He smoked his joint, looking right into Maurice's eyes.

"Ha ha," Maurice replied.

"Two thousand years old," said Amado. "Turned Reginald to save his life, because you thought a big fat guy you barely knew was worth more than food. Worth risking *your* life for, too."

"Look, I don't know what Harrison told you, but—"

"Discovered he's got more vampire talent up *here*—" Amado tapped his head. "—to make up for what's not out *here*." He waved vaguely at his own body.

"Vampires don't exist," said Maurice.

"Of course they don't. Say. Do me a favor." Amado reached into his pocket. "Hold this for me while I re-light my joint?"

It hadn't gone out. And what Amado was extending toward Maurice was a necklace of pure silver. Amado liked his bling. When he wasn't Marty, he was always dripping with jewelry.

"I'll drop it," Maurice said, knowing he was fooling nobody. "You'd better keep it."

Still without taking his eyes from Maurice, Amado put the silver necklace away.

"It doesn't bother me, Maurice," he said. "I've been watching you. You're friendly and you're humble. There are more things on Heaven and Earth than are dreamt of in the usual philosophy. Honestly, vampires are a lot easier for me to believe than mass shootings. Than wars. Than partisanship. Than an epidemic of hatred."

"Look," Maurice said, panicked now. This wasn't an ordinary threat. He couldn't glamour or fight his way out of this one. The show had to go on, and Amado was core to the show. No force would fix this. Only begging could save it. "You can't tell anyone. Please. It's fun to tell stories about fake monsters. It's entirely different when the monsters are real."

Then Amado smiled. He offered Maurice the joint.

"You misunderstand me, Maurice," he said. "The world is *full* of monsters. More monsters now than ever before."

Maurice took a puff and handed it back.

"But you, my friend, are not one of them."

Hours and hours later. For Annabel, had she been on her old schedule, the time would have felt early. She'd been on Celeste and Maurice's schedule for almost three full weeks now, though, so instead it felt very late.

The house phone rang just shy of 10am.

"That's Maurice," Annabel said.

Without moving, Celeste said, "I know."

Since they'd returned to the mansion, Maurice had called Annabel's cell phone half a dozen times. Calls to the home line had begun shortly after, now numbering another half dozen or more.

"We should answer it."

"Answer it, then."

It was a good bluff for Celeste to call, because she knew Annabel wouldn't answer the phone any more than Celeste herself would. If Maurice wanted to talk to them, they both felt he should get his ass back home — sun or no goddamn sun — and grovel. The fact that he seemed to think *calling* was enough after failing them so completely was insulting. She and Celeste had nearly died. What had been so goddamn important to Maurice back when they'd needed him?

She rose and walked into the ironically-named sunroom, which at this hour was awash with sun. It felt safer where vampires couldn't go, and right now she wanted to be alone.

A text message arrived: I KNOW YOU'RE THERE.

Annabel ignored it.

Another came shortly after: ANSWER THE PHONE. I NEED TO TALK TO YOU. Then the phone rang. She ignored it until it stopped.

IT'S IMPORTANT.

Annabel didn't give a shit. If it was so fucking important, he'd be here in person. Only: *No, no ...* if it was important, he'd *never have left.* At first it'd made all the sense in the world for Maurice to use the TV show for cover, but these days Maurice seemed to be enjoying his cover a bit too much. His whole manner told the world, *You want to make me a big shot? Okay, twist my arm.*

A new text message: I REALLY NEED TO TALK TO YOU.

Then the phone rang again, and this time Annabel decided on impulse to answer. Why not? She was tired from losing so much blood and had very little willpower left. Being angry for as long as she had — angry enough to keep up with Celeste — had worn her down. She wanted sleep, not resistance.

She opened by saying, "I'm only answering to tell you to stop calling."

"We need to talk," Maurice said. His voice wasn't confrontational or conciliatory. It was something in between. *"Both* of us need to talk. To each other."

"I don't want to talk," Annabel said.

"What would you have told me in one of our sessions," Maurice asked, "if I'd said that to you?"

She gripped the phone tighter. *Oh, no. Don't you dare get cute with me, motherfucker.*

"I wouldn't say anything. A person is allowed to have preferences."

"So you wouldn't point out that I could have blocked your number? That I didn't need to answer 'just to tell you not to call'? Are you seriously pretending, Annabel, that you're not posturing right now?"

Her thumb moved to the hangup button. Then Maurice said, again in that in-between voice, "Just give me five minutes."

Her thumb retreated. She supposed she *was* posturing, but she didn't like him pointing it out.

"Is Celeste nearby?" he asked.

"No."

"Good. Because this is just between you and me. Look: I know I fucked up. Don't worry; that's abundantly clear. But Celeste and I have been together for over a thousand years. We've been through rougher times than this."

"That's no excuse, Maurice."

"I know. But I can only take back one thing at a time."

In the silence that followed, Annabel felt a cool flutter of breeze. The sunroom's windows opened to screens, and one had been left open to the screen.

"Please," Maurice said. "Please just go somewhere she can't hear you."

"I'm in the sunroom."

"Farther. She listens in."

Annabel stepped through the door and onto the lawn, then sat in one of the wrought iron chairs where they sometimes had midnight tea. "It's ten AM here, Maurice. The sun's been up for almost three hours. I'm sitting on your back patio now, in bright sun. She's nowhere near any of the windows. She should be sleeping, but she can't. This is far enough. It's as far as I'm going."

He must have accepted that, because the next thing he said was, "I know what happened."

Surprise shoved Annabel's anger aside. "You do? How?"

"I called Brian. Brian knows from Logan. Logan obviously doesn't know Brian told me, or that he *would* tell me. Look. I'm sorry the two of you felt you had to take things into your own hands. I assume Celeste wanted to go out looking for Ophelia. Thought she could sense dark magic. Ants in lines. Spiders in piles. Is that all correct?"

"How—?"

"She tried to talk me into doing something similar before you came to stay with us. I know the Council Guards saw you last night. I know they saw—"

"—*Victor?*" Annabel said, her voice turned bitter. "Feet away from us, ready to shove some sort of wood pole through Celeste and take me away?"

Maurice paused, then said, "Yes."

"Celeste reached out to you. You didn't answer."

"I know. I couldn't concentrate on anything inside myself. I was running very fast, for a long time. I could have reached out after I stopped, but by then the call had ended and Celeste was ... *busy* somehow. I couldn't reach her. I wasn't even sure I'd heard anything in the first place. That there even *was* a call. I knew that if whatever Celeste needed was urgent, her blood cry would be unmistakable. I made a bad call. I figured it was okay."

"Running? Where?"

He paused again, then said, "Victoria."

"Canada."

"Yes."

"To your TV show. *That's* where you were when we were fighting for our lives."

"I didn't know you were fighting for your lives. I never heard a life-or-death call, and I should have if there was that much danger. I don't understand it. Something was going on with Celeste, and I don't know what it was."

Annabel thought she had the answer to that. When the worst part happened, Celeste had essentially been in a Thrilloglobin frenzy, no more cognizant than a junkie. Her state had probably scrambled her signals — maybe turned them into undifferentiated noise. Not that she intended to tell Maurice that, and let him partway off the hook.

"We almost died, Maurice."

"It was a mistake," he said, and she could hear the regret in his voice. "I should have stopped right away and made sure. Celeste doesn't usually use blood ties. I made a choice, and it was stupid, and it was wrong. I didn't want to deal with any more bad news, was the truth."

"This is some apology, Maurice."

"It's just an explanation. But I am sorry. *So* sorry. Tonight — it ... it gave me a whole new perspective on things."

"What are you talking about?"

He took a breath as the conversation took a step toward civility.

"The show is just a stupid story, but the story matters. It *matters* to everyone I met up there last night. Not just because it's a paycheck, but because of what it's a metaphor for. I understand why I saved Reginald now. I thought it was just instinct, but last night I got to thinking of the things we talked about. Things you told me in our sessions. Do you remember, Annabel? You said there was more good in me than bad."

She huffed and shook her head. "Hell of a time to dig for compliments."

"Please," he said. "Please try to see through what I've done and hear what I'm saying. God knows I've done plenty. To you, to Celeste ..." He sighed. "Every hero is tempted. Every hero has a flaw. Every hero has to find his own way."

Annabel was about to snipe back at him (*Hero? Now you're the* hero? *How big is your ego, Maurice?*), but her inner psychiatrist stopped her. Patients were often difficult, and it was the therapist's job to see past the difficulty and be the bigger person. Annabel had been yelled at by patients, and blamed, and made the recipient of many misplaced emotions. She couldn't take what Maurice was saying personally — not if he was coming to her in therapeutic spirit, asking her for help.

"I thought this TV show was nothing more than something we were building," he told her. "Harrison and me. It didn't feel any different from putting together a model airplane. We just had to stick enough 'production assets' together, using money as glue, and that's how we'd build our armor against Logan. The thing itself hardly mattered. It *could* have been an airplane model made of plastic. The substance of it just didn't matter to me at first."

"But that's not how it is now?"

She could almost imagine Maurice shaking his head. "The people I met ... they had to *decide* to do this," he said. "They chose it for a reason. Maybe for some of the crew, it's just another job. For the director, though, and the creatives, and the writers, and especially the cast?" He sighed. "Harrison screwed up, Annabel. I told him to pay them as much as it took to get them involved, but one of the actors I talked to said the pay isn't very good at all."

"Shouldn't they complain to the producer instead of you?"

"That's not what I'm saying. She wasn't complaining. She was saying it like a fact. Even the big star, Amado, didn't get as much as I told Harrison to pay him. Harrison knows we needed this done and done fast, but he can't help what he's used to, and he's used to trying to save money where he can. I was up there until just before sunrise, and when I got back I looked up everyone's salaries. I told Harrison to pay Amado ten million dollars just to be sure we got him. The first offer caught his attention, but somehow he still ended up making average pay for a job this size. His family apparently is friends with Harrison, so my hunch is he brought that number down on his own. Everyone else is making what Delilah said: 'not great pay.'"

"So ... What?" Annabel asked. "You told Harrison he could keep the rest of the budget, right? Are you saying he's being cheap so he can line his own pockets?"

"No. He's going to rebate the rest back to me. Apparently something he and Jerome are discussing, involving a possible network sale, requires that the budget isn't inflated. I won't end up spending a fifth of what I told Harrison I was willing to spend."

"Speaking of Jerome ..."

Maurice stopped her, but politely so. "I can't see how he's under anyone's spell, Annabel. He's not a vampire. Not a glamoured human. Just about the only thing he could be is an incubus. Maybe a wendigo. But that's not even why I don't think he's what Celeste thinks. If he was Ophelia's puppet — and if Ophelia is looking to destroy the show because Logan wants her to — why isn't Jerome doing anything to hurt us?"

"Maybe he's hurting you behind the scenes," Annabel said.

"The point I'm trying to make," Maurice went on, "is that I started this whole thing thinking we could just put actors in place and put a crew in place and in the end we'd have a machine that'd do the job. After tonight, though, I see that was never the case. When you build a model out of wood or metal or plastic, the wood doesn't get a choice. The metal and plastic don't get choices. Only the modeler matters, and if the modeler wants to use those things to build a plane, he builds a plane. If the modeler wants to build a tank instead, those same raw materials becomes a tank. But the show isn't made of inanimate building materials. It's made of *people*. People who *chose* to do this project ... not because it pays well, but in spite of the fact that it *doesn't* pay well. Our situation created so many obstacles for this thing. The deadlines were impossibly short, we had trouble getting permits, it's cold in Canada, and Harrison's mistake put our mega-budget on a shoestring instead. *Marty the Vampire* should have been really unappealing to the human beings who got to choose whether they wanted to be part of it or not, and yet still ... here they are, doing it anyway."

"What are you saying?" Annabel asked.

"I'm saying the project has taken on a life of its own. To me, it was just a tool. But to them, it's becoming a movement."

"Isn't that a little dramatic?"

"Maybe. It *is* still a job. It *will* still be sold, once we can afford that much attention. People *will* still make money, and if it's done well, the people involved will be able to use their *Marty* experience to land other jobs. But I saw something bigger than those things last night on opening day. They're good people, Annabel. Every single one of them."

Annabel waited.

"I'm so sorry about last night. If Celeste will talk to me, I'll tell her the same thing and more. But it's not just tonight. It's all of it. I've been an asshole — and *because* I've been a pompous, self-involved asshole, you had to go through Hell without me even lifting my head to look in your direction. The way I've behaved is unforgivable. Now that I see it, I hate myself for it. I hate who I've been. All I can say is that there was at least a reason, though I didn't know it until now. I let my ego get the best of me. I let you down. Both of you. But this is me, here, trying to do what you taught me. I don't know if anyone will forgive me, but I'm saying I'm sorry anyway."

"Are you sure this isn't just a self-aggrandizing concession?" Annabel asked him. "Are you sure *the apology itself* isn't your way of grandstanding? Maybe you're virtue-signaling. You got what you wanted, so it's no big deal to take it back now. Maybe that's what this is: a way for you to make yourself the center of attention by throwing yourself at my feet."

Maurice was quiet for a while. Then he said, "Well ... is it working?"

It'd been a long night. Annabel was too tired to be angry any more, so she laughed instead. Her laugh went on far too long. Now Maurice would think she was the crazy one.

After she calmed down, Maurice pivoted. "Brian said Celeste bit you. Was it to wake Macht in her blood?"

"How the *hell* did you know that?" Annabel asked.

"Because it worked. I see him plainly now, through

Celeste. It's as if his memory suddenly decided to become a Thrill addict. He's loud and proud, as the saying goes."

Annabel was shocked. In the hours since they'd returned, there'd been no signs of hope from Celeste. No signs of progress. No signs that even though they'd gone through the Hell Maurice mentioned, *their* part of this, too, had at least been worthwhile.

"It *worked?*"

"Celeste didn't say?"

"She's pretty occupied with hating you. I don't think she's allowing herself any good feelings right now."

"Do you think I should come home? Any ideas how I can make this up to her?"

"I haven't forgiven you quite enough to give you marital advice just yet," Annabel told him.

The line was silent for a while.

"I have some fences to mend," he finally said. "For Celeste to suggest doing what the two of you did, she must have been a lot more desperate than I realized. I knew things were bad for her, but ... well, shit, she told me what Ophelia did to her back then so I guess I understand. But ... Exposing Ophelia to us through her bond with Macht means that *we're* exposed to *her* now, too. You understand that, right? What Celeste did under hypnosis was just poking the bear. What she did last night was more like waking it all the way up. No, wait; it's more than that. Bringing Thrill into the mix is like shoving a branch up the bear's ass."

"So we're in danger?" Annabel said.

"All of us were already in danger. A *lot* of danger. The only good news about how much danger we're in is that there's no point in being more cautious. It almost literally can't get worse."

"But .. If it worked, we *can* at least track Ophelia now?"

"Yes. And Ophelia can track us."

But that was still their advantage, wasn't it? If Annabel understood this right, Ophelia was and had always been bound by her need to remain hidden. Celeste, Maurice, and Annabel had no such need. In fact, the more their group was out in the open, the better.

"So what's the plan?" she asked. "Now that she's onto us, are you coming home?"

"Not yet," he said.

"Why not?" Then she double clutched. "Do you mean to tell me that even after everything you just said, the TV show—"

"If *any* of what Celeste says is true," Maurice interrupted, "Ophelia's work is happening here, too. She's after you in Ohio, yes ... but if Celeste is right, Ophelia and Logan have a second prong of attack here. In LA. Or in Victoria. Destroy us, destroy the show. The goals are one and the same."

"But *we're* here! You have to help *us*, not them!"

"I don't think it's that black and white," Maurice said. "It's not just a question of what we protect. It's also a question of what protects us."

Annabel was on her last nerve, ready to explode. "What the hell does *that* mean?"

"It means we need to take the fight to them," Maurice said, "because even though we have enemies on the west coast, the good news is we have allies as well."

THIRTY-THREE
HOPELESS

Two weeks passed.

Maurice begged Celeste's forgiveness and didn't get it. He begged again and was refused again. After the third time, Annabel suggested he knock it the hell off because it wasn't working. Maurice asked what he should do, then, and Annabel told him he'd have to figure it out on his own. So he let it go. She'd either forgive him eventually or not, and in either case there was work to do.

Maurice began dividing his time more or less equally between Columbus and Victoria. He didn't bother much with LA anymore, especially now that Harrison was on-set most of the time. He made himself a fixture on set, trying to shore up the show's community so it'd continue to grow into something worth fighting for, showing up only when they shot at night. Harrison and Amado, as the humans who knew Maurice's secret, made subtle excuses to cover his weird schedule: *Mr. Toussant has other books to finish; Mr. Toussant is a bit of a night owl.* Maurice countered this by insisting nobody call him "Mr. Toussant." Amado changed his tune right away, but Harrison turned out to be surprisingly professional on the job. He referred to almost everyone by their last name.

Because he was around so often, Maurice got to know pretty much everyone. Reginald had proven that vampirism could strengthen the mind as well as the body, so Maurice put his to use memorizing everyone's names. Turned out he wasn't gifted that way and remembered very few names — only faces. To compensate, he called everyone "dude" or "what's up?" He made himself useful whenever he was around, constantly delivering beverages from Crafty for whoever wanted them.

The director eventually put Maurice in the background of a scene, as an extra. His job was to fake-sip a fake slushy while fake-talking to another extra he hadn't met before. Fake-talking was hard. They weren't supposed to actually speak out loud, so they just mouthed words to each other. It was hard to come up with enough pretend conversation after a while.

His entire time on set he kept making the rounds, making sure everyone was on the same page theme-wise. Not everyone cared about theme. A lot of the crew just kind of wanted to do their jobs and get on with life, and that was okay with Maurice. Still, a surprising number of cast and crew were totally on board with Maurice's idea of "theme," which was basically this:

This show is a microcosm of modern life. If life and society and friends and family decide that you're nothing but a fat vampire, do you accept the label as the insult (or at least the condescension) it's usually intended to be ... or do you re-claim the term as your own? Do you slump your shoulders, stare morosely at your feet, and say, "Yeah, you're right, I'm a big fat vampire"? Or do you stand up tall and say, "I'M A FAT VAMPIRE; HEAR ME ROAR!"

It was actually Amado who said it that way first, not even bothering to substitute terms. That's what made Amado a baller in Maurice's mind. He could just ask everyone if they were *fat vampires* or *FAT! VAMPIRES!* and everyone somehow understood that "fat vampire" was a metaphor for any societal label that might be used as a weapon against someone or in their favor. Take "production assistant" for instance. Technically speaking, PAs were lowest on the production's totem pole, running here and there whenever anyone needed the coffee that Maurice had already gotten them. So: Were they *lowly, pathetic PAs?* Or were they instead PRODUCTION MOTHER-FUCKING ASSISTANTS! "PA" therefore became a label to be as proud of as "director" on set. Because every one of them was a fat vampire — hear their motherfucking roar.

It wasn't long before the wardrobe people were distributing black shirts with the show logo on the front and *I'm a fat vampire, bitch!* on the back. Delilah thought it was hilarious and wore her shirt half the time. Jerome complained that fat empowerment was a problem, so Delilah asked for three more shirts and began wearing one of them *all* the time. Jerome compensated by calling her "Sweetie" and asking if she needed help understanding obvious things. Delilah compensated back by spilling coffee on him a lot and pretending it was an accident.

Maurice, unwilling to make the same mistake twice, was extremely careful not to let the ego trip of being Big Man On Set become too seductive. That's why he got everyone coffee. It's why, when the crew needed an extra hand putting up any sort of screen or rigging, Maurice helped despite it being a flagrant violation of union rules. It's why he kept hiding the chair Jerome had ordered for him with his name on it, despite well-meaning people constantly pulling it back out in deference to how much he was around. It's why he refused to go by "Mr. Toussant." It's why he bought his own weed and smoked it with anyone, of any station, who'd talk to him.

He needed to touch base regularly with Reginald (and Nikki and Claire, who were still maintaining Reginald's information blackout), so he spent a few hours most days at work. Then, once Reginald buried himself in a job, Maurice would sneak away and run home to make sure the mansion was secure and to check in on Celeste's progress tracking down Ophelia. The bond had remained open after Macht's blood memory became an addict (and that was good), but Celeste now suspected it was because Ophelia was *keeping* it open, and that was bad. Ophelia seemed to have realized that as long as Logan was in charge of the Vampire Nation, she'd have an impregnable fortress around her. She was a prisoner, but a well-protected one. The only way she'd become vulnerable to Celeste's attack would be if she was stupid enough to come out of wherever Logan's work had hidden her — a place that couldn't be triangulated other than by vague feelings Celeste couldn't localize.

After the infusion of Annabel's blood, Celeste could tell only two things about Ophelia. The first was that she was almost for-sure hidden inside Logan's compound: somewhere in Columbus, its exact location fogged and impossible to pin down. The second was that even from within the compound, Ophelia could do her necromancy. She knew this because Ophelia's necromancy had become visible to Celeste when she closed her eyes and focused. It made a line of light ... and that light stretched without diminishment from Ohio all the way to British Columbia.

Where Jerome now worked full-time — not on set, but in *Marty the Vampire*'s offices.

And Maurice was starting to change his mind about Jerome.

Jerome's support of the show had, from the beginning, been on strange and erroneous grounds. That much was clear now. At first Maurice had felt that *any* enthusiasm from Jerome was good because enthusiasm made him do the right things. But those things, it turned out, weren't actually being done and had probably never been done. Before he'd changed his tune, Maurice had been certain Jerome was out in the world drumming up support for the show, giving updates to those who needed them, and gladhanding anyone whose hand demanded gladding so that when the time came for the show to air, it would have a home. The idea that the show might actually air — after Reginald's trial, when it would be safe — was a real thing now. This despite Jerome, not because of him.

And despite Jerome's farce of action and complete lack of actual promotion, the "everyone can be a hero" vibe that had become so popular on set was now leeching into the wider community and across the internet. "Chubby," thanks to the pro-Reginald Chubby Chasers, was increasingly a good thing to be. Self-acceptance was good now, too. A growing number of the show's fans who saw things that way kept demanding: *When will this oh-so-unusual show air? What network will it be on?* Hearing this, Harrison again lamented that they couldn't take the show to Comic Con in San Diego. A panel there would *kill*. Was Maurice sure they couldn't just let Reginald in on the secret and take his story — even pre-trial — to the masses?

At the start, *Marty the Vampire* had only been for Maurice's protection — a way to keep his brain from being fucked-out by Logan's Mentalists. Already, however, it'd taken on its own life.

"It belongs to the masses now," said Harrison.

Fortunately for the Reginald blackout, the show's pride had mostly localized, creating its largest fanbases in niche online quarters known for their obsession with TV. Its obscurity wouldn't last long, though. If the show got too much more acclaim in nerdy areas of the World Wide Web, word of it would reach critical mass and go mainstream. If that happened, it'd spread too fast to keep the news from Reginald.

As things stood, the main thing keeping Reginald ignorant was his disinterest in pretty much everything. He worked, he slept, he ate human food that made him barf all over the place, he spent time with Nikki, he tried to drink blood and mostly failed, and he hung out with the real Claire because her mother was gone constantly and they both needed friends. He didn't care about the news and lived inside an internet bubble that was being carefully curated by Claire's weird tech skills. He had a small social circle, and almost nobody inside it wanted to flatter him by, say, telling him that a shitload of strangers who didn't even know him loved him to death.

"Word's going to get out eventually anyway," Nikki said one time to Maurice. "Can't we just tell him, like Harrison wants? Get it over with?"

But until something broke, Maurice saw no reason to fix it. For now, Reginald's bubble was intact. He'd deal with the fallout of it popping if — and only if — it ever popped. For now, keeping Reginald ignorant continued to make sense. If Reginald found out he had fans, he'd try to interact with them if only to thank them for their fandom. If he found out that his antics were giving people joy (even if it was sometimes shameful joy), he'd do more antics.

But those weren't even the main reasons Maurice didn't

want to tell Reginald the truth. He still had a trial coming up, and the trial — unlike overt action against Maurice or pursuing Thrill — was one thing Logan *could* admit to. There was no vampire law against calling Reginald names and running smear campaigns against anyone who thought he "wasn't that bad." There were no laws against prejudice or bigotry. There was nothing at all to keep Logan from pulling out all the stops on the defamation front, training all his guns on Reginald to make sure pre-trial public opinion was as against him as it could possibly be. Right now, at least some of Logan's attention was still (quietly) on finalizing the Thrillery and (just as quietly) on plans to separate Maurice from his posse and disappear him. But that would change if Reginald made more of a spectacle of himself than he already was — which *would* absolutely happen if Reginald learned he was famous.

And *famous* — at least in a small way — Reginald was.

Even vampires were starting to wonder if Logan's physical standard made sense — something the Vampire Nation hadn't actively questioned for decades. Why *did* vampires have to be muscular and ripped and look like models? Why *did* candidates for turning need to spend so much time preparing ahead of time: training, sculpting, dieting, and even sometimes undergoing plastic surgery in order to perfect the bodies they'd live in forever?

Seeing this, Logan began his campaign of public opinion. He made a lot more progress changing vampire minds *against* "unfit" vampirism again than he should have, though — probably thanks to Ophelia.

Everything Celeste had learned from Amadeus Macht about necromancy told them what they already knew: Necromancy could be directed broadly or narrowly. Broadly, a necromancer could sway opinion the way Logan wanted to sway opinion. Or, focused like a laser, a good necromancer could make individual vampires, werewolves, and other beings do pretty much whatever they wanted. That's how Macht had died, after all: Ophelia's necromancer made him walk into the sun.

If Ophelia's abilities were similar (and Celeste's vision suggested they were), that would explain why so many vampires who came *close* to acknowledging Reginald's worthiness suddenly changed their minds and decided he was too fat again. It became public-opinon Whack-a-Mole: Good vibes coming off the TV show changed a few vampires' minds in Reginald's favor, but then Ophelia's influence changed them back.

Ophelia, if she was indeed behind it, was the stronger force of the two. The way things were going, Reginald would face an extremely unsympathetic audience once he got to trial ... and that trial's delay had almost reached the end of its leash. It was almost here.

Jerome, meanwhile, had become a much bigger problem. He'd gone from helpful to lazy to actively harmful.

He didn't understand that the story was ironic, was the problem. Even the label "Fat Vampire," from the YouTube videos, had been mostly ironic. There were those in the comments who mocked Reginald, of course, but most just found him amusing. As time went on, a majority became positive if a tad condescending: Reginald was "cute," "cuddly," and "like a big ol' bear." Later his fans evolved the whole thing, turning "Fat Vampire" on its head. The phrase came to mean the way the world saw Reginald rather than the way sensible people saw him. It became more a comment on the shallowness of society than a dig against Reginald.

But Jerome didn't understand any of that and never

had. He thought the point of the show was to roll "Marty" around in fried dough and laugh.

He started coming to the set and making jokes nobody laughed at. Everything Harrison and Ella had written with great satire was lost on Jerome. He rooted for the show's bullies and booed the heroes, thinking that was what viewers were meant to do. At one point he walked up to Matt, who played beautiful Isaac, and asked why he was wearing a shirt that said *I'm a fat vampire, bitch!* on the back. After all, *Matt* wasn't fat. *Matt* didn't eat Cinnabon frosting as a food group. *Matt* wasn't funny whenever he bent over.

So Matt explained. Unfortunately, it was the one time Jerome *did* understand the irony — and didn't like it one bit. He banned the shirts on set. He announced at the morning meeting that they all had a job to do here, and hierarchies needed to be respected so work could be done. Anyone seen wearing shirts with the word "bitch" on it would be fired because such language had no place here. He was wearing a shirt that said "Ask me about my faggy brother" at the time.

"I have an idea," said Celeste. She was halfway talking to Maurice again, which he took as a good sign. "Maybe you should kill him."

"I can't kill him. He's the line producer."

"What's that mean?"

"It means he says no to things that cost too much."

"The show is 65 percent under budget," Celeste pointed out.

"Yeah, well."

Then Celeste said, "I'm actually serious. I don't think the world will miss him. Did you know he green-lit four Pauly Shore movies? *FOUR*."

"Four?"

"*Four.*"

"Are you including *Encino Man?* Because I'd call that a Brendan Fraser movie."

"You know what I thought when I got to know Harrison?" Celeste continued. "I thought, 'This man is nothing like what I thought LA guys were like.' He's not a smarmy dickbag. He doesn't strike me as chronically disingenuous. I don't want to throw up when I'm around him. I don't lose hope for humanity whenever I hear his name. If I learned his grandmother was pushed in front of a subway train in exchange for a Shake and Bake coupon, I wouldn't suspect him at all."

"Harrison's a good guy," Maurice agreed.

"Now. Do you know what I thought when you took that Zoom meeting with Jerome?"

"I get it," Maurice said.

But eventually Celeste changed her mind. She hated Jerome, but her research suggested a reason not to kill him beyond his being the line producer. That part was no big deal; another line producer could be hired. Not-at-all-hilariously, the best reason *not* to kill him was exactly the same as the reason he needed to die in the first place.

"If Ophelia's controlling Jerome when you kill him, it turns out his death will echo back through her blood," Celeste explained, consulting her notes. "Killing him will basically make her stronger. Do that a few times with a few other of her puppets and she might even wind up strong enough to control *you*, Maurice."

"I'm inoculated. I've seen necromancy before. A necromancer can't control someone who's seen her tricks."

"I think that logic breaks down if you kill a few people the necromancer is piped into."

"You don't know that," Maurice said.

Celeste tapped her head. "Macht does."

Ah, yes. Amadeus Macht. Creator of Ophelia. Thanks a lot for that, asshole.

"We're still not sure Ophelia is behind him," Maurice pointed out. "Maybe he's just a dick. Maybe he just spreads bad juju and kills joy wherever he finds it for purely non-supernatural reasons. In that case he kind of needs to be hit by a bus. Repeatedly. You know what he said after he took his vacation to Mexico?"

"What?"

"'Too many Mexicans.'"

"How does the cast feel?" Celeste asked.

"They want him burnt alive. Especially Delilah. He keeps asking her to sit on his knee. She's tried a few times to stab him with a fork, but she can't quite make it look like an accident."

"Harrison said he calls the makeup girls 'fluffers.'"

"Don't believe everything Harrison tells you," Maurice told her.

"Oh."

"Except for that. That one's true."

"Oh." It was a different *oh* this time.

"So yeah," Maurice said. "Misogynist. Racist. Classist. He throws donuts at homeless people."

"Well, at least he'd doing a *little bit* of good."

"Not *to* them. *At* them. Hard."

"Oh."

"Fortunately there's not much he can *do*, really, other than say No and puff his chest. I don't even think he has the authority to tell people not to wear the shirts Deborah made for everyone. He's not HR. He's certainly not keeper of the brand. He's pretty much just a salesman. The contract says he's allowed to make suggestions and sign things on the production's behalf. Or sign *for* things. I'm not sure which."

"That's a pretty big difference, Maurice. Signing *for* something is like receiving packages. *Signing* things, on the other hand ..."

And Maurice said, "I'll check the contract.

He returned to Celeste a half hour later. Frowning, he said, "Jerome can sign things."

"What kind of things?"

"*Most* things."

"Tell me it's souvenirs, Maurice," said Celeste with a hint of *you'd-better-not-be-saying-what-I-think-you're-saying* and *I-told-you-so in her voice.* "Tell me he's legally authorized to sign his autograph on collectibles like posters and DVDs and coffee mugs and—"

"Contracts."

"Contracts," Celeste repeated.

"Contracts," Maurice confirmed.

"So. He can cancel the show."

"No, *that* he can't do," Maurice said, proud of at least one thing but deciding it was probably too meager a victory to celebrate. "Our other contract contradicts it. The contract I already have that says only I can cancel the show because I'm providing all the money."

"Can he fire Amado?"

Another point scored. "He can't fire anyone on the cast. Nor most of the crew."

"*Most* of the crew?"

"He can fire the electrician."

"Why the electrician?"

"I don't know. Maybe electricians are special."

This was definitely not the spirit of the real question Celeste was asking. Just when Maurice thought he'd begun clawing his way back toward her good graces, he found a way to slide all the way back to the start.

Celeste launched into a full-fledged conniption. She demanded to know all sorts of unreasonable things like: Why was Maurice signing things he didn't understand? and Why had he given power of unknown scope to a random guy he and Harrison didn't actually need? Maurice's only rebuttal was that things had been happening quickly at the time and contracts were long.

Celeste was further displeased when she realized Maurice hadn't had a lawyer review anything. He'd simply trusted Harrison's barometer and been mollified when Jerome assured him their agreement was "boilerplate." It'd turned out to be boilerplate in the way the medieval tradition of Prima Nocta was boilerplate: possibly standard, but super shitty in practice.

The contract, once duly reviewed, turned out to resemble indentured servitude dressed up with fancy language. The only saving grace was that Jerome probably didn't understand it either. It'd been drafted by his lawyers, but Maurice could fix that: his lawyers probably weren't vampires and could therefore be glamoured into forgetting to inform Jerome of his rights, or to deceive him about the rights he already knew.

That wouldn't stop his mouth, though, and Jerome's mouth was formidable. Maurice had been duped, but he'd been duped by a master. Anyone could fall under the spell of a guy like Jerome. He was one of those people who could talk paint off walls. He could talk ice cubes into not being cold anymore. When loosed in the wild jungle of television network executives, his words could make or break promotion for *Marty the Vampire*. The way he talked about the show could make or break the advertising budget. He could probably convince distribution partners that the show would go nowhere unless the name was changed to *Marty's Sodomy Hour*.

"Maybe this is okay," Harrison said after Maurice brought him the news, a little pissed-off that Harrison hadn't seen this train wreck coming. "The original plan was to shoot the show on spec. We don't need to sell it. I know you want it to air after Reginald's trial is over, but it doesn't have to. We could shoot it, then just keep it in the can. Put it on ice. Or *he* could ice it. What's it matter? You wanted camouflage to keep Logan off your back and you've got that either way."

It was half true. Shooting was scheduled to take two months, and they'd already burned three weeks. Maurice, as keeper of the money, could pay for extra footage and prolong their timeframe by a month or more. But even then, Maurice would be out of this particular spotlight in six months at the most, even if he milked post-shooting spectacle to the max. If the show wasn't picked up by Jerome's network, chances were it wouldn't be picked up by *any* network. A "pass" by one buyer had a way of killing a project in the eyes of other buyers, at least in the short term. And if it wasn't picked up by anyone after Reginald was dead or could know about it — if everyone stopped talking about and clamoring for and being interested in *Marty the Vampire* soon after shooting wrapped — how long would Maurice's popularity endure? Even under extremely generous circumstances, he'd be a nobody again by the end of the year. Logan could abduct him easily then. He'd have bought the world a year without Thrill. No more than that.

But there was a bigger problem, and Maurice had been pretending it didn't exist. Thrill's rollout could be delayed, but Reginald's situation had an expiration date. They couldn't run from it; unlike the back-alley dealings for Thrill, Reginald's situation was legally sanctioned by the Vampire Nation. Trial was unavoidable unless Maurice and everyone he'd ever known wanted to spend the rest of their lives on the run.

Time was running out for Reginald, the show notwithstanding. There was no way around the logjam that this new wrinkle with Jerome was already beginning to cause. Jerome couldn't be outmaneuvered in time to make a difference. He had a big mouth, and if he wanted to ruin the show's chances single-handedly, he probably could. And that was a huge problem because there was more at stake now than ever before: Maurice now felt responsibility not just to Reginald and a world without Thrilloglobin, but also to the show's cast, writers, and crew. *And* to its growing fan base — the potential tens of millions out there who deserved to see someone who looked and acted like themselves being respected for a change. Being a hero.

But what to do? Maurice couldn't kill Jerome without empowering Ophelia. Nobody could kill Logan unless they were smarter than supercomputers and willing to incur the Vampire Nation's wrath.

As long as Logan was alive and Maurice was alive, Thrill remained a ticking bomb. Maybe his idea to kill himself — hence erasing the last copy of the formula — had been the right one all along.

Stupidly, and maybe because of the weed, he confessed this to Amado.

"You can't kill yourself," Amado said.

"Sure I can." It wasn't even tragic. At this point it would be easy. The alternative was assholery and legal entanglements and paperwork and waiting for other shoes to drop.

"You can't do it because of Celeste."

Maurice really shouldn't have told Amado about Celeste.

"She'll survive."

"I don't think she will," Amado told him. "You said you can get at this Macht guy's memory, right? Including what he knows about necromancy?"

Maurice *definitely* shouldn't have told Amado about Macht and necromancy. Damn kid was just so easy to talk to, and Celeste still hated him too much to chat.

"Yeah, we can," Maurice said.

"Well, then won't Logan think maybe he can still get at your memories after you're dead, through her, in the same way you got information out of Macht?"

"It doesn't work that way," said Maurice. "The last copy of Thrill's recipe dies with me."

"Uh-huh. And are you sure *Logan* is convinced that's how it works? Are you sure he won't try with Celeste anyway, just in case, after getting it out of you stops being an option?"

Fuck. That was true, and he hadn't even considered it before now. *Way to go, Amado, for adding to my substantial list of worries.*

"Way I see it, you're screwed pretty much no matter what you do," Amado went on.

"True. Thanks for pointing it out."

"Logan won't stop coming after you as long as he's alive, and you can't kill him."

Maurice nodded. "It would take a genius to even get close to Logan. The security algorithm protecting him is intense."

"So Logan will be a factor forever, for you, Celeste, and anyone tied to you."

"For the foreseeable future," Maurice agreed. *Forever* was a pretty big word when you were immortal.

"On top of that, Reginald's in trouble. He's got that trial coming up and you can't delay it much longer."

"I'm pretty sure I can't delay *any* longer." He'd used up every filibuster he had.

"Except that there *is* help for that," Amado pointed out. "It's already happening. People are excited by the show. They see in *Marty* what we see in *Marty*: a real chance for the underdog. This is the story of the unlikely hero — which pretty much everyone can relate to."

"Ophelia is changing minds back against Reginald as quickly as we can change them for him."

"*Vampire* minds," Amado corrected. "Not *human* minds."

"Humans aren't the ones trying to kill him."

"And besides, that's only true right now. Who out there even *knows* about the show right now? I mean, it's a big deal to you and it's a big deal to me, and it's a big deal to everyone involved in the show itself. It's a big deal to a small group of hardcore nerds, and it's a big deal to another small group in Columbus thanks to your press conference. Compared to the world as a whole, though, that's nothing. Can't be too hard for your necromancer to keep changing *that* amount of minds to the other side. There just aren't that many of them."

"Mmm," said Maurice, not seeing much point in discussing this. Or hope in general.

"But if the show hits? If people love it?"

"You mean if it airs."

"Yeah," Amado said, passing yet another joint — a standard thing they'd fallen into. "If it airs, and if people start talking about it and loving it … Then *man*, you'll be famous forever."

"For the foreseeable future," Maurice said again.

"And Reginald," Amado went on. "People will *love* Reginald. You said vampires already know that 'Marty' is Reginald, but at some point you'll let Reginald in on the secret. At that point you could always announce to everyone that Marty was inspired by Reginald. He'd become an insta-star. Do you really think one little necromancer can undo the amount of love that'd come Reginald's way if *that* happens?"

Maurice puffed. "He'll be dead by then."

"You can't find a way to delay the trial any longer?"

Maurice almost sensed possibility here. He wasn't sure why yet. "I don't … *think* so?"

"Maurice," said Amado, looking right at him.

"Amado," said Maurice.

"I may be one one-hundredth your age."

"Close," said Maurice.

"But I still think I'm smarter than you on this one."

"Asshole," said Maurice.

"You've circled the problem so many times, you've lost sight of all its pieces. Look how you came into this. It wasn't even a TV show to you at the beginning. You signed a contract blind because *it would take you too long to read it.* After a guy fucks up *that bad* — and that's *bad*, dude — like *face-up-the-butt-looking-for-gold* stupid—"

"This is helping a lot," Maurice said. "Really making me feel better. Thanks."

"After you fuck up that bad, you probably feel like you can't ever do anything right again. But you're missing what's right in front of your face. It's so obvious, I can't believe you can't see it."

"What?"

"We just have to *help you*, man," Amado said. "Every one of us just has to climb aboard the Good Ship Maurice and start to row like hell. You aren't in this alone, brother. *Tell* me you haven't been around this set for like a month now, watching the magic. *Tell* me you seriously can't see that this is more than a job to almost everyone here."

Maurice lifted his head, interested now. "How can you help me?"

"Help *all* of us," Amado corrected. "And the answer is: by taking this show all the way to the finish line no matter *what* Jerome does. Then making it a hit — fighting claw and fang, if we have to."

Annabel was sleeping when a knock came at her window.

"Psst."

She blinked awake to see Victor floating outside. At first she thought it was a dream, but then she realized it was real.

She shot upright, clutching her chest to keep her heart from hammering its way through her ribcage. Her internal clock had already started counting the seconds to her death. She eyed potential worthless weapons around the room, including her watch and a pillow. This was probably already over, but hey — might as well go down swinging.

But Victor hadn't moved. He was still just hovering there.

"So are you going to say hello?" he asked.

"CEL—!" Annabel started to yell, but something about Victor's casual gesture as she did stopped her. He simply put one finger in front of his lips, not bothering to move otherwise.

"Are ... Are you *shushing me* right now?" Annabel asked. "Who does that?"

"If you want to yell, yell later," he said. "Hear me out first."

She almost shouted Celeste's name anyway, but Victor's was such a stupid request that she felt compelled to explore it. She wasn't and wouldn't be glamoured; she'd been carefully avoiding his eyes. Glamour was sort of a "fool me once" situation for Annabel.

"Why the hell would you think I'd want to hear anything you have to say?"

"Because I can help save Maurice's friend. Reginald."

Annabel wasn't expecting that. She said, "You're lying."

"Just give me a few minutes to explain. I won't hurt you. You stay there and I'll stay here. All I'm asking is for you to give me a chance."

She said, "You have no power over me."

He rolled his eyes. "Oh. Okay. What is this, a kids' movie? If I *did* have power over you, you simply *announcing* that I didn't wouldn't really change anything, now would it?"

Annabel lowered the weapon she realized she was holding. It wasn't her watch or a pillow, but instead a superior bowling trophy. Apparently Maurice bowled. Who knew?

"You can fly?" she asked, just now finding it noteworthy.

"I can *float*. It's not always on purpose."

"I don't think Maurice can float, and he's two millennia old."

"The vampire gift is different for everyone," Victor snapped. "Floating isn't usually something you grow into. It's something you grow out of, like wetting the bed. So, yeah. Sometimes I float up like six inches. I'm a little sensitive about it, so I'd thank you let it go."

Annabel looked out. Yes, six inches. Her window was on the ground floor.

"I'm not going to look you in the eye, Victor."

"Good for you."

"And I'll yell for Celeste if you try and come through the window."

"I *can't* come through the window. For fuck's sake, Annabel." He sounded like an exasperated husband, which she'd so recently believed him to be. "Do you think I'd go to all the trouble to come here and wait outside your room, in full view of anyone who walked by, just so I could *float* here if I had any choice in the matter? Do you seriously think I have nothing better to do with my time? I almost died trying to grab you in the park. You're just insulting my intelligence by implying this is a choice."

"Well ..." She really shouldn't ask this. It was like when teenagers in horror movies went into scary basements despite a clear mandate not to. "*Why* can't you come through the window?"

"Because you haven't invited me in."

"But this isn't my home."

"No, but it's your *room*."

"In *Celeste's* house. A vampire house, not a human one." Annabel put her hands on her hips as if he was being stubborn or dense. "You aren't seriously telling me that just because someone lets me stay in their house, I get some sort of anti-vampire protection over whatever room they give me."

"It's a squatting thing. You've been in the room for long enough that it's considered yours now. It's treated like common-law marriage. Time makes it real."

"Whose rule is that?"

"I don't fucking *know!* The magic? I planned to take you

out of this same room two weeks ago, but apparently now you've stayed too long and fucked it up!"

"Well ..."

"Anyway, I came here to say—"

"... what if I was in a hotel?"

"*What?*"

"I said, 'What if I was in a hotel?' Do I get protection in a hotel?"

"Depends on the hotel. What kind of hotel are we talking about?"

"I don't know." She thought. "A Days Inn."

"Oh, sure. I could grab you from a Days Inn."

"What about a Ramada?"

"Internal or external hallways?"

"Internal. External is a *motel*. Obviously *anything* goes at a motel."

"Maybe if I did it in the first two days?"

"You're saying vampire magic works like travel points?"

"It's complicated."

"Do I get extra protection and a parking space if I join the Platinum Club?"

"Hey," Victor said. "Do you want to hear this or not?"

Annabel regarded her floating ex, still without making eye contact. There was very little point in him lying. If he could break through the window and grab her, he would have done it by now.

"Okay," she said. "Talk."

"Maurice is trapped between a rock and a hard place. There are no good ways out of this for him anymore."

That much was true, at least.

"Reginald's trial was originally supposed to be simple and fast," Victor continued. "The law says Council was supposed to call him in with a casual invitation, like no big deal. The infraction wasn't big enough for them to just grab Maurice or Reginald off the street. Once they had Reginald at their facility, *that's* when they could move him to testing. So you see, there's no formal 'trial' date. Can't be. It has to start as an invitation that can't be reasonably refused."

"Why?"

"Invitations are a big deal vampire-to-vampire, just like with human-to-vampire invitations to enter a home or room. It's the vampire way of getting around due process. And yes, there's a lot of arbitrary-sounding nuance involved. Do you want to quiz me for twenty minutes about it?"

"Maybe later," Annabel said.

"I learned a lot about Reginald's case while I was staying with Logan. For instance: Logan wanted to hold the trial something like six weeks ago, but then Maurice screwed things up for Logan when he started working with you. Logan had invited him in the way protocol demands, but it was on the same night I sent him to see you for the first time. So Maurice said he was busy; he'd have to reschedule the invite. They asked again the next week and Maurice said he was busy again. It was just dumb luck. Vampire laws — not just magic laws — are kind of stupid. A trial has to be preceded by an interview, and an interview is basically just a heavy-handed meeting. I'm guessing that whenever it ends up happening, *if* it happens, three cronies of Logan's will show up at one of their homes: Charles and two others. Only after that can they formally require Maurice to bring Reginald in."

"That *is* stupid," said Annabel.

"Pretty much all religions have stupid rules like that," Victor said. "Think of vampirism as an anti-religion. In a weird way, most of us are more devout than die-hard Catholics. A *lot* more. That's why so many vampires can't look at crosses. 'Collective mind' is a real thing. If enough of us believe things need to happen a certain way, even if it's an idiotic way, then that's how it has to happen."

"Anyway," said Annabel.

"Anyway, the law's given Logan a way around Maurice's scheming. You told me Maurice mentioned the trial in his first session with you. If you'd been thinking clearly, you'd've noticed that the trial date kept moving. Maurice knew the rules, so he was planning conflicts in advance. The TV show is now the ultimate conflict, effectively occupying his entire schedule for an indefinite period of time."

"Clever."

"It used to be clever," Victor said, "but now it's backfired. Because *Maurice* is chronically unavailable, Logan was able to get legal permission to invite *Reginald* instead. Reginald has no excuse. Because of it, the 'invitation' date — effectively the *trial* date — is finally set in stone. He's got one week left now, no more delays. Knowing Maurice, he'll create a hole in his schedule so he can come with Reginald, now that it's inevitable."

"But the TV show ..."

"Public opinion matters for the trial, and yes, the show's demonstrated that it can influence public opinion. But it's too little too late. The show can't change enough minds in the remaining week to make a difference. Not with Ophelia changing them back. *Nothing's* going to change Reginald's trial date now. Nobody can run away and nobody can stop it. Do you believe me about everything so far?"

Annabel wanted to run through the scenarios, but she and Celeste had done that a billion times. She didn't want to believe Victor, but she did. She nodded.

"If you believe me," he said, "then you also know there's

no scenario where Thrill doesn't come back after this farce is over. After the trial, chances are Maurice's world will shake apart enough that Logan will have no trouble getting him. Even if Maurice *doesn't* go to the trial with Reginald, the Guards will probably grab him in all the confusion. Logan's already built three distilleries, Annabel. He had to let a lot of vampires know about his plan for Thrill in order to make that happen. They don't know where the formula is or even if Logan's telling the truth, but they *do* know he's really breaking the law. Once he has Thrill flowing, that won't matter. He'll have enough money and power that everyone around him will get rich. But if he *doesn't* get the formula soon, the people he made promises to will mutiny. That means *Logan's* between a rock and a hard place, just like Maurice. Sooner or later he's going to get desperate enough to make a move even if it's risky."

"What's your point?" Annabel asked.

"The return of Thrill is inevitable. But Reginald's death isn't."

The smug, I-know-what's-coming-and-I-don't-care expression slid from Annabel's face. She said, "You want to make a deal, don't you?"

Victor nodded. "I scratch your back, you scratch mine. All I need is to make Thrilloglobin before Logan does. *Someone's* going to make it; we just need to be sure it's me. If I can make it first, I'll end up with enough money to buy myself all the support I'll ever need."

Annabel felt cold. "Support for what?"

"To overthrow Logan."

She didn't trust herself to speak.

"Here's what I propose: I'll get the formula from Maurice—"

"It won't work," Annabel interrupted. "Do you

remember the *last* time you tried to 'get the formula from Maurice'?"

"This time it's different. This time, you'll help me."

She laughed. "Go fuck yourself," she said.

"Are you sure?" Victor wore a salesman's smile, knowing she hated him but that his argument could wear her down. "Think about it. *No matter what,* Thrill is going to be made by someone unless you want Maurice to die to keep it from happening. *No matter what,* whether your friends live or die will be decided by the Deacon." He smiled wider. "But if *I'm* the Deacon instead of Logan, I'll pardon Reginald. He can live, if I say so."

"Like you'd keep a promise," she said.

He chuckled. "If you think that, you don't know me *at all,*" he said. "I *never* break promises. You can't do what I do without help, and I can't get help with things this dangerous unless people *know* I always keep my promises."

"Just because you bite my finger again doesn't mean—"

Victor waved it away. "I'm not asking for a blood link. Maurice's defenses are too strong now; I'd never get past them. What I have in mind is something else."

"What?"

"You surrender. You walk outside, and let me take you."

Now Annabel laughed harder. "You're insane."

"I promise not to hurt you. I can frighten your blood without harming you in any way. It's a ruse, see? Maurice only has to *think* you're in danger. If he thinks you're in danger, he'll talk. You're like family to him. He's unreason-able that way, just like a human."

Annabel turned in disgust. But then she stopped, and went nowhere.

She wanted to call Celeste to dispatch Victor, but instead she found herself running through his perverse logic. It was true that their current detente couldn't last forever. It was true that Logan was desperate now, and that his desperation put Maurice in far more peril than before, spotlight or no spotlight. It was true that Reginald would be tried in a week and would be executed because of it — and that Maurice might well be executed along with him. It was true they couldn't run. Couldn't hide. It was true that the return of Thrill now felt inevitable. Technically speaking, it was also true that any Deacon could pardon Reginald, but that Logan never would. If Victor became Deacon, though …

But the show, she told herself. *The show can still sway public opinion. That's what Maurice said Amado told him just last night. They can make everyone love Reginald. If the world loves Reginald and Ophelia's power isn't strong enough to stop them from doing it, he could still win his trial.*

But that was a pipe dream and she damn well knew it. The trial was set in stone now, its date hard and fast. A single week just wasn't enough time to make the show a big enough hit to matter. Amado's enthusiasm was too little too late.

Rock.

Hard place.

Annabel didn't like Victor's idea at all, but a coldly logical part of her saw a sliver of his point. It might actually be the only way to lessen the damage.

But her anger was boiling.

"I'll give you a ten second head start before I call Celeste," she told him.

"This is the only way, Annabel. You know it's the only way."

"Ten."

"Come on. Don't be stubborn!"

"Nine."

"What do you think is going to save him? *Unicorns and sweet fucking dreams?*"

Now Annabel was glaring at him, almost daring him to try his glamour. She said, *"Eight."*

Victor threw her one last angry look, then sprinted for the trees.

It wasn't long after that that Annabel laid back down, unable to stop shaking.

THIRTY-FIVE

QUITTER

The day after Maurice's talk with Amado, he felt a lot better. There was a way out of this after all.

Yes, Logan had issued his deadly invitation to Reginald directly this time. And yes, that meant they had a week left before armageddon. Still, Maurice was unreasonably optimistic. Maybe they'd find a way around it. Maybe Reginald could delay and delay, just like Maurice had delayed and delayed. Maybe it wouldn't matter that Reginald was under a mandate as a brand-new vampire and therefore had to do anything the Council wanted him to do no matter *what* he had on his calendar — no delays allowed. Maybe, somehow, a miracle would happen.

Miracles seemed to be happening already, so why not?

But it wasn't all pink smoke and roses. Jerome, for one, continued to be a problem.

Since the last time Maurice had checked in, Jerome had soured two deals. Under Harrison's direction, *Marty the Vampire* had been creating a lot of buzz in Europe and was beginning a slow rise he hoped would peak at MipCom next May. Unfortunately, amongst all those good vibes,

Jerome had acted like Jerome in a meeting with the Germans, comparing fat camps to concentration camps. A brief PR nightmare followed. To mitigate the damage and avoid protests, the network quietly killed the deal. Just like that, a few million potential eyeballs left the show. And that was only Jerome's first strike.

Soon after, and without prior notice or reason, Jerome cancelled the production's lease on the Home Depot in which all of the sets had been built. It was a costly cancellation, too: In addition to locking the producers out of the building, the plaza's landlord was suing for breach of contract. Maurice solved part of it by paying the lease off in full, but they still weren't allowed to enter and use (or somehow retrieve) the sets until the landlord found it convenient to let them back in — which was also the reason Maurice couldn't find and glamour him. "Maybe next week," the landlord told Harrison on the phone. "I'm on vacation this week." He wasn't, though. He was German, and had heard Jerome's German news, and was basically just being a dick.

Maurice had been pumped up by Amado's enthusiasm, but the truth of things was starting to dawn on him. No matter how enthusiastic everyone was, one week was one week and now they had no sets on which to film — a doubly-bad thing because Harrison had called in favors, inviting press to visit the set in order to get them talking. The remaining locations were all exteriors except for Angela's mansion, and the weather had turned foul. They couldn't even shoot inside the mansion because the main room was all big windows. Storms were coming, and those big windows would make both light and sound impossible to control.

The weather gave them all the finger. Shooting slowed

to a crawl, and what little press they could attract to their now-limited production did little to help *Marty the Vampire*'s image.

"Fuck it," said Harrison, handing Amado a new script while Maurice pouted beside him.

"Fuck what?" Amado asked.

"*It,*" Harrison answered. "I rewrote the confrontation scene so it takes place in a deluge. You're now fighting in the rain. It's going to mean an assload of ADR in post to put your dialogue back in, but it'll be fun to watch."

"For us?" Maurice asked.

"For my friends at the *LA Times.*"

"But we're in Victoria."

"What can I say," Harrison said. "I made it sound really compelling."

Unfortunately, the trip was nixed from the *Times*'s calendar. Jerome had called the news office and told them shooting was rescheduled, which it hadn't actually been. *Can you come yesterday instead of tomorrow? No? Well, that's too bad.* And then when tomorrow came and cameras rolled in a beautiful natural downpour that required no expensive rain machine, the press was absent. Jerome did give the *Times* one choice tidbit, though: He told them he was pushing hard for the show to have a laugh track. And a lot more fat jokes to go with it.

"This is Logan's doing," Maurice told Celeste, meaning Jerome. He'd done a one-eighty. She'd been right all along.

"*Ophelia's* doing," Celeste corrected. "If we can find her, I'll kill her. I *want* to kill her."

That surprised nobody.

"If we kill Ophelia, that's like yanking weeds out by the root," she explained. "If you then want to kill Jerome after she's dead, it won't matter."

"Jerome is just a puppet," said Annabel. "The real threat is Logan."

"*And* Ophelia."

"Yes," Annabel said, "but if you kill *Logan*, it'll be easier to kill *Ophelia*, right?"

"Look who's wearing her killing pants today," Maurice said, looking at Annabel. Her fingers were covered with metallic gold paint. Recently she'd been addressing her boredom by making jewelry, or painting, or maybe painting jewelry — Maurice wasn't sure which it was. His human therapist casually discussing vampire murder wasn't even the weirdest way her claustrophobia had been showing itself recently. She really needed to get outside more.

"I'm just wondering why we've stopped trying to figure out how to get rid of Logan," Annabel said.

"He's protected by hundreds of Guards," Maurice said — something he'd told Annabel several times before. Why was she bringing up the idea of killing Logan again recently? "A secret, unbreakable algorithm determines a different random location for the Vampire Council, and for his house, at regular intervals. That means that in addition to being unreachable, he's also unfindable."

"Victor could find him. He hasn't moved since Victor."

"I'm *sure* he's moved since Victor," Maurice said.

But Annabel barely let him finish, as if she'd been thinking a lot about this. Reading all the vampire trade magazines. Watching vampire CNN.

"*No,* he hasn't," she said. "His Guards all gave Victor free run of the property despite the fact that he shouldn't have been there at all. Logan couldn't tell them he was there for Thrill for obvious reasons. That right there made the Guards raise their eyebrows. It meant that when Logan turned on Victor, Logan had no way to explain why.

Moving the house would make it look like Logan had decided all of a sudden that Victor was a security risk, and that's not something Logan could admit, again because Thrill's a secret. Logan's basically gambling that Victor, working alone, can't break back into the house. The Guards are on duty, but the house is still right where it was."

Everyone was staring at Annabel. That was far too much information for her to have.

"He told me when he was in the bushes at the park," she said looking caught. Then she turned to Celeste. "You were too whacked out to hear him him say it."

Still everyone stared.

"I'm just saying," Annabel went on. "Maybe Victor will kill Logan for us. Maybe he'll convince the Guards to turn on him."

"Why would the Guards turn on Logan?"

"I don't know. Maybe he has something they want."

"Like what?"

"Hey!" Annabel said. "What do you want from me? It was just an idea. I'm just some dumb human! What do I know?"

Maurice thought he knew what was going on. Annabel had talked more than usual about Victor over the past 24 hours. It might be Stockholm Syndrome. Her life as a refugee in the Toussant home wasn't very satisfying, so maybe some ill part of her wished she was back how things were: oblivious but at least nominally happy under Victor's control.

Maurice's mood soured again. Making the TV show popular really had felt like the way to solve all their problems, but disrupting Logan's plans using public opinion required a level of popularity they weren't even *close* to having.

"Well, we can't just *give up*," Alexander told Maurice the next day in Victoria. They weren't on-set because filming had stalled out again, again thanks to Jerome. They'd stopped to chat anyway at the production office, where Maurice had gone to see Harrison and Alexander had stopped by to grab his paycheck.

Maurice forced himself to remember the official version of things before responding. In the official version, the show was in no rush. Amado had concocted a cock-and-bull story about them needing a whole lot of good vibes within the week because Amado knew about Reginald, but for everyone else the deadline was arbitrary: *a lot of good vibes right now just because.* It's not like Alexander or anyone else knew there were real vampires involved.

So Maurice said to Alexander, "We're not giving up. We're just taking a hiatus."

"I meant giving up on *Reginald,*" said Alexander.

Maurice wasn't sure what to say. So he said, *"What?"*

"You're two thousand years old and you still haven't learned persistence?"

"What?"

"It's cool, Maurice. Amado told me."

"No he didn't," Maurice said.

"It's cool. So you're a vampire. You're still the same person inside."

"I'm not a vampire."

"Of course not," said Alexander. "Unrelated, hold this for me."

He handed Maurice a charm bracelet. Maurice took it, no problem.

"Wait. Is that not real silver?" Alexander snatched it back. "Dammit! She told me it was silver! Pretend I did this like Amado did it."

"Did what?"

"*Look,* man!" Alexander told him. "It's cool! I have two friends who are trans."

"Being a vampire isn't like being trans," Maurice said. Apparently he was giving up on denying the vampire part, choosing instead to argue what wasn't remotely relevant.

"Oh yeah? Well, what if you're a *trans vampire?*"

"Well, then," Maurice said. "Then obviously that would be *exactly* like being trans. Because you're *trans.* You really don't see the flaws in your logic? Join the debate team or something."

Alexander laughed and embraced him.

"You know. The debate team in school."

"Relax, Maurice. We're on your side."

"Because you're young. Because all of you are like fucking babies or something."

"Good comeback," Alexander said. "I love you anyway."

"You can't tell anyone I'm a vampire."

"Of course not. I'd never do that."

"So nobody else knows? Just you and Amado?"

"Well, Delilah knows. Obviously *Delilah* knows."

Maurice pulled away and put his face in his hands. He was up to six humans now who knew his secret, counting Nikki and Claire. He was bad at this. Bad at laying low.

"Look," said Alexander, wrapping a companionable arm around him. "You're *Maurice.* Who cares what else you are? Not me. Not me at all."

"I'm not a vampire, Alexander."

"So anyway. I had an idea," Alexander told him. "You know — *if* you're not ready to give up. Because I'm not going to tell you if you're ready to give up. Are you giving up, Maurice?"

"I'm serious. I'm honestly not a vampire. I held your shitty charms."

"Okay. But are you a quitter?"

"I ... what?"

"Get this," said Alexander.

"Get what?"

"Comic Con."

"What *about* Comic Con?"

"Well, you know it's coming up, right?"

"No."

"It's this weekend. Come on, man; how do you not know? Harrison talks about it all the time. He's got a Comic Con boner. Like, it probably has Batman tattooed on it."

"I've heard him talk about it. I just haven't paid much attention. What about it?"

"Amado thinks he can get us in," Alexander said.

"Get us in *where?*"

"To Comic Con! Are all vampires this slow?"

"Oh, I don't know," Maurice said, understanding. "Comics aren't really my thing. Besides, it's not a good time for a road trip. My wife needs me around to—"

"Not to *go!* To *present!*"

"Present what?"

"You know. To be on a panel? To sit at the front of the room and talk about *Marty the Vampire?* Presenting in front of Comic Con would be like setting off a nuke in the publicity department. If we do it right, it'll generate so much sympathy for outcast vampires that your boy Logan will *never* get a consensus. He'll have to postpone, or cancel, or something. Everyone will love Reginald after we do our thing. It'll give us time if nothing else."

Maurice sat upright. That actually sounded true, if unlikely. "Comic Con cares about TV?"

Malcom nodded. "Anything geek culture. Of course the schedule's packed way in advance, but Amado's got an in with Marvel. They still want him for that movie he put off to do this instead. He thinks he can pull a favor. Marvel has a slot they might not use. Maybe we can get it."

Maurice had heard "superheroes" at the start of Amado's tenure with the show, but not "Marvel." Had Amado seriously delayed a *Marvel* movie to do *Marty the Vampire* instead? Maurice didn't know if the truth of it was flattering or stupid — if he should be heartened by the power of this dumb little show or worried by Amado's poor judgment.

"You seriously think we can put together a Comic Con panel about the show on this short of notice? That we can seriously present it this weekend?"

"Amado does. Oh. And get this. The slot is Saturday evening. So you can go. Because you're a vampire."

"I'm not a vampire, Alexander."

And Alexander said, "Sounds like quitter talk to me."

THIRTY-SIX
ENDGAME

Saturday became the nexus date for absolutely everyone.

Amado was able to do as he'd hoped. Marvel had planned to use their bonus slot on Saturday evening for a general Q&A to augment their larger Comic Con sessions, but they apparently wanted Amado for their next movie and so handed it over when he asked.

After that, preparations came easy. Travel was simple if expensive, handled in a jiff for their panel of five: Amado, Alexander, and Delilah as numbers one through three on the show's call sheet, Ella as representative showrunner (the plan needed Harrison elsewhere), and Maurice as the "book's" supposed author. There was no need to organize material. They only needed to sit at the front of the room and have an engaging but unscripted discussion. The editing department rushed together a trailer they'd show during the panel to pique the audience's interest. It focused on how wonderful the main character was: the kind of guy you wouldn't want dying in a vampire trial, for instance.

So the four humans booked their tickets and Maurice

planned to run as usual. They were able to plan without subterfuge because after Harrison learned that Alexander and Delilah also knew Maurice's true identity, he figured he might as well tell Ella. Ella alone had some skepticism about vampires that'd been lacking in the other four. She seemed to be humoring them. This was just one big game to the cast and her partner, but she was willing to play along. There was basically no chance she actually believed he was supernatural. Either way was fine with Maurice at this point.

One big benefit of Comic Con was that the sheer amount of humanity present would keep Logan from attacking. He wouldn't do it publicly — not if he still hoped to get his Thrill train going after Reginald was gone.

If the show and Maurice got their way, though, Reginald would not be dying on schedule.

Maybe the world would even come to love him, and he wouldn't have to die at all.

BUT THE PLAN was not single-pronged, and Maurice's group was only one of its pincers.

Maurice and the humans' goal was creating publicity and good vibes. As such, all they had to do was to go onstage and be engaging. With luck, Comic Con's many attendees would like what they heard, go out, and spread the word. Press was thick at Comic Con, so with even *more* luck, interviews and media coverage would help spread the word even faster.

That was prong number one: to boost the show's image and blow a lot of smoke in Logan's face by doing it. If that part went well, Logan would have to delay the trial or risk Reginald's winning it. But there was also prong number two, and that one was Harrison's responsibility. If Jerome was being controlled by Ophelia — and if Ophelia was, in turn, being ordered around by Logan — Jerome would surely do his best to torpedo the Comic Con panel the way he'd torpedoed Germany.

And that was bad, because Jerome's contractual power meant he could demand a seat on the panel with the rest of them. To prevent that from happening, Harrison was in charge of keeping Jerome busy and distracted until the panel was over — if necessary, to outright hold him down. Maurice didn't want him risking life and limb, so he'd told him to be extremely careful, always choosing passive resistance over confrontation. He should be okay; even under Ophelia's control, Jerome was still just a man — or, more accurately, whatever unimpressive supernatural being he'd have to be for a necromancer to control him in the first place.

The plan was straightforward. Maurice even thought it might work.

Now, they just had to do it.

BUT OF COURSE Celeste had no plans to sit still and stay home while Maurice was away. She'd tried that already. She was tired of trying that. Ever since Annabel had helped rip the Band-Aid off her old memory, Celeste had been obsessed in a way she'd never been obsessed before.

"My idea works *with* them, not *against* them," she told Annabel as if Annabel might object.

Annabel, who was also sick of playing for the B team, nodded. They were both rationalizing and knew it. Maurice and Celeste has mostly patched things up, but a core wound still remained between them.

"He doesn't get to tell me what to do just because he's a man," said Celeste.

"*Never!*" Annabel replied. They'd been making plans of their own, and now that the endgame had come, Celeste kept walking pump-up circuits around the house with Annabel trailing her like a hype squad.

"I know their success at Comic Con is all that matters right now," Celeste told either Annabel or herself, "but this matters too."

"It matters!"

"My hiding inside while Maurice saves Reginald and saves us all from Thrill doesn't help anything. My going out hurts nothing. This is my choice, Annabel. My choice!"

"It's your choice!"

"But don't tell him anyway."

"I won't tell him!" Annabel echoed.

Celeste's idea was simple. It threatened nothing at Comic Con. She didn't so much as plan to leave the city, let alone trek all the way to San Diego. And the plan was this:

Amadeus Macht's blood presence inside her was still strong thanks to Daisy's infusion of Thrill back at the park. Since then, Celeste had trained herself to see the sire bond between Macht (aka, *herself* right now) and Ophelia as if it were a beacon. It wasn't entirely true that Logan's compound, where Ophelia was hiding, was impregnable. It was probably pregnable, once you knew where it was. The problem was finding it ... and that's why Celeste had been watching the bond, listening to her blood, and gathering every bit of information she could that might help her triangulate.

So far it hadn't been enough to narrow down Logan's location, but on the night of Comic Con, all that would change.

Maurice's stunt in San Diego was the last Hail Mary. Because it might actually work, Logan would do his best to stop it. It meant he'd focus Ophelia's necromancy *hard* on San Diego in order to manipulate whatever needed manipulating — Jerome most of all. Focusing *that* strongly would leave a trace Celeste should be able to see. If that was true, she could back-trace the signal now that Macht's blood had shown her what to look for.

That made Celeste the secret *third* prong of the plan. While Maurice was raising the show's profile and Harrison was keeping Jerome from ruining it, Celeste would be back home trying to cut Jerome's influence off at its source. At Ophelia, who was pulling his puppet strings.

Find Ophelia. Kill Ophelia.

That way, everyone won.

BUT ATOP CELESTE'S secret third prong, Annabel had a *doubly*-secret *fourth* prong that nobody knew about except herself.

She was aboard for Celeste's revenge quest. Really she was. But in addition to supporting Celeste for Celeste's sake, the main reason Annabel was supporting Celeste was so she'd leave the mansion on Saturday night. Once Celeste left, Annabel would be home alone.

That way, she could meet with Victor.

Things had spun way too far out of control. No matter how Annabel looked at the situation, it was a clusterfuck — and was getting worse all the time. Far too many innocents had become involved. Once upon a time, this had involved only three people: herself, Maurice, and Victor. If Victor's initial plan had worked, he would have snatched the Thrilloglobin recipe from Maurice's mind that first night, run off, and made his vampire version of crack. That would have been bad; Annabel knew from Maurice that Thrill caused problems. But on the other hand, humans dealt with illicit substances already. Vampires may have gotten by a long time without addictions of their own, but they'd survive even with them. It would be okay.

You're rationalizing again. It wasn't Daisy's voice. This shameful knowing was her own.

But she'd tried to do things the sane way over and over and it hadn't worked.

At this point, the insane choice she'd already made was the least of evils.

MEANWHILE VICTOR, from his home high in the garbage-bag-draped rafters of a freeway overpass, bided his time. He knew when he'd be meeting Annabel, and he knew what he'd do once he had her. He hadn't been lying; keeping his word really was a weasel's stock and trade. So no, he wouldn't harm Annabel. He'd just use her. It was *Maurice* he planned to harm.

He'd also built himself a technicality: He hadn't told Annabel *when* he'd let her go. On that, he'd left no promises. It wouldn't be glamour that held her this time.

First, he'd get the recipe for Thrill.

Then he'd erase its last copy by killing Maurice. He'd only promised to pardon *Reginald*. It was Annabel who kept adding Maurice.

He'd have a monopoly after that, and although he'd keep his batches small at first, the Thrill he made would be more than enough. Very quickly, he'd be able to buy himself some allies. He'd start making deals and buying promises. Promises to Guards who agreed to help him, for instance. To Guards who would, in exchange for payment or drugs, allow Victor to enter Logan's home unseen.

After he dispatched and replaced Logan as Deacon (and freed Reginald; promises were promises), Victor could use the infrastructure Logan had built to expand his operation.

Then he could make all the Thrill he wanted — and rule this city.

LOGAN, who'd mostly forgotten about Victor now that he was gone, said to Ophelia, "Stop them by all means necessary."

"All means necessary" might require a public brawl. Logan still didn't want that to happen, but his priorities had changed. He now cared a lot more about losing control than he cared about the optics of taking Maurice. Focusing Ophelia's talents on San Diego risked exposing his necromancer, but Logan had an exit plan if anything went wrong: If Ophelia was discovered, he'd simply blame her on Maurice. He'd kill her (easy enough considering her restraints, the trance she'd be in, and how long he'd kept her prisoner), then publicly dump the clues connecting her to Maurice's wife. Ophelia was a lot more believable in the Toussants' hands than she was in Logan's anyway — or at least, that's how the Nation full of angry vampires would see it.

Besides, it was probably time to get rid of Ophelia regardless. He'd never liked keeping someone so dangerous as a pet, and in recent years her influence had become less necessary to him anyway. The abduction might go well, yes. He hoped it would. But if things went bad, it would be a case of two birds, one stone.

Ophelia told Logan she'd do as she was told.

Grudgingly. Lethally.

Like an attack dog on a fraying leash.

THIRTY-SEVEN
CONVERGENCE

"Small problem," Ella said. "We're not on the program."

She handed Maurice a conference guide. The slot they'd booked for the *Marty the Vampire* panel still showed as a Marvel Q&A.

"I'll see if I can get it fixed," Harrison said.

Ella shook her head. "No, it's okay. I'll check on it. You have to stay by Jerome. Where is he, anyway?"

Harrison looked back. Then looked again.

"He was just there!"

They both looked back. Into the crowd. Which was absolutely massive.

HARRISON RUSHED into the throng of people.

Jerome had been standing beside a big Spider-Man display just moments ago, but now he was nowhere to be seen. Harrison wondered if he'd been outplayed. He'd been following Jerome for hours, keeping his distance, staying out of sight. Jerome, meanwhile, had been doing Jerome things. These consisted mainly of ogling women in cosplay outfits, hitting on women, and rubbing up against women. It was so gross and ordinary for Jerome that Harrison had let his guard drop. He'd stopped thinking of Jerome as a threat and started thinking of him as just another sleazy executive who regularly traded casting couch blowjobs for acting jobs. Jerome apparently didn't see a problem with that sort of thing. Harrison had overheard him saying it was the way of the world. Everyone did it.

Now, though, Harrison was starting to think Jerome had been playing dumb. He *knew* Harrison was following him. If that was true, maybe Jerome's obviousness was only playing. It might even have been Jerome who'd removed the *Marty* panel from the program. Harrison had followed Jerome yesterday, too, but had lost him briefly in the East wing, which just so happened to be near the program director's office. Everyone knew Jerome in that office. If he'd poked his head in and said, "Marvel wants their slot back; we're not doing the vampire panel," they'd have stricken it right away.

Harrison's phone buzzed. It was Ella: *FOUND HIM YET?*

Harrison was preparing to reply in the negative when he finally saw his quarry. He replied:

JUST DID. HE'S AT THE NETWORK BOOTH.

Ella typed back: *!!!* Which basically meant *OH FUCK.* Asshole was probably up there talking to all the right people in all the wrong ways, trying to fuck up their network deal.

Harrison ran. He arrived at the booth just in time to hear Jerome tell the Black head of programming that *Get Out* was "Pretty good for one of your people's movies."

"*Harrison!*" Jerome said, *faux*-cheery. His voice and mannerisms were drunk but his eyes were steely, as if lit from behind. It was a hybrid look that said *sloth* and *hawk* at the same time. "Harrison, what did *you* think of *Power*? Did you believe Black people in suits, or did that strike you as 'off'?"

"I'm sorry," Harrison told the others in the booth, red-faced. "He doesn't speak for us."

He dragged Jerome away. He needed to find the others. Jerome played stupid very well, but Harrison wouldn't be fooled again. He had Jerome by the arm and wasn't planning to let go. Maybe he should just go nuclear. Tie Jerome up in a back room somewhere. Beat him with a sock full of quarters. That wouldn't let Ophelia and Logan know Maurice was on to them, would it?

His phone buzzed again. He looked down and saw a new message from Jack the Driver, who'd been planning to attend Comic Con anyway and offered his eye.

I'M HERE. WHERE DO YOU WANT TO MEET

Fucking Jack. It really peeved Harrison when people didn't add question marks to their questions.

MAIN LOBBY ENTRANCE, Harrison replied. ELLA IS FIXING THE PROGRAM. NEED TO KEEP JEROME AWAY FROM THE BOOTH SO HE DOESN'T TAKE US OFF THE SCHEDULE AGAIN.

From Jack: OK

Harrison looked up.

Jerome was gone again.

CELESTE STOPPED ON A HIGH RISE, her mind sweeping the city for signs of Ophelia's necromancy beacon. Finding nothing, she looked at her watch. It was three hours earlier in California, and that meant the panel would be starting soon. Maurice had texted Annabel not long ago about a problem at the conference center: the panel moving rooms or moving times or not being advertised correctly. Whatever the problem was, it'd sounded in-hand. And so while Annabel was replying, Celeste had waved, given her a knowing nod, and walked into the darkness outside.

Still on the rise, Celeste closed her eyes. She scented the air, but in truth this wasn't about senses. It was closer to being entirely *without* senses. The new trance felt like hypnosis while standing up.

She had to find the blood tree on which she'd seen Ophelia the first time. She had to walk along its branches.

Come on, Macht. Show me the bond. Ophelia is focusing somewhere down there. Her mind is reaching out, through blood you shared. Reaching all the way to San Diego. That reach is the reason you died. So show it to me. Help me find her.

When Celeste reopened her eyes, she could see a broad blue haze coming from the north. It was the beacon she'd been looking for, visible at last. It wasn't focused. It wasn't crisp. It was just a broad swath, not a laser beam.

She followed it anyway. The night was young, and Celeste was determined.

She'd find the one she sought.

ALL ANNABEL HAD to do was step outside. The grounds of Maurice and Celeste's house weren't protected — only Annabel's room.

Victor zipped into existence seconds later. Annabel looked at him, still avoiding his eyes.

"I have one request," she told him. "Since I've done this for you, the least you can do is grant me one request."

"What?"

"If you lied — if you plan to kill me — I want you to do it quickly."

"I don't want to kill you, Annabel."

She went on as if he hadn't spoken. "I know vampire bites contain a sedative. I remember how it felt, when Celeste bit me. So if you're going to kill me, I want to go that way. I want to just go to sleep and not wake up. We lived together, Victor. I think you owe me at least that much."

He looked almost offended. He said, "I made you a promise."

"Promises are meant to be broken. Just because we made a deal doesn't mean you'll honor it."

He looked in her eyes even though she kept looking away — sincerity, not glamour — and said, "I will honor everything I told you. You live. Logan dies. Reginald is pardoned."

"And Maurice? What happens with Maurice and Celeste?" She suddenly realized Victor had said nothing about either of them.

"I keep my promises," Victor said.

Which, of course, told her nothing at all.

"I told you I won't harm you, and I won't," he continued with the air of changing topics. "But it will take a bit of pain for your blood to call out to Maurice." He pinched her left pinky between his thumb and first two fingers, pulling its skin taut. "Are you ready?"

Annabel nodded. Horrid thoughts were swimming in her mind.

He opened his mouth. His fangs descended.

"Then one. Two. And *three.*"

. . .

MAURICE SUDDENLY SCREAMED. He'd felt a lot of pain in his life, but the bolt he'd just experienced was totally out of the blue. Worse, it wasn't even *his own* pain. Self-pain could be managed, but the pain of others felt profane: the suffering of an innocent.

"Are you okay?" asked the man at the front of the Q&A line. The standing microphone magnified his words: a strange question to ask a Comic Con panelist.

Delilah, three chairs down at the on-stage table, shot Maurice a look. She didn't understand, but seemed willing to roll.

"He's fine," said Delilah. "You were saying?"

"I was asking which vampire lore you used for the show," the man asked. "Is this, like, *Nosferatu* rules, or more like *Vampire Diary* rules?"

It was exactly the kind of nerdy question Ella loved. She leaned toward her mic and began to answer while Alexander leaned toward Maurice, staying low.

"*Are* you okay?" he whisper-asked, eyeing the crowd. It was a good crowd. Ella's work had borne easy fruit. The printed program was all that had turned out wrong; Jerome's interference had neglected the online schedule, which was what almost everyone used. Their session wasn't packed, but it was reasonably full. If they did well with this group, the blog-and-podcast types among them would no doubt rush to their rooms after the panel was over eager to tell their friends. This could work. It really could.

Instead of answering right away, Maurice winced and shook his right hand. The pain there was diminishing, but a shadow of it remained. It was in his pinky finger ... and as he'd felt the pain, he'd smelled human blood.

Oh. Oh no.

"I think Annabel is in trouble," Maurice whisper-replied.

"Who?" Delilah asked, overhearing.

"My psychiatrist," Maurice whispered to both of them.

"Oooh, I *love* my psychiatrist!" Delilah said a bit too loudly. The mic picked her up. The audience, confused, frowning to one another.

"I have to help her," Maurice said.

"I'd *totally* help if my psychiatrist was in trouble," Delilah said, keeping her voice lower this time. Apparently none of this was weird to her. It must be an LA thing. Maybe it could even inspire a show: *Psychiatrists in Danger*. The whole Valley would watch it.

"Go, then," said Amado, now leaning into the huddle. "We got you, Maurice. Anyone asks, you went to the bathroom."

A woman to one side had had enough of their chatter. "*Shh!*" she hissed as Maurice rose from his stool and exited stage right.

"WAIT," said Ophelia. Logan knew the trance, so he waited patiently. She was probably looking through a hundred pairs of eyes right now, doing her cognitive best to zero in on something that'd happened in front of just one of them.

Her eyes opened. They were so brown, they almost looked black.

"What?" Logan said. "You opened your eyes. Get back out there!"

"I'm not sure you care about the Comic Con crowd anymore," Ophelia told him.

"Why?"

"Because according to one of the vampires I'm seeing through out there," she said. "Maurice just left."

BECAUSE ACCORDING *to one of the vampires I'm seeing through out there,* said Ophelia's voice, *Maurice just left.*

Celeste's concentration broke. The broad beam of blue light washing over most of north Columbus had blinked out a few seconds ago, but even if it returned now she wouldn't be able to see it.

Maurice had left Comic Con? Why? What would make him do that?

Celeste closed her eyes, looking inward. Forgetting about finding Ophelia for the moment, she sought her blood bond with Maurice instead.

At first she saw nothing, but then she saw Daisy's blood atop Maurice's. The bond, so far as she could tell, was doubled. But why?

Then she understood.

Beneath Daisy, she saw Annabel. And Annabel was in trouble.

MAURICE WAS PLANNING to run as fast as he could toward Annabel, but he never made it out of the convention center. He was stopped at the door, surrounded by humans. Jerome had him by the wrist.

"Where do you think you're going, you little bastard?" Jerome hissed. His voice wasn't its usual idiotic, happy-go-lucky timbre. This was what Business Jerome must sound like. Maurice had underestimated him. Jerome could be cunning after all. He wasn't so harmless, in the end.

"Let go of me," Maurice said.

"Why? You have somewhere more important to be?"

Maurice whipped his hand free, but Jerome grabbed it again. He would have to leave this place at human speed and only accelerate once alone. Jerome's delay atop it was the tick of deadly seconds.

"This job isn't just about being a diva," Jerome told him. "You have work to do in the panel room. I made room for you. I put myself on the line."

"It isn't your goddamn show!" Maurice growled.

"It became mine when you brought me into it. You remember our agreement. It's your asset, but it's my tool. I swung my bat for you because I needed something to attach my reputation to. Remember that?"

"I said, *let me go.*" Annabel's wail had become a fever pitch. It would take Maurice fifteen minutes to reach her from here, but he couldn't even start until he was free of Jerome and away from all these prying eyes.

Already people nearby were eyeing their struggle. Their argument.

"You agreed to be here," Jerome went on. "You're the face of this thing, second only to Amado. Everyone seems to love you." He gritted his teeth. *"You're not running out on me now."*

"Let me go," Maurice said evenly, "or I'll break your arm."

"Really," Jerome said, smiling at Maurice's thin limbs. He looked like a shrimp. It wasn't always easy to believe how strong he could be.

Maurice nearly broke Jerome's arm and moved on, but people were still staring.

Jerome dragged him away from the doors and toward the center of the room. The place was mobbed: wall-to-wall bodies pressing in and stealing all the oxygen. But what could Maurice do? Any chance he'd had to leave unseen was gone. He could get away from Jerome easily ... but not without everyone seeing him for what he really was.

"*LADIES AND GENTLEMEN!*" Jerome bellowed once they reached the mob's middle. "I just talked Maurice Toussant, creator of *Marty the Vampire*, into doing an *impromptu, middle-of-the-crowed Q&A!*"

People cheered in a knowing way, and that was a good thing because it meant word was spreading: The world knew the show. The smokescreen he'd hoped for was growing ... but still he was trapped; he couldn't reach Annabel now.

And that wasn't the only thing now striking Maurice as wrong.

Some of the eyes turning toward him were *vampire* eyes.

They'd been watching him.

Waiting.

Like sentinels.

ANNABEL HAD SPENT a lot of time thinking about Alicia over the past two weeks. Not Maurice. Not Celeste. Not Thrill or Daisy or the vampires of the world. She'd thought about all of those things and more, of course, but recently her present-day concerns had fallen into the background. Her old friend Alicia had come to the fore again to replace them. It'd taken Annabel a long time to understand why.

Alicia had always been a good friend to her. They'd bonded over just about everything, sharing life's pains so that those pains, though twice as frequent, were half as intense. It was a system the two women had always had, ever since the problems with Alicia's mother. They were like sisters, and always had been.

When Annabel first came out of her glamour fog, she'd been lucky to remember her own name. She'd cracked Victor over the head with the award on what now felt like faith. She'd only vaguely understood what she was doing at the time, or why. Mostly she'd had to trust her instincts, the way she'd had to trust the return of her memories since.

But not all of her memories had returned quickly. She kept finding little bits of glamour in her mind. Little pieces of forgetfulness and neglect that'd been left behind.

Like her connection to Alicia. Her questions *about* Alicia.

It wasn't easy to notice the absence of a thing. Annabel had learned that much when she'd come partway out of Victor's glamour, gasping at real life like fresh air from the surface. At first it hadn't occurred to her that her normal routine was gone. She hadn't remembered that she wasn't married. And she hadn't remembered Alicia at first. Those memories, from the past, had returned slowly.

Like the memory of Alicia coming to her house to check on her, then being glamoured so she would return no more.

It took Annabel some time to remember that she, Annabel, had never followed up after her glamour was gone. Moving in with Maurice and Celeste — especially under duress — had kept her mind full. Only in recent days — now six or seven weeks from Victor — had that particular open loop returned. How could she reach Alicia and undo her glamour the way Annabel had undone her own? Or an even larger question: What had become of her? Victor had only told Alicia to go home. To sit and do nothing. So what'd come next? What was happening *now* with Annabel's best friend?

So Annabel called her. There was no answer.

She texted. No answer. Emailed. No answer. She couldn't bring herself to leave the house again after what'd happened the first time, so eventually she'd gone draconian and sent Alicia a letter. Again there'd been no answer.

Finally, unsure what else to do, Annabel had done an internet search for Alicia's name. That's how she'd learned the county coroner believed her to be a mentally-ill shut-in who'd forgotten how to take care of herself. A neighbor had found Alicia dead in her kitchen, fatally dehydrated. Victor's twisting of her mind had caused her to go home, sit down in a chair ... and then do nothing else. Nothing at all.

Three days later, having eaten nothing and drunk nothing, Alicia simply fell out of her chair and died. She'd had three children, all away at camp. Fortunately the neighbor's grim finding came before they returned home.

All because Victor wanted to be rich and powerful. All because motherfucking *Puffed Wheat* had seen fit to steal a month of Annabel's life ... and, consequently, all of Alicia's.

It had all come together for Annabel three nights ago: the night after Victor first visited her window with a deal, and the night before Annabel decided, finally, to take him up on his offer.

Now, while Victor watched the distance and waited for Maurice's arrival, Annabel wrapped her fingers around the dangling charms of a gold bracelet that long, long ago her best friend had given her.

She'd left her phone behind and walked outside to rendezvous with Victor, yes.

But not on his terms.

On hers.

.   .   .

"WHAT'S HE DOING NOW?" Logan demanded. "What's going on? Do people like the show? Are people reporting on it? Am I fucked?"

Ophelia, listening to Logan but ignoring him, breathed slowly. She'd suffered him for hundreds of years in partnership because they'd struck a deal. She'd then suffered hundreds more in servitude after it dawned on Logan that staying with him was her only option. After he became Deacon and grew paranoid, even servitude had soured. Logan started locking her door. Putting her in chains whenever he felt she couldn't be trusted. Weapons cut both ways, and Logan was no fool. So for decades now he'd done everything he could to protect himself from his best asset, even if it meant making her a slave.

"Jerome has Maurice in the middle of a crowd, answering questions," she answered. "He seems to want to leave, but for some reason he's not going."

"*Leave?*" Logan asked. "To go where?"

"I don't know. My sight is diffuse. I don't have eyes everywhere."

"Well, do people like the show? Their stupid fucking fat show?"

Ophelia took a breath. She wanted to dismember Logan, but that wasn't new. It's how she usually felt.

"I still have eyes in the room. People seem to be enjoying the panel. There's a lot of laughing and smiling."

"Make the vampires you're seeing through look around for mobile phones," Logan told her. "See if people are posting updates."

"Of course," Ophelia said. "Would you like me to wipe your ass for you, too?"

He glared, but her attitude wasn't new either. Logan knew he held the upper hand. He always had the upper hand.

"You're wasting time," Ophelia told him. "Jerome has Maurice Toussant by the wrist like a naughty child. He's not even running away because he's afraid of how it'll look. Do I have to draw you a picture?"

"What's your point?" Logan asked.

"We should unleash them and attack," she said. "He's vulnerable now. You'll never get a better chance."

THIRTY-EIGHT
ALL HELL

Harrison's cell phone rang. As if he didn't have enough to keep track of. He'd already lost Jerome, and he couldn't shake a feeling that Jerome was up to absolutely no good whatsoever.

He looked at the phone's face. It was some random Ohio number. 614. He ignored it.

Then it rang again.

And again.

He slammed the phone to his face, so frustrated he'd become livid.

"What?" he demanded.

"Where's Jerome?" the female caller demanded.

"What?"

"Stop saying what! Where's Jerome!"

Harrison thought he might recognize the voice, but not at all its tone. "Is this ... *Celeste?*"

"Where's Jerome, Harrison?"

"I don't know. Around. What's this number you're calling from?"

"A phone," she said. "I stole it. Then I called directory

assistance and got your office number, then got your answering service." She was talking faster, faster, and faster. "When they wouldn't give me your number I told them to transfer me to you, and when they wouldn't do *that* either I ran all the fucking way home and got your number off the fridge *so will you stop wasting even more goddamn time and tell me where Jerome is!*"

"Okay, okay," Harrison stammered. "I ... um ..." He cleared his throat. "I sort of lost him."

"You *LOST HIM?*"

"Relax! I'm sure I can find him!"

"Let me talk to Maurice!"

"Why do you want to talk to Maurice?" He affected calm, knowing it was stupid. "Maurice is answering some questions. He's working the crowd. He's—"

"Harrison!"

"Yes?"

"Something's happening with Annabel. It has to be Logan."

Harrison dropped the act, snapping to serious. "Are you sure?"

"No. I'm not *sure* at all." She'd sounded angry before; now she sounded closer to breaking down — lost all of a sudden. "I felt her. I felt Daisy's blood." The name "Daisy" meant nothing to Harrison; she seemed to know it and scrambled on. "Annabel needs me. Me or Maurice. But I lost her. The line I had on her just ... it just *vanished*. I can't feel her anymore, Harrison. She needs me and I can't find her. Just like you can't find ... *fucking Jerome!*"

Harrison heard an audible attempt to pull herself together. Then Celeste went on.

"I think Logan has her. I know she's not dead, but there's no reason a blood cry should just ... *cut off* like that.

She can't have suddenly just ... *stopped being afraid.* It has to mean her blood ties are being blocked. Only a necromancer could do that. So Logan must have her. Logan and Ophelia."

"Okay," Harrison said, standing up straight for no one to see. "What can I do? What do you need?"

"Find Jerome," she said. "Once you find him, tell him something that will really piss him off. Something Logan would *hate* to hear."

"What, though?" Harrison asked.

"Come up with a big lie about the show and its success. Something that looks astronomically good in our favor and astronomically bad for Logan. Something that will make him want to kill the world."

Harrison felt cold just thinking about it. "Are you serious? You *want* Logan that pissed off?"

"Yes." She sounded out of breath. "Because if he's angry — if he thinks he's lost and has no other options but to lash out — he'll have Ophelia do something drastic. Something bad enough and chaotic enough that the humans and vampires here won't even be able to *think* about some dumb TV show. They'll be too busy being horrified. Too busy fearing for their lives."

"But Celeste. There are *tens of thousands* of people in this building. Maybe *hundreds* of thousands. If we make Ophelia do something extreme ..."

"It'll never get that far," Celeste said. "The second Ophelia tries to do anything, it'll strengthen her beacon. When that happens, I'll find her. Find her and kill her. Once she's dead, there's no more threat."

Harrison was still unsure about the idea of provoking mass chaos, and clearly Celeste knew it.

"Listen to me, Harrison," she said, forcing her voice to

calm. "The only reason for Logan to take Annabel is to try and use her tie to Daisy to break into Maurice. If Logan breaks into Maurice, it's all over. This is the only way to stop him. The only option. Do you understand?"

"Yes," he said. Then, more strongly: "Yes, of course."

"You have to hurry, Harrison. *Hurry!*"

THIRTY SECONDS LATER, Harrison was running into bathrooms, across concourses, into offices, up and down stairs. He wished he had one of those magic beacons the vampires seemed to have. It'd make finding people a whole lot easier.

He wasn't as young as he used to be, unused to running. He ran anyway.

Finally, desperate, he shoved himself through the gap stage-left from the *Marty the Vampire* panel. Ella, Delilah, Amado, and Alexander were still holding court at the time, the crowd laughing hysterically.

Then the crowd stopped, staring at Harrison's sudden onstage appearance.

Amado whipped around in his seat, saw Harrison, and decided to improvise. He gestured and said, "Executive Producer Harrison Cardiff, everybody!"

The crowd applauded, but Amado's face, seeing the look on Harrison's, fell away.

"What is it?" he said away from the microphone.

"Have you seen Jerome?"

"No. Why?"

The crowd, seeing this, started to murmur.

"Why do you need Jerome, Harrison?" Delilah asked.

She had a small purse on her crossed legs. A moment ago, she'd looked ready for a delightfully cute magazine photoshoot. Now, though, she looked ready to grab a sword and start lopping heads. Harrison thought he knew why. Amado and Alexander were enamored of Maurice's vampire stories, but those same stories made Delilah furious. While the boys were saying "cool," Delilah was seeing the bullies behind the *cools* and asking "how dare they?" Either she'd been bullied as a kid or had simply been born a defender. All it'd taken, to sharpen her, was the look on Harrison's face.

Jerome. Delilah, more than any of them, hated Jerome with a passion.

"*Harrison* ..." she said when he didn't answer. It was a warning tone. A get-out-of-my-way tone.

"Ophelia has Maurice's psychiatrist," Harrison blurted.

"*HIS PSYCHIATRIST?*" Delilah spoke-bellowed. "*That's* the trouble she's in? With fucking *Ophelia?*"

She was far too loud for the audience not to hear. Harrison's eyes darted, trying to balance his need for urgency with his need for discretion. But it was too late. Delilah was standing already, grabbing her purse, stalking off like rolling up sleeves for a beatdown.

The crowd began to murmur at this turn of events. Amado put on his PR smile and was about to try and explain it all away when a terrified yell came from the lobby.

"*VAMPIIIIIRES!*"

There was a beat. Then all Hell broke loose.

AMADO HAD SEEN many strange things in his seven years as an actor. As a rule, acting put a person into more contact with weirdness than the average person saw in a lifetime. He'd watched giant aliens cross a room while he hid inside a shipping crate. He'd watched angels take flight. He'd seen more RPGs explode than anyone in a war zone. Special effects could make the impossible possible, both post-production and pre.

But he'd never seen anything like this.

The main hall of the convention center was crawling with creatures. They were scaling the walls like Spider-Man. They were rounding people into groups. People, then, were running hither and yon, screaming in all directions.

Amado rooted his feet and watched two of the so-called vampires pass. They had big, sharp teeth. They were very fast. But in contrast to all the stories Maurice had told, they weren't feeding on the conference attendees and they didn't seem to have killed anyone. *Why not?* The big room looked more like a show than anything truly dangerous.

Delilah, who'd always been sweet, was in the middle of this sitting atop Jerome's chest, beating him with both fists while Maurice stood by with his eyes wide.

"You're still here," Amado said, coming up alongside Maurice.

"I think I have to be here."

"Harrison said someone has your friend. Doesn't that usually make you want to ..." He made little flapping motions with his finger: Maurice flying off to settle a score.

"It should. I heard her scream. But then the scream was just ... gone."

"Gone?"

"Gone."

"Maybe she's okay, then."

Maurice slowly shook his head. "She's not okay."

They looked around the chaotic room from their strangely-undisturbed oasis in its center. Jerome, it turned out, was handled. He'd gotten up and run from Delilah, but

Alexander had grabbed him around the feet and he'd fallen on his face. Alexander's hold had caused his pants to slide down. Now his ass was out.

Harrison was nowhere to be seen at first, but then Amado spied him: Across the room, laying low while a group of vampires prowled. He was staring at Jerome as if he very, *very* badly needed to reach him. Hadn't he said something onstage about needing to find Jerome?

"Look," Amado said. "I don't mean to tell you your business, but shouldn't you ..." Now he gestured around the room.

Maurice took a moment, then said, "Maybe."

"What do you mean, 'Maybe'? There's friggin vampires all over the place!"

Maurice was watching it all. Then he said, "Something's wrong."

"Hell yeah something's wrong!"

Alexander shouted. Jerome had gotten free again. Harrison was with them now, saying something to Delilah and Alexander about instructions Celeste had given for using Jerome to track down Ophelia. Amado didn't hear it all, but he did notice that Jerome was trying to get away. So as he rose, Amado punched him in the kidney.

"Take our shirts! Tell us what to do!" Delilah was screaming, raining punches on Jerome's chest once he hit the floor again. *"I'M A FAT VAMPIRE, BITCH!"*

Jerome wiggled enough to partially unseat her, so Amado sat on his head.

It was all downhill from there.

BUT FOR MAURICE, things had gone still. He'd heard what Harrison said. What Celeste seemed to think. He didn't like the way Annabel had stopped screaming either, but he couldn't square Harrison's report with what he was seeing here — and even more, he couldn't square *what he was seeing here* with logic. Not at all.

The things climbing the walls and rounding people into groups were real vampires; Maurice knew that much. He could feel their coldness as they passed, and he smelled no human blood on them. Strangely, though, they weren't actually attacking. Everything Maurice saw around him was a parody of a melee, not the melee itself. It was someone's attempt to create the *feeling* of a vampire attack without relinquishing the ability to deny it all later — to say there'd been no such thing, and it was all just special effects.

Real vampires that weren't attacking. Out of their minds as if controlled — orchestrated *en masse* — by something. Or someone.

Ophelia. She was controlling them: a lot of supernatural minds influenced only a little. Which meant she couldn't be influencing *ONE* mind a lot.

The fact that Ophelia had made the vampires revolt proved Jerome wasn't her puppet. He never had been. And that meant that the cast of *Marty the Vampire* attacking Jerome wouldn't do what Celeste wanted. It wouldn't light a path back to Ophelia, so she could follow that light to Logan and Annabel.

Ophelia was putting on a show here, nothing more.

It wasn't an attack.

It was a distraction.

OPHELIA HAD PULLED up the live video feed in advance, then shown it to Logan. A few bloggers were streaming Comic Con despite clear prohibitions against it

— something Ophelia had made herself sure of before suggesting any of this. As usual, Logan thought the plan was his idea. It wasn't. It was *her* plan. And here he was, falling for every bit of it.

"*Good*," Logan said now, watching humans scatter and vampires climb walls. "*Very* good."

The asshole sounded hungry. Or horny. He was seeing exactly what he wanted to see, same as always. He hadn't noticed that none of the vampires were doing anything particularly vampirish other than climbing walls — something that would surely be explained-away later as clever wire work. Right now Logan thought he was witnessing the return of his precious *terrifying vampire order* and putting the human population in its place after so much time spent ogling Reginald Baskin's imperfect form. He was incorrect. Tomorrow, chances were excellent that the media would look back and see all of this as nothing more than a publicity stunt. Chances were excellent that after tomorrow, the world wouldn't be cowering and afraid. Instead, they'd love *Marty the Vampire* more than ever.

Ophelia had led Logan like the dog he believed her to be. She'd told him they should attack the convention center, so that's what his brain was showing him. He couldn't see that nobody was hurt. That nobody, once the smoke cleared, would even be frightened. *Those weren't real vampires. There's no such thing as real vampires,* the humans would say later. *What we thought were vampires were actually acrobats and actors, hired by the Con's favorite new drama.*

Ophelia held the bubble in mind for a few more seconds, then let it drop. Immediately the vampires climbing the walls came back down. Then, together with the others on the main floor, they walked out into the darkness.

"What's happening?" Logan asked, watching the feed. "What's going o—?"

He stopped when a shard of silver entered his voicebox. It was one of Ophelia's fingernails. He kept his slave close and guarded her, but he also gave her access to the home's treasures: a morsel of luxury he seemed to think might impress her. And while the vampires here didn't use the old mansion's silverware, Ophelia had. It'd taken months to flatten the shard so completely without touching it. A long time to fashion herself a protective under-nail to separate her body from the silver itself. She'd painted it red like the rest of her nails.

Now it'd stopped Logan's ever-babbling mouth, his body unable to heal around it.

"Remember that I spared you," she whispered as he sagged, weak, to the ground. He stared up at her with disbelieving eyes as she snapped the nail away from the under-nail, leaving him impaled. The silver shard was too deep to remove without a knife. "Remember that I could have taken your Deaconship but didn't want it. You're *my* dog now, Logan ... and if you make a single move to find me, I'll tell the world what you used me for. Then we'll both burn. You. And me. Together."

She used Logan's key to exit the room. Then, instead of dropping her necromancer's influence entirely, she turned it from San Diego to the mansion for a handful of seconds.

She didn't need much time — just long enough to make every Guard look away, uncaring, while she exited.

. . .

CELESTE ARRIVED where the blue signal seemed to terminate. Harrison must have done what she'd asked, because soon after speaking to him the beacon had reappeared between Ophelia and the necromancy she was doing in San Diego. Celeste had used her Macht-sense to back-trace it to its origin.

She found herself at the front gate of a house she now knew to be Logan's current residence just as the signal died again.

She waited, unsure how to proceed. She'd wanted to surprise Ophelia in her necromancy trance, but it seemed the necromancy had ended. She had her bandolier of stakes, but she also had Annabel's old crossbow.

She was just about to leap the gate when her vampire eyes picked out the form of a woman emerging through the large front door.

She knew right away that the woman was Ophelia. Ophelia looked over at Celeste and then, as if unsurprised, smiled and waved ... and then was gone into the night.

Instead of trying to follow, Celeste rushed toward the house to find Annabel. Before reaching it, though, she stopped as she felt something new coming from her surrogate daughter.

It wasn't fear she felt from Annabel this time.

It was laughter instead.

THIRTY-NINE

BRIMSTONE

No one was coming. Annabel understood that now.

With Daisy more present than ever in her veins, she felt like a thing that was half human, half vampire. What Celeste had done, by drinking not just Daisy's blood memory but also Annabel's own, had solidified the bond between them. Before, she'd been linked to Maurice and Celeste only weakly. Now, even though Annabel was human, their blood tie had become iron. Annabel wasn't special; that's not how it was possible. It was *Daisy* who'd been special. Daisy, who Celeste painted as a girl always full of life — always wanting more, and more, and more.

It seemed that need for *more* had survived her death. Daisy, even as a memory, was a ravenous presence.

You see it, don't you? Daisy's voice asked Annabel now. *You see why Maurice won't come. Why Celeste won't come. They only hear the scream of your blood you when you are weak, when you need their help. But you are no longer weak, are you, Annabel? You don't need them anymore.*

It was untrue. She needed them as family. She needed them as friends. But she needed nobody for this.

Victor had taken her to an old warehouse with small broken windows far above. The building would leak sunlight during the day, but at night it was the perfect hideout. It was quiet. Likely far from the town center; she didn't know for sure because he'd carried her at speeds too fast for her mind to clock. It was just Annabel and Victor. Victor and Annabel. The old married couple, just like in the good old days. The days after Alicia had decided on Victor's suggestion that she didn't need water anymore. The days in which Victor had held Annabel captive and Annabel had gone to work for only one client: Maurice, on whose mind she'd been ordered to spy — to forge a key of blood, while Annabel's oldest friend lay rotting in her kitchen.

Victor had tied one of her legs to a pipe. Annabel didn't know if his binding her was insulting or flattering. He'd never been afraid of her — or about her in any way — before now.

He'd bled her finger, then brought her here. Maurice was supposed to hear her cry of pain and come running all the way from San Diego. What Victor hadn't anticipated was that Annabel might *stop* crying out after his initial bite. He hadn't anticipated her not being afraid anymore ... maybe because she'd *never* been afraid. Maybe now she was too angry to be afraid. Victor couldn't hurt her anymore.

The fact that he'd tied her? Maybe it meant he thought she'd run, which was crazy. Or maybe it was something else that'd done it; maybe something had spooked him tonight. Annabel had winced for only a second over her finger, and after that her gaze had gone hard. She'd dared to stare him in the eye, glamour be damned. She knew he wouldn't try. Wouldn't think he had to bother. Meanwhile Annabel met his eye, her head full of steel, thinking about all this man had taken from her. All he'd done for power and fame.

Maybe that's why he, not she, was the spooked one tonight. Annabel was just a human, but she was also his shadow. And now that the shadow had found its power, Victor couldn't stand to face it.

"He should be here by now," Victor said.

He'd been pacing for twenty minutes. They'd been inside the building for forty or more. She had no idea what was happening wherever Maurice found himself, and she had to assume Celeste was still out on Ophelia patrol. They'd probably both heard her first scream, but it was Annabel — not fate, or magic, or vampire law — that had silenced that scream. She didn't want to be interrupted. This was her time. Her place.

"Maybe he's not coming," Annabel said. "Maybe he doesn't want to give you the formula. Maybe he's seen the forest for the trees: Protect Thrill, not little old me."

Victor said nothing. He paced a bit longer, then said, "Shut up."

But she could tell: Victor was worried. This was the only plan he had. The only plan he *could* have. He was doing what evil people always did: counting on the good-heartedness of others to ensnare themselves. If he was wrong, though, what then? He'd made an enemy of Logan ... and if Maurice wasn't coming, maybe it was because Maurice had gone to Logan as well. For all Victor knew, Maurice knew all about the deal he and Annabel had made. Maybe this was even a setup. Maybe Logan would come at him hard now, for daring to plot an overthrow. An attempt on Logan's life.

Annabel looked inward. Recently, the trick of blood came easier and easier.

Inside herself, she saw Celeste. Celeste was worried about her. Looking for her. But then Annabel thought, *I'm just fine. Just hanging out, Mom.* And then she laughed, and it was like Celeste's blood tie lifted its head. Had Celeste heard her laugh, the way she'd hear her scream? She was new to this. She had no idea.

"Untie me," she told Victor.

"Shut your mouth."

"Untie me. I can't run. I can't fight you. I'm just a little girl, at your mercy."

He looked at her. Looked away.

"Victor."

With hesitation, he looked again.

"What story did you tell me, about our honeymoon?"

"What?"

"You glamoured me into thinking we were married. The night I met Maurice, I remember thinking you were home watching football. You don't like football. So I got to thinking: Maybe *I* invented the football thing. Maybe you didn't tell me anything. So tell me something. If that's true, are you the creator of my reality? Or am I?"

Victor looked at her. Paced. Looked out the window. He was holding a shotgun. A plain old human-killing shotgun. His idea was simple: aim it at Annabel when Maurice came, daring him to see if he could outrun buckshot. Maurice would have a simple choice: do as Victor said and reveal the Thrill formula, or try his luck at single-shot roulette. It was a good plan, but right now he didn't look very confident of it all.

"I said shut up."

"I think we went to Hawaii," Annabel said.

"What?"

"I think we went to Hawaii on our honeymoon. I don't think you told me otherwise, so that's what I choose to believe. That makes it real, Victor. So you see? I'm a necro-mancer, too."

He walked purposefully over. She had a gag around her neck that she'd persuaded him to remove a while ago, but he kept threatening to return it. That's what he was going to do now, to stop her yammering mouth.

But before he could grab the gag, she grabbed his wrist. It was ice cold. She stared into his eyes.

"What did we drink on the beach? Was it margaritas? Was it mai tais?"

He shook her free, but she grabbed him again. This time it was more hand to hand, less hand-on-wrist. Sensual. Like a lover's touch.

"You didn't take advantage," she said, "did you?"

"Let go of my goddamn—!"

"It's okay," she said. "I'm not shy."

With this she gripped his hand very hard, then used her other hand to slide her gold charm bracelet from her wrist to his.

Victor staggered. It looked like he couldn't breathe. He swatted at Annabel as she released him, but he could barely touch her. She pulled the shotgun from his hand as sweet as picking a daisy.

"Key," she said, aiming the gun at his head.

He sucked air. Made faces. Tried to grab her and failed.

"*KEY.*" She poked him with the weapon. "I know you can heal, but I'll still bet having your head blown off hurts like hell."

Victor flapped useless hands at his pocket, eyes bulging chest hitching. He looked like a fish trying to survive on land.

Annabel got the hint. She set the gun aside, then crawled forward until she could pull the key for the chain binding her from his pocket. When it was done and she was free, she stood up.

He looked up from the ground at her, barely able to move. His eyes went to the bracelet she'd slid onto his wrist. The bracelet he was now too weak to remove.

"The bracelet?" she asked him. "Do you like it? My best friend gave it to me. She gave it to me before she forgot how to stay alive. But don't get excited. It's not *real* gold. Just gold paint over top." Then she leaned in and whispered like a secret, *"It's actually silver."*

Weakened so completely, Victor could only lay still and stare. The bracelet was so loose it was almost falling off, but he couldn't even lift his hand enough to let it drop away.

Annabel walked to a busted table in the room's corner among some other debris. She wrenched at the leg until it broke, shearing into a wooden point.

Then she walked to Victor and put the tip of the thing over his chest.

"I wonder what it's like, to die of thirst," she said.

She poked him. These lines had sounded so good in her head when she'd been planning them back at the house, but something inside herself was ruining them now that they'd reached prime time. She didn't feel quite as victorious or vindicated as she'd hoped. There was a hollowness to her play. A dark thing inside tugged at her as if trying to pull her down. Into a pit. Where sorrow lived.

"I wonder," she said, shocked to feel a tear leaking down her chin, "if dying of thirst is anything like feeling wood enter your heart ..."

An image flashed before her eyes: Alicia, dead and still open-eyed on her linoleum floor. The neighbor had found her, but for some reason Annabel could only imagine one of

Alicia's own children behind the body, sinking to its knees and sobbing.

"… inch …"

Then a memory of Alicia in life. As her friend. The two of them traveling together. Laughing, in easier days.

"… by inch."

She shoved. The tip was sharper than she'd thought. Victor's chest began to bleed.

"*ANNABEL!*"

She looked over her shoulder. Standing it the warehouse's doorway was Celeste Toussant.

"I have this," Annabel said. She wiped her face. Goddamn tears, coming from nowhere.

Celeste came forward. She said, "Give me the stake."

"*I SAID I HAVE THIS!*"

But did she? She wanted to sound strong. She sounded petulant instead. She was hollowed-out, like a gourd. She felt a sliver of her usual self.

"Listen to me," said Celeste. "You don't want to do this."

"I do. I want to do it so much."

"It's not just about him. It's also about you."

"It's him. It's *her*." Annabel snorted back phlegm, feeling a mess. She pushed the stake into him again. He winced. He bled.

"You can't undo this kind of thing," Celeste said. "Killing changes people. If you want to be free of this man, killing him in cold blood is the last thing you should do. Push that stake into him and he'll *never* leave you. What you're doing might feel right, but it's not. Whatever he did, however he hurt you …"

"Like you know!"

"*I KNOW!*" Celeste bellowed. The wave of sound that came from her was like a wave. It concussed the beams.

Shook dust from the rafters. "Believe me, I know. You were there. You more than anyone know the score I have to settle."

Annabel shook her head. Defiant. She hadn't let go of the stake. "Then I have to settle mine, too."

Celeste came another step forward. She said, "Let me do it."

"No."

"Let me do it, Annabel. My soul is already black. I've done this before."

"I want it. This is mine."

Gently, Celeste said, "You don't want this."

Something broke. Annabel found herself stepping back, her stake falling to the floor. Then the tears came without hesitation, hard and strong.

Celeste picked up the stake.

"If you're staying," she said to Annabel, "don't look right at him as he burns."

"You aren't going to tell me to look away?"

Celeste shook her head. All she'd say was, "I was human once, too."

Celeste used her foot to roll Victor fully onto his back. But in the rolling motion, Victor's hand flopped sideways ... just enough for the gold-painted silver charm bracelet to slip from his wrist.

There was no hesitation. None at all. Victor was up in a partial second, his body wrapped completely around Annabel's from behind. He wasn't bothering with the shotgun anymore; he had a hand on her chin now, his fingernails sharp and rough like jagged steel. He'd rip her head off, if Celeste took one more step.

He began to back up, away from Celeste. Celeste eyed him and paced with him, teeth bared.

"Let her go."

"You had your chance."

"Let her go or you won't believe how slowly you die." Annabel kept watching Celeste's eyes. She was a mother bear, protecting a cub.

"Then find your husband," Victor said. "You both know what I want. Tell me how to make Thrill and I'll let her live."

He was almost to the door now. The door through with Celeste had entered. Now Celeste was ten feet from him, daring to come no closer. Celeste was old, and age made her fast and strong. Was she old enough to undo Victor before Victor undid Annabel? Probably not, and she seemed unwilling to take the chance.

He reached the door. Once out, he'd turn with her. Run with her. Maybe smash her to paste with the G-force of vampire acceleration, or maybe just save her to torture else-where until he got what he wanted.

"Get Maurice and bring him to me," Victor said, squeezing Annabel's neck. "No one has to die."

Something seemed to strike Victor from behind. He went very still, and then black bile began to run from between his lips.

"He's already here," said a new voice. It was Maurice.

Maurice stepped inside the warehouse. He very gently pulled Annabel away from the burning body.

Brimstone ash filled the sky as Victor departed.

Ten feet away, Maurice and Celeste wrapped Annabel like a blanket as the fire grew hotter, embracing her like the daughter they'd lost long ago.

FORTY

UPPERCUT

The rest of the day should have collapsed like a top-heavy house of cards. Instead, it folded neatly in on itself like a closing pop-up book. Maurice didn't understand. Amado, who'd accepted Maurice's vampirism in the way he'd accept a person's birthmark, was strangely the only person wise enough to express what had happened.

"Sometimes we push against the world and sometimes the world pushes against us," he said, "but in the end, all it really wants is surrender."

Not "surrender" like giving up. This was the surrender of letting go. This was standing in the middle of that house of cards, taking a deep breath, and taking hands from the walls to see what came next. Surrender was something Maurice never, ever practiced. It was also, he'd realized as he ran back across the country, the issue he'd taken to Annabel in the first place.

He'd been forever troubled by an inability to surrender. An inability to have a bit of faith for once, and just let go. These were not easy things, for an immortal born of darkness.

"How old are you again?" Maurice asked Amado after he spoke, thereafter folding his hands sagely like the Buddha.

"Twenty-five."

And Maurice said, "Fuck you."

He hated that it'd never occurred to him. Life so far had been a two-thousand-year test of strength requiring his every attention in every minute. You survived by micromanagement; that was how a vampire got so old in the first place. Annabel knew that; her therapeutic pokings and proddings of Maurice had been all about forgiving himself for failing to contain the inevitable. For failing to anticipate and prevent every negative thing — and for having the arrogance, in any given moment, to be so sure of what was negative and what might, in time, turn out otherwise. Forgiving himself — in words that were still metaphorically accurate if technically a lie — for being *human*.

That was the root of everything. Annabel had seen it right away. Maurice felt guilty about Daisy because he'd felt responsible for her. He'd been so dragged-down by H. H. Holmes because he'd thought himself able to kill the killer, yet was unable. All of Maurice's problems came down to things he felt needed to be handled, but that he couldn't handle all by himself. His guilt came down to things he wanted controlled that couldn't be controlled by anyone.

What if there was no way to control everything? What if Maurice wasn't responsible for everything? What if he was just one person, with flaws like anyone else?

After the warehouse, Maurice had gone with Celeste and Annabel back to the mansion for a while — not because they needed him, but because he'd begun to realize how badly he needed them. When Maurice then said he had to return to San Diego to help clean up the mess he'd left there, Annabel had cupped her palm over his cheek and said, "The mess was left. *You* did not leave it."

She fell asleep almost immediately after, so Maurice couldn't ask questions. Had that been a personal observation? It felt like a philosophical one, on par with the sound of one hand clapping. But then as he left, he decided her words might just be the most direct therapeutic advice she'd given him in all their sessions, though she'd probably only said it like Confucius because she'd been half asleep. In everyday words, it meant, *Everything isn't about you, asshole.*

Fifteen minutes later, after thinking over Annabel's words while his feet churned meditatively beneath him the whole run back, Maurice discovered he'd ground himself a new pair of lenses through which to see the night's remainders. It was suddenly so obvious. This wasn't about facing his own consequences — *Maurice Toussant's* consequences. There were other people here, and they were facing consequences, too.

That's when Amado said the thing about surrender — so much wiser than his years, the asshole. After something like eighty of Amado's lifetimes, Maurice still hadn't figured that out.

By the time he re-entered the convention center, the crowd was gearing down for the night. Maurice wasn't sure if this was the natural end of the day or if the commotion Ophelia's vampires had caused had been a little too much excitement, prompting an early close. He decided it was the first one. The likes of San Diego Comic Con didn't shut down because of a few nightcrawlers — especially after everyone decided the whole thing was a *Marty the Vampire* publicity stunt, which was already the internet's consensus. And why wouldn't it be? The author of the thing had been in the spot-light when the "vampires" broke loose and started climbing "invisible wires." The stars of the show were those who'd come to the rescue rather than security staff ... and after they did battle, the whole thing ended. *Of course* it was a stunt.

The geeks loved it. *Marty the Vampire* and the balls it'd displayed, by pulling off something so spectacular, had made the show an instant favorite. It was Saturday's best session by far. Maybe the entire con's.

Maurice, Amado, Alexander, Delilah, Ella, and Harrison had found each other and were comparing notes when Alexander suddenly looked across the emptying room and started laughing.

"I'll be damned," he said. "Who knew you could be arrested for being a dick?"

The others looked. Jerome was in handcuffs, being led off by two SDPD officers. Not security guards. Cops.

Ella stepped forward with an air of authority. She didn't flash an ID to show she was with the production that Jerome worked for, but her body language did the exact same job. She addressed the police politely but with expec-tation of an answer. She told them this man was an employee of hers (Delilah tittered at that; in truth, despite the stick he usually swung on set, he'd never actually been the boss) and asked what he'd done.

"We found him sharing alcohol and illicit substances with minors, ma'am," said one of the cops. "If you'd like, you can follow us to the station while we process him."

Alcohol. Illicit substances. Minors. It turned out to mean Jerome had gotten into a vodka-and-MDMA party with three sixteen year-old female attendees he'd been trying to impress with his show credentials. Apparently the plan was to sleep with all three of them at once. In a pile. Stacked long like Lincoln Logs.

"Nah," Ella told the cops.

Jerome turned to Maurice. He looked humbled: a look Maurice had never seen on his face before. Now that Maurice knew Jerome was a red herring (Ophelia had never controlled him after all; her bubble's attention was on the diffuse task of influencing vampire opinion instead), it was like his whole presence had changed. He hadn't been trying to tank the show. He'd been indulging in hedonism and power trips for his own reasons, tanking it accidentally. Before, when Maurice thought he'd seen Ophelia in Jerome's eyes, the man had struck him as intimidating. Now he was just pathetic.

"Maurice. Harrison. Guys," Jerome said. "Tell them it's a mistake. I wasn't going to do anything. Those girls brought the drugs, not me. They told me they were eighteen!"

Maurice couldn't bring himself to answer Jerome's request. He found himself looking at him the way he'd regard a cockroach.

"Celeste was wrong about you," he said. "You're not a vampire."

Jerome wasn't sure what to say to that.

"No," Maurice went on. "You're just a monster."

Jerome looked to another of their party. "Harrison?"

Harrison shook his head.

"Amado. Amado, please."

Nothing.

Then he looked at Delilah and said, "Come on, Tits."

Delilah dipped at the knees, then drove upward hard enough to deliver an uppercut to his testicles.

"*Miss!*" said the second cop, moving to grab her as Jerome dropped.

But Maurice got there first. He looked into the second cop's eyes, then the first.

"'Good job, Miss,'" he said.

"Good job, Miss," the cops said together. Then they dragged Jerome to his feet, and dragged him away.

Delilah put an arm around Maurice. "Let's talk," she said, "about you meeting my ex."

FORTY-ONE

THE WAY WE ARE

Reginald's trial was postponed. Celeste was not surprised.

"I should have gone in," she said, meaning the time she'd stopped short of Logan's gate after Ophelia emerged from the house. "I just assumed Ophelia had either killed him or done some necromancy to make him strong enough that he'd never need her again. I chose to follow Annabel. That felt more important. While I was standing there, I heard her laugh."

"Of course you followed Annabel," Maurice said.

"I wish I'd gone inside. Brian says they found Logan with a silver fingernail in his throat. Couldn't move. I could have changed 'two-week delay' to 'cancelled forever.'"

Maurice repeated some of the lessons he'd finally learned from Annabel, pointing out that Celeste wasn't the center of the universe any more than he was. They needed to control what they could, then surrender the rest. Celeste thought most of Maurice's recent proclamations were obnoxious new-age assholery. She told him to stow it. *Of course* she should have killed Logan. Where was the

Maurice she'd married, determined to be the lone voice of morality and reason in the hedonistic vampire world?

But it was really just breaking balls. They were better now, and Celeste had finally forgiven him.

Annabel went home. With Victor gone and Logan missing his necromancer, Annabel had become a non-issue to the vampires of Columbus. Nobody but Celeste and Brian knew Maurice had even gone to therapy in the first place, and Logan — who was in spin-control mode trying to explain what'd happened without admitting to the necromancer he'd been keeping — didn't have room on his docket to care about some random human doctor. Logan's regime had lost a lot of its teeth on Saturday night. Although only Maurice and Celeste knew why, Logan would be a lot less influential now. He would have an uphill climb with the Council, though he was bully enough to whip them back into line in time.

Maurice was still skeptical about Reginald's chances despite Comic Con's success.

"We can't air the show," he told Celeste. "You know that, don't you?"

It was a fact that nobody wanted to face. Filming on *Marty the Vampire* had just been picking up steam when Comic Con happened, and everyone was excited. The convention itself added afterburner to the production, thanks to the confluence of three things: Jerome's removal (he'd been fired, then charged as a sex offender), the cast's bonding (it was much more exciting to fight fictional vampires after you've fought real ones), and a huge upswell of public interest and support for the show. Because that too had happened: The show's *idea* was a hit well before anyone viewed a frame of footage, seeing as its idea ticked all the "misfit hero" boxes that'd drawn cast and crew to this "very special" production in the first place. Even amongst vampires, Maurice saw more interest and more acceptance. In that way, *Marty* was doing its job far better than Maurice had hoped.

But at the same time, it was too much risk. Too much spotlight. Logan was in trouble and needed a scapegoat to take some heat off himself. Maurice — who in vampire eyes would be exposing their world's secret if the show went forward — was the perfect target.

"What about Thrill?" Harrison asked when Maurice laid it all out for him. "You *needed* exposure. The exposure was *why you did this in the first place.* We all banded together to go gung-ho with the goal of making the show *so* popular, Logan would never be able to put his hands on you. *Maurice. Buddy.* If you put this light out, they'll come for you tomorrow. What's changed?"

And Maurice answered, "Victor's changed."

Ah. Yes. *Victor.* Logan and Ophelia had comprised such an impressive threat (especially if the good guys thought Jerome was in that mix) that Victor tended to get lost in the shuffle. But Victor was the one who'd made the blood key, and that key had died with him. Victor's plan, once he realized he wouldn't be able to use his own key without Logan's help, had been to use Annabel as leverage: a way to get Maurice to give up Thrill's formula voluntarily. But Victor had wanted to keep an ace all to himself — something Logan didn't know and that Victor could therefore use against him — so he hadn't told anyone about Annabel's connection to Maurice, through Daisy. Thanks to Victor's selfish discretion, nobody knew about Daisy now beyond those who'd loved her.

Without a key and without Daisy's leverage, Thrill was safe inside Maurice. For now.

"'For now'?" Annabel repeated.

"Logan knows I have a copy of the Thrill formula in my head," Maurice explained. "The *only* copy. He won't stop trying to get it out of me until one of us is dead."

"Him," Annabel suggested. "I like *him* as the dead one."

But it was a joke, because the window in which assassinating Logan had been possible had closed. Celeste hadn't known Logan was alone and defenseless that day. If she had, their problems would be over. But she'd played it safe, and for now that was good enough. Maurice was tired of holding up the house of cards. A person couldn't keep all threats at bay all the time, so maybe it was best not to court threats in the first place.

Which Celeste was still doing, by the way. She hadn't given up on Ophelia at all. Most nights she circled the city, trying to feel Macht's finally-waning bond, looking for the blue light of Ophelia's necromancer spell. But Ophelia was smart. She'd hidden for a very long time. And so now that she was free of Logan, she didn't seem to be *using* her spell. She'd gone quiet again. Dormant again. Celeste didn't want to accept it. Missing her chance at Logan bothered her, but missing Ophelia *consumed* her. It'd been easier for her to let Ophelia go back when Ophelia had been merely a concept. Now, however, Ophelia had a face that Celeste remembered as clearly as her own. Just as Celeste's sisters' faces and even that of the baby she'd lost — equally remembered in life and death — were just as vivid.

"I have dreams of them," Celeste said. "Lucid dreams. My sisters and I walk the Earth looking for her. In the dream, they know where she is. They can feel her. They can feel what she did to us."

And then quietly, when she thought Maurice could not see her, she would cry. She had a thousand years of mourning to catch up on: a spot rubbed sore inside her that might never heal.

"Lucid dreams are *prescient* dreams," Amado told Maurice on his last visit to the *Marty* set. "In time, she'll find her."

The crew — but mostly the cast — had convinced Maurice to let them finish shooting. The money was already out of Maurice's bank account and he had so much left that a few million simply didn't matter. Although Maurice would need to keep his distance from the show for reasons of discretion (and the production would need to be very low-profile and shoot mostly indoors where they couldn't easily be seen), the show still felt like a hobby to Maurice. Nonetheless, cast and crew still seemed to feel it was important to finish Reginald's story in a good way seeing as the real story would probably end poorly. It was tribute to the way the world should be. *Could* be. And maybe one day *would* be.

"Which is difficult, if nobody ever sees it," Ella grumbled. Having never really believed in vampires, Ella saw their surrender as a big, dumb cost-sink.

"You never know," said Maurice. "If you finish the season, you'll have it ready. You can always air it later."

"Oh, yeah? And when exactly would *that* be?"

"I don't know." Then, spontaneously: "2022."

"Why 2022?"

"Why not?"

But that was the future. One *possible* future. Although, while he sat across a table from Maurice inside the Slushy Shack set between shots, the star of *Marty the Vampire* seemed to be claiming to know the future.

"'Lucid dreams are prescient dreams,'" Maurice repeated. It had a nice ring, that zinger about dreams predicting things yet to be. "Is that another piece of your wise philosophy?"

"Yeah. Some yogi said it."

"Which yogi?"

Amado sipped the real slushy he'd bought at 7-11. You couldn't sip the fake Slushies. They were toxic somehow, maybe made of gasoline.

"Okay, fine," he said. "I made it up to fuck with you."

Lucid dreams are prescient dreams. In time, she'll find her.

Maurice liked the first part and decided to believe it anyway. The second part, he didn't like at all. It sounded exactly like Celeste. He really *did* think she'd find Ophelia eventually, if for no other reason than she'd never give up. When she did, Ophelia would still be a necromancer. Still able to perform vampire-bending magic, and chances were Celeste's mind wasn't fully immune. Ophelia's coffin could show up right next door one night and Maurice still wouldn't want Celeste to walk over and stake her. It was too dangerous. Simply existing made Ophelia dangerous ... which, paradoxically, was the exact reason Celeste would eventually give for ending her no matter what the cost.

To Amado's witticism, Maurice said, "Asshole."

It was the last time they'd see each other. Maurice had already said his goodbyes to the rest of cast and crew. For safety, those who knew Maurice's real story and background — including about Reginald — had already been glamoured. Amado would be the last. They'd all remember Maurice, but only as a guy who'd had an idea. They wouldn't know he was a vampire. They wouldn't know anything that mattered.

"But the show will still exist," Amado said as they circled around to the inevitable final glamouring. "Isn't that a problem? We won't understand why we're working so hard on something that we know will never air. How will that make any sense to us? We won't do any more publicity. We won't tell people about it. It won't show up on our IMDB pages unless it ever goes on-air. Maurice, shit ... we're going to spend another — what? a *month?* — shooting a show that goes nowhere."

"Some things go nowhere. Some things exist, then just sort of stop existing." He was thinking of the Reginald videos on YouTube. Using that weird tech ability of hers, Claire had somehow erased them. He'd thought they'd return (someone had posted them after all, and he couldn't glamour everyone who'd ever seen them), but so far they hadn't. Some surely wondered, but the internet — like the world — had simply moved on.

"But won't we wonder?" Amado said.

"Do you wonder at the *other* things you can't explain? Or does your mind rationalize and fill in the blanks? Yeah, you're shooting a TV show with an unknown destiny, but you're also living a life with an unknown destiny. People get themselves into situations they shouldn't even when they know better. People get into the same bad relationship over and over. People can't stop procrastinating. Can't stop overeating. Can't stop using their cell phones at the dinner table. If you think you understand the reasons for all you do, you're living in a dream world. If we can invent a story about why we're walking past someone starving on the street, we can invent stories about why we're doing all sorts of things. There's a saying: 'We don't see the world *the way it is.* We see the world *the way we are.*' The world that matters to us isn't out there, Amado. It's the one in here." Maurice tapped his head. "You're thinking in terms of objective facts, but that's not how glamour works. Glamour understands that in the end, we all believe what we want to believe."

Amado was processing it, seeming to accept it.

"'We don't see the world *the way it is.* We see the world *the way we are,*'" he repeated. "Who said that?"

"I made it up to fuck with you."

And Amado said, "Asshole."

Neglect started the remaining bridges burning even faster than Maurice expected. Information moved quickly, and a side effect was that anything that wasn't fed a constant stream of fuel immediately began to die. Less than a week from the big "publicity stunt" at Comic Con, news about *Marty the Vampire* was already dwindling because the production — led by a glamoured Ella and Harrison — failed to follow it up.

Apathy worked better than erasure. Of course people out there would know the show existed … but the world was a very big place, and unless anyone specifically went looking for it, the TV-show-that-almost-was would disappear in the shifting sands of time. Until 2022, at least.

"I guess that just leaves us," said Annabel when Maurice returned from his final visit to the set.

"What *about* us?" Maurice asked. The two of them were back at the mansion, Celeste probably out looking futilely for Ophelia again. Annabel had moved home, but evening wine had become a cross-species tradition that couldn't possibly last forever.

"The cast forgot," Annabel said. "The entire production forgot. Victor's dead. You can't touch Logan, and Ophelia might be underground for good. That leaves the three of us.

We're the last three who really know what happened. Even Reginald doesn't know."

Maurice nodded. Claire and Nikki sort of knew, but not everything. The depths of it all were back in the heads of the vampire couple who'd lived Thrill's story in the first place ... and the psychiatrist with their lost progeny's blood, who held it all together.

"I guess it's our secret," said Maurice.

"Our burden to bear," said Annabel.

Burden. Yes. That was the right word. It was true that Ophelia might never return to bother them beyond the taunts that continued to plague Celeste's dreams — *directed* taunts, it seemed, possibly sent by the old bitch herself. Chances were excellent that Ophelia, who technically had no grudge, would find no reason to visit Celeste, who had all the grudge in the world.

But Logan. Ophelia might be gone, but Logan remained.

"If it becomes a problem again," Maurice said, "we're doing things my way."

"What way?"

"I have the only copy of Thrill inside me," he said. "It's a ticking bomb. So if Logan comes ..." Then he made himself say it, because he knew it was true. "*When* Logan comes. I won't risk you or Celeste or anyone else. This is my burden, and mine alone.

"No," said Annabel, understanding.

"Logan won't stop chasing me as long as the recipe exists. There's no other way to erase it, Annabel. No other way to be free."

Footsteps entered the foyer. They all looked up to see a large man: a visitor, escorted by Celeste. The big man embraced Maurice, who was surprised to see him. Then he turned to Annabel and introduced himself: Reginald the Vampire, finally in the flesh.

"I told Reginald about Thrill," Celeste said as if it explained her bringing him here. "I told him *all about* Thrill ... after he called me up, and said he'd met Daisy."

Maurice's jaw fell.

"We found out I can read fast. Memorize fast. Think fast," Reginald told his maker. "I kept doing those things while you were away, and I learned something new. You kept saying I'd probably be good at blood ties." He paused. "And at glamour."

"You saw Daisy when you looked inside yourself?"

Reginald nodded. "At the blood tree. She stood out like a flame, addicted to a blood I'd never seen before." Then he looked knowingly at Annabel. "She was awake inside a human. A *human*, Maurice. So I decided to try something. I tried to talk to her."

"But she's—"

"—distant. Gone. Not real anymore. I know; I can see it. I asked her questions anyway. She gave me answers. I know you're hiding things from me, Maurice. I know you've been hiding for a while. It's okay. It was better if I didn't know. But it was Daisy who gave me the idea. Daisy who asked me to try something. On her."

"But Daisy is just—!"

Again Reginald finished Maurice's sentence. "—a memory. But the thing is, the lines blur, Maurice. I can see that now."

Maurice considered his progeny. He knew they'd only scratched the surface of Reginald's mental gifts. The exercises they'd done were memory tricks, parlor games, nothing more. Maurice could barely see one fork down his blood tree, but now here was Reginald, delving deep. Fully lucid inside. It was a phenomenon that wasn't supposed to be possible. A phenomenon possible only in a vampire forced to turn his gifts inward, lacking as they were on the outside.

"Daisy asked if I could glamour her. And I could."

"Not for real, Reginald. Vampires can't be glamoured."

"I think they can," Reginald said, "and that means there's another way."

It seemed to have worked. Maurice closed his eyes beside Celeste, willing himself into a blood fugue. With effort, he was eventually able to see the old Thrill distillery back in Chicago. He was able to see the office, the desk, and Malone standing beside him. He was able to see the papers on the desk. To read through them. One was a memo. One was a requisition for toilet paper — odd, because vampires didn't usually eat, and hence rarely needed it.

But when Maurice reached the paper with the Thrill formula written on it, he found it blank — entirely erased, thanks to one fat vampire.

"It's gone. The Thrill formula is gone," he said, opening his eyes again. "I don't understand."

"You do, though," Reginald replied. "Someone told me once that we don't see the world the way it is. We see the world the way *we are.*"

"*I* told you that. But—"

"You also told me that we believe what we choose to believe. That we're the makers of our own realities. That our lives are our memories. All this out here?" He waved his hands to indicate the whole of existence. "It's just fly by wire."

"Reginald ..."

"Let me ask you a question," Reginald interrupted.

Maurice waited.

"It's been a little over two months since you turned me. A crazy two months. A *messy* two months. You didn't trust me to know all that happened in that time, did you?"

"Reginald, I—"

Reginald held up a hand. "I'm not offended. You were right to keep it from me. But you screwed up. *Both* of you screwed up." He looked at Celeste. "You finally told me the truth, and after that I *knew*. At first I only knew what you told me, but the rest came behind it. I can't *not* look at the blood memories inside myself, Maurice. Have you seen?"

Yes, Maurice had seen, though he'd tried not to look. Looking into Reginald's blood without being invited was like peeping through his window, but he was Reginald's maker; he'd seen just the same. And so he knew: Reginald's was a world without blinders. His mental abilities were so intense, it seemed there was nothing he couldn't learn. He could find anything. He could glamour vampires. He might even be able to trace down the world's vast but singular family of vampires to the first of them on the blood tree — the original ancestor, who'd begun it all. So yes. Reginald *couldn't* not look at the blood memories inside himself. As soon as Celeste told him the first thing, he'd probably learned it all.

"You were right to keep it from me, for my own and everyone else's safety," Reginald said again. "But now I know everything. So. Would it be safer, do you think, if I *didn't* know? If I didn't know about you and Annabel. If I didn't know about Victor, and Ophelia, and what's happened with Logan. About the TV show. About Thrillo-globin. About Daisy. Even the fact that I seem to be able to glamour vampires."

"But you *do* know those things," Maurice said.

"Maybe I do," Reginald said, "or maybe I'm seeing the world not as *it is*, but how *I am*. Maybe we really *do* believe what we choose to believe. Maybe our lives really *are* our memories. Maybe … just maybe … I truly *am* the maker of my own reality."

"Those are just expressions," Maurice told him. "They're only figurative."

"Maybe they *are* only figurative," Reginald said, "but maybe I choose to believe they're real."

And so Reginald did.

By the time he left the mansion, Reginald had made himself forget everything. It was safer that way, he explained before he began. He'd replaced two months of his life with a simple lie: *A week ago, I was human.* Glamour — even though it was *self*-glamour — would fill in the gaps. Unless Maurice meddled, Reginald's mind would forever fold tomorrow back to the beginning. The inconsistencies and contradictions that should result from removing a block of experience would, as far as Reginald was concerned, resolve on their own. The mind didn't look for loose ends in itself. It was blind when it wished to stay blind.

"I still don't understand," Maurice told Celeste when he was gone. "None of it. Not one tiny little bit of what Regi-nald did today."

And Celeste replied, "I suspect there's a lot about Regi-nald, if they allow him to live, that nobody will understand."

It made Maurice think of the future. Of evolution.

. . .

LESS THAN AN HOUR LATER, Celeste was asleep. And in that sleep, she saw the gift that Reginald had given her — the secret gift that even Maurice would never know about. The gift that had convinced Celeste to seek Reginald. To find him. To tell him the story of Thrill, which ended up telling him everything.

And the gift was Daisy.

Personified.

Awake.

They met in a meadow.

"I can't believe this," Celeste said. "I didn't believe it when he showed me in trance, and I don't believe it now."

"You don't need to believe it," Daisy said. "It's a dream."

"But what kind of dream? One that tells truth? Or one that lies?"

"Mother," Daisy said with a laugh. "You act like it matters."

The scene changed. Now they were walking along the streets of old Chicago. Daisy was wearing clothes she'd worn when they'd known her in life. Flapper dress. Flapper headband. Short hair, pretty smile. The dream was real enough to touch.

"Ophelia is dead," Daisy told her.

Celeste turned her dream head. She couldn't have heard that right.

"*I know, I know,*" Daisy said, rolling her eyes theatrically. "You'll say that you wanted to see it. You'll say you wanted to *do* it. But you didn't. It's like you told Annabel: Revenge changes you as much as it changes the present. Ophelia died, but you would have carried her on. She would have stayed with you, like dirt on your shoe."

Even in the dream, Celeste felt anger. Ophelia was her life's biggest plague. It wasn't satisfying enough that she'd died. *Died* was past tense — and in this specific case, it was an almost dismissive past tense. More fanfare should have been made. Just as Annabel had done, Celeste had wanted to press the stake against her heart. Then push it forward, inch by inch. She could picture it now: Ophelia angry, then Ophelia pleading, then Ophelia begging for her life. In the end she would have burned so slowly, the agony would have been impossible to witness.

Which, interestingly, was exactly what she'd told Annabel. The exact reason she'd told Annabel not to do it: not because of what it'd do to Victor, but because of what it'd do to herself.

As if reading Celeste's mind, Daisy said, "The world has seen enough suffering. Now, it's time to heal."

"I've dealt death before. Annabel hadn't."

"All the more reason, Mother. She's gone. That's all that matters."

"My sisters deserved vengeance. Ophelia deserved what *they* got."

Daisy almost laughed. "Oh, they *got* their vengeance. How many times have you dreamed of them? How many times have you spoken with your sisters in the same way you're speaking with me now?"

The answer was that it'd been constant: dreams of the girls, dreams of them alive and not at all suffering. They were dreams of remembering who Anna and Nell had been, not how they'd died — which, before now, was all Celeste had had. But in the recent past, Ophelia's presence had always shown up to ruin those dreams. She'd poke her awareness in from the extended tree of blood, prodding like a tease. Ophelia was always able to see in; Celeste could never see out. That was necromancer magic at work: the exact reason Celeste, if she'd found Ophelia, would probably already be dead ... while Ophelia lived to gloat another day.

"Ophelia woke them up, just like Reginald woke me up," Daisy explained. "Strictly speaking, I don't suppose any of us are real. But who cares? Strictly speaking, *you* aren't real, either. Nobody is. Nothing is."

"It's not?"

"Where do any of us live," Daisy said, "other than inside our minds?"

It was too difficult a thought. Celeste's logic didn't work as well in the void, which was probably just as well because she got the feeling Daisy's statement wasn't based on logic. She let it go.

"You didn't tell me *how* Ophelia died. *Why* she died. Who killed her."

"A blood clot killed her."

"Vampires don't get blood clots."

"Then perhaps the intelligence *inside* that blood clot killed her. Maybe the blood itself decided to pull into a cluster. Because it was angry. Because it'd been wronged."

"How can *blood* be wronged?" Celeste asked.

"*Your* blood was wronged. Two sisters. *Blood.*"

"That's not the same," Celeste said.

And Daisy replied, "Oh yes it is."

What did that mean? Celeste didn't know. But then again, she also didn't know how Reginald had reached deep inside Maurice and erased the last dangerous piece of his vampire mind. She *doubly* didn't know how Reginald had done the same thing to himself. She didn't know how Reginald had seen Daisy from inside his own blood; they were connected, but separated by generations and ages. She didn't know how, if Reginald was telling the truth, he'd managed to glamour Daisy, which meant glamouring a blood memory. It was true, though, because here Celeste was, talking to a dream that had far more substance than it should. So who knew? Maybe this was another gift Reginald had given the world.

Celeste's sisters had seemed just as awake in her earlier dreams as Daisy seemed now. With Reginald's impossible blood-navigating on board, maybe they really *had* been able to reach back: all the way over the bridge of Amadeus Macht and finally into Ophelia. It was a ludicrous journey for any vampire to take, but Reginald was far beyond special. So maybe it was true. Maybe all blood had intelligence. Maybe Anna and Nell had whispered to Ophelia's blood. Maybe they'd convinced it, somehow, to disobey.

So had Ophelia burned after the clot seized her? Had it happened like a stake in the heart or a walk in the sunshine? Or had she just suddenly become inert and lifeless, dying like a human?

But then again maybe, Celeste decided, she didn't care how it'd happened. Ophelia was dead. Celeste, if she'd tried to do it herself, would probably be the dead one. Maybe *that* was all that mattered. The world had seen enough suffering already. Now, perhaps, it was time to heal.

The scene changed again. Now there were three women with her: Daisy and both sisters. Then in a blink there was one more: Annabel, here inside her despite being very much alive.

"I don't understand what's happening," Celeste said.

"That's okay," the being that might or might not be Annabel told her. "Nobody does."

BUT WHAT ABOUT REGINALD?

If you're wondering what ended up happening with Reginald, his trial, and the future of Logan's elitist Vampire Nation, you might have missed out on my book ***FAT VAMPIRE*** — Reginald's story, which started it all!

Check out Fat Vampire (adapted in 2022 on the SyFy Network as Reginald the Vampire, starring Spider-Man's Jacob Batalon)!

ENTER THE TRUANTVERSE

When it comes to stories and the worlds they live in, books are only the beginning.

Visit JohnnyBTruant.com/join to get my best books sooner and cheaper than the other stores.

My list doesn't suck like so many author email lists. Seriously. It has unicorns.

Open Meadows

The Unforgotten

The Magic Bunch

Unicorn Genesis

FAT VAMPIRE:

Fat Vampire

Fat Vampire 2: Tastes Like Chicken

Fat Vampire 3: All You Can Eat

Fat Vampire 4: Harder Better Fatter Stronger

Fat Vampire 5: Fatpocalypse

Fat Vampire 6: Survival of the Fattest

The Vampire Maurice

Anarchy and Blood

Vampires in the White City

Fangs and Fame

Game of Fangs

INVASION:

Invasion

Contact

Colonization

Annihilation

Judgment

Extinction

Resurrection

Save the City

Save the Girl

Save the World

Longshot

THE INEVITABLE:

Robot Proletariat

The Infinite Loop

The Hard Reset

Cascade Failure

Reboot

En3my

DEAD CITY:

Dead City

Dead Nation

Dead Planet

Dead Zero

Empty Nest

THE DREAM ENGINE:

The Dream Engine

The Nightmare Factory

Null Identity

COMEDIES:

Everyone Gets Divorced

Greens

Fiends

Decoy Wallet

NONFICTION:

The Fiction Formula

Fiction Unboxed

Iterate & Optimize

The Story Solution

Write. Publish. Repeat.

The One With All the Writing Advice

www.ingramcontent.com/pod-product-compliance
Lightning Source LLC
Chambersburg PA
CBHW020322010826
48973CB00005B/1082